C0-DYB-233

THE LOIN CONNECTION

A NOVEL

BY

AJOBI BROWN

Copyright ©ⒶAjobi Brown

All Scripture quotations are taken from
the New King James Version unless otherwise stated.

All rights reserved solely by the author. The author guarantees that the contents of this book do not infringe on the rights of any person or work. No portion of this book may be reproduced mechanically, electronically or by any other means, without the written permission of the author.

For copies, please visit: www.womanonpurpose.org
or your online book store.

ISBN: 9798355977177
Published by

Improved
...the improved you

www.improved2life.com

To Contact the Author
Email: ajobiakinrinsola@gmail.com

DEDICATION

To God Almighty, who gave the idea and fortitude to write the book in the first place. To my darling husband, whom I met seven years after I started this book project and who encouraged me to finish it and get it out there! You made me experience the *other* side. Thank you for believing in it and making it happen. I love you! Finally, to all the seemingly broken women out there in the world, I hope you discover that there really is life after trauma. May this be your testimony...too.

ABOUT THE AUTHOR

Though an Attorney with a brief stint in legal practice, Ajobi Brown ventured into the entrepreneurship world a few years ago. Amongst other things, she is a retail fashion business owner, with her own plus-size fashion line, a design and image consultant with various interests in other areas of creativity such as, interior design, drawing, building and cooking. Ajobi has an avid passion for young people and is also keen for women, in particular, to develop, foster, and maintain a sound emotional balance, regardless of their past experiences. Ajobi stumbled into the writing world when she realized she had stories within her worth telling. ***The Loin Connection*** is her debut novel and broadly addresses narratives of human experience and the courage to keep going, even after emotional trauma and unexpected realities. The book has taken her nine years to write, and she claims the stories just poured out of her. Ajobi and her husband currently live between their homes in Lagos, Nigeria and Pennsylvania, USA.

CONTENTS

CHAPTER ONE

Labake woke up in fright. Her heart raced wildly, and her head ached badly. She could feel the sweat drip down her neck, and it felt like blood rushed through her head and entire body all at once and at an uncontrollable speed. She gasped for breath and struggled to do the breathing exercises she had been taught at the clinic. It was a weird but familiar feeling that she now knew had a name. She had a *panic attack* but what was strange about this particular episode was how it had awakened her from sleep. Until now, she had only ever experienced them whilst fully awake. She felt like she was suffocating and could feel the panic grow.

Suddenly, she shot off the bed, and as her feet landed on the foot mat beside it, she squealed like a wounded puppy. She held her head in both hands as if to keep it from exploding and shut her aching eyes. This had been the norm for the past few weeks, and it seemed to worsen by the day. The last doctor at the clinic had assured her that she was not losing her mind as she had thought. He had explained its causes, symptoms, and treatment and mentioned that a lot of people experienced them too.

Labake rose slowly from the bed and swiftly grabbed the bedpost to steady herself. Her head and eyes were heavy and spinning as though she had just got off a roller coaster. She felt her knees buckle, and her whole body felt like it was on fire. She could not think of a part of her being that was not aching in that moment. Slowly, she got to the medicine cabinet in the adjoining bathroom, opened it and scrambled around for the strong painkillers that had now become a part of her daily routine.

She tried to avoid looking into the cabinet mirror as she shut it but found she was unable to. Seeing her reflection in the mirror caused tears to well up in her eyes and slowly slide down her purple and blue, bruised cheek bone. She had a split lower lip, and she could see another shade of purple appearing just above her collarbone. Her arms felt like lead and trembled as she reached to get some water from the tap to help swallow the pills.

The time was now *eleven-nineteen* in the morning. Labake had gone back to bed after Vince and Ella left for the day. She got up at five-thirty every morning to make both her husband and daughter break-fast and, of course, to get Ella ready for school. Ella had not noticed anything different in her mother's appearance and had chatted all through their usual morning routine. She was a happy six-year-old who loved school. It was as though she could not wait for day-break so she could hurry off to school. It was never a problem getting her up in the mornings, and Labake was grateful for that right now. She could not imagine struggling with Ella each morning in her present condition.

By the time Labake was done with Ella's hair and she was seated at the table for breakfast, her father came down the stairs with a scowl on his face, causing Labake's heart to skip a beat the minute she noticed it. That was usual for her. In fact, she did not need to see her husband to feel panicky; all she had to do was hear his footsteps or just remember that he would be home from work at any moment, then her nerves would start the *Macarena*.

"Good Morning, Daddy," Ella greeted her father cheerfully with a mouth full of *cocoa pops*.

"Morning, my Angel," Vince replied to his daughter and gave her a peck on her forehead. He always referred to her as His *Angel*. She was his pride and joy, the only person Labake believed he ever truly loved.

"Ready for school?" He asked her. Ella bobbed her head enthusiastically in response. She was every bit a *daddy's girl*. For a six-year-old, Ella was well aware of her father's deep love for her and got away with anything, even when she was being naughty. Vince had the patience of a priest when he handled his daughter.

"Morning Vince...er...should I... should I serve you breakfast?" Labake asked her husband of five years, ten months and six days nervously. Vince threw her a deeper scowl and carried on with his daughter softly, ignoring his wife's question. Labake nervously stood where she was, unsure of what to say or do next. This was the usual trend when she dealt with Vince. Uncertainty just always seemed to be the order of the day. She wondered how he could be so mean to her yet so tender towards his daughter, all in the same breath. How was *anyone* capable of that?

Still unsure of what to do, Labake stood rooted to the spot awkwardly. She contemplated repeating the question, serving his simple breakfast of eggs and toast, or just playing her usual *avoidance* card by disappearing into the kitchen. This was the effect Vince had on her most of the time. She always felt the need to avoid being in the same room with him for fear of doing something which could ignite his temper. The last thing she needed was a repeat performance of last night, as she knew she could not survive another beating this morning. She was in physical pain already, though she had taken painkillers before calling it a night in the guest room last night and popped a few early this morning when she got up. That was another common occurrence in their household. Often, Vince would send her out of the bedroom they shared after he had given her a beating.

Labake wondered what she would do without the painkillers and if she was addicted to them. She was aware that there was a likelihood of getting hooked on the *extra strong* painkillers she took, but she found it hard to face a day without them. She could not remember a time when she was not in pain recently. Not just physically but emotionally and mentally too. Unfortunately, she was yet to find antidotes for the latter two.

Staring at her reflection in the mirror, Labake's mind drifted back to this morning's event.

After what seemed an awkward moment, Vince finally answered in an icy tone, "Get me a cup of coffee." It was an order, and Labake scurried off to obey it as fast as she could, without question. She walked with a slight limp, one she had sustained a year and a half ago when Vince knocked her into a wall, shattering her left knee cap. She had lied at the hospital that she had tripped and fallen down the stairs. She had been in hospital for weeks and had worn a cast for months. In fact, she had been told by the orthopedic doctor that she would require a cane to get around for the rest of her life but thankfully, that had not been the case. Her knee had healed in a matter of months, and she found that she did not require the cane after all. The limp was, however, here to stay, be it ever so slight.

Turning away from the mirror, Labake wondered why her husband was always so angry with her. She really did try to do everything right, trying to be the best wife she could to him, but it just never seemed enough. She felt as though the harder she tried, the angrier he got as she was never able to please him. He was never tender with her, the way he was with their daughter, and Labake wondered why. She had once tried to broach the subject with him and perhaps make amends if he was aggrieved over something she had done, but he had shut her up with that familiar scowl of his.

Labake was never able to initiate a conversation successfully with Vince, except when it had to do with Ella. Vince was all ears when it had to do with his beloved daughter. Even then, Labake would stutter so badly out of nerves that she ended up being incoherent, causing Vince even more anger. He would shout at her and rain curses on her for being so dumb, making it even worse for her to spit the words out. To say she was a bag of nerves around him was an understatement. She was terrified of her husband and lived in constant fear.

Labake often found herself second-guessing every action she took lately. *Should she do it? If so, how should she do it? Was it enough? How much would he want? He's always preferred it this way, but the last time, he slapped her for doing it his preferred way.* The questions were unending, and they consumed her thoughts daily. They spanned every single decision from food, cleaning, their daughter, and the list went on. She just did not seem able to get her husband's approval over any single decision she made. Vince gave many mixed signals, making it impossible for her to predict him or what he wanted at any given time. This made her unsure of herself around him all the time.

Labake had been with Vince all these years and still could not say she truly *knew* him. He would complain, yell, cuss and eventually resort to violence regardless of what she did to placate him. There were absolutely no triggers. He would flare up at will over the slightest thing. Labake, therefore, trod carefully around him to avoid upsetting him. His temper went from *zero* to *a hundred* degrees in a matter of seconds, such that she often did not even know what he was upset about until after his blows subsided.

Labake loved Vince in the beginning and believed he loved her too in his own way. He just had difficulty finding expression for it. At least, that was the excuse she made for him. In the months following their actual wedding, however, fear had swiftly replaced whatever love she once felt for Vincent Ebodo. In actual fact, she was terrified of her husband. Many times she was afraid to the point of confusion when dealing with him, and he was aware of the effect he had on her. Labake believed he even got a kick out of it. When he started, It was as if he enjoyed the look of fear and powerlessness in her eyes.

The shoves had quickly turned into unexpected slaps, and in time, the slaps had grown into full-on beatings within weeks of their marriage. The beatings ranged from her being punched or kicked to being whipped with one of Vince's leather belts or objects being thrown at her when he flew into one of his rages. She would beg and plead with him to stop, but the more she did, the worse the beatings got. It was as though his ability to hurt her and get away with it, coupled with her inability to stop him, excited him. Labake was beginning to think her husband was a sadist as he displayed all the symptoms of one.

Another tear slowly rolled down Labake's battered cheek as she remembered the first time Vince had hit her. She had been shocked by it and held her stinging cheek with a startled look. She had forgotten to pick up his suits from the dry cleaners, and he flew into a rage. The experience had made Labake vow never to let that happen again. She always had a *to-do* list handy now. It helped a lot as she had become really forgetful since she had been with Vince. Having a list helped her complete all her tasks, thereby reducing the risk of being attacked by her husband. She had read somewhere that forgetfulness resulted from depression, and Labake knew she was depressed. She felt helplessly trapped in a loveless, violent, emotional, and mentally abusive marriage.

Labake had thought of upping and leaving Vince many times but was too scared to do so. She had been a teenager when they married and had never worked a day in her life. What would she do for an income, particularly with a young child? She had no work experience, no family or friends in whom she could confide as they had all been cut off since her marriage. Vince hated her family or anyone who tried to maintain a relationship with her. Her mother, *Maami,* as Labake and *Laide,* her sister, called her, had tried to mend bridges several times but to no avail. She had since died a few months back, and Labake only had Laide, her elder sister. Laide had managed to remain diplomatic and sucked up to Vince so that she could maintain some kind of contact with her sister, but even that was tedious as Laide now lived outside the country.

Vince had finally barred Laide or any of his wife's friends from coming to his house. Labake thus had a secret relationship with her sister, one her husband was unaware of as he would kill her if he ever discovered they were as in touch as they were. He had forbidden her from contacting her sister without his knowledge. Labake now knew it was his way of keeping her in check and free of any external influence. She and her sister, however, spoke every day as Laide usually rang on weekday afternoons when she was certain her difficult brother-in-law would be at work. Labake was sure to delete every trace of their communication off her cell phone, just in case Vince checked, as he often did.

There was also Ella to consider. What would Labake do without her daughter? This was what Vince held over her. He had told her in no unclear terms that she could leave whenever she wanted but that she would never set her eyes on their daughter ever again if she did, and Labake believed him. The thought of that frightened her to no end. She could bear Vince's brutality and did not care about the numerous affairs he had, affairs he never even bothered to hide from her. What she could not imagine was living her life without her daughter. Ella was what kept her sane, and she bore her husband's cruelty only because of her. Ella was the only valuable thing Vince ever gave her, and there was no way she was going to let him keep her away from her. Labake knew she would die first than have him do that, which made her feel even more trapped in her marriage to him.

Last night, Vince had come home from work in a foul mood. Labake's heart had started racing when she heard the way he slammed the front door as he walked into the house. That was another skill she had mastered in the years she had been married - the ability to gauge her husband's mood even before she set eyes on him, usually by the way he shut a door or came down the stairs.

Labake had wondered if she could avoid a beating once Vince got in last night, as that was often the eventual outcome when he came home in a bad mood. He took his anger out on her and would somehow find a way to link her to his aggravation, whether she was the cause of it or not. She knew he struggled with a difficult boss at work. She was well aware that his foul moods on his return home from work were often a result of an altercation with *Mr. Singh*. Mr.

Singh was Vince's Indian boss, the CEO of the Insurance Company where he worked.

Labake's hands jittered, and her adrenalin got pumping in trepidation of what was to be the inevitable outcome of Vince's obvious foul mood. She had spilled a glass of water all over him as she was unable to control her shaky hands, and in an attempt to mop it all up, she stepped on his foot too. At first, he had shoved her away in pain and anger, causing the pitcher of water in her hands to fall to the tiled floor and shatter into tiny pieces. Then there was too much salt in his food which was not *hot* enough in the first place.

All these *atrocities* on Labake's part had got Vince ticking like a time bomb, waiting to explode any second. Usually, at this point, Labake could do nothing right, and Vince's mind was already made up to use his fist to remind her of how useless she was. It would only take a few minutes for him to unleash the dragon, and Labake sensed it and waited in apprehension for it.

The final straw was that they had run out of beer, unknown to Labake. Somehow, that had not made it on her *to-do* list that day. Vince usually had a beer with his supper, but she had not remembered to stock up on them. Of course, at this stage, Labake knew what was to come. It was inevitable. The lack of any beer was a *sacrilege* and her third strike. She was savagely attacked within seconds of her husband's discovery.

Vince had turned red with rage spitting out curses and yelling how useless Labake was as he delivered each blow. She, on the other hand, did the usual. She cowered and tried to shield herself from his punches. She pleaded with him in hushed tones as she did not want to awaken Ella, who was asleep upstairs. The more she did, the harder the blows came. Labake stiffened and moaned in pain with each blow Vince delivered as she tried not to cry out loudly. She had mastered the art of stifling the urge to cry out. The last thing she wanted was to damage her daughter by having her witness her father's brutality. She curled up into a ball on the floor and bore Vince's blows, hoping the episode would end soon. When he was done, Labake had a bloody face and ached all over. The evidence of last night's ordeal was even more obvious this morning by the ugly bruising that now appeared all over her body.

Snapping out of her deep thoughts, Labake suddenly remembered she had a few errands to run before she picked Ella up from school that afternoon and decided to take a quick shower and get on with the day. She did all this with difficulty as she was in so much pain and found it hard to get around easily. It was as if her mind moved faster than her body such that she willed herself to go faster but her body just could not keep up with the pace. She rechecked the time and hoped the painkillers would take effect soon.

After what seemed like forever, Labake got into the car but realized she had forgotten her sunglasses. She could not go anywhere public without them; they were all she had apart from the make-up and long sleeve clothing she wore to help conceal the bruising on her face, neck, and arms. She made a difficult dash into the house again to get the oversized sunglasses and a neck scarf to hide the purple blotches around her neck, then made her way out of the estate where they lived.

CHAPTER TWO

Omorewa Ilo pressed and held her car horn impatiently again. This time, longer than the last. She wondered why it always took the security guards at the main gate so long to open it. It seemed as though she had been waiting outside her parents' house for longer than usual today. *Where are they?* She impatiently pushed the car horn again, holding it down a little longer this time. She was about to reach for her cell phone when the gates swung open. She hissed and ignored the guard's greeting as she drove passed him, leaving a cloud of dust in her wake. She parked her car in her usual spot on the large, well-tended grounds of her parents' mansion and gathered her things to vacate the car. She was aware that she was rather irritable today. Was it just the guards at the gate that annoyed her or something else? She wondered.

As she got out of the car and walked up the short flight of steps to the large oak front doors, Rewa wondered why the guards still had jobs with her parents. They clearly did not value them. She hissed again as she put her key in the lock and let herself into the lusciously furnished hall way. She walked the short distance into the large living room where her mother was seated with her best friend, *Mrs. Thomas*. They were examining what seemed to be yet another *aso-ebi* fabric. Her mother looked up as she walked in and said, "Hello dear, how was work today?" Mrs. Ilo asked, smiling at her first daughter.

"Good, thank you, Mum," Rewa replied and then greeted Mrs. Thomas with a smile, "Hello, Aunty," She said.

"Rewa dear, how are you? Hope you've had a good day," She asked. Most people referred to her as *Rewa* for short as opposed to her full name - *Omorewa*.

"It's been good, thank you, Aunty," Rewa answered her mother's friend of over fifty years. Mrs. Thomas and Mrs. Ilo were old school friends from way back and were inseparable.

"This is the *aso-ebi* for Gbubemi's wedding," Mrs. Ilo explained to her daughter. "What do you think, dear?" She asked Rewa.

Gbubemi was Mrs. Thomas's twenty-nine-year-old son. He was the last of her four children to be getting married, and his parents were planning a really big society wedding.

"Nice, very pretty, Mum," Rewa answered and decided to leave them to it. She was tired and had been in traffic for what seemed like ages, not to mention the hard day she'd had at work. All she wanted to do was have a shower and put her feet up before she turned in for the night.

"I'm going to take a shower, Mum," Rewa announced and bade Mrs. Thomas a good evening. She, in response, prayed for her as she usually did, "We will surely gather to celebrate your own wedding soon, dear. On that day, my head tie would be the highest and biggest by God's grace, my darling." Omorewa smiled at her sweetly and said, "Amen, Aunty."

"Amen," Mrs. Ilo added.

"Would you like your supper brought up to your quarters, dear? *Cook* made your favorite *pasta,*" she asked Rewa.

"Thanks, mum. I'll have it upstairs, please," Rewa replied and then asked,

"When is dad due back from his trip?"

"It was supposed to be yesterday, but he rang earlier, saying the meeting had been postponed till today, so I guess he'd be back tomorrow," her mother answered. Rewa nodded and then headed upstairs to her bedroom.

Chief Benjamin Ilo, Rewa's father, had been away for a couple of days. You could tell when he was away. The house was a lot quieter when he was away. He had a larger-than-life personality, was very funny, and wanted everyone around him to be happy. He was every bit a generous soul. Usually, when he was around, you could hear the roar of his laughter ring through the house, and there would be a fleet of cars parked in the driveway outside. There were always people either having meetings with him or waiting to see him for personal reasons, mostly financial.

Chief Ilo was a renowned philanthropist and was highly influential in society. He was a very busy man, and his wife and daughters knew it. They had grown accustomed to his endless meetings and having people coming and going around the house. That had been the case since Rewa could remember. The place, however, seemed like a *ghost town* today as the only visitor present was Mrs. Thomas.

As she climbed the grand staircase to her quarters on the east wing of the first floor, Rewa thought about her father and how he needed to slow things down. He was not getting any younger, and she thought he needed to understand that. She knew her mother felt the same way too, as they had talked about it the other day. He'd had a heart scare a couple of years before, and though he got through it and was given a clean bill of health, Rewa believed someone needed to get on his case about taking things easy or even retiring. She was going to have a conversation with him about it when he returned.

Rewa was quite aware that her father certainly did not need to work for the money. He had made more than enough for generations to come, and even the tabloids knew it. Besides, her immediate younger sister, *Omosede,* and her husband, *Larry*, were quite capable of running the Ilo Empire. They had both worked with Chief Ilo for a while now. In fact, he had said many times that he was pleased with the fresh ideas they brought as young people and how he was quite happy to hand over the reins of his group of companies to them. *Well*, Rewa thought, *there was no better time than now to do just that!* It was a conversation she believed they needed to have.

When she got into her bedroom, Rewa kicked her shoes off and flopped on the bed with a thud as her mind drifted back to Mrs. Thomas' prayer. She was used to them. Her aunties and uncles on both sides of the family prayed the same way whenever they spoke to her, particularly on her birthdays. If only they knew how fed up she was with such prayers and how embarrassing she found them too. She knew they were said in good faith, but they only served as a reminder that she was *'the odd man out'*, the one who was of marriageable age but was still single, the one no one clearly wanted and was therefore perpetually displayed on the *spinster* shelf, year in and out.

Rewa sighed, thinking about it again. Being single at her age, particularly in this part of the world, certainly made her feel extremely sensitive to comments made about it, even when they were aimed at encouraging her. She sometimes felt like she was the only one in her situation though she knew so many others like herself.

The thought of yet another wedding ceremony that was not hers made Rewa feel sad. When was it ever going to be her turn? She wondered. What was it about her that made it impossible to find someone to like her long enough to marry her? She had never imagined being single at her age, let alone *living* with her parents. She had erroneously believed she would be married by age twenty-five and would have had her three children by the time she was thirty at least. "*Ha*!" She laughed out loud. If only all things went according to plan. Instead, here she was, a week to her fortieth birthday, still very *'single and searching'* as Faith, her old school friend, had described herself the other day. They had both laughed at how true that was.

Omorewa and Faith were the only two left unmarried in their group of friends. They hung out together and talked a lot about their single status. It was nice to have someone to talk to about it, someone who was going through the same thing and understood how it felt. Rewa sometimes felt no one else really did get it. Certainly not her sisters or even her parents. In her head, she felt people looked at her pitifully and had labeled her *'the unmarried one'*. It was all she thought about these days, and the degree to which it occupied her thinking worried her as everything she did or that was said to her seemed to revolve around it.

Rewa was beginning to feel like a leper or physically handicapped in some way. She was successful in all other areas of her life except in the area of getting *hitched*. It was almost as though she had been marked with a *'do not marry'* sign on her forehead. She was anxious about her age as well; if she had not found a nice guy when she was younger, what were the odds she would in her forties?

Moreover, her biological clock was ticking, and that compounded issues. First, she had to worry about meeting and marrying the *right* guy, and then there was also the issue of bearing children early enough before her eggs became literally *fried* because of old age. She sometimes encouraged herself, thinking that it just was not God's time yet, and she sometimes succeeded, feeling hopeful that one day, she would get what she desired most in the world. For the most part, though, she was unable to draw courage from any *pep talk* she gave herself or anyone else's for that matter.

Omorewa was the eldest of three daughters. Both her younger sisters were happily married, and between them, Rewa had three nieces. Her youngest sister *Omorien*, was pregnant with her second child, and the family was expecting a call from the United States soon with news of the latest addition to their family.

The Ilos were a close-knit, wealthy family, which had always been the case since Rewa was born. Chief Benjamin Ilo, the patriarch of the Ilo dynasty, had made wise business investments that had paid off early in life, and Rewa and her sisters had wanted for nothing growing up. They were considered *spoiled* by outsiders who did not know them well enough. However, the truth was that the Ilo girls were nowhere near spoilt. They were all professionals, quite successful in their careers, and had been raised with good values and strong work ethics.

Rewa had a degree in Pharmacology from a reputable University in the United Kingdom. She had graduated with honors but found her real passion in interiors and had carved out a great niche for herself in the industry. Her area of specialization was business premises, and she thoroughly loved what she did. She was not just great at it; she was quite successful too and had clients from all walks of life, in both government and private sectors. One would have expected that her job would perhaps afford her a great avenue to meet single and equally successful men, especially with her good looks. Still, she had not met anyone notable or eligible through her work.

Rewa was an attractive, honey-complexioned lady with an hourglass figure. She was of average height and had a great sense of fashion. She was confident and had an air of cool calmness about her, which a lot of people mistook for arrogance. She had been described as *unapproachable* by some guy she had dated in the past but did not know how to change that about herself. It was just the way she was and had always been. Besides, she agreed with her immediate younger sister Omosede that when she eventually did meet *her* man, he would be fully equipped with the skills to *'peel away'* at the onion known as Omorewa Ilo, as he would love *absolutely everything* about her.'

Rewa chuckled now at her sister's summation of the subject. *Sede,* as everyone called her, had always had a way with words, and Rewa knew it was her way of describing her as *somewhat complicated*. She, however, did not mind her illustration at all. In fact, she quite liked the idea of being *peeled away like an onion*.

Lately, Rewa had felt like she had overstayed her welcome in her parent's home. She had recently found herself a lovely apartment in a nice gated estate close to her office. She was in the middle of renovating it and was looking forward to moving soon. Her parents had tried to talk her out of it. They felt odd that any of their children would live anywhere else but their family home and, worst of all, whilst still unmarried. It just went totally against their culture and beliefs.

Mrs. Ilo, in particular, believed only wayward unmarried girls lived by themselves, especially when they had parents who lived in the same city. She was not pleased with the idea and made this clear to her eldest daughter, who was of the opinion that her mother's view was not just old-fashioned but ridiculous. Times had changed, Rewa had patiently explained to her mother. Besides, her mind was made up to move out, and nothing anyone thought about her decision would change it. Her parents knew how difficult it was to persuade her once she decided on anything.

A few months ago, a neighbor had parked his car right in front of the entrance to the Ilo mansion, obstructing the main gate, thereby making it impossible for anyone to have access in or out. On her arrival from work that evening, Rewa had been unable to gain entry into the house through the gate. She was livid, especially as he had taken his time coming out of his house to move the offending vehicle. When she complained to him about it, he responded, "Surely this should be the least of your worries at your age." She had not quite understood what he meant and looked at him as though he had lost his mind.

"Should you still be here, living with your parents at your age? I mean, how old are you? Forty, forty-one, or two? Your peers are all in their husband's homes, and here you are, lamenting over gaining entry into your parent's!" He said caustically, shaking his head disapprovingly before he got into his car and drove off, leaving a stupefied Rewa in his wake.

Tears now stung Rewa's eyes as she remembered the horrible incident. She had decided that very instant to move out of her parents' house. She was convinced the rude neighbor had expressed the views of the entire neighborhood, though she had never even met him or any of the other neighbors prior to that evening. Theirs was quite the upscale and affluent neighborhood, and residents generally tended to mind their businesses. However, It was obvious that this particular neighbor *knew* her, and Rewa found the thought that he did worrisome. Worst still was the thought that if he did know her and was aware of her marital status, the odds that the other neighbors did not was unlikely. Rewa did not even bother wondering how he knew that much about her. Domestic staff within the neighborhood were rather chummy with one another, and there was a lot of information sharing amongst them.

Rewa had rung a realtor friend of hers the minute she got into her quarters with instructions to find her an apartment that evening.

"I mentioned a while back that I thought you should move out, sis, remember? And not to any of the properties owned by Mum and Dad either!" *Omorien*, Rewa's youngest sister, had said when Rewa recounted the story to her on the phone a couple of days later.

"If not for anything, then just so you can at least feel independent and put some space between you and the folks! Even if they complained in the beginning, they'd get used to it eventually *and* respect you more for it too. The guy was a jerk for saying that to you, but at least it's set the ball in motion," Omorien concluded wisely.

Rien, as they called her, was the youngest of the Ilo girls and also the rebel of the family. She had never conformed to any of her parents' rules and had wondered how Rewa had managed to live with them all these years. It was alright when they were younger, but as an adult, she felt it would be stifling! Their parents were too interfering and meddled in all of their daughters' lives. She loved them and knew it was a price to pay for being as closely knit a family as they were, but Rien did not envy her eldest sister in the least. She knew it would be impossible for Rewa to have any privacy living at home with their parents.

Rien herself now lived in Texas with her husband and young daughter. Rewa was sure she would have done exactly what she had advised her to do months before if she were in her position. Rien was just that way inclined. She was the most independent of the Ilo girls.

Rewa was not one to care what anyone thought about her normally, but this was different, especially because it was a *touchy* subject. She had already begun to feel like a guest in her parent's house anyway. Not because of anything they had said or done but because she believed in her mind that she did not belong there anymore. It felt strange, too, to be picked up on dates from her parents' home. In her mind, she seemed like the spoilt brat who had refused to grow up and flee the nest, especially being the eldest of her siblings! She was, however, now ready and looked forward to leaving the Ilo Mansion once her new apartment was completed.

Rewa was also tired of the weird pastors and odd prophets her parents invited to the house for endless vigils, particularly over her seemingly *prolonged* single status. She was a Christian and believed in God and the bible, but her parents believed in seeing visions and *helping* oneself. They believed one needed to physically do something in order to get what one wanted. Praying and waiting for God's timing just seemed too easy and could not be enough. Rewa was fed up with it, and they knew how she felt on the subject. Her mother had referred to her as *cranky* the other day because she refused to put in an appearance at one of such *'prophetic'* meetings.

Rewa sighed now as she remembered. Hopefully, in a few weeks, she would be out of here and probably gain some respect from her folks once she put some distance between herself and them, just as Rien advised. She loved and respected her parents and was grateful for everything they had done for her and her sisters, but it was now time to grow up, and she looked forward to being by herself, in her own space.

The knock on her door brought Rewa back to the present. "Yes?" She answered. It was Emeka, one of the resident stewards of the Ilo household. He popped his head through the door and asked,

"Good evening *Aunty*. Should I bring your food up now?" He asked.

"Not yet, Emeka. I'll ring for it when I'm ready. Thanks," Rewa answered. Emeka nodded and left the room.

That was another thing. The entire domestic staff at the Ilo mansion referred to Rewa as *'aunty',* and she hated it! It made her feel like an *old maiden* and made her presence in her parents' house seem all the more unusual, considering her age. Or perhaps she was just being too sensitive, as Sede, her immediate younger sister, had said when Rewa complained to her about it. Anyhow, Rewa thought within herself, all that would soon come to an end.

It really was a lonely life being single at her age, particularly because there were hardly any of her friends who were. Except for Faith, but she had enough troubles of her own and was not available in recent times. She shuttled between Lagos and Abuja often, visiting her ailing mother.

Asides from the loneliness Rewa felt, there were also the string of *could-have-been* relationships she'd had in the past, the endless *hook-ups* and match-making attempts that ranged from hilarious to dodgy, and of course, the gold-digging guys in between. The truth was, there seemed to be a shortage of decent men in circulation. It seemed all the good ones were married, engaged, or simply *commitmentphobe.*

Then, of course, there was another category of men who had either been recently separated or divorced. *'The rebound guys',* Rewa called them. They usually started out with so much intensity but suddenly ran out of steam once they finally got your attention. She felt she could write a book on being a *'mature single'* lady in the twenty-first century. She chuckled at the term *'mature single'*.

Just as she got off the bed to undress for her shower, her cell phone began to ring. It was Faith who was in Abuja at the moment.

"*Girl*! You won't believe what I'm about to tell you! Got some *sweet* gist for you!" Faith said, sounding so excited and happy.

"Really? Hit me with it, girl. I *need* to hear something *sweet*!" Rewa replied to her old friend, chuckling. She sat on the bed again and smiled in anticipation. God knew she needed any good news to cheer her up at that moment.

"Hmmm, I met this good-looking chap on the flight from Lagos to Abuja yesterday! He sat in the seat right next to mine, and we got talking. Initially, I was a bit aloof when he started the conversation as I was tired and just wanted a quiet trip. But as we talked, I realized we had a lot in common and then took a proper look at him at some point during our conversation and realized he wasn't bad looking at all-not to sound shallow-but you know what I mean!" Faith exclaimed and laughed.

Rewa laughed with her friend and said, "You were always a sucker for *fine boys*. What did you talk about?" She asked Faith enthusiastically.

"Life generally. The conversation was so refreshing; we really connected in a matter of minutes! He was easy to talk to, and he said the same about me! He asked for my number and, of course, I gave it to him. He's rung me this morning already!" Faith exclaimed in exhilaration. She was a bit of a *drama queen* and had quite a bubbly personality. It was what Rewa loved about her. Faith was one of the *realest* people Rewa knew with nothing but pure gold within her heart, and Rewa was genuinely happy about her news; she grinned from ear to ear. "What does he do for a living?" She asked her friend animatedly. Then added, "Er...not to sound too shallow!" Both ladies burst into laughter at Rewa's mimicry of Faith's comment earlier.

"He's a lawyer, apparently. He seemed really nice and is even Christian too! He said he was forty-six and had never married as he'd never found the right person," Faith continued.

"*Really*? Do you mean the conversation went *there*? That's great news! Watching this space from here on then!" Rewa clapped excitedly. They chatted a bit more and bade each other a good night.

Rewa was truly excited for her friend. Faith deserved to be happy, especially at this time in her life. She had a lot on her plate at the moment, with her mother being ill. Faith was the first of five siblings. She had lost her father at a very early age and had struggled to put her younger siblings through school once she left University and got her first job. She was a banker and needed help in shouldering some of her responsibilities, emotionally at least, Rewa believed. She only hoped this was an answer to her friend's prayers as she needed the relationship between Faith and this new chap to become serious and perhaps even end in marriage. It did not matter who met a life partner first; it just had to click for either her or her friend. If it happened for Faith, then she would be encouraged and keep hope alive that she could also find love at her age.

Rewa sighed again, but this time, it was out of satisfaction and hope. She stepped into the warm shower and got lost in her thoughts again, remembering the last date she had been on with a guy named *Lucky*. She met him through a client *Mr. Koye*, who had initially expressed an interest in her himself. Rewa had, however, politely declined not only because he was married but because he really was not her type. They had become good friends after that, and once Mr. Koye knew her stance on the subject, he thought she was too pretty to be alone. He appreciated her values too and decided to introduce her to a single and equally successful friend of his named *Lucky*.

Unfortunately, *self-absorbed* Lucky had talked about himself and all of his great achievements as an architect non-stop from the beginning of the date. He had not bothered to ask Rewa any questions about herself or even pretended to want to know anything about her. He had *talked shop* all night, and by the time their main meal arrived, Rewa was ready to leave. She, however, managed to get through the meal just out of respect for Mr. Koye, who had introduced them. At the end of the date, Lucky had the effrontery to ask if he could see her again. She had smiled sweetly and said he could ring her whenever he wanted and wished him a good night. She never answered or returned any of his calls after that evening.

Rewa wondered how many more dates like that she would have to endure before *'Mr. Right'* came along - *if* he ever did. Did he even exist? She was at a point now where she was beginning to doubt if she would ever meet him. Perhaps it was not in God's plan for her life, she often wondered. She had read somewhere that if one had a desire to be married, then it was put there by God, meaning marriage was a part of one's destiny. She really did hope so as the waiting did get to her at times.

There were times when she just needed to be held by a man, times when she sometimes felt overcome with these strong sexual urges. Sometimes it got so bad that she contemplated ringing one of her old male friends just to satisfy the overwhelming need for sex. It was worse just before her periods, during her monthly ovulation. She was uptight and cranky a lot these days and wondered if it had anything to do with that too.

A colleague at her former job had once suggested she got herself a *'dildo'* to help ease her frustrations. This had been after she snapped at him over something so trivial. He had asked jokingly, "When last did you get laid, girl? You're so *high-strung*! You don't need a man these days, you know. I suggest you get a *dildo* online or something." He had then given her a knowing wink and walked away. She could not deny that she was even more irritable than normal lately. She just seemed to have lost her sense of humor and overreacted at the slightest remark or comment.

Rewa was no virgin. She'd had her fair share of guys while at university and shortly after. That was before she began to take her relationship with God more seriously. She decided eight years ago that the next person she got sexually intimate with would be her husband. *Hebrews* chapter thirteen, verse four of the bible came to mind again, especially *'...the bed undefiled'* part of it. She had believed when she made that promise to herself and God that He would reward her by sending her a husband early enough so she would not have to '*burn with passion*' for too long or give into sexual temptation. However, that was not the case as she was still in the same position as she was eight years ago when she made that commitment. Alone and starving for companionship, someone to love and call her own.

Rewa had come close many times to faltering on her promise to stay celibate till she got married but found she just could not go *'all the way'* with any man, no matter how much the desire to do so was. She sometimes felt she would burst with all the love and affection she believed she was capable of showering on a husband. She had unfortunately been taken advantage of in the past by guys who considered her *desperate*. Some of such experiences she could never bring herself to share with anyone, not her sisters or even Faith, as they were far too humiliating.

Rewa knew her faith wavered when it came to her meeting a life partner, especially as she had a strong faith in other areas of her life. However, she did not seem able to muster up any hope, least of all *faith,* when it came to the subject of her marriage or finding the right man. It was getting to the point where she rarely really prayed about it. She guessed somewhere in her subconscious. She had left it to chance, which in itself was also a source of worry.

CHAPTER THREE

Labake was seventeen and had just finished high school when she first met Vincent Ebodo. Her mother owned a small canteen opposite Vincent's office at the time. He was twenty-seven and had just started work as an insurance broker. He had taken an interest in Labake the minute he laid eyes on her during one of his lunch breaks at the canteen. She had been helping her mother out at the canteen, seeing as she had just completed her 'O' level examinations and was waiting for the results.

Labake was the most naturally beautiful girl Vince had ever seen. She was young, bright, and intelligent. She had big dreams of studying Medicine at University. Once her exam results were out, she still had to sit and pass the Joint Admissions Matriculation Board (JAMB) Examination too to be admitted into the university.

Something about Labake's innocence appealed to Vince. She was friendly and liked by the patrons of the canteen, not only for her beauty but because she was polite and well-mannered. She would greet and converse with them when it was not busy. She was intelligent and had a great sense of humor. Labake just made going to the canteen more fun, when she had the time. She was light-skinned, tall, slim, and shapely in every way. Vince thought she had the nicest long, slender legs and the tiniest waist he ever saw. He thought she had all the physical attributes of a supermodel and had said so to her a few times. In fact, it was one of the reasons he kept a tight rein on her to date.

Vince was aware Labake had a lot of male admirers at the canteen, and even some of his work colleagues from the insurance company passed comments about her on their lunch breaks and at the office. It was a fact that irked him at the time as he liked Labake a lot and had claimed her as his in his head, though he had not quite spoken to her about his feelings for her. She was a natural beauty even with cornrows in her hair and a make-up bare face. She was stunning. She walked gracefully back then, until the limp which she had sustained as a result of her husband's violence.

Labake had never known her father. In fact, rumor had it that she and her older sister, Laide, were products of illicit affairs *Maami* had with two different married men. *Maami* had never spoken about Labake's father, but Labake remembered that *'daddy'* as they referred to Laide's father, had been mean to *Maami* too. He had slapped her around a lot while Labake and Laide waited in fear outside the one room they shared with her, in the ***face-me-face-you*** style house they lived in as young girls.

'Daddy' had left *Maami* a year after Laide was born and returned into her life a few years later when Labake was about four years old. He resented that *Maami* had moved on and had another child with another man in the seven years he had been gone and showed it with his fist from time to time. Laide and Labake would often overhear *Maami* beg and plead with *'daddy'* not to leave her whenever he got upset about something. He would often beat her up, leave her for weeks on end and resurface again into her willing

and open arms whenever he desired, until he finally left one evening and never returned.

To date, Labake's elder sister, Laide, hated her father and had never felt close to him, even as a little girl. In fact, the first time he had been introduced to her as her father had been when he came back into *Maami's* life when she was seven and Labake was four. He, in return, never even pretended to love or care for Laide. He ignored her for the most part whenever he resurfaced again in their lives. The only thing Laide remembered her father ever buying her was ***puff-puff*** once or twice when he had done one of his disappearing and reappearing acts.

Laide had not seen or heard from her father since she was nine years old and had never bothered to search for him since she became an adult. The memories and images of him hurting her mother had stayed with her and had kept her from marrying and settling down herself. She had been hardened by the experience and had vowed never to let any man treat her the way *Maami* had been treated by her estranged father.

Maami was a strong woman and though shattered by *daddy's* final disappearance, had found a way to cope after his abandonment. Moreover, she had two young daughters to cater to. She had managed to gather some money and started her small business of selling ***'Jollof rice'*** outside their communal house. Eventually, she made enough money to rent the small shop opposite the Insurance building where Vince worked at the time. She had converted it into a *pseudo* canteen and introduced two or three other dishes to the menu. It was by no means a five-star restaurant, but the food was good as she had always been a great cook.

Labake and Laide had nobody but each other and had fostered a very close bond with their mother, who had raised them to be decent girls. They did not have much growing up, but they had their mother's love. *Maami* made enough to provide accommodation and put her girls through school, vowing they would have better lives than she did.

After a year of visiting the canteen, Vince summoned up some courage to ask *Maami* for Labake's hand in marriage. Prior to his asking, he would come into the canteen on his lunch breaks, bearing little gifts for Labake from time to time. He would bring her gifts like hair clips and novels as he knew she loved to read. She was appreciative of these gifts and looked forward to them. They made her feel like one of the girls she read about in the ***'Pacesetters'*** stories he bought her. At this point, she had turned eighteen and had re-sat her ***JAMB*** examination again as she had not made the required ***cut-off*** mark to study medicine at the University.

At first, *Maami* had been reluctant to let Labake marry at such an early age. She was worried about her education as she knew her daughter was a clever girl. She wanted to ensure she achieved her dream of becoming a Medical Doctor one day. She was also worried about the ten-year age difference between Labake and *'Mr. Vincent'* as she referred to Vince but Vince had assured her not to worry about all that. He said he loved Labake and was happy to take on the responsibility of looking after her. He promised to allow her further her education and did not mind putting her through university himself.

The relationship between Labake and Vince became formal after that, and a couple of months later, Labake, who had been a virgin, fell pregnant by Vince. He had invited her to his flat for the first time with *Maami's* permission. She had agreed, as Labake was now somewhat betrothed to him. Of course, Vince had taken advantage of the situation as it was the first time they had ever been alone. He had cajoled her into having sex with him, and Labake had willingly obliged as she was already head over hills smitten by him at that stage. He had been nice to her in the beginning, and she could not believe how lucky she was that he wanted her.

Labake's first sexual experience had been unpleasant as Vince had been rough with her even then, paying no mind to the fact that it was her first time. What she had been unaware of at the time was that it had been a deliberate plan on Vince's part to impregnate her, thereby making her permanently his so that her mother could not refuse their marriage. Indeed, *Maami*'s hands were tied by Labake's pregnancy.

Vince and Labake were married at the Marriage Registry a few months before Ella was born, causing Labake to defer her entry into University. Eventually, she sadly settled for a part-time course in Microbiology at the Polytechnic as there just was no time to commit to a full-time, six-year medical degree with a husband and child to care for. Vince had managed to convince her that she could study Medicine once Ella was older. He was always able to manipulate her into doing what he wanted without her even knowing it.

Labake gave in to Vince's every wish without question because she had loved him back then and wanted to please him. She never argued with him as she never wanted to upset him. She also never wanted to *rock the boat* in her new marriage, especially as she considered herself fortunate to have met a man who was willing to be responsible for her and her child, a fact *Maami* always reminded her of.

The first time Vince had shown any violence towards Labake was when he angrily shoved her out of his way because she brought the subject of going to Medical School up again. He had been livid and shouted, "Why are you so selfish? Don't I provide enough for you? I will not have a stranger raise my daughter because you want to go to school! *Never*! Do you hear me? *Never!* I will not hear of it! Don't ever talk to me about that again!"

It was at that point that he had roughly shoved her out of his way, the force of which had knocked her against the kitchen wall. Labake had been shocked by Vince's reaction and could never bring herself to broach the subject again with him. That had been Vince's aim, and it had worked. He had successfully bullied her into silence over her life-long dream. Her sister Laide, who was in her third year at University at the time, kept pushing her to ask Vince about her going to medical school, but Labake had never been able to after that last experience. She had never been able to stand up to her husband. Not then and certainly not now; even the thought of it made her shudder.

Labake had begun to understand about a month into her marriage that her husband was not as easy going as he had appeared prior to their marriage. Immediately after they wedded, he had managed to cut her off from both her mother and sister. He banned *Maami* from visiting them at the apartment where they lived at the time just because she, too, had enquired about Labake's education. *Maami* had tried to no avail to appeal to Vince's better side, but nothing had worked. Instead, she had stayed away from their home and only communicated with her daughter by telephone as she had not wanted to create more trouble for Labake.

Maami heard several times from Labake that Vince had grown more difficult as the days fast ran into weeks and months of their marriage. She, however, always advised Labake to forebear and stay with him because of Ella. She did not want her daughters to suffer like she had as a single parent. She wanted an entirely different life for her girls, one where they were secure in marriages with husbands who cared for them. She, therefore, advised Labake to persevere and make the most of her marriage. She was optimistic that things would improve with time. Unfortunately, they never did. Instead, things got increasingly worse in the months and years to follow.

Vince had gradually become a terror to live with. He was extremely possessive, jealous, and irrational, particularly when he and Labake went out to events or even to the shops together. Labake dreaded going out with him as she almost always received a beating on their return. Vince would convince himself that she had flirted with any and every man they came in contact with on their outings together and then resort to violence to remind her whose she was.

On one such occasion, at his mother's sixtieth birthday party, Labake had been helping out with serving guests food and ensuring everyone had enough food to eat when she bumped into an old school friend who was also at the party with her husband. Her friend's husband had embraced her in a hug when they were introduced, and Labake thought nothing of it. As far as she was concerned, it had been an innocent, friendly gesture. Vince had seen it and immediately became cold towards her throughout the rest of their stay at the party. Labake, on the other hand, had been in the dark about what she had done to upset him and had been nervous because of his sudden change in attitude towards her.

On their way home from the party, Vince slapped her across the face in the car while Ella slept in the back seat. He accused her of flirting with her friend's husband. Shocked, Labake denied that ever happened and said she would never cheat on him or humiliate him in that manner, but that was not persuasive enough for her very angry husband. He had beaten her mercilessly when they got home that evening, calling her a whore, and as if to put his stamp of ownership on her, he dragged her into their bedroom and brutally raped her.

That was also another usual occurrence in the Ebodo household. Having sex with her husband made Labake feel dirty. He made her do things she was not comfortable with. Vince also had a very high sexual libido and was a selfish lover, taking a lot but never giving anything in return. It was always about him, and to prove she was his and no one else's, he took her forcefully and at will. He wanted sex almost every night, never considering her mood or if she was tired or ill. He demanded it, and she could not ever refuse.

Labake remembered trying to explain how tired she was once, having had quite a busy day, hoping he would understand and let her be for that night, but Vince had turned on her instead. He had beaten her and raped her, claiming he would not beg or be held to ransom to sleep with his own wife. Labake had learned never to deny him sex after that and yielded to his every whim. It was whenever he wanted it and however he needed it. Vince dominated every aspect of Labake's life, her mind, body, and even her soul.

Labake had dreamed and had wonderful expectations about making love to her husband before her marriage to Vince. She had been a hopeless romantic at heart and had read a lot of novels, giving her high hopes and lovely ideas about love making, particularly with someone she loved. However, she now knew they were *illusions of grandeur* as Vince had ruined her sexual experience in ways she could not even describe. She abhorred having sex with him and considered it a most unpleasant chore, one she had learned to endure and engage in mindlessly.

The light in Labake's eyes had long since gone dim, and something in her had shut down and perhaps even died since her marriage. She had grown a lot quieter, her youthful, bubbly nature had disappeared, and she had become a shadow of who she used to be. She did not just have a hollow look in her eyes; she felt hollow within too. Most women gained weight after childbirth but not Labake. She had lost quite a bit of weight and had not gained any during or after her pregnancy. She also became hypertensive and required medication at her young age to manage her blood pressure.

Vince's violence had cost Labake three pregnancies since Ella's birth. There had been some complications with the last miscarriage, and the doctors had advised her not to ever try to conceive again. A fact that had saddened Labake greatly but one she had quickly come to terms with as she was determined not to have any more children with Vince Ebodo. She had resolved that it would only further tie her to him, and she did not think her marriage was healthy enough to bring another child into anyway. Vince was never violent towards Labake while Ella was around or awake. He was far too calm and calculating for that. He usually waited for her to go to bed before he *unleashed the dragon.*

Recently, Vince had begun talking about having another child even though he was aware the doctors had advised against it. He knew having another child would jeopardize Labake's life as she had nearly died after losing the third pregnancy. The doctors had even contemplated giving her a hysterectomy due to complications she had developed because of the extent of injury Vince had inflicted on her while she was pregnant. He, however, seemed to have forgotten the doctors' astute warnings. The doctors had decided she could keep her uterus against all odds, with strong warnings for her never to attempt pregnancy again. She was now beginning to wish she'd had the hysterectomy as it would at least have kept Vince off her back for another baby.

Wanting another child seemed to be another reason for Vince's wrath lately, and Labake wondered how long she would have to bear the beatings that were sure to follow. The other day, he had called her *infertile*. Labake sometimes felt like she lived with an imbecile or someone who lacked the cognitive ability to reason properly. He acted like *he* was not *the reason* for their inability to have more children.

Labake had no friends whatsoever, as Vince did not encourage it. She led an isolated life, and no one knew what she endured with him. Her sister, Laide, had her suspicions but had no real proof, seeing as she now lived and worked outside the country in The Republic of Benin. Laide was not allowed to visit her sister without prior notice or permission from Vince. She, therefore, did not know the full extent of hardship Labake suffered at her husband's hands.

Laide worked for The Ministry of External Affairs as a diplomat and had been posted out of the country a few years ago. She and Labake had not seen each other since their mother's funeral a few months back, and Labake missed her and the life they'd had with their mother before it all changed. Laide was all the family she had left since *Maami's* passing, and she had not been able to fully confide in her about her husband's cruelty, especially because of the distance between them.

Labake had never mentioned her husband's violence to Laide or anyone at that. Even the hospitals where she received treatments for injuries inflicted by Vince were unaware of her situation. This was because she visited several different hospitals and clinics just so there was no trail of evidence to prove that she was being routinely battered. She found it shameful and humiliating to even think of telling anyone about her predicament.

Labake believed she had no options, Vince was *her cross,* and she had to carry it till he hopefully realized he had anger issues and sought some help for it. In the meantime, she tried to stay out of his hair as much as possible and do everything he wanted for peace's sake. She prayed that someday, things would be different between them. In the meantime, she kept busy with picking Ella up from school and doing other domestic chores.

CHAPTER FOUR

"Hey Rewa, how are you?" Rewa stopped in her tracks, thinking the voice sounded vaguely familiar. She turned round and recognized him right away. How could she ever forget him? It was *Banjo Adetunji.* Cautiously, she took a step towards him to confirm she was not being deceived by her eyes.

"I knew it was you the minute I saw you. I can never forget that figure of yours. You haven't changed a single bit. In fact, you look better than I remember!" Banjo said appreciatively. His roving eyes voraciously ran up and down her body in a way that made Rewa feel she needed a shower.

She stared at him blankly, unsure how to react to him or his comment. After what seemed a moment, she said, "How are you, Banjo? It's been a while." It was a rather lack luster, flat greeting. One that did not even pretend to be anything else. Rewa stared at him with the same blank expression on her face, thinking it uncanny that they were bumping into one another *again*. In fact, she thought silently, if her memory served her correctly, this would make it the second time they would run into each other since their rather *unfortunate* incident. She was amazed at how he was able to act like she was a long-lost friend. In fact, it was hilarious, she thought within herself and really could have laughed out loud at that moment.

Suddenly, something about the way he appraised her made Rewa feel self-conscious, and her hand went to her hair as if to smooth a stray strand into place. She was surprised and found it annoying that Banjo unnerved her even after all this time and all that had happened between them. His eyes ran the length and breadth of her form brazenly, clearly unabashed, as though they were simply old acquaintances between whom nothing but sex had transpired. The look he gave her was a dirty, lustful one, and it annoyed Rewa all the more. *How dare he?* She wondered.

Banjo's smile deepened when he realized the effect he had on her. *The effrontery!* Rewa thought. She averted her gaze and looked round the store sheepishly. She suddenly felt dirty and ashamed and could not explain why. *Talk about an eclectic mix of feelings* she thought within herself.

"What are you doing here?" Banjo asked in his usual feigned interest. They were standing in the furniture section of *Homeware Super Store*.

"I...I just moved into my own place...I'm looking for furnishing for my guest room," Rewa replied and thought, *that was way too much information, silly*. She chided herself.

"*Wow*! You mean you finally fled the nest? Banjo asked, teasing her with a wicked look in his eyes. *God! He was just as handsome as ever!* Rewa thought. Banjo was one of those strikingly handsome *brothers*. Like something out of a *GQ* magazine. He personified the words *tall, dark and handsome*. His pearl white teeth gleamed against the contrast of his very dark, shiny skin under a perfectly groomed mustache that was above dark, luscious, full lips. *Oh, how I remember those lips*. Rewa thought within herself.

Banjo was lean and had a very distinguished look about him. That charm was almost irresistible, and Rewa knew that too well. He had this false look of humility about him. *False* because it was ingenuine. It was one he *put on* and was not immediately apparent to the naive sister she had once been. *Banjo Adetunji* had a deceptive, caring, and concerned disposition about him too. It was, however, all a façade; sadly, Rewa could testify to that. The realization made her sigh almost loudly as she studied him now. He looked rather dapper in a striped pink shirt and blue jeans. What a waste of a fine specimen he was, she thought silently.

"I guess I did," Rewa answered quietly, having finally resolved within herself to play it *cool, calm,* and *collected* with him.

"Where is it?" Banjo asked in that phony, very interested way that only he knew how to pull off.

"Where is what?" Rewa asked blankly. She had been studying his face so intently that she had missed the train of conversation. *Gosh,* she thought! Her mind just went to mush around this guy, even after all this time! That irked her a lot.

"Your new place, *silly*!" Banjo laughed.

"Oh, It's in *Crossway Estate*. Just a small two-bed flat," Rewa supplied without thinking. Again, too much information, she thought when she heard herself.

"*Wow!* My sister lives in that estate. Nice one. *Congrats*! How are you finding it...living by yourself, I mean?" Banjo asked interestedly.

"Your sister lives in *Crossway*? The world really is a small place," Rewa answered dryly. "It's a welcome change if I'm being honest...liberating in a way. How about you? Are you still at *Medlake Hospital*?" Rewa asked, attempting to stir the conversation away from herself.

"Yes, that's where I'm still at. They made me *Medical Director*," Banjo answered rather distractedly as if that was not the most paramount issue at hand.

"Congratulations," Rewa said quietly, still with the same blank but now resigned expression on her face.

Suddenly, they did not have anything more to say to one another. They just stood there, face to face, looking into each other's eyes. After what seemed an awkward moment, Rewa took a glance at her watch and said,

"Er...I should probably get going. Nice seeing you again, Banjo." Then as if he suddenly found his voice too, Banjo asked for her number, and she obliged him, contrary to what her head was telling her. She wanted to ask more questions but did not want to appear interested. Strangely, she was pleased he asked for her number. *Why?* She wondered.

Just as she turned to leave, Banjo reached for her hand and held it. Looking deeply into her eyes, he said, "I'm really sorry for the way we left things the last time, Rewa. I know I hurt you, and I would do anything to undo that. I'm sorry." Again, he said it so convincingly that no one would have doubted that he meant every word.

"That's ok, Banjo. All water under a *very high* bridge now," Rewa answered, cracked a half smile for the first time, and turned to leave again but not before hearing the magic words.

"Let me make it up to you and buy you dinner some time...?" It was a half question, half statement kind of sentence. *He just had to ruin it by asking,* Rewa thought within her. It was so like Banjo

Adetunji to further complicate issues. She really could not believe he was asking to take her out. *Was he serious right now?* Rewa wondered.

Well, not again! It had taken her several months to get over him and work him out of her system. To her amazement, however, she heard herself say, "Any time, Banjo. You have my number." Obviously, her head and heart were not in sync. She shook her head slightly as she walked away.

You foolish girl! When will you learn? She scolded herself as she walked away. *He broke your heart a few years ago, and you want to travel that same road again?* The attraction or chemistry was just too strong between them, and Rewa found herself unable to resist his charm. She ignored her head completely and did what her heart wanted. She was supposed to hate him, to want to scratch his eyes out for what he did to her, but she did not do that. Instead, she held her head up and walked away gracefully. She hoped.

Rewa had first met *Doctor Adebanjo Adetunji* at *Medlake Hospital,* where she had worked as a pharmacist shortly after she returned from the United Kingdom. He had been a resident doctor there at the time, and they'd had an instant attraction to one another. They dated on and off casually, and though Rewa had been unaware at the time, Banjo had meant more to her than she had to him.

These were the days before she became a more serious Christian. She immediately fell for his charm, throwing caution to the wind, and slept with him on their first date. Making love with Banjo had been magical, just as she had anticipated. It was, however, one of the biggest mistakes she ever made. She had regretted it for months after, as he began to avoid her after their *rendezvous* together. The embarrassing thing for her was that she had not realized it had been *just sex* for him. She had acted every part of the silly, gullible girl she was.

A week later, Rewa had eventually caught him in the hospital elevator. He had not returned any of her calls, and she had wondered why. When Banjo realized he was trapped in the elevator with her and could no longer avoid her, he suddenly got angry when she asked him why he had not returned her calls.

"Look, Rewa, I like you and everything, but what we had was purely sex. I thought you understood that. I am engaged and very happily so, I might add. I'm getting married in a couple of months. Weren't you aware? The entire hospital is, for crying out loud!" He snapped at her in a frustrated tone as if this was all her fault.

One could not tell by the expression on her face at that moment, but Rewa was shattered inside. She gathered herself together swiftly, looked at Banjo in that cool, blank way that only she understood, and said quietly,

"I wasn't aware that *it was purely sex* for you...I certainly wasn't aware of your engagement but never mind, I get it now." She got off the lift on the next floor, not caring that it was the wrong one as she needed to put some distance between them desperately. The tears stung her eyes as she made her way past people to the staircase.

Rewa thought she would die of heartache and humiliation after that meeting in the Hospital elevator. She felt rather foolish and now understood why she had been the recipient of some weird stares from her colleagues and other staff at the hospital. She remembered a conversation with *Chichi*, one of the nurses she was chummy with. In her own way, Nurse Chichi had tried to warn her about Dr. Banjo and his notorious philandering ways with unsuspecting ladies at *Medlake hospital* and beyond. Her warning had, however, come too late as Rewa had fallen for the handsome doctor on the fifth floor such that Nurse Chichi's message had gone right over her head! She had later remembered exactly what Chichi had said,

"Miss Ilo, please be careful about dating anyone here at *Medlake,* and don't be fooled by its size either...news spreads like wildfire here. Some of the staff, especially the *male* doctors, aren't to be trusted, and many unknowing *female* staff members have had their fingers burned for dating them," She had stated quietly.

Rewa had not got the message at the time and had waived it off as usual hospital gossip. It had all become clearer to her in the following months that nurse Chichi had actually attempted to warn her of Banjo in particular. Rewa wished Chichi had been more direct about the subtle but vital message she had tried to pass to her. Perhaps it would have saved her from months of pain, shame, and humiliation.

Apparently, Banjo was a serial womanizer and heartbreaker, and almost everyone at the hospital knew it. Rewa's nasty experience with him was one of the factors that eventually informed her decision to leave her profession. Apart from the fact that she never found fulfillment in Pharmacy, her nasty affair with Banjo made her dislike it even more. She had resigned that month, to her parent's chagrin, and never saw Dr. Banjo Adetunji again until a few years after. Anyone would have thought she would have learned from that last experience with him, but no, not Omorewa Ilo. *He was the thorn in her flesh!*

Rewa and Banjo had bumped into each other after *Medlake*, a few years later, on a flight from Lagos to London. She was on her way to an annual Interior Design Exhibition in Northampton while Banjo was attending his cousin's wedding in Manchester. He had spotted her at the boarding gate of the airline and came looking for her once the plane took off.

"Hey, gorgeous!" He said, just as Rewa got settled and turned the page of a magazine. She recognized him instantly. *"Hey!"* Banjo said again, playfully tapping her shoulder like an old friend would and jumping in the vacant seat next to hers before she could respond. To the on-looker, Banjo seemed like a long-lost friend who was pleased to see his friend and was about to catch up with her. Rewa, of course, had matured since her last entanglement with him, and as hard as she tried to maintain a cool demeanor, in spite of herself, she gave him a half smile and said.

"Hello Banjo, it's been a bit..." She was rather surprised to see him and her heart lurched, but she managed to feign a calm exterior.

"It has! How have you been?" He asked her. *Exactly where you left me!* Was what she wanted to spit at him, but she did not. Her heart had begun to do the usual thing it did each time she saw him, and it was as if she completely forgot the heartache and pain she suffered because of him.

She noticed his eyes went straight to her wedding ring finger and wondered if she imagined that he seemed relieved there was no ring on it. Suddenly, Rewa remembered the emotional wreck she had been after their last incident in the elevator at *Medlake Hospital*. Though the pain was not there anymore, what she felt now was embarrassment at how naive she had been back then.

"How is your wife, and how many kids do you now have?" Rewa went straight to the point though what she really felt like doing was to go for his jugular! She heard from Nurse Chichi that he had got married, just as he mentioned to her, after his outburst in the elevator at *Medlake*.

"*Wife*?" Banjo repeated, "It didn't work out." He answered in a rather cavalier way. "We've been separated for two years now. I have two lovely daughters though, *Four* and *Two*." He pulled out his wallet and showed her photos of them.

"They are lovely indeed," Rewa said. Something about him being separated from his wife made her feel good. She was unsure if it was because she felt he deserved the pain of a failed marriage after the way he treated her or because that meant he was single and *available* again. Either way, she thought it was wrong that she was pleased about it. The truth, however, was that she was, and the fact that she even cared worried her.

"Must say, I'm not surprised she left you," Rewa found herself saying suddenly, causing Banjo's eyebrows to shoot up. He seemed surprised she possessed the courage to be as outright. That was not the Rewa he remembered. She had been soft, sweet, and perhaps a bit *wet behind the ears*. He looked at her with new eyes now. She had clearly done some growing up, he thought. He did not remember her being quite as vocal, and the thought made him smile as he asked.

"*Really*? Why? And what gives you the feeling that *she left* me?"

This time, it was Rewa who laughed.

"You *really* have to ask Banjo? We have a bit of *history,* remember? I suffered unbelievable shame and humiliation at *Medlake* before I eventually resigned. I mean...I was labeled *husband snatcher* because of you. Why wouldn't I assume she *left you*? You had sex with me a couple of weeks before your wedding!" Rewa looked around the cabin nervously, hoping none of the other passengers heard her sarcastic comment. She lowered her voice and then continued.

"A leopard can't change its spots. Surely it was only a matter of time before she caught on to the *real* you," she concluded sardonically. Rewa struggled to control her emotions at that moment. She thought she had dealt with all that had happened between them but found she was still hurt and angry with how he treated her.

"Sorry I hurt you like that back then, Rewa. I never meant to. I would have rung you to explain things properly if I had your number, but you disappeared! I felt terrible that I never got the chance to make things right between us. Point of correction, though, *I left her,*" Banjo said.

He sounded sincere enough, and that made Rewa feel better. She *had* changed her phone number after leaving *Medlake Hospital.* She did not want anyone from the hospital to contact her as she left in what she deemed a shameful manner. She had bumped into Nurse Chichi a year or so later, and she had filled her in on the news about Dr. Banjo's wedding. He certainly would not have been able to contact her even if he had tried.

"It doesn't matter now. Besides, there was really nothing left to explain as you were quite *honest* at our last meeting in the lift. That was enough explanation. I'll just blame my misunderstanding of the situation on my naiveté and the fact that I was a *'Johnny just come'* at that time...I learned from the experience, though," Rewa said with a resigned smile. God, she thought, he was still just as good-looking as she remembered.

"That makes me feel terrible now. I hope I can make it up to you somehow. How long are you in the UK for?" Banjo asked, and that had been it again.

They talked from then on till they landed at *Heathrow* Airport. During the six-hour flight, they had talked about everything from hospital politics to personal relationships like his failed marriage and her business. Rewa found she still had a strong attraction to the man who had broken her heart a few years back.

They shared a taxi into town from the airport and talked all the way to Rewa's hotel in the city. Rewa had known it would be too late to carry on her journey to Northampton when she arrived in the United Kingdom. Therefore, she planned to pass the night at a hotel in London and continue her journey to Northampton the following morning. Banjo decided to do the same and catch the train to Manchester the next morning. He also decided to get a room at the same hotel where Rewa was booked to pass the night but could not as he did not have one reserved like her. He was asked to sit and wait for the next available room as the hotel was fully booked that evening.

Rewa thought it ridiculous that he should wait for a room when she had one with twin beds. She offered her spare hotel bed to Banjo, and he did not hesitate to take it. They were not exactly strangers, she had thought at the time. They were both adults and had buried whatever hatchet there was between them. What harm could possibly come from them passing the night in the same hotel room, in different beds? Besides, they both were tired from the flight and needed rest.

Today, nearly five years later, Rewa still wondered why she had offered Banjo the extra bed that evening. Had it actually been a genuine act of kindness on her part, or was it that she enjoyed his company so much on the plane that she felt it awkward to say good night at the hotel lobby? Or perhaps, somewhere in her subconscious, she had hoped to rekindle their relationship, especially now that he was no longer with his wife. Or again, was it just simply that she had suffered a bout of *the itch*? *'The itch'* was

Rewa and Faith's terminology for a strong urge to have sex. These were questions Rewa still could not answer to this day.

When Rewa and Banjo got into her hotel room, he offered to order them some dinner from room service, and Rewa went straight into the restroom to have a shower. By the time she came out of it, Banjo was eating, and she joined him in a hotel robe. Banjo glanced at her freshly scrubbed face and knew he had to have her, even if it was just for *old time's sake*. She was gorgeous and looked so innocent without any make-up on. Besides, what was the point of two consenting adults *with* some sexual history, alone in a foreign hotel room, if it was not to relive their past experience together?

They began to talk again as they ate, and Banjo eventually disappeared into the shower after their meal. When he came out of it, Rewa was already tucked in one of the two beds in the room and had started drifting off to sleep.

"You look like an angel when you sleep, you know," Banjo began. "Haven't changed one bit either," he added. His eyes travelled down her form hungrily. He needed her badly in that instant.

"Really?" Rewa answered in a sleepy voice, but they could both feel the proverbial *elephant in the room*. Desire was written all over Banjo's face, and it was contagious as Rewa knew she needed him in that instant too. It felt like she would die if she could not have him. The sexual tension in the room was suddenly heightened, and before she knew it, she was in the arms of the man she had loved for so long. The same man who had shattered her heart into tiny pieces a while back.

They made sweet, passionate love that night, and Rewa knew for sure that Banjo Adetunji was her weakness, the *thorn in her flesh*. She was his for the taking, and she gave herself willingly.

Something deep within her knew he was wrong for her, but she carried on with him regardless. She found him overwhelmingly irresistible. She had hated him for the way he treated her back then at *Medlake*, years before, but now, she just felt a rush of love for him. No wonder they said *it was a thin line between love and hate.* In an instant, Rewa had forgotten the pain Banjo caused her, the heartache and shame she had suffered, and how she felt she would die if she had to live without him. The memory of it all vanished, and she wilfully opened herself up to Banjo at that moment.

They slept in each other's arms that night and made love two more times before morning. The last time just seemed better than the first. For Rewa, it was simply *magical*! The following morning, they made love one more time in the shower. It was as though they could not get enough of each other, and Rewa felt on top of the world! She beamed from ear to ear on the train to Northampton after she and Banjo parted ways.

She could not believe how lucky she was to have boarded the particular UK-bound flight on that particular day! What were the odds of her and Banjo meeting again and spending time together after what had transpired between them? She was happy they had another chance at a relationship again and felt strongly that this was it! Perhaps she *was* destined to be with Banjo Adetunji. Their meeting again just made the hurt she had felt in the past all worthwhile suddenly. She was so happy and excited! She could not believe how a single day could turn things around!

Banjo had insisted on paying for the hotel room, their supper, and breakfast the following morning. He was so tender with her, and she felt so loved by him. He treated her like a queen that morning. They exchanged numbers and shared a passionate farewell kiss before he put her in a cab to the train station and said he would ring her later.

Rewa did not hear from Banjo again until two nights after. She had almost lost her mind wondering why. She tried the number he gave her over a hundred times, but it was switched off. She had been distracted for the first two days of the exhibition in Northampton as a result of his failure to contact her as promised. Not hearing from him was ruining her entire trip! She had chided herself several times to get a grip, but it did not help the feeling of confusion she felt. Had it been *just sex* for him again? She wondered in the back of her mind. She, however, willed herself not to think about that; it could not have been. Not after the way he had loved her barely forty-eight hours ago!

"*Banjo*! You gave me such a fright! I've been wondering what happened to you in the last couple of days! Are you alright? Your phone was switched off!" Rewa ranted on breathlessly when Banjo eventually rang her two days after he said he would. She was relieved to finally be speaking to him.

"I know, my phone has a problem, and it's just been terribly busy here, wedding and all. I haven't had time to catch my breath!" Besides.., I only just found ...only just found the piece of paper I scribbled your number on...I've been looking for it since I got to Manchester. Anyway, how are you? How's the... meeting going?" Banjo asked in a distracted, rushed and hushed manner.

"*Meeting*? What meeting? It's an *exhibition,* silly!" Rewa laughed. Only too happy to hear from him after two days of agony. "You sound distracted. Where are you?" She asked, but the phone suddenly went dead before she could get a response.

"Hello...hello Banjo...can you hear me?" Rewa cried into her phone as if it was a lifeline. She tried ringing him back several times, but the automated voice on the other end sounded Chinese or something each time she did.

That had been it. Rewa never heard from Banjo again on that trip or after, and she had not seen him since that night in London either until now, today in the furniture section of *Homeware* Store, almost six years after. It had been her second, nasty encounter with him.

What Banjo had failed to mention to Rewa then and what she would never know was that he had actually been in Manchester to visit his estranged wife and daughters and not to attend a cousin's wedding as he had said. His wife had moved to Manchester after they split up the year before. She and Banjo were trying to patch things up for the sake of their daughters but had failed to do so, especially because Banjo refused to relocate and live in the UK. Instead, he had returned to Nigeria with the intention of filing for divorce.

Banjo was not entirely sure why he had lied to Rewa. Had he felt bad at the way they had parted ways at the hospital years before, or perhaps he just really thought he would get lucky and achieve the proverbial *'leg-over'* while they were both in the United Kingdom, far away from home and both their real lives? It did not really matter now; he had got lucky and was certain they both had fun while it lasted.

Banjo found Rewa too sexy to resist! Her innocence was what he found rather appealing and nothing more. He had not meant to hurt her feelings *again*. As far as he was concerned, she was a good lay, and that was his only real interest in her. Moreover, he had not actually asked her out or promised her a relationship. They had just done what any two adults who'd had sex with each other before did when they were alone again. What was it with girls these days anyway? Whatever happened to *friends with benefits*? Why did they always assume a guy wanted a relationship with them when all he really wanted was sex with no strings? Banjo wondered.

CHAPTER FIVE

Labake fidgeted in the kitchen, trying to get Vince the glass of water he had requested as quickly as she could. She was her usual jittery self around him and walked on eggshells to avoid annoying him. If she tried hard enough, she told herself, she could at least avoid igniting her husband's temper tonight. She struggled but failed to calm her nerves as her hands just would not stop shaking.

She had put Ella to bed earlier than usual and was tidying up before she retired for the night herself. She was dead tired as it had been a busy evening for her. Two of Vince's friends had turned up at their house to watch the *Nigeria-Zimbabwe* football match earlier on. They had turned up unannounced, and Vince had not bothered to mention to her when he got in from work that he was expecting them. She garnered, from the way he greeted them, that their visit was actually a planned one.

Labake had been on her feet all evening, running up and down to ensure her husband's guests were comfortable. She was glad that she'd had the sixth sense to make some extra food for supper this evening, as she would usually make just enough for herself and Vince. There had been just enough to feed Vince and his *unexpected* guests. A fact that made Labake sigh with relief. The last thing she needed was to have Vince blow his top because there was not enough food available to entertain his friends.

Labake remembered the last time that had happened and how her husband had beaten her for it. Somewhere in his head, he believed she had intended to humiliate him as there was no extra food to offer his friend who had turned up unexpectedly. She had learned from that experience and always ensured there was a little something she could rustle up to offer any unexpected guests.

Vince was never discreet about the way he treated Labake, even when they had company. He yelled at her regardless of who was present. Labake had grown used to it, though she still jumped each time Vince shouted at her in anger. She did not just feel like a glorified maid; she was treated as such by her husband, particularly in the presence of his family and friends. He derived some pleasure knowing that everyone knew he was in control of his wife and home.

Labake had learned early on in her marriage that complaining was never an option. She did what she was told when she was told, and as quickly as possible, without asking any questions. Sometimes, even after she had done all she was asked to do, she still got beaten and that largely depended on her husband's mood. Most times, he did not need a reason to beat her, especially once his mind was made up. She was beaten at will. What was worse was she did not see it coming sometimes. She only hoped and prayed it would not happen as often as it did.

"*He is a bully,* and you allow him to get away with the way he treats you!" Laide, her sister, had said over the phone once when Labake mentioned that her husband was being difficult about Laide paying them a short visit. Labake had snickered in response as she knew Laide did not know half of it. The truth was, Labake wasn't *allowing* Vince to *get away with anything*. She just did not have a choice in the matter.

Labake remembered one Sunday afternoon, on their way home from church, when Vince decided to make a stop at his mother's house. Labake hated going there and would usually hide in the kitchen or in the background, somewhere, when they got there. She did this to avoid her husband, who usually flared up and humiliated her in front of his family at the slightest irritation.

On this particular occasion, *Mama,* as they referred to Labake's mother-in-law, had guests over from her Church, and a small prayer meeting was being held in one of her living rooms. Two of mama's other daughters-in-law, *Kara* and *Vero,* were also present. They were wives to Vince's younger brothers, Victor and Sebastian, respectively, who were also present. Labake had never been close to either of them, and they treated her like an outsider.

Though their husbands were younger than Vince, Kara and Vero both had children older than Ella, as Vince's brothers had both married earlier than he had. Their wives and Vince's entire family believed Labake had intentionally gotten herself pregnant by Vince in order to entrap him into marrying her. As far as they were concerned, she was a *gold-digger* and deserved whatever cruelty he meted out to her.

Labake had overheard Kara and Vero gossip about her several times, so she knew what the entire Ebodo clan thought of her. She had never confronted them over it and did not intend to. As far as she was concerned, they could think whatever they liked. She could just imagine the look on Vince's enraged face if he found out that she had even tried to confront her sisters-in-law. She knew what the repercussions would be and would not even dare think about it.

Labake had been in the restroom when she suddenly heard her husband barking through the door. "*Where* is her mother? *Labake*! *Labake*!!" Vince yelled at the top of his voice. She could also hear Ella crying in the background. She wondered what had happened but knew from Vince's tone that she was in trouble, at least when they got home. Heart pounding frantically out of panic, she flushed the toilet and literally ran out of it to answer her husband. When she opened the bathroom door, she could see everyone gathered around Ella, who was crying.

"I'm he...here, I was in the..." Labake started, but before she could finish the sentence, she received a blow to the side of her head. Right there, in front of her mother-in-law, her guests, and her family. It was as if Vince had forgotten himself and where he was. He yelled at her, "What are you doing? Why did you leave Ella unattended? We've all been looking for you! Now, look at her arm!"

Vince yelled at the top of his voice, clearly enraged. Eyes dilated, nostrils flaring, Vince looked like he could throttle her in that instant. The look in his eyes frightened Labake as her husband appeared to have developed a form of temporary insanity. He grabbed her and was about to deal another blow when Mama's Pastor intervened and dragged him off her. The force of the first blow had sent Labake across the small toilet doorway and back into the toilet.

That was the first time Ella ever saw her father hit her mother or anyone at that. It frightened the poor child, and she screamed and cried even louder. Everyone, including Labake's brothers-in-law and their wives, had turned back quietly to what they had been doing as if nothing had happened whilst members of Mama's church rushed to help Labake off the toilet floor.

Labake hated the attention she had drawn and was quick to let them know she was alright though she had sustained a bloody cut to the side of her head. Slightly dazed from the blow she received from Vince, she rushed to her daughter to examine the tiny injury on her arm. Somewhere in the corner of her eye, Labake could see the Pastor having a quiet word with Vince as he struggled to calm himself down.

Mama had said nothing until the following day. Labake was in the hospital receiving treatment for the extra injuries Vince had inflicted on her after they got home from Mama's house when her call came in. Whatever counsel the Pastor had given Vince had clearly gone in one ear and come out of the other because Labake received the beating of her life when they returned home. As usual, Vince accused her of deliberately humiliating him in front of his family and his mother's guests.

"You have been married to your husband for some time now, Labake. Surely by now, you should know his temperament," Mama had started. "A good wife should study her man and know what irritates him to avoid getting on his wrong side. The incident with Ella yesterday could have been avoided if you had been careful. Ella could have sustained a more serious injury because she was playing without any supervision!" Mama concluded in her usual condescending tone.

That was typical of Vince's mother. Her sons could do absolutely no wrong in her eyes. She always defended them, even when she knew they were wrong. Labake had not bothered with an explanation as she knew she could never win with her mother-in-law. Besides, the last thing she needed was to be reported to Vince by Mama for being argumentative or rude. The thought of that ever happening was tantamount to asking for a death sentence. All

Labake could muster was a "Thank you, Mama" before the call ended.

Before the hullabaloo the evening before, Ella had been in mama's other living room, playing with her cousins, when Labake stepped into the restroom. She was aware of her daughter's boisterous nature and always kept a watchful eye on her wherever they went. Labake was never careless with Ella. She was all she had and cared about, particularly because she was aware she would never bear any more children. Mama's suggestion that she had been careless with her was just typical, and Labake did not expect anything different.

Suddenly, the kitchen door swung open, and Vince walked in, startling Labake back to the present. She cowered and stiffened, an alarmed expression on her face when he drew her to him roughly and backed her against the sink. Her heart jumped into her throat as she wondered what she had done wrong this time. She raised an arm to shield herself from what she foresaw to be an impending blow but instead, Vince turned her round forcefully. Labake winced in pain as her bad knee jammed against the cabinet, and he roughly pushed her head down so she was bent over the cabinet. He pinned her in that position with one hand, making it difficult for her to move, and then lifted her skirt with his other hand. Suddenly, Labake's panic doubled when she realized what he was about to do.

"Please..." She begged in a terrified tone. "Please, Vince, not...not like this, please... Vince..." Without a word, he undid his trousers and forcefully inserted himself into her from behind. Labake tried to stifle a howl but could not. The pain was excruciating, and it shot through her body like an electric current as her husband pounded away savagely.

After what seemed an eternity, the ordeal was over, and Labake slid to the floor, curled up and trembling with her arms wrapped around her knees. "That's what you get for flirting shamelessly with my friends right under my nose!" Vince yelled. He zipped himself up and strolled out of the kitchen as if nothing had happened.

Labake whimpered, shuddering violently. She felt dirty and ashamed. What was worse were the feelings of helplessness and hopelessness she experienced again at that moment. She did not know who to turn to or what to do about her predicament. There did not seem to be a way out of her horrible situation with Vince, but she knew she was at the end of her tether. She was unsure of how much more she could take of her husband's violation of her and suddenly realized she would not live much longer if she stayed in her marriage. It occurred to her for the first time that her life was in danger. She could not bear to think of what would happen to Ella if she died. It occurred to her there and then that she had to do something about her predicament. Vince *was an animal!* Nothing but a savage animal, and she hated him with every fiber of her being. Her fear for him had morphed into pure hatred, and she wondered how she could ever have loved him.

Labake wiped her tears away and got off the floor slowly. Her knee throbbed badly as she struggled to put her weight on it. She finished clearing up like a zombie and left the kitchen, heading for the guest room. She quietly limped past Vincent, who sat in front of the TV like nothing had transpired between them a moment ago. He caught her in the corner of his eye and asked, “Hey, where’s my glass of water?” She had completely forgotten about it. “Actually, get me a cold beer instead,” Vince ordered, and Labake instantly turned back like a robot and limped towards the kitchen again, without a word.

When she finally got into the guest room, she had a shower, took some pills, and lay on the bed. For the first time in her marriage, Labake was convinced of what she needed to do. Vince's violence seemed to get worse as the days went by, and it was now obvious to Labake that praying and hoping he would suddenly see the light and stop hurting her was no longer a plausible option. It seemed to her now that the longer she stayed with him, the worse his violence got. She had to do something about her situation if she wanted to live. Her thoughts raced as she tried to hash out a plan.

The following morning, Labake got up early. As usual, she was in physical pain and went about her morning routine slowly. Ella was being particularly fussy this morning, and her father seemed to be in an unusually good mood. Labake had overheard him through their bedroom door a few days earlier, talking to someone who appeared to be one of his many concubines.

"Don't worry, my darling," she'd heard him say, "You can tell me all about it when we meet. My flight is at ten-thirty pm on the fifth. Yes, it's the British Airways flight. I'll transfer at Heathrow and should be in Denver by the afternoon of the sixth. See you soon, darling. I love you too."

Labake was aware of most of Vince's affairs and knew he never traveled alone. He was either with a female companion or was traveling to visit one who lived abroad. It was no secret either as Vince talked to them openly, even with his wife present. He did not respect her enough to hide his extra-marital activities. Labake was thus aware that he had quite a few, and it had never bothered her. She had never confronted him about them or anything at that in the years she had been with him.

Labake was all too aware of how insignificant she was to Vince. He had told her countless times how he had done her a favor by marrying her, usually between punches. He would say she was useless and no other man could ever tolerate her. He would remind her that she would have ended up in the gutter had he not rescued her from the life of squalor and penury that was bound to be her destiny. The irony of it all was that she had heard it so many times that she could not remember a time when she did not believe it. She had always felt inferior to Vince and had believed from the beginning of their relationship that she could never deserve him or his affection. In fact, until now, she had felt lucky he had found her and married her.

Today, Labake was thankful in a way for the incident the evening before. It was what she would call a *light bulb* moment. She suddenly felt an urgency to do what she should have done a good while ago. She was jittery about her decision though, as she had not quite thought the details through yet. She was scared to hash out a full plan for fear of losing the nerve to carry them out. She was uncertain of the outcome of her hasty decision but was desperate and knew she had to take the risk.

Labake did not sleep a wink all night, thinking of ways to execute her plan. It particularly helped that she was armed with the little piece of information about Vince's trip to Denver tonight. Of course, Vince was unaware she knew about his impending trip. He never revealed his travel plans to her until the morning of the day he was leaving and only because he needed her to do his packing for him and drive him to the airport.

Labake did not have it all planned out yet, but she knew she had to get away, especially after last night. She could not take it anymore. Vince had done and made her do some degrading things in the past, but yesterday took the cake, and she felt that was her limit, her breaking point. She decided that come what may, she was leaving her husband and marriage of almost six years *with* her daughter. Labake believed this to be her opportunity as her life and her daughter's future depended on it.

Though terrified of the consequences of what she planned, Labake willed herself not to give too much thought to it. She had to at least *attempt* an escape from Vince. Sitting down, arms folded, waiting to be killed by him clearly was not going to help or do her any good. She knew she had to do something, *anything* to spare her life and, ultimately, Ella's too. She silently assured herself.

Once she dropped Vince off at the airport and got back home, Labake immediately rang her sister Laide, who was surprised to hear from her at that time of day.

"I've decided to leave Vincent," Labake blurted out as tears began to slowly roll down her cheeks.

"Really? Are you alright?" Laide enquired of her younger sister, slightly alarmed.

"I am. I haven't...thought it through properly...but I have to get away from him...I'll pack a few things for Ella and myself and travel by road to The Republic of Benin... to you...if that's alright...I just can't take it anymore...!" Labake broke down and began to sob. Laide felt sad to hear her cry.

"Labake, please stop crying. This is not the time for tears. You need to be strong at this point so you can think straight!" Laide scolded. She had always been the stronger and more focused one. She took after their mother in strength, and Labake was grateful she had her to turn to at a time like this. Laide was smart and fearless and always seemed to know what to do in any given circumstance.

"What about Vince? You know he won't just fold his arms and watch you leave with his child. You have to be reasonable, sis; a getaway requires some serious planning, you know," Laide asked.

"He's traveled out of the country...*Denver,* I heard him say," Labake replied between sobs. "I just dropped him off at the airport. He's going to be back in two weeks...this is my only opportunity...I'm scared, Laide. What should I do?" She asked her sister agitatedly.

"Thank God you finally realize that you can break away from this sham of a marriage. I've been praying for God to open your eyes before he kills you one day! Thank God you now see. It's great that he's going to be gone for some time. Did he leave you any money"? Laide enquired from her sister.

"Yes," Labake said, blowing her nose, "He left an open cheque for me to cash. I'll cash it first thing in the morning." Vince usually left Labake an open cheque whenever he traveled for any emergencies, and Labake knew he did it only because of Ella. He never took any chances where his beloved daughter was concerned.

"That's good," Laide said, "Just make your way here safely first. We'll decide what to do next when you arrive. I'll take the day off work and pick you up at the border. The Immigration Officers there can be difficult, but I'll get one of the facilitators from the High Commission to come along to make things easier. Keep me posted regarding timing, and keep your cell phone on and with you so I can ring you at different intervals. Do not tell a soul where you are going. Oh, I almost forgot to ask, do you have your passports?"

"I do. I snuck them out of the bedroom when I packed his things...for his trip this morning," Labake answered, wondering how she'd had the presence of mind to remember the passports and how she had taken them while Vince showered that morning. He usually kept them under lock and key, but by sheer providence,

Labake had found the drawer where he kept all their passports unlocked. Perhaps because Vince had opened it to retrieve his own passport for his trip. She had been shaking so badly that she dropped both passports twice. Labake was thankful she had made a note to collect them the night before. She was glad she got the opportunity too, as her entire plan would have been ruined without hers and Ella's passports.

"That's great! Travel light so as not to arouse any suspicions. See you soon and do try not to worry. Everything will be alright. I promise you, sis," Laide assured her sister before ending the call.

Labake felt a sense of relief after her conversation with Laide. She was glad she had Laide's support at a time like this. She hoped Laide was right when she said *everything would be alright*. Her predicament seemed so bleak at the moment, and she could not quite see any light at the end of the tunnel, but she knew she had to take the chance. Whatever happened, she knew she owed it to herself and Ella to at least make her escape from Vince's cruelty. She wished she had saved herself such enormous pain all these years and just taken the plunge! Even the thought of planning her escape gave her a weird feeling of liberation. It was as though she finally realized that she could! Surely she deserved it, and her life and Ella's were worth it. She tried not to think too hard about it and, for once, needed to be spontaneous about her decision.

The one thing Labake knew was that she was petrified. Vince knew many people in the Security Services and in most governmental agencies. She wondered how far she would get till he caught up with her. She willed her mind not to worry about that at the moment. For the very first time in her life, she was going to take her chances. Surely, it would be worth it in the end. She hoped and prayed it would.

CHAPTER SIX

Rewa stood at her apartment window, watching the lady who lived in the house across the way from her drag a half-opened suitcase to a waiting taxi as she struggled to talk on her cell phone all at the same time. Even from the distance, Rewa could see she appeared rather rattled. She looked as though she was running late to catch a flight or something.

Crossway Estate was a beautiful gated community consisting of different types of dwelling houses. This included a block of twelve condominiums, twelve duplexes, and twelve bungalows, all built around a huge common courtyard at the center of the estate. The entire estate was surrounded by tall palm trees, adding to its aesthetic appeal. The courtyard also included a gazebo hut where residents could hang out outdoors.

The Estate was considered a high-brow place to live, and Rewa felt proud and lucky to own an apartment within it. She had not quite met her neighbors yet except the angry-looking man with the Jeep who had almost rammed it into her the other day. He had seemed to be fuming and rushing somewhere too. He had stopped to apologize and introduced himself as *Vincent*. She wondered if he was married. He was kind of cute, she had thought within herself at the time.

Rewa's phone began to ring, and she left the window to answer it. It was Banjo. It had been a few days since they bumped into each other again at the *Homeware store*.

"Hi Rewa, how are you? He asked.

Rewa's thoughts drifted back to how she had struggled to put the pieces of her heart back together again when Banjo Adetunji broke it a second time after their brief but memorable encounter in London. She had heard a preacher say once before that taking a wrong decision could be deemed a mistake the first time; to do it again would be stupidity, and a third time, however, would be complete madness. Rewa totally agreed with him.

If only Banjo knew the amount of trouble he had caused her, Rewa thought sadly. She remembered the enormous sense of pain and loss she had felt in the months following her return from the exhibition in Northampton and how alone she had felt. It had been dreadful, and she did not wish the bitter experience on anyone. To date, it was the most difficult time of her life, and she prayed she never ever had to relive it again.

Thinking about it now, remembering the guilt she still carried from that brief episode with Banjo in London and its resultant effect, how he had used and dumped her a *second* time without a head turn, made Rewa hang up on him at that moment. She had never told a soul about it and was quite prepared to go to her grave with it. Besides, it was not anyone else's business. It was her life, her story, and there was no use telling anyone who could do nothing about what had already been done, and Rewa intended to keep it that way.

Banjo rang back again, and this time Rewa snatched up her phone in anger and snapped when she answered.

"What do you want, Banjo?" She almost shrieked into the phone out of sudden fury. She was not entirely sure why she was angry. Was she angry at Banjo for his horrible ways with her in the past, or was she angry at herself for the fact that he still stirred something deep within her? Perhaps it was a little bit of both, she told herself.

"What do you want with me, Banjo?" She asked him again. "What if we hadn't bumped into each other at the furniture store? Would you be ringing me now?" Rewa spat the question into the phone as her anger rose. She did not bother to disguise the irritation in her voice either.

"Er...sorry, Rewa, have I caught you at a bad time?" Banjo asked innocently. He was confused. After all, she *did* give him her cell number at the store the other day. She should have expected he would use it. He concluded that he must have caught her at a bad moment.

"It is *not* a *bad time* for me at all, actually. I asked what you wanted! What are you ringing me for, Banjo?" Rewa almost screamed out of frustration now, especially as he appeared to be patronizing her.

It suddenly dawned on Banjo at that moment that Rewa's anger *was* directed at him. Clearly, she still bore some resentment towards him after their last meeting in the UK. She had not shown any signs of anger when they bumped into each other at the store a couple of days ago. She just appeared somewhat aloof, but he was certain he had not picked up any anger in her demeanor while they spoke and got reacquainted at the store. He was surprised at her present reaction. Realization set in for him very quickly, and he decided to play it easy.

"Rewa, please calm down. I know this must seem strange to you especially considering the way we left things the last time we were together. Please let me make amends by taking you out. I'd like to see you again if that's alright with you. Please...I know I don't deserve to ask anything of you but please just consider meeting me for drinks or something so we can talk," Banjo cajoled.

Perhaps it was the way he said it. Rewa immediately felt her heart begin to melt again. She suddenly realized she was tired of the anger and resentment she had bottled up inside all these years. She heard herself sigh and reply in a resigned tone this time,

"Okay, pick me up at seven this Saturday evening." *Sucker!* She scolded herself quietly.

"Cool, thank you, and see you then," Banjo hung up before she had the chance to change her mind.

It was after she hung up that Rewa realized she had just had yet another weak moment with Banjo Adetunji. Why was she such a sucker for heartbreak, especially where he was concerned? She wondered. There and then, at that moment, she decided she was going to blow him off on Friday night. She was going to avoid Banjo Adetunji like the plague. Yes, she still found him irresistible, but she was not going to put herself in a compromising situation with him ever again. She reckoned he would eventually get the message and leave her alone for good if she stood him up once or twice. *Players* like Banjo Adetunji did not wait around for too long once you caught on to them and their schemes.

On Friday night, Rewa sent Banjo a text *to cancel* because *'something came up'*. He, however, did not reply to her text but turned up at her door at exactly six-fifty nine pm on Saturday evening as planned. Rewa heard the knock and was surprised when she peeped through the pigeonhole to see him standing outside her apartment. Heart racing, she paced back and forth in her hallway, unsure of what to do next. For a brief moment, she thought about ignoring the doorbell and pretending to be asleep, but she had instinctively asked who it was before she got to the door, so he knew for sure that she was home. She gave herself a quick look in the hallway mirror. Satisfied with the red, sleeveless, floor-length lounge dress she had on, Rewa swung open the door with a slightly flushed, *embarrassed-but-trying-not-to-show-it* expression on her face.

"Banjo, what are you doing here?" She asked pointedly. But before she could say anything further, Banjo, dressed in a pair of jeans, brown loafers, and a nice pale blue shirt, pulled her into his arms and locked his lips with hers in a hungry, wet kiss. Slightly dazed by his actions, Rewa nearly forgot herself and melted into his arms. After what seemed a moment, she suddenly stiffened when she realized what was happening. *How dare he?* She wondered.

Both hands on his chest, Rewa pushed hard at Banjo, broke free from his grip, and, with a look of horror on her face, took two quick confused steps backwards as if he were poisonous or had a contagious disease. Then, feeling violated and embarrassed at the same time, she took another step towards him and slapped him hard across the face. She then turned away a bit too swiftly and suddenly felt dizzy and had the beginnings of a headache. She also became slightly disoriented and wondered what had come over her at that moment. He had managed to get to her in the familiar way that only he did, and she hated it, hated him more for it too.

"What do you think you're doing?" Rewa asked in a shaken voice, her rigid back still to him.

Slightly stunned by her reaction, Banjo entered the flat uninvited and shut the door behind himself. "I'm sorry, Rewa, but I couldn't help myself...seeing you in that dress, without any make-up on..." He trailed off, speaking in a pleading tone. There it was again, that false apologetic *act* that only he knew how to put on so perfectly. Rewa thought, spinning around to face him.

Glaring at him, she said in a quiet tone, "I sent you a text...*I couldn't make it this evening as planned...something came up*...didn't you get it?" She asked him angrily.

"I did, but very late...thought I'd take my chances and drop by anyhow. I didn't know your house number, but one of the security guards pointed to your flat," Banjo replied with a slightly amused look on his face now. He was clearly beginning to enjoy himself and her reaction to the situation. He gave her a knowing look as if to say, *I see through you, Rewa, and know what you were planning all along.*

"Well, the security guard *shouldn't* have done that...he should have given me a buzz first. I wish you hadn't come here, Banjo," Rewa said sternly. It was a wonder she was audible enough as her lips were tightly set as she spoke.

"Why? Why are you trying to avoid the inevitable Rewa? Admit it. You *want* me just as much as I want you, so why play hard to get now? Let's be adults about what we both *really* want and get it out of the way," Banjo answered in a rather cocky, *matter-of-fact* manner. His true nature was out and had now replaced his pretentious one. The *real* Banjo Adetunji had finally put in an appearance.

Rewa was stunned by what he said though. *God! He was brutal!* She thought. He had not even bothered to keep up the pretense for much longer. She felt as though he had returned her slap. She could not believe what he had just said. Was that truly how he viewed her? Did he think all she ever wanted with him was *just sex* too?

After all, he had said that much to her in the elevator at *Medlake Hospital* many years before. Was that all she ever was to him? A plaything, someone to toy with, dump and forget about and then pick up at will whenever he bumped into again? Was she really that easy and weak where he was concerned? She felt humiliated and regretted giving him her number at the store. In fact, she regretted ever having anything to do with him in the first place.

Rewa realized at that moment that she had somehow, freely given Banjo a measure of power over her, and he had done the inevitable, used it to her detriment. He sensed her weakness for him and capitalized on it. *Well*, she thought within herself, *not anymore*. She decided in that instant that *enough was enough*. She was taking whatever power he had on her back; right this minute, she resolved silently. Whatever hold Banjo had on her was coming to an abrupt end here and now, she determined within herself.

It was as if Rewa's eyes were now suddenly open, causing her to see more clearly how foolish she had been and how she had meant absolutely nothing to Banjo from the get-go. She had foolishly let her heart rule her head for far too long, believing she loved him. *Love*! Rewa could have laughed out loud at the word at that moment.

"I really can't blame you for that comment, Banjo," Rewa started icily with that familiar blank expression on her face. "After all, I did give myself to you cheaply in the first place. I mean, I slept with you on our first date back at *Medlake* Hospital and threw myself at you again in London...even after you treated me like dirt the first time. I'm not surprised that you consider me cheap and maybe easy. I mean, let's face it, I did offer myself to you *on a platter*." Rewa paused momentarily for what she was saying to sink in. She spoke quietly, but the look in her eyes sent a different message. She raised her hand abruptly when Banjo attempted to interject, indicating she was not done speaking and then continued.

"Not sure you've noticed, however...but I *have* done a bit of *growing up* since. I'm not that naive, *wet-behind-the-ears* girl who fell for you way back then. And contrary to what you may think, I do see you for the cad you are now. Please do me one last favor, leave my house and don't *ever* contact me again...in fact, let's make a pact...if we happen to bump into each other again because, for some weird reason, we always seem to, please ignore me and move on, and I'll do the same," Rewa finished coolly. She was quite proud of the extra chill in her voice as she spoke.

Banjo had the nerve to look pained at the words she spoke and attempted to reach for her hand, but Rewa pulled back. "Rewa..." He started, "I'm sorry for what I just said and the way I treated you in the past. You didn't deserve any of it, but I thought you understood that what we had at Medlake and in London were purely physical. I didn't realize you wanted more. I am truly sorry if I led you to believe it was more," he said, dropping his outstretched hand and putting on again what Rewa now knew to be his *false-sincere* look.

"Isn't it funny how you apologize each time we *'bump'* into each other, Banjo? Is it just me you do this with, or are there a string of other silly, clueless ladies whom you take advantage of? I mean, is this a *pattern* with you, Banjo?" Rewa asked pointedly. She was looking at him very intently now, as though she really needed to know. Then, without waiting for an answer, she carried on.

"You pretend to want something deeper, capitalize on the weakness of your *prey*, do a runner the minute you get what you want, and then the first thing you do when you bump into the prey again is to *apologize* with the silent aim to repeat the cycle of *hit and run* all over again." Rewa paused again, looking at Banjo the way a shrink would look at an ailing patient with the sole aim of unraveling the mystery of what their issues could possibly be.

Banjo, on the other hand, had a look of what Rewa deemed *'confused remorse'* on his face. When he did not respond to any of her questions, she continued,

"Your silence suggests I'm on the right track. That's all right now...because...though it was a terribly painful journey getting here, I finally have you figured out. Banjo, there's no need for any apologies or pretense here anymore. See yourself out and do have a good life. Good-bye." Rewa finished with a hand gesture that literally said *scram*.

Banjo shook his head and replied, "Come on, Rewa, don't pretend you didn't know it was just sex between us. We both enjoyed it while it..."

Before he could finish, Rewa burst out,

"It *wasn't just sex* for me, you idiot! I was *in love* with you! I would have done *anything* for you! But what did you do? You took advantage of me and my feelings, messed me up, left me to pick up the pieces, and didn't bat an eyelid! What was worse was the *miscarriage*!" Rewa glared at him and continued when she saw the look of utter confusion on Banjo's face.

"Yes, I got *pregnant*...with *your* baby! I had a miscarriage out of heartbreak! I miscarried *your* baby!" She screamed at Banjo and then broke down and began to sob. They were deep, heart-wrenching sobs. She shuddered violently, sliding to the floor, her hands covering her face as she wept.

It was out, the secret she felt she would never tell anyone. She wept for the shame of falling for Banjo and not seeing him for who he truly was, for the guilt she still carried for not knowing she had been pregnant, and for the extreme sense of loss she felt after losing the baby. Finally, she wept for the anguish of what she had been through and what she once felt for Banjo, who clearly had never had any real feelings for her and was audacious enough to admit it.

Banjo was beyond shocked by Rewa's revelation. Omorewa Ilo, *Ice queen,* as most of the male doctors at *Medlake* Hospital had referred to her back then, had been pregnant with his child and had actually *loved* him all along. He was stunned beyond words. He felt a rush of shame and guilt for what he suspected she had been through. For a brief moment, he just stood there in her hallway, looking down at her as she wept on the floor in disbelief. He struggled to absorb all she had just screamed at him. It was as if he actually saw her for the first time as flesh and blood, as a person with feelings and emotions that could be crushed. She was not just some random girl whom he could have his wicked way with and then dump. Banjo suddenly felt ashamed of himself. His heart went out to Rewa for the very first time since he met her. He knelt on the floor beside her and said softly.

"Did I hear you correctly? Did you just say...you were...*oh my God, oh my God!* I'm terribly sorry, Rewa, so, so sorry, I never knew...why didn't you tell me?" He tried to take her in his arms, but she brushed him off and got off the floor rather quickly. With her back to him again, she said in a quiet, shaky tone, "Please leave." The last thing she needed was his pity.

"No, Rewa! No...please talk to me..." Banjo said. Rewa was not quite sure if this was the real dumb-founded and genuinely apologetic Banjo or if it was part of his usual act. You just never knew with him, but it did not matter now. She did not care to know at this point; it was far too late.

Turning to face him with hot eyes, tears running down her face, Rewa said, "Leave my house now, Banjo," in a dangerously firm tone. What was there to talk about after all that had transpired between them? The secret was out, and the baby was long gone. There was absolutely nothing left to discuss. Rewa just wanted Banjo gone from her apartment and her life too.

Banjo got off the floor and looked long at Rewa. He looked rather defeated for a moment and then said, "For what it's worth, Rewa, I am truly sorry I hurt you." He hesitated a bit, then turned and left.

Rewa shut the door behind him, slid again to the floor, and cried some more. This time the sobs were gut-wrenching. She had held them back for far too long.

CHAPTER SEVEN

Labake stood in the doorway of her daughter's bedroom, watching her sleep. Ella looked like an angel when she slept. She had always looked that way, even as a baby. Labake had a mixture of emotions standing there, watching her most treasured possession. They had been through a lot in the last year. She felt terribly guilty that Ella was growing up without her father and sometimes wondered if she had been selfish and thinking just of herself when she decided to run from Vince.

She wondered how she was ever going to explain it all to Ella when she asked later on in life why she had left her father. So far, it had not been easy to make her understand. She was too young to comprehend it and had asked repeatedly on the trip to the Benin border where they were going and if her father would be joining them. Labake had not known how to answer her at first. She had not thought that bit through when she planned her *get-away*. She, therefore, did not have an answer prepared. She had lied to Ella that their destination was *a surprise* to keep her quiet, but Ella asked about her father again a day later and every day for a week until Labake had explained that they would not be seeing daddy for some time. When she asked why, Labake had said a tad too curtly, "Finish your breakfast, Ella." But she knew it would come up again. She only hoped to have found a more permanent answer when it did.

Labake still felt confused about what she was going to do in the long run. She knew she could not keep running. It did not help her psyche in any way as everything just seemed so *up in the air* even after a year. It was not good for Ella either. *A child needed some stability* Labake would chide herself every now and again. Even she felt unsettled and as though someone was watching or after them. Labake found that even after all these months and after a couple of moves, she still looked over her shoulders. She felt nervous and uncomfortable about her current lifestyle, and no matter how she tried, it still felt as though it was all temporary, like she was on vacation from her real life.

She still had trouble sleeping, still had the anxiety attacks, still woke up in a panic, and the nightmares were even worse now. It was what had awakened her early again this morning. It was three-seventeen in the morning, and she had woken up after a nightmare of Vince chasing her with a murderous look in his eyes. She wondered if the nightmares would ever stop. She had them every time she fell asleep, regardless of what time of day it was. All she needed to do was shut her eyes for a bit, and she would see Vince's enraged face. His hatred for her in her dreams was palpable!

Labake was immensely grateful to her older sister. Laide had been there for her and Ella over the past year. Labake could not think of what her fate would be right now without her help. She did not know that Laide had secretly vowed never to allow her sister to go through what she had been through ever again. Laide had silently made that vow when she saw Labake at the border on her arrival in The Benin Republic. Laide could not believe the image of her sister she had seen.

Though they had spoken almost every day, Laide had not seen Labake since their mother's funeral almost a year ago and was shocked at her appearance. Labake was a lot thinner than she had been, her walk was awkward because of the slight limp in her step, her skin was blotchy, and she looked like a frightened puppy. Laide could not see her eyes as she had large, dark sunglasses on and was almost too frightened of what she would see in them once the glasses came off.

Laide had been rather distracted at *Maami's* funeral, and she and Labake were too distraught by their mother's sudden death for Laide to have noticed what she now did about her younger sister. However, She had observed that there was something different about Labake at the funeral. There had not been enough time for a good chat with her as they had both been inundated with all the burial arrangements at the time.

Prior to their mother's death, Laide had not seen Labake in over two years because she had been posted to Portugal by the Foreign Office at the time. She had only been at her present post in the Republic of Benin for just over a year. She, therefore, did not have the full details of her sister's difficult marriage. *Maami* had mentioned before she passed that Labake was having some issues with Vince, but she had brushed it off as the usual teething problems which accompanied any young marriage. To her utmost dismay, Laide was entirely in the dark about what her sister had actually gone through in her marriage.

At the Benin border, Labake held on to Ella amidst the crowd as though she were her lifeline. Laide's eyes flooded with tears once Labake's sunglasses came off in the car Laide had picked them up in. Labake's eyes were lifeless and sunken. She had a fading black eye and an angry-looking scar at the top of her brow. She looked lost and confused, but most of all, she looked deeply sad. Her hands trembled as though she was catching a chill even in the hot West African sun. Her head was hung over like one defeated, and she scarcely looked her sister in the eye. To Laide, Labake seemed utterly bereft and ashamed.

Temporarily forgetting that the driver, the facilitator from the high commission, and her young niece were also in the car, Laide cried, "*My God!* Labake! What did he do to you?" She wondered where her beautiful, confident, lively sister had disappeared to. Labake was a ghost of who she used to be. This was not the sister Laide had grown up with. Labake had been the playful, cheeky one and had loved life and living even as a young girl. Laide remembered her as a carefree, happy-go-lucky child but all that had disappeared. Labake definitely was not the same person Laide knew. She was distant, resigned, and seemed nervous too.

Labake and Ella had stayed with Laide for ten days in *Port Novo*, after which Laide decided it was not safe for them to remain with her. She needed to move them to a place that was not as obvious. The *Benin Republic* would be the first place Vince would check once he discovered his wife had run off with his daughter. Though Labake had assured her that Vince was unaware Laide had been posted there, Laide was not taking any chances. She was convinced she needed to move her sister and little niece to a more remote location, where they did not have any relatives or ties. She was going to make it as hard as possible for *Vince Ebodo* to find her sister and niece. Laide believed she owed it to Labake and their late mother to keep them from him. She also needed Labake and Ella to settle into a brand new way of living as soon as possible. She believed it would help her sister regain some of her confidence if she was far away from any threat of being found.

Labake's situation reminded Laide too much of her father and how he had treated *Maami* when they were children. He had beaten her many times to their hearing and sometimes, even when they were present. Laide still had a vivid recollection of *Maami*'s blood-curdling screams as *daddy* dealt her blow after blow, especially when he returned into their lives after Labake was born. He had been gone for seven years, and Labake had been born during his absence to another man, and that angered him.

Thinking about it made Laide wonder if witnessing all that violence between *daddy* and *Maami* was the reason Labake had stayed with Vince and his violence. Was the vicious cycle being repeated as she had read it sometimes did? She had read somewhere that girls who grew up in abusive homes often tended to marry abusive husbands. Was that the case with Labake? Laide wondered.

She herself had taken the extreme, opposite stance of never going through what their mother had been through and had decided she was never getting married. But was she also a *statistic*? She had based the rest of her future on what she had witnessed as a child, which also made her a victim just like her younger sister. Laide pondered on these thoughts while her sister had been with her, and she found them rather unsettling.

Laide had an old colleague who had become a very good friend in Accra, Ghana. They had met at her old post in Portugal, and he was one of the few men she trusted. *Kwame* was Ghanaian and had moved his family back to Ghana, where they now lived. Laide had decided to ask for his help in relocating Labake and Ella. She explained the situation to him, and he was all too willing to help an old friend. He was a decent, kind-hearted man, and he understood the situation perfectly. He himself had grown up with an abusive father and had been a *God-send* to Labake and Ella. Laide felt she would forever be indebted to him and his family for helping her sister and niece settle into an entirely new and foreign environment.

Kwame helped find a nice school for Ella and had even helped Labake get her very first job. Labake worked as a back office administrator in Kwame's brother's five-star hotel. She had been excited at the prospect of working and earning her own money for the first time in her life. The job was perfect for her as it also came with an apartment within the hotel staff quarters, which meant she did not need to worry about accommodation or child care.

The housekeeping staff at *Dolphin* hotel loved Ella and were always keen to keep an eye on her when Labake had to work. It was a perfect arrangement. The pay was not bad either and was more than Labake needed, especially since she did not have to pay for accommodation in the city. She was able to put some money away for emergencies, giving her a feeling of security.

Labake knew she owed a lot to Kwame and her sister, whom she spoke to every night over the phone. So far, there had been no news from home, and Labake hoped it stayed that way. She was managing to get a grip on her life and was finding her feet slowly but surely. It was a bizarre feeling for her at first, as she had never taken full responsibility for herself in her entire life. She had gone from her mother's care at eighteen into the hands of her controlling and abusive husband. She had never been alone or fended for herself but knew she had to *pull herself up by her bootstraps* as she also had a young daughter who depended solely on her now. She knew she had to swiftly become the adult she had never fully grown into.

No one at the hotel knew much about Labake or her past life. She had not made too many friends, and her colleagues found her to be polite but private. She kept a low profile and focused most of her attention on her work and raising her daughter. She still struggled with her insecurities and battled with her lack of confidence, but these did not affect her efficiency or ability to learn quickly on the job.

The Dolphin hotel was a vast five-star hotel that was busy all year round. It was especially popular for its large conference rooms and banqueting halls. There were events scheduled for every weekend of the year, and this kept Labake busy and on her toes. Her sole responsibility was managing the hotel diaries and bookings. It was also her duty to order the equipment needed for each specific event. She was good at it and had got a lot of commendations from the Hotel Manager, *Mrs. Ofori,* to whom she reported directly.

Labake sighed and left Ella's room, tip-toeing back to hers. Ella was a light sleeper, and Labake did not want to awaken her as she had school in the morning. Thankfully, Ella had adjusted to her new surroundings and new school. Her love for school had not diminished in any way, a fact Labake was grateful for. It distracted her from constantly asking about her father, giving Labake a breather from her boisterous nature.

Labake was finally off the painkillers but still had trouble falling and staying asleep, especially because of the nightmares. She was not as shaky as she used to be, and the physical pain and dizziness she had grown accustomed to when she was with Vince were all gone. Whatever pain she had now were emotional and mental, and she hoped that those would go away in time too. Her memory had also improved, and she was not as forgetful as she had been when she was with her husband. She, however, still kept the *to-do* list. It was part and parcel of her now, and she had a list handy at all times.

Labake laid back on her bed and tried to think of what she would do with the rest of her life. She thought about medical school and how she still nursed dreams of becoming a doctor one day, but she knew she was not quite settled enough to make such a huge commitment. Besides, she did not have the money to enroll and put herself through a continuous course of study. She had to work and earn a living to feed Ella and pay for her school too. Laide had offered to pay for *Med School* if she still wanted to tow that line, but Labake had declined. She believed there was still a lot to do in restoring some normalcy in her life and Ella's too.

Labake sometimes felt overwhelmed by her newfound independence and was at times scared that she would not be able to do life on her own without any guidance. It was as if she needed to be directed on how to live her life. This was the first time she had made decisions for herself and Ella. It was scary, but she was slowly getting accustomed to it. She still second-guessed her decisions and hated being so indecisive sometimes, even over the minutest thing.

She wondered if she would ever be able to return to her home country again. She worried about a number of other things too. Her daughter's future was a matter of primary concern to her. She was all Ella had now, and she wanted to raise her properly. She wanted her daughter to be as well-rounded as possible, particularly now that her father was not in the picture. She had, however, decided to heed Laide's advice and take each day at a time and not worry too much about the future, but that was easier said than done.

Labake's mind drifted now to Vince, and she wondered if she would ever see him again and shuddered at the thought. Even after all this time, the thought of Vince still made her heart beat faster. She realized in the months she had been away from him that she did not even know how to be herself without him. She had married him when she was rather young before she became a proper adult. She did not know any other life as an adult. Vince had groomed her into what he wanted, fit for his purpose only and no one else's, not even hers. He had formed her entire life around himself and what *he* wanted so much that she did not even see herself as an individual or a separate entity with personal desires of her own. He had managed to affect her so deeply that it was a wonder she had even thought of escaping. She felt lucky and proud that she had though, *all by herself*.

Labake was unable to fully trust or relax with anyone as her guard was always up. The other day at the hotel, a male colleague had stretched over her to retrieve a file from the cabinet above her desk, and she had almost jumped out of her own skin! He had been surprised at her reaction and had apologized profusely for having startled her. Labake had been terribly embarrassed by her shaky overreaction. Ghosts from the past often reared their ugly heads, she thought and wondered if they would ever die.

Her mind drifted to the immediate future and Kwame's daughter's fifth birthday party, coming up this Saturday. She was planning on taking Ella and had stopped at the mall near the hotel to get her a new outfit for the party. Ella was growing up fast these days, and Labake thought she would need a new set of clothes soon. She was going to turn seven next month and was getting really tall for her age. She had even outgrown most of the clothes they had managed to bring with them to Accra. Labake made a mental note to take Ella clothes shopping soon. It was her last thought before she drifted off to sleep again.

* * * *

Vince was infuriated! He never saw it coming. He never conceived that Labake was capable of planning *anything,* least of all a *get-away*. He also could not believe how clueless he was about where she would have run to. He had tried everything, had used every resource within his reach, but it appeared his wife and daughter had vanished off the face of the earth.

What baffled him most was how she had even managed to *think* of running off *with* his daughter. She knew how he felt about *his angel* and was convinced Labake had taken his daughter to spite him. It was a wicked thing she did - snatch his daughter from him without a trace. He was going crazy just thinking about it. He was beginning to feel like he had lived with the most devious, evil person these past few years. She had planned it all, and he had completely underestimated her.

He wondered how she had managed it. He knew she had to have had some help but wondered who could have helped her. She did not have any family or friends except Laide, her sister, and even that relationship was virtually non-existent as he had seen to that. He had made Labake know how he felt about any external interference in their lives.

Now, Vince wished he had been a lot friendlier with his sister-in-law because, as things stood, he did not have the foggiest idea of where she was either. In fact, it was as if Laide never existed. He knew she had done a post-graduate course at the *University of Lagos,* but that was years back. He had kept the little family his wife had at arm's length, and he now realized it was to his detriment. But then, how was he to know his wife would *make away* with his daughter someday?

The police had asked about Labake's family when he went to report his child missing. He had said she only had her elder sister, whose full name he did not even know. He was not even sure he ever knew Laide's last name as he was aware that both she and Labake had different biological fathers, and even if he did, Laide could have married and changed her last name. In this part of the world, people were difficult to trace even with the most up-to-date information on them, and here he was, unsure of his sister-in-law's current name! He knew he would need nothing short of a miracle to find Laide as he knew absolutely nothing about her. It was a hopeless situation. He had tried *Google*, *Facebook,* and *linked-in* but found nothing. It was as if Laide was a figment of his imagination. So much for *social media,* Vince thought and swore under his breath. *The world wasn't such a global village after all,* he thought angrily.

He remembered how angry he was that he had been unable to reach Labake by phone to let her know when she was to pick him up from the airport on his return from Denver. He had been even more furious that she had not even bothered to contact him in the two weeks he had been away. He had initially become worried a couple of days after his arrival in Denver when he had rung Labake to speak to Ella but had been unable to get through to her. Vince had thought of ringing his mother to find out if she had heard from Labake since he had been away but thought against it. He never wanted any member of his family to think he was unable to control his wife or home at that. He had decided to take an airport taxi home on his arrival, not wanting to involve anyone else.

When the taxi entered *Crossway Estate,* where they lived, everything seemed normal, and nothing was out of place. When he pulled up to *House Seven*, Vince noticed Labake's car was parked in its usual spot but could not see any lights on through the windows of the house. He had assumed she had gone to bed as he had arrived home rather late due to his flight being delayed. He knew something was out of place the minute he let himself into the house. The place was in pitch darkness, and a stale smell was in the air. The house was neat, but there was a film of dust on everything. Thinking about it now, a closer look at Labake's car outside revealed it was dusty too and did not appear to have been driven in a while.

Angrier now, Vince marched into their bedroom, the guest room, and Ella's bedroom but was shocked that all three rooms were empty and in the same dusty condition. He looked around for a note or something to explain where Labake and Ella were, but there was none. Suddenly alarmed, he looked in the closet, and Labake's things seemed intact. He then rushed back to his daughter's room again. At that point, it dawned on him that Labake had left him and taken his daughter with her. The chest of drawers in Ella's bedroom was open, and it was obvious that some of her clothes were missing. *'Mr. Snockels'*, her beloved teddy bear was gone too.

Apart from her car keys which had been left on the console table in the living room, Labake had not even had the decency to leave him a note! Vince was trembling at this point and felt a rush of emotions all at once - anger, hatred, panic, humiliation, but most of all, shock. He still could not believe Labake had the effrontery to *make away with* his child. *His Ella!* He wondered now how long they had been gone.

Though tired from his trip, Vince had not slept a wink that night. He had been on the phone with his mother and siblings immediately, wondering if anyone had heard from Labake in the two weeks he had been away. He had also silently hoped that she would have left Ella with a member of his family before she disappeared, but she had not. In fact, no one had seen or heard from her recently, and because she was not exactly the most favorite in-law, no member of his family had bothered to check on her or Ella, not even his mother.

The following morning after his return, Vince had rushed to the main gate to inquire from the security guards, but none had noticed anything except that they had not seen *Mrs. Ebodo* lately. The estate close circuit TV was virtually useless as it had not recorded anything new in weeks.

Next, Vince rushed to Ella's school, but her teacher said she had not been in school since they resumed after the mid-term break the week before. It was at that point that he decided to go to the police station to make a statement that his wife had kidnapped his daughter. He had also gotten in touch with an old school friend of his who worked for the *State Security Service*. The friend had suggested that they post pictures immediately at all borders and airports in the country, but Vince had said that was not necessary as Labake did not have access to her international passport or Ella's.

It had taken another three days before he discovered that both Labake's passport and Ella's were missing from the drawer where he hid them. He had been flabbergasted. He had rushed back to inform his friend, who concluded that they could be anywhere at that point, seeing as they had almost a three-week head start. He suggested putting pictures of Labake and Ella in the newspapers and on TV, but Vince had declined, not wanting to air too much of his dirty laundry in public. Vince's friend had said they would check with all the airlines to see if his family traveled on any of them. So far, nothing had been found. There was no trace of his wife, child, or even his sister-in-law, Laide. There was no record of their passports having been scanned at any of the international borders in the country either.

Vince was angry and felt slighted by Labake. He still could not believe that she, of all people, would have succeeded in pulling a fast one on him. She was the most foolish person he knew! How had she managed it? How long had she planned it? Who had helped her, and where in the world had she taken his daughter? These were the questions he had spent most of the last year asking himself. He was beginning to lose hope and wondered if he would ever see his daughter again. The thought that he would not frightened him beyond comprehension.

His mother was also deeply troubled by the news that her daughter-in-law had kidnapped her grandchild. "I never trusted that girl for half a second. I always knew she was capable of anything!" She had said and asked her Pastor and members of her fellowship to pay Vince several visits and hold prayer meetings with him, hoping that by some sheer miracle, Labake would bring her granddaughter back.

CHAPTER EIGHT

After Banjo left on the evening when Rewa had revealed to him that she had fallen pregnant by him but miscarried his baby, she developed a bad migraine that lingered for days. He had opened old wounds she erroneously believed were long healed. She cast her mind back to how it all happened and suddenly realized it was all still rather fresh in her memory.

Rewa had been back from the exhibition in Northampton for a few weeks and had been miserable and listless since her return. She had not heard from Banjo since her last phone conversation with him in Northampton. She had tried his old number on her return home, but it was no longer in service. She also left messages for him at *Medlake* Hospital, but he had not returned any of her calls. It had finally dawned on her after a few more attempts at contacting him that Banjo Adetunji was not interested in keeping in touch with her. He had played her yet again.

The realization that Banjo had broken her heart a second time made Rewa ill. She could not understand how she deemed herself relatively intelligent yet unable to see through him. She clearly had not learned from her prior, nasty experience with him and had compromised herself yet again. How many chances was she prepared to give Banjo to her detriment? She had finally accepted that he clearly never had and would never have any good intentions towards her. Rewa was sickened by her own stupidity and perhaps shocked and disappointed that anyone could be as heartless as Banjo Adetunji. She really did believe she had grown up and was not as naïve as she had been when she first met him, but Banjo had proved her wrong *again*.

Rewa had not only fallen physically ill on her return from Northampton, but she was also an emotional wreck. She lost so much weight and was so depressed that even going to work seemed too much of an effort. She managed to drag herself into work each morning, but it was not enough distraction. She was not interested in doing anything socially and her inability to speak to anyone about it made it even worse. Her mother had been worried about her too, as she clearly was not eating or sleeping. She looked terrible, and Mrs. Ilo commented on it one evening when Rewa returned home from work.

"What's the matter, dear?" She had enquired worriedly of her daughter. "You look dreadful!" She exclaimed. She had suspected something was not quite right with her daughter since her return from her trip abroad but did not quite know how to broach the subject. Rewa was a bit of a closed book on her personal issues and had always been since she was a child. Mrs. Ilo knew that getting any information out of her would be like trying to get water out of a rock. She was unlike her younger sisters, particularly Sede, to whom she was closest. Mrs. Ilo now wondered if she could get Sede to find out what was going on with her elder sister. Rewa looked ill and sad, and she wished she knew how to help her.

"Thanks, mum, trust you to tell it as you see it," Rewa had responded sardonically to what she viewed as her mother's insensitive comment.

Mrs. Ilo had ignored Rewa and, instead, touched her head and whistled. She became frantic and said. "That's it! You're burning up. Get up. I'm taking you to the hospital this instant!" She was suddenly alarmed and ignored all Rewa said to reassure her that she was fine.

"I'm alright, Mum...really, I just need to rest a bit." She said in an attempt to calm her panicked mother, but Mrs. Ilo pulled out her phone from her handbag and dialed her husband first to let him know what was going on and then her driver, *Sule*.

"Can you manage to get up so Sule and I can help you down the stairs?" She asked Rewa after she got off the phone.

"That's hardly necessary, mum; I'm alright..." Mrs. Ilo didn't wait for her to finish the sentence. She answered the door to Sule and practically bundled Rewa to the hospital despite her protests.

Looking back now, Rewa wished she had not been rushed to the hospital by her mother on that dreadful day. She had been immediately placed on *anti-malaria* tablets by the young doctor who had seen her. It had been late in the evening, and Dr. Pat, the family doctor, was off duty. The young doctor who had treated her had not checked or asked if she could be pregnant, and it had not even crossed Rewa's mind that she could be. She had never been pregnant before, so she completely missed all the signs. All she knew was that she had been tired a lot since her trip and seemed to lack the energy to do anything. She had blamed it on the state of her heart and perhaps the stress of the entire trip to Northampton.

A week later, Rewa was rushed back to the hospital after she passed out at work on a client's site. It was at the hospital she had been informed about her pregnancy and subsequent miscarriage due to the anti-malaria medication she had received the week before.

"Were you unaware that you were pregnant?" Dr. Pat asked her in the private hospital room.

"*Pregnant*?" Rewa had asked the Doctor in bewilderment. "I can't...can't be pregnant...are you sure about that?" She had further enquired of the doctor. Her pale skin had grown ashen from the shock of what Doctor Pat was saying to her.

Dr. Pat smiled and asked gently but pointedly, "Have you had unprotected sex recently, Omorewa?" Rewa looked away, slightly embarrassed and confused. She had known Dr. Pat since she was a teenager, she was the Ilo family doctor, and Rewa found the situation she was in at that point rather embarrassing, but she answered with a confused look and said,

"Yes, but that was...that was about four months ago." She looked up at Dr. Pat who was a motherly figure and one of the best physicians in the country. Rewa hoped to God that she was wrong and that she would realize her error, apologize, and say she had made a terrible mistake and was reading from another patient's chart. However, she did not. Instead, Dr. Pat said, "It couldn't have been four months ago because if I'm to give an estimate by your last known period, you were probably about ten or eleven weeks pregnant."

Rewa suddenly had a light bulb moment when she recalculated and realized she had been with Banjo about two and a half months before. She immediately felt utterly confounded by what was now being revealed to her.

Dr. Pat proceeded to give more details of what she believed had caused the miscarriage. Thinking back now, what she had said had all been a blur as Rewa had not heard anything else at that point. The knowledge that she had been pregnant with Banjo's child and had unknowingly lost it saddened her beyond words. It was almost as if she was losing her grip on her life, and everything was spiraling out of control. She was immensely frightened but, most of all, shattered. How could she not have known she was pregnant? She thought about it over and over again to this day.

Rewa had been so consumed with disappointment and heartbreak when she had not heard from Banjo since the UK trip, and it had caused her to totally forget that she had missed her period. She never really kept a record of her periods or her menstrual cycle in general, seeing as she had not been sexually active prior to meeting Banjo on the London-bound flight. Missing a period was therefore the last thing on her mind and until it was confirmed by her doctor, it had not occurred to her.

She and Banjo had, after all, had spontaneous, unprotected sex, a fact that Rewa found even more embarrassing when Doctor Pat had asked. She had been so overcome by the *itch* that she had not taken the necessary precautions. There was therefore no one else to blame but herself. How careless could anyone with her level of exposure be? She asked herself to this day. She was lucky she had not caught any STDs off the *idiot* in the process - God knew he would sleep with anything at the drop of a hat. Rewa frowned at that last thought.

A few months had now passed since Rewa revealed her pregnancy and miscarriage to Banjo at her flat. Apart from the bunch of flowers he had sent to her a week after, with a card which simply read *'Sorry'*, Rewa had not heard from him again. She hoped she never did, as he reminded her of things she wanted desperately to forget.

The worst of it was over; Rewa sighed at her desk now. She sometimes thought it was perhaps all for the best that she had lost the baby. She did not think it would have been wise to co-parent a child with someone as inconsistent as Banjo was. To do that would be unfair to the child, she believed.

The idea of being a single parent also was not one she found appealing. What would her parents and entire family think of her? She was the first child of her parents; what example would she have been to her younger sisters? Never mind that they were both grown and way past the age where they needed one.

Rewa, however, still secretly grieved the loss of her baby and the loss of what could have been had she known she was pregnant. She, however, managed to pick up the pieces of her life yet again but still lived with the guilt of her carelessness in not knowing about her pregnancy. She had never told a soul about it until her outburst with Banjo the other day, and she intended to keep it that way. She had said as much to Dr. Pat and hoped she understood the confidentiality issues involved. She was not just the Ilo family doctor; she and her husband were very close friends with Rewa's parents. Rewa hoped she would respect her wishes not to mention the pregnancy or miscarriage to her parents.

In a bid to forget it all, Rewa threw herself into her work and helping Faith plan her wedding. The gentleman Faith had met on the plane, *Stephen*, had proposed to her after only six months of dating, and they were getting married in a couple of weeks. They were planning a quiet *civil* ceremony in Abuja as most of Faith's family lived there.

Faith was beyond ecstatic at the prospect of getting *hitched,* and so was Rewa for her friend. She deserved to be happy, and Rewa wished her all the best. Of course, she was going to be one of her witnesses at the registry wedding and was therefore working hard to try and finish her current renovation so she could take some time off work to make the wedding in a fortnight.

The current project Rewa was working on involved renovating the offices of a large, reputable law firm in *Victoria Island,* and her workers were trying her patience on it. It was getting clearer that she was not going to meet the stipulated deadline for completion, which was something that never happened. She usually gave more than enough time for completion on all her projects just to accommodate the shenanigans of her workers and any other unforeseen circumstance which could cause delays. However, in this particular case, Rewa was convinced that shifting the completion date was unavoidable. She was dealing with a carpenter who just took his time in delivering anything, and there were delays already in the arrival of some imported furniture which she ordered from overseas too.

Rewa had an appointment booked for tomorrow to see the Head of Chambers or the *HOC,* as everyone at *Princes Chambers* referred to him. He had requested the meeting. The firm's lease at their current location was coming to an end in a matter of weeks, and they were eager to move into their new permanent site which had been purchased three months earlier. Rewa was therefore being *summoned* by the boss to give an explanation as to why there was a need to push the deadline by an extra week.

Hitherto, Rewa had dealt with the firm's Managing Partner, *Mrs. Atta*. She was Rewa's main contact person on the project, and Rewa found her quite easy to deal with. Though Mrs. Atta was under pressure from the top to get the job completed as quickly as possible, she never let on to Rewa until yesterday when she informed her that the *HOC* had requested a meeting with *the designer*.

"He can be a very difficult man at times, you see, Ms. Ilo," Mrs. Atta whispered to Rewa yesterday as she set up the appointment. “He wants to be involved in absolutely *everything*...I wonder how he's able to keep up given his hectic work schedule," Mrs. Atta laughed. She was a huge, heavy-set woman whom Rewa judged to be in her late forties. Rewa had found from her dealings with her over the last few months that she was extremely meticulous herself. The firm had put her in charge of the new designs, and she and Rewa had been back and forth over every minute detail without any major hick-ups so far. Mrs. Atta was an amiable woman and had handled things in the most mature, diplomatic, and professional manner. From what Rewa was hearing about the *HOC*, she hoped those traits trickled down from the top.

"Underneath all that bravado though, is a really nice man but be prepared for some sort of opposition to your shifting the deadline. He is a bit spoiled and rather impatient too, you see..." Mrs. Atta continued with a half-smile. She was obviously very fond of her boss and had a huge admiration for him, being one of the oldest partners at the firm and the one person who knew him all too well.

Rewa had done a bit of investigating herself. She had *googled Chief Ralph Eke* (SAN) the minute she was assigned the job. She usually did that with her new clients just to have an idea of who she would be dealing with and, of course, for some general knowledge. In her pursuit of information, she had discovered that Chief Eke, though in his mid-fifties, had founded *Princes Chambers* after a few years of successful legal practice with other firms. He had been an avid member of the *Bar Association* and had been its president at some point. He had also sat on the board of several government agencies and had a large number of *VIP* clients too. He had won several highly publicized and controversial cases involving private individuals, top corporations, and even the government and was a highly acclaimed and sought-after legal icon. He was very popular within the legal system of the country, particularly for some of the controversial cases he had taken on and won. He was considered smart, hardworking, and unbiased in his dealings with his clients, regardless of who they were.

Chief Ralph Eke had bagged the prestigious title of *Senior Advocate of Nigeria* (SAN) barely a decade into his practice and was well respected amongst his colleagues and peers. He was definitely a major *mover and shaker* within the country's legal system and had a lot of money and property to show for it.

Though he made a number of social appearances in the tabloids and was renowned for his philanthropy, successful practice, and numerous achievements, Rewa also garnered in her quest for more information on him that the Chief was a very private man, and very little was known about his personal life.

Rewa thanked Mrs. Atta for the heads-up and decided to be forearmed for her meeting with Chief Eke tomorrow. It was slated for one-thirty in the afternoon; she therefore had enough time to gather the paperwork and details of the project and make adequate arrangements to get there early enough. She had loads of paperwork on the project and needed to get them organized before the dreaded meeting.

CHAPTER NINE

The party was in full swing when Labake and Ella walked into the *Children's Fun Centre* where Kwame's daughter, Nana's birthday party was being celebrated. A bubbly and happy Ella hopped and leaped excitedly in the pretty new denim dress her mother had purchased for the occasion. Labake found it hard to restrain her and tightened her grip on her wrist in an attempt to give her a silent warning to behave herself.

There were colorful balloons of all different shapes and sizes at the Centre, the place was beautifully decorated, and there were all kinds of side attractions and rides for the children present, who all appeared to be having a great time. Kids were playing in a huge bouncy castle, and over twenty other noisy children of different ages were running around the place.

It was not too long before Ella spotted a friend from her school and broke free from her mother's grip to go and play with the familiar face. "Be careful, Ella...!" Labake called after her as she almost knocked a boy down in her haste to get to her friend. Labake shook her head in slight frustration, wondering what the point of the talk they had on their way to the party was. She had asked Ella to behave herself at the party and even promised her a treat to the pizza place tomorrow if she did. It was clear now that she had not been listening.

Labake spotted Kwame and his wife, Adia, handing out ice cream cones to a bunch of eager kids and went over to say hello and see if she could help with anything. Adia, completely inundated, was grateful for Labake's help and asked her to distribute some cupcakes to another group of patiently waiting children.

Labake's mind drifted to Ella's first birthday party as she passed the cakes around. It had been one of her worst days ever as Vince Ebodo's wife. She had done all the cooking in preparation for the party Vince insisted on throwing and had been out with him very early on the morning of the party to get some more supplies for the big party. The party was to be held as usual at Vince's mother's house as she had more space in her yard for it. They had dropped a cranky Ella off with her grandmother so that they could put the finishing touches to the shopping before the guests began to arrive.

Labake, having been married to her husband for only a little under a year at the time, was not fully aware of how bad his temper was, but she found out very quickly on this fateful day. She had bumped into an old neighbor's son whom she and her sister, Laide, had known growing up. *Mufu* and his parents had lived in the same building as they had when they were kids. He had been like a brother to them, and Labake had not seen him since he went away to University. Mufu had been the first to spot her at the meat market, and they were both excited to see each other. They were catching up on old times when Vince suddenly showed up from the other side of the market and, without a word to Mufu, literally dragged his wife out of the market for the viewing pleasure of all present.

Labake, confused by Vince's rude actions, had tried to explain to him who Mufu was, but her effort to do so had fallen on deaf ears. Vince was enraged at that point and was unable to see past the fact that his wife had warmly and openly embraced another man publicly and right under his nose. He had shoved Labake into the car and driven away. He was so angry that he completely forgot about their shopping!

Labake wondered why her husband had been so possessive. She had never given him a reason to be. Nevertheless, he had always believed her to be interested in other men and always ensured that she remembered whose *property* she was.

Bumping into Mufu at the meat market had ruined the entire celebration for Labake as Vince picked on her throughout their daughter's birthday party. Her mother, who had been alive at the time and also present at the party, had noticed how rude and mean Vince was to Labake and had enquired about it. Labake had reassured her that everything was alright and made the excuse that Vince was under a lot of pressure because of the party.

That evening, after their guests left and they returned home, Vince got the opportunity he had wanted all day to physically show his wife whose she was. Labake had landed in the hospital with two black eyes, a split lip, and two broken ribs. The beatings were usually worse when they were fuelled by Vince's jealousy. As he dealt each blow that evening, he told her how she was the cause of his violent behavior. That she always provoked him as she was such *'a useless whore who flirted with every man she met.'*

Thinking about the many times she had been physically attacked and brutalized by her husband still made Labake's stomach churn. She still felt nauseous when she remembered his punches, slaps, whippings, and kicks. Not to mention his cussing and swearing or the evil glint in his eyes when he had determined within himself to get his pound of flesh.

Labake remembered how panicked she got when she knew she could not avoid a beating. Even after all this time, she still felt afraid and froze each time a man came near her. It still felt as if she was doing something wrong if a man so much as spoke to her, and though she knew it was silly, somewhere in her subconscious, she hoped Vince had not noticed. Even now, thirteen months since her escape, far away from her brutally abusive husband, Labake was still afraid. She desperately wanted to stop being scared, but old ghosts died hard. In the meantime, she lived with them helplessly, praying they would *rest in peace* one day.

Labake had maintained a low profile since her arrival in Ghana. It was what she was used to even when she had been with Vince. He never encouraged friendliness or any form of outgoing behavior, and she did not have any friends as a result. It was, therefore, easy for her to maintain a low profile in her new life and surroundings. She was quiet, extremely cautious, not trusting or saying much to anyone, and kept to herself a lot.

Labake sometimes felt timid and wondered if she had ever been able to stand up for herself even before her marriage. She had been so young and naïve when she married Vince that she did not even remember what her personality was way back before they were married. She had been *indoctrinated* or perhaps *'brainwashed'* in a sense, groomed to behave a certain way, not to talk back to her husband or anyone, to do as she was told without question, to speak only when spoken to, and the list went on. She often felt like a zombie or an automaton, even now, over a year since her escape.

In the ten days Labake had spent with her sister before her move to Ghana with her daughter, Laide had felt as though she was a stranger. She had found Labake rather withdrawn and uncommunicative. Laide was disturbed and concerned for her sister's mental well-being too. The sister she grew up with had been quite chirpy, cheeky, and full of life. Labake was, however, a totally changed person now. She had been replaced by this somewhat distant, quiet, jittery person who lacked any confidence or clarity of purpose.

Laide had silently observed Labake for days, hoping to see a glimmer of who she had been when they were younger, but that person appeared long gone. Eventually, when she could not bear it anymore, Laide suggested therapy. She felt her sister needed to talk to someone, a professional counselor. She was secretly worried that the old Labake she used to know would never be found again.

"You need some sort of therapy, Labake, you've been through a lot, and it's made you a different person," Laide had insisted and offered to get her sister some help. Labake had declined, saying all she needed was an income in order to provide for her child. She believed time to be the best healer and was willing to wait it out. That was over a year ago, and nothing had changed except she had not been beaten during the period and therefore was not in any physical pain. The mental and emotional scars, however, were still very fresh and present. Healing in this area seemed rather slow in comparison, but Labake was hopeful that in time even that would be history.

"Your little girl appears to be having a lot of fun." Labake literally jumped back to the present at the voice behind her. She was startled and her deep thoughts were suddenly interrupted by the male voice, which she found when she turned abruptly, belonged to a tall, rather light-skinned man of medium build. Labake took a frightened step back with a hand on her chest as if to stop her heart from jumping out of her throat. She looked at the man with an alarmed expression on her face.

As if to put her at ease, he immediately stretched a hand out to her with a slightly worried but reassuring smile.

"I'm sorry, I didn't mean to startle you. I am Earl, *Earl Tetteh*," The man said with his hand stretched out to Labake.

Labake judged him to be mixed-race as he was far too light-skinned to be purely African and his hair, though cropped, had a slight waviness to it. He seemed to be in his late thirties or perhaps early forties, with a pair of keen amber-colored eyes. He wore an African print dashiki with a pair of blue jeans and sandals. She noticed the latter when she took a further couple of quick steps backwards and stopped only because she bumped right into the cake table behind her.

Hesitantly but speechless still and not wanting to appear rude, Labake took the hand he offered, which she observed again was quite soft as he shook hers warmly. *Definitely not pure African.* She thought within herself.

Not waiting for an actual response from Labake, Earl said, "I presume the little girl in the blue dress is your daughter?" Turning as he spoke in Ella's direction. She was in a group with four other children, playing excitedly with hoops. Labake could see her from where she and Earl now stood.

Labake suddenly became alarmed and wondered what Earl's interest was with her daughter. "Yes," She answered in a hesitant and quiet tone. She attempted to move around him and away from the table in an effort to put some distance between them, but what she really felt like doing was snatching her daughter up and running. She, however, controlled the urge to do so, thinking it would be silly of her. Instead, she smiled politely and, at the same time, moved to walk away from Earl Tetteh. Just as she turned to find a seat, she bumped right into Adia, who said,

"I see you've met my brother; let me introduce you properly." She held Labake's hand and practically pulled her back to where Earl Tetteh still stood, smiling. *So he was her brother?* Labake thought within herself and relaxed a bit. She, however, had a puzzled look on her face to which Adia responded,

"...*half-brother,* I should say actually, we share the same father," Adia further explained to Labake and continued, "Earl, this is Labake. She's a friend of ours. Labake, this is my beloved elder brother, *Earl Tetteh*. He recently moved back home from Canada". Adia smiled at him, and Labake said rather breathlessly,

"Nice... to meet you *again*...Mr. Tetteh".

"*Earl,* please...call me Earl. It's a pleasure to meet you too, Labake, and please pay my naughty sister no mind. I've been back home for over two years now. I couldn't help noticing your daughter when you arrived. The little girl just seemed so happy to be here and couldn't wait to join in the fun," Earl Tetteh mused.

"Yes, that's Labake's daughter, Ella. She's such a joy to have around," Adia added.

Labake smiled in response. Relaxing a bit more now that she knew Earl Tetteh was a relative of her host. She understood his explanation and his reason for taking an interest in Ella too. At that moment, Adia was called away to gather the children around, to sing the *Happy Birthday* song to the celebrant, and Labake found herself alone again with Earl Tetteh. She felt rather awkward as he looked at her as if trying to unravel the mystery before him.

He asked her if she'd had anything to eat and offered to get her a drink as he led her to a table with two empty chairs. Labake said she had a piece of cake and did not want anything more. She wished Earl would move on to someone else as she really was not in the mood for small talk. She wanted to sit quietly and enjoy the party. She had been planning to leave in another hour and was already trying to muster up the strength to handle Ella's tantrum once she knew it was time to go home. She, however, resolved to be polite but not too friendly with Earl, who pulled his chair closer to hers so that they could have a conversation amidst the noisy party.

"So Labake, if you don't mind my asking, what is it you do apart from being the mother of that lovely, eager little girl of yours?" Earl asked with a smile in those keen amber eyes of his. Labake noticed he had nice teeth, and his smile was disarming. She averted his gaze, looked away nervously, and answered,

"I work in a hotel...accounts and admin..." She trailed off as though she had said too much. She did not like the feeling of being interrogated, especially by a complete stranger. She pondered on a polite way to let him know she was not in the mood for a conversation or any attention and began considering leaving the party earlier than planned. The feeling she had of snatching Ella up and gunning for the exit became overwhelming again, and she had to struggle to suppress it.

"I'm sorry..." Labake heard herself say as she rose clumsily from her chair, without a plan as to where she was going. "I...really need to...need to get going...it was nice meeting you..." She trailed off again. Earl immediately got to his feet too, slightly confused by her sudden need to get away. "Er...likewise. I hope you're not leaving on my account...?" He asked, concerned that he had made her uncomfortable.

"No...no, I just remembered I have to stop at the...at the supermarket on my way home..." Labake mumbled almost to herself. It was obvious she had just fobbed him off. She said, "Good day." She picked her bag up and hurriedly went to fetch Ella and search for her hosts to let them know they were leaving.

CHAPTER TEN

Omorewa Ilo took another impatient look at her watch. She had been sitting in the Lobby of *Princes Chambers* for over forty minutes. *Gosh!* She thought angrily about how she hated to wait. She took another look in the direction of the *Head of Chambers'* secretary and wondered if she needed to remind her that she was still waiting to see him but decided against it. She did not want to appear unprofessional. The secretary, a young lady in her late twenties, had informed Rewa when she arrived fifteen minutes before her scheduled appointment with the HOC that,

"Chief Eke sends his apologies as his meeting is taking longer than expected. He is aware that you are here and will be with you shortly."

That had been forty-five minutes ago, and Rewa was already irritated. *Princes Chambers* was a good paying client, but she did not appreciate the time wasted sitting there, doing absolutely nothing. Why did people give you an appointment and then make you wait so long after the scheduled time? As far as Rewa was concerned, it was highly disrespectful. It was as though they felt their own time was more valuable than yours. She shook her head and looked away irately from where the secretary sat, typing away profusely on her desktop.

Rewa's thought drifted to all the things she needed to do before Faith's Abuja wedding next week and sighed again impatiently. She had a lot on her plate at the moment and could not afford to sit around waiting to see anyone. She declined the tea or coffee she had been offered on her arrival and wished at that point that she had asked for a glass of water instead. She was beginning to feel dehydrated now. Perhaps it was due to the fact that she was nervous about this meeting, especially knowing who she was there to see and why.

This was Rewa's very first time meeting the Head of Chambers or *HOC,* as they referred to him here at *Princes* Chambers. She had dealt with Mrs. Atta all through the instruction-taking process and inspections that had followed in the last five months. Mrs. Atta had been the person she had shown samples to and got feedback from with regard to choices and decisions to be made on the entire project. Rewa knew Mrs. Atta reported back to the *HOC* whom she had heard was a bit of a *control freak.* It was rather surprising that he had not requested a meeting with her sooner. She, however, knew why he asked for one now and shifted nervously in her seat again.

Meeting the *big boss* himself was nerve-wracking, to say the least, as Rewa had insider information that he could be difficult, was spoilt, and used to having things done his way. She was asking for a week's extension of time within which to complete the decoration of the firm's newly acquired office building not too far away from their present location. Though she had done some personal snooping on him at the beginning of the project, she did not feel any better about meeting Chief Ralph Eke.

Rewa was proud of the work she had done so far on the new office premises. It was a building on five floors, and she had been assigned the contract to redesign every inch of it. Though slightly unfinished, it looked spectacular already. The furniture and fittings were all state of the art. Mrs. Atta and some of the other partners had been pleasantly shocked at what they had seen on their last inspection. Rewa hoped the boss, the one who mattered most, the *HOC,* in the person of Chief Ralph Eke, would be pleased too. She had gone beyond the call and overextended herself on this project. In fact, there were going to be a few more pleasant surprises when the firm eventually moved in as Rewa had put in a few extra details that were not in the original plan, at no extra cost to the firm.

Rewa needed the extra week to put a few finishing touches on the place and hoped the carpenter would speed up the process of delivering the last few pieces of furniture. She was also expecting the boardroom table from Italy, which had been delayed in transit for about four weeks, particularly because of the nationwide airport staff strike. The strike had gone on for almost a month but had recently been called off. The shippers had assured her that the table, along with a few other accessories, would be delivered today or tomorrow, and Rewa had her fingers crossed on that.

Rewa never asked for an extension of time from her clients as she generally had a good sense of timing and was able to predict correctly how long a project would take. She included extra time in her delivery dates just to accommodate unforeseen eventualities such as this one. Before now, she had always made the deadline or usually even delivered way before the stipulated time.

However, this project had been a huge one, and she and her crew had been working on it for over five months. Rewa had to decorate all five floors, and though she had enjoyed every bit of it, it had been grueling at times, especially because of some of the contractors she engaged who had no sense of timing or urgency. She was quite ready to take a holiday after it was finished. She believed she had earned herself one.

The door behind the secretary's desk opened, and three young men in business suits came out of it. They stopped to speak to the secretary for a moment before leaving. The intercom on the secretary's desk beeped almost immediately, and after she answered it, she got up and walked the short distance to the sitting area where Rewa was.

"Chief Eke will see you now. Apologies again for the delay," she said and led Rewa to the door. She knocked on it and opened it after Rewa heard the *Enter* on the other side of it. The secretary then motioned for her to go in.

Rewa composed herself and walked into the large office. It had a huge mahogany desk at the center of the room and was packed with a large screened computer, leather-bound books, files, papers, newspapers, pens, and every form of stationery one could think of. One kind of got the impression that the owner of this office was busy. Behind the desk sat a very dark, very tall man of a slim build. Rewa watched as he rose from his chair politely the moment she entered and extended his hand to her across the large desk for a handshake.

He had on a crisp white shirt that had been loosened at the neck and a blue tie. His shirt sleeves were rolled up to his elbows, and the shirt itself was tucked into dark slacks that fit his lean body perfectly. He had on a pair of spectacles which he removed before the handshake, and Rewa could not help but notice the grey hairs at his temple. He was a rather good-looking man she observed and, for a split second, was tongue-tied.

Chief Ralph Eke certainly did not look anything like a chief. Rewa had not seen a picture of him in her quick search, so she had envisaged a short, stocky, pot-bellied, sweaty middle-aged man. *Why*? She wondered now. Chief Ralph Eke looked nothing like that. For someone in his mid-fifties, he looked unbelievably young, at least ten years younger, Rewa gauged. She clumsily dropped some of her papers on the wooden floor of his office as she was completely thrown by how wrong her expectations were of the HOC of *Princes' Chambers*.

Rewa took the hand he offered, shook it briefly, and immediately knelt to gather the papers she had dropped, trying to hide the fact that she was now terribly embarrassed. *He must think I'm a klutz!* She thought silently. Chief Eke stooped to help pick some of the papers off the floor, handed them to her, and said,

"Hello, Ms..." He stopped mid-sentence, replaced the spectacles on the bridge of his narrow nose briefly, and moved back to his desk swiftly so he could take a quick glance at the paper on his table before he continued. "...*Ms. Ilo*. Good to meet you. I apologize for the delay in seeing you. We had a pressing issue to sort out in the last meeting, which, unfortunately, ran into our appointment." He gestured to one of the four chairs opposite him, indicating that Rewa sat in one of them before he took his own seat.

A gentleman. Rewa observed silently, getting over her initial embarrassment quickly. *A gentleman without a smile.* She further observed. He had not cracked a smile since she entered, not even when he shook her hand. She found it hard to read his *expressionless* face and decided to play it cool and professional herself. She thought he seemed rather tired and a bit aloof. *Well, that works well for me,* she thought and said finally, "Pleased to meet you, Chief Eke." Rewa took the seat he offered and said,

"Thank you." Without a smile. She had *her* expressionless face on too and waited for him to speak first.

"Please call me *Ralph,*" he said and continued, "Right, I hear you've done quite a phenomenal job on the new place. I haven't seen it personally, but I trust the judgment of my people whom you're dealing with. They say it's great work you've done so far. I'm, however, uncertain as to why we need to extend our original deadline. I presume you're aware we're under a tight schedule to vacate this place. So, why the extension, if I may ask Ms. Ilo?" Chief Eke asked in a very *matter-of-fact* way.

Rewa observed that he did not check the paper in front of him to confirm her name this time. It had clearly registered. He leaned forward and folded his arms on his desk, looking at Rewa pointedly. There was no doubt that she had his unflinching attention now, Rewa thought. He was quite *straight-to-the-point,* Rewa noticed too. Did she detect a slight cockiness in what he said and how he said it? She wondered and then answered in the same direct manner.

"*Omorewa,* please, but you can call me *Rewa* for short. Er...I apologize for the extra time we need to complete the project. I usually never need an extension, but we've had some issues with the shipment of some of the furnishings we ordered abroad. They're being brought in from Italy, but the personnel strike at the airport, which has now been called off thankfully, had a major role to play in the late delivery." Rewa had decided to keep mute on her erring carpenter and blame the delay on the strike instead. She believed that to be a more palpable excuse, especially as it showed the situation was out of her hands and could not be helped.

"We, however, have been assured of..." She continued and was mid-statement when the chief's phone began ringing. He lifted a finger up to Rewa, indicating he be excused for a moment before he answered it. He spoke for about five minutes on the phone and beckoned for her to carry on when he finished. Rewa was extremely irritated by his actions. She considered the hand gestures rude and hated the interruption to what she had been saying as she could not quite remember what she had been saying now.

She cleared her throat as if to swallow what she would rather have said and continued. "I was saying that we hope to receive the last few pieces of furniture in a couple of days seeing as the strike has now been called off," she concluded.

Rewa noticed Chief Ralph Eke took a quick glance at his watch as if to say he would rather be doing something else or that he had spent too much time with her at that moment, which irked her even more. He had kept her waiting for almost an hour and now appeared to want to rush things along.

"Er...*Rewa*...right?" He asked and continued when she nodded, "What I usually find with people wanting to extend deadlines is that such extensions never seem adequate. What's the assurance that the furniture you're expecting will be delivered within the extension period? I gave my word to the owners of this property that we would vacate in a few days...we also have to consider that we would require at least a few extra days within which to pack up and move out of here. You extending the date of completion means I can't keep my word because your extension eats into the number of days within which we have to vacate. I mean, packing up the library alone is bound to take more than a couple of days. These are the things I wish you would take into cognizance - the fact that *we* are also under pressure to vacate these premises."

Rewa was not aware of it, but Chief Eke paused when he saw what he perceived as a flash of anger pass through Rewa's eyes. He spoke in a steady tone, one that could even be described as mild but to Rewa, what he said seemed like a *telling-off* of sorts, and something about that annoyed her.

"I assure you that we *did* take your predicament into *cognizance* and will receive delivery of the expected furniture this week. It's rather unfortunate that the airport staff have not functioned in over three weeks. Besides, we are only proposing a week's extension...give or take, as we may not even need it. I have also given Mrs. Atta the number of a reputable removal company that we use on a regular basis. They are quite prepared to work overnight if required," Rewa replied, struggling to maintain a cool demeanor and also take the edge out of her voice as she spoke.

She believed in professionalism and did possess good customer handling skills, but she was no push-over. She certainly was not going to let Chief Eke give her the *run-around,* never mind that she had received more than an adequate remuneration for the job she was doing for his firm. There was no doubt he was a good-paying client, one who had even paid the entire amount for the project upfront, but she could not allow him, or *anyone* at that, to treat her in a disrespectful manner.

Chief Eke observed all Rewa struggled to hide but said nothing about it. Instead, he took what appeared to be another impatient, quick look at his watch, slid his chair backwards and got to his feet as if to indicate the meeting was over. He extended his hand again to Rewa and said, "Thanks for coming in, Rewa. I do hope things turn out just the way you envisage. We appreciate the work you've put in."

Was that it? Rewa wondered. Had she spent almost an hour waiting to see this pompous individual for a five-minute meeting? She was beyond irritated at this stage but tried her hardest not to show it. Instead, she gathered her papers in the file she brought them in and held it firmly in one arm. She picked her clutch purse off the floor, rose to her feet gracefully, took the hand Chief Eke offered with her other hand, nodded, and left his office with her head held high.

Rewa fumed inside as she walked past his secretary. She was not sure exactly what to feel by the time she got to her car. She was not even certain of how the meeting had gone. Had it been successful or not? Had she got the extension she wanted or not? She hated being dismissed. He had indeed treated her as though his time was more valuable than hers. It was as if he had dragged her all the way, only to brush her off. *Who did he think he was?* She decided to ring the shippers and sit on their necks so that they knew how urgent the deadline had become as she definitely did not want to have to plead for a further extension. She hated it! She dumped the now *unnecessary* file with the papers she had painstakingly searched for, gathered, and organized the day before, all in preparation for the meeting, on the passenger seat angrily and started her car.

* * * *

Rewa's phone rang, and she answered it on the second ring. "Hello, Ms. Ilo. This is Mrs. Atta of *Princes Chambers*." Rewa smiled when she recognized the familiar voice.

"How are you doing, Mrs. Atta? I wasn't expecting to hear from you this soon," Rewa said, thinking out loud. It had been over five weeks since the completion of the new *Princes Chambers* building. As far as she knew, everything had gone according to plan, and they had moved and settled into their new offices. Rewa had not needed the one-week extension she had requested after all, as the furniture she had been expecting arrived the day after her meeting with the

HOC. She wished that she had never asked for an extension, but there was no point crying over spilled milk; the deed was done, and all concerned were happy. So, why was Mrs. Atta ringing her now, over a month later? Rewa wondered.

"I know you weren't...don't be worried, it's nothing to do with the decoration as such. This is more of a social call if you like. I've been asked to invite you to the commissioning dinner we're having next Friday. We believe you should be a part of the celebration, considering you were the brains behind our *new look*! In fact, an invite is being dispatched to you as we speak. It's going to be at six pm and will be a black tie event. Please say you can make it..." Mrs. Atta pleaded and paused for an answer.

"Wow, what a great idea!" Rewa laughed. "You get to create some awareness of your new location and, of course, *show off* your new premises!" She teased Mrs. Atta, who had become a new friend.

"*Exactly*!" Mrs. Atta exclaimed. "Please say you can make it...I have a few people to whom I'd like to introduce you, some of our associates abroad, and what have you. You really should come and bring your business cards along as it promises to be a big networking party for your business too," she added cheekily.

Rewa had been thinking of declining until that last statement by Mrs. Atta. She heard herself say,

"Oh well, now that you put it like that, I'll definitely be there. Thank you for the invitation, and see you next Friday!"

"*Great*! We're sending you a couple of invites. Do feel free to bring *a plus one* along. See you then!" Mrs. Atta said excitedly and hung up.

CHAPTER ELEVEN

Earl Tetteh pulled up to the gas pump at the filling station. He was on his way home from work after a visit to his newest building site. He had just been contracted as the construction engineer for a new hotel that was to be built right in the Airport Residential Area of Accra. It was a project that ran into Millions of dollars, and the owners, a group of four friends, were not about to spare any cost in accomplishing the *seven-star* hotel they had in mind.

It was going to be the first of its kind in Africa and was going to be completed in fifteen months. Earl knew it could be accomplished before then, provided the resources were readily available. He had received a tip-off by a close friend of his, who was a cousin to one of the owners, that the funds required for completion were more than available. Earl was, therefore, certain that they could complete construction well within time and had already rounded up his best men, in and out of the country, for the job.

Today had been their last meeting with all the stakeholders. All drawings and planning details had been approved and signed off as work was scheduled to begin the following Monday. It was a great project, and Earl could not wait. He loved new challenges and was quite ready to break ground and start construction right away.

As Earl paid the attendant and started his car, he noticed her immediately. Though she had her back to him, there was no mistaking who she was as she had been on his mind for over three weeks since his niece's birthday party. Earl thought there were not too many ladies around with a figure like hers, or at least he had not seen many. It was Labake, in a blue print dress that fit her tall, slim body like a glove. He could never forget those long slender legs and her thick, long, jet black hair that shone now, even in the early evening sun. She had an unusual beauty Earl thought within himself. He found her fascinating, and something about her appealed to him. He was unsure of what it was exactly at the moment, but it was way more than her physical appearance, and he knew he needed to find out. He purposed in his heart to do just that.

Labake stood helplessly on the other side of the road, opposite the gas station, next to a rickety-looking car with its hood open. She looked into it as though trying to figure out what was wrong with it. "Talk *about a damsel in distress,*" Earl murmured under his breath, excited at another chance to meet and speak to her. Their first meeting had not quite gone so well, and Earl had wondered why she suddenly bolted when he attempted to converse with her at Nana's birthday party. Well, he said to himself, *I won't miss another opportunity to get to know her.*

Earl drove out of the filling station and parked his car a few feet behind the errant old *Toyota Corolla*. It was a faded grey hatchback, and it looked rather tired. A bit like its owner at that moment, he mused as he got out of his car. He could see that Labake was yet to see him as she still had her back to him. One hand on the opened car hood, Labake had a puzzled expression on her face as she looked down into the car's engine intently.

"Hi, Labake," Earl called out from the short distance between their two cars, trying not to startle her this time. But she appeared not to hear him as they were on a busy road, and there was quite a bit of noise from passing vehicles.

"Hi, Labake," Earl repeated as he got to her side. Labake jumped at the interruption. Her frown deepened the moment she realized who he was.

"Do you make a habit of frightening people *every* time?" She asked angrily, moving away from him in irritation. She was barely audible as her voice sounded breathless. It was a cross between a squeal and a whisper. She clearly was not expecting him or anyone for that matter and was already upset by her predicament. Being frightened out of her wits seemed to have sparked her anger. Earl observed. He could tell she was annoyed and could understand why too. After all, this was exactly how they had met the first time. He had interrupted her thoughts and startled her at Nana's birthday party.

Earl smiled and said, "I'm sorry. I know how this must seem, but I did call out before I got close to you. I guess you didn't hear me for all the noise." He waved his hand at the busy road distractedly. He wondered how he would get in her good books now that she was clearly irritated with him.

Labake turned her glare away from him and back into the engine. Evidently struggling to disguise the anger she felt and the familiar feeling of vulnerability that was slowly taking its place. Earl observed both emotions in her eyes before she shifted them back to the car. He wondered how old she was as she seemed pretty young and rather transparent to him. There was a childlike innocence to her, and he had wondered how she seemed too young to have a daughter of Ella's age after she hurriedly left Nana's party. He judged Ella to be about seven and Labake to be in her early twenties. Her reaction at that moment also proved she did not have the *worldliness* of most ladies her age either. *Who is she?* Earl wondered silently.

"Engine troubles?" He asked, moving closer to look into the car engine.

"It suddenly started making this weird sound...and I thought to park and see what was going on with it. Nothing appears out of place, but when I went to start the engine again, it wouldn't start," Labake explained in a resigned manner. ".I'm supposed to be picking my daughter up from school in about ten minutes," she added in a low, absent-minded tone. It was another semi whisper that sounded like she was talking to herself. She was clearly thinking out loud and looked rather worried, Earl observed.

After fiddling with a few things in the car, Earl said, "I'm afraid it needs to be towed. I think there's a leak somewhere, but my mechanic isn't too far from here. I'll give him a ring, and he'll get a tow truck and sort it out. Just give me a minute." Earl walked a few meters away to make a phone call. After he was done, he said, "The mechanic would be here in no time with a tow truck. When he gets here, we'll go get your daughter...*Ella*? I think it is, from school." Earl easily concluded as if they had a prior agreement or plan.

Labake was thrown aback by a couple of things. First, the fact that he remembered her daughter's name. Second, the fact that he had come to her aid without her asking for his help. *How annoying!* She thought within herself. Typical male behavior! Who did he think he was, coming over and making plans for her? He just sauntered over and took control of things without her input! No way was she going to put herself in a situation where he or anyone could take charge of her life *just like that!* She was not going to feel obligated or indebted to him or anyone. *Absolutely no way!* Labake concluded vehemently within herself and then said quietly but stiffly,

"No, thank you. I'll just get a taxi from here once the tow truck arrives. Thank you so much for your help, though." She then steadily shut the hood of the car. Though she felt vulnerable at that moment, the last thing she wanted was to appear so to this man who was just a stranger. After all, she told herself, she only met him once, never mind that he was Kwame's brother-in-law.

"Please let me help. It's no trouble at all, honestly...I insist. Besides, I've finished for the day anyway. We'll be on our way once the tow truck gets here," Earl said reassuringly. He had contemplated visiting Kwame and Adia this evening as he wanted to find out a bit more about Labake from his sister, but as God would have it, they would bump into each other this evening.

Though unplanned, Earl suddenly looked forward to spending some time with Labake and her daughter this evening. He wanted to be her friend, but he needed to find a way to make her feel more relaxed in his company. What about him made her want to bolt each time they were together? Earl wondered as he observed from her gait that Labake looked like she was about to run off in the opposite direction again. He also noticed that she found it hard to look him in the eye and seemed uncomfortable accepting the help he offered. Earl again wondered why, as she did not appear to be the difficult type. Far from it, actually. She just seemed to want to get away like she had the first time they met. It was as though she was afraid of him. Was it him, or did she generally react this way to people? He asked himself silently.

Earl reached out to place a reassuring hand on Labake's arm, but she flinched as though he had touched her with a hot iron. Eyes bulging in alarm, she moved out of his reach and said in that breathless whisper,

"What do you...what do you think you're doing?" Labake asked, stuttering. He had clearly caught her off guard, and she seemed suddenly frightened. She instinctively walked around the passenger's side of the car and snatched her handbag from it. She rolled up the car windows hastily, locked the car door with her keys, and said,

"Thanks, but I will sort *my* car out *myself!*" She then turned in the opposite direction and motioned to flag a taxi down.

Earl went after her. With his hands held up, he said gently, "I'm sorry that I have upset you. I was only trying to reassure you as you seemed uneasy. I apologize if you consider my gesture a forward one. I really do advise that we wait for the tow truck. It isn't safe to leave your car here. Besides, I've rang the mechanic who is on his way with the tow truck anyway."

Labake felt rather silly now at her overreaction and the fact that she was certain she appeared really rude and overly presumptuous. She just became so jumpy and confused each time something unplanned like this happened. She knew she had to get a grip on herself and act maturely. She tried to calm her racing heart and considered that he was right; the car was not in a safe place. They were right in the heart of town, and there was a likelihood that if she left the car there overnight, it would not be there or be in one piece in the morning. Never mind that it was an *old banger.* She had purchased it from a colleague, so she could get around easily, and until now, it had done just that. Labake decided to relax a bit and forced herself to be practical and accept Earl's kind offer.

* * * *

Some twenty minutes later, they were on the way home from Ella's school. They had picked her up an hour later than usual, and Labake had explained to her teacher that she had car troubles. Ella had been excited to ride in Earl's nicer, sleek car as opposed to her mother's jalopy. She bounced up and down the back seat of it and chatted all the way with *'Uncle Earl'* as her mother had introduced him.

"Sit still, Ella, and please be quiet. You ask far too many questions," Labake said sternly to Ella, who was her usual bubbly self, not minding that she was one of the last to have been picked up from school. She showed off and asked Earl questions non-stop.

"I don't mind, really," Earl said to Labake and said to Ella," "So Ella, what's your favorite subject in school?"

Labake tuned off at that point. She was already thinking about their destination and was uneasy about Earl knowing where they lived. She did not want to create any type of friendship between them or encourage him in any way. Dropping them off at the hotel, she feared, would do just that. She really did appreciate his help with the car, picking Ella up from school, and dropping them off at home. However, she did not want to feel obligated to him in any way and was already thinking of a nice way to let him know she appreciated his help but did not want his friendship.

As he drew up to the hotel entrance, Earl asked if that was where they lived, but before Labake could answer, Ella yelled, "Yes! We live at the back, in the *Staff Quarters*!" She announced proudly.

"Wow! Lucky you...it's a pretty grand hotel. I've never been inside it before. How do we get to the Staff Quarters then?" Earl asked, and again, Ella answered before her tongue-tied mother could.

"You have to drive to the back, through the back gates, just there," Ella said, pointing animatedly at the gate.

"Ok, just keep pointing me in the right direction so I don't miss my way," Earl responded playfully. "I don't want to get lost; it's huge!" He teased Ella, who rose to the task of *tour guide,* believing she now had the very important job of ensuring *Uncle Earl* did not miss his way.

Earl was aware that the *Dolphin Hotel* was owned by Kojo, Kwame's extremely wealthy brother, and though he had heard a lot about it, he had never been inside. It was a sight to behold, not just in the day but at night too. It was spectacular. There were huge white columns in front of the hotel building, which served as a sort of arcade through which cars drove up to the main entrance to drop off and pick up guests. The grounds were covered with freshly mowed grass, and there were beautiful flowers and green hedges planted around the hotel and around a water fountain that sprung from the center of four large, gold dolphin statues. Earl thought it was a magnificent-looking place and wondered what the rooms looked like inside.

It was already dark when they drove into the premises. The lights were on through the windows and outside too. They shined brightly, providing a rather elegant view to passersby and visitors, exuding a rather overwhelming sense of opulence. Earl was eager to have a wander around the grounds and the insides of the hotel. He wondered if he could get some inspiration for the Hotel project he was about to embark upon himself.

He drove through the second set of gates as directed by Ella and parked in the small parking lot in front of an impressive-looking apartment building. It was also surrounded by flowers, and there were security lamps on there as well. Earl also noted the small *'Staff Quarters'* sign on the gate as he drove past the security guards there. Though separate from the main building, it was located at the rear of it and was painted white, just like it. It was obvious to Earl from the look of the building that *Dolphin hotel* held its staff in high regard and perhaps cared for their well-being too.

Labake had sat quietly and rather stiffly in the passenger's seat for the best part of the journey. She turned to Earl when he parked the car and said, "Thank you for your help today. I really do appreciate all of it. Can I please get your bank details so I can pay you back for the tow truck and mechanic?" She asked Earl, who smiled in response as he got out of the car and opened the back seat door to let Ella out. Before he could respond, Ella grabbed his hand and literally pulled him toward the stairway leading to the first floor, where their apartment was located within the building.

Labake could not believe what was happening and how fast it was too. She called out to Ella to wait for her as she struggled to get out of the car as swiftly as she could. But she was too late as both Ella and Earl entered the apartment building before she could do anything about it. Labake shook her head in frustration and hurried after them. It was bad enough that Earl now knew where they lived. The last thing she wanted was for him to know which *exact* apartment theirs was.

She had been planning to end the evening by wishing Earl a goodnight in the car, hoping he would get the message and get on his way, but Ella clearly had other plans and was making things rather difficult. She acted as though Earl was a long-lost playmate of hers. *Kids can be annoyingly innocent* Labake frowned as she followed them. She made a mental note to have a proper conversation with Ella about trusting strangers and talking too much with them.

Labake was cordial but cautious with her colleagues and neighbors at the hotel. Whatever relationship she had with them was a result of Ella's boisterous nature. She was quite popular with the staff at the hotel and was loved by them all. They found her adorable, especially for her intelligence and friendliness too. It, therefore, made it virtually impossible for Labake to keep much of a low profile at the hotel.

She had managed beautifully on her own since she started what she hoped was a new life with her daughter. She had worked hard to get here though she still lacked confidence and self-esteem and knew she had a lot more work to do on herself, but she certainly did not have room for close friendships. Kwame and Adia were her closest friends here in Ghana, the closest she had ever had in her adult life. She trusted them because her sister Laide did. However, she did not feel like she needed any more friends.

Labake was unprepared for any type of friendship with Earl or anyone else, for that matter. She just needed to get his bank details and send him on his way. What did he want anyway? Surely he could tell she was not keen on being friends with him and now wondered if she had encouraged him in any way. She felt a familiar panic about to grip her heart when she sensed things were about to get out of her control.

Earl and Ella were waiting outside the apartment door when Labake got there. Instead of opening it to let them in, Labake stood awkwardly and said to Earl, "Thank you again for your help today...er...it is late, and I need to get Ella settled for the night. There's also homework, I'm sure..." Labake started and trailed off, expecting Earl to take the hint and leave them outside their flat, but

Ella said, "No, Mummy, I don't have any homework today, and I want to show Uncle Earl my..."

"Not tonight, Ella," Labake said, cutting her daughter off a bit too curtly. "We've taken too much of Uncle Earl's time already...now, wish him a goodnight, dear." She reached for Ella's hand and drew her to her side.

Earl received the unspoken message loud and clear. He cleared his throat and said, "It was nothing, really. I'm glad I was able to help." Then he turned to a sulking Ella and said, "You can show me your books another time Ella. Goodnight, ladies." He turned towards the exit and left.

* * * *

What was her problem? Earl wondered. The least she could have done was offer him a glass of water. She had not even *attempted* to be friendly; she was as cold as a dog's nose, but that just made her even more intriguing! He wanted to get to know her, but Labake made it palpably clear she was not interested. She appeared scared of him and acted as though she expected him to pounce on her or something. She was like a wounded kitten, and Earl wondered what her story was. He decided to visit Adia and Kwame after all. He wanted to know more about Labake as he did not think she would be willing to give him any information herself. Perhaps he would catch a glimpse of who she really was and why she was overly cautious. He just could not get her out of his mind. He had been unable to since the day he met her.

CHAPTER TWELVE

The new office building of *Princes Chambers* had been aptly named *Princes' Place*. A lovely gold plaque bore the name and address of the building on the wall just outside the entrance. It had been unveiled earlier, and Rewa had spotted it when she arrived. That had been over an hour and a half ago, and she'd had enough of the lovely event so far and was already planning her exit.

Rewa had been introduced to a number of potential clients by Mrs. Atta. She had mingled with staff and associates of the firm generally and had struck up a conversation or two with other invitees. She had also listened in on a rather interesting conversation between two well-known legal luminaries on issues within the judiciary and how they could be resolved. There had been several short presentations by other dignitaries, and Rewa had garnered that several judges, the Attorney General, and some other government ministers were present too. One of the State governors had also just been ushered in, and there were reporters all over the very elegant event.

It was indeed a grand affair. Rewa judged there to be over a hundred invitees present. The event was taking place at the penthouse of the building, on the fifth floor. It had been mentioned at the instruction stage of her brief with *Prince's Chambers* that the firm held a few social gatherings, including an elaborate end-of-year party. They therefore required a large space on the premises to accommodate such events.

Rewa had decided that the fifth floor would be ideal as a *quasi*-conference hall. It was perfect, particularly because it had its own private lift at the rear end of the building. This enabled visitors to be conveyed straight up to the fifth floor without access to any of the other floors within the building. It was ideal, Rewa thought, looking round now. She knew it was one of her best works so far. She had used muted colors on the walls and hung three huge chandeliers from the suspended ceiling.

There were large, gold-framed pictures of past and present *Chief Justices of the federation* hanging on the walls. Rewa had done her research and come up with the idea for the pictures herself. She wanted something that still showed they were within the premises of Law Offices and had run the idea by Mrs. Atta, who also thought it a brilliant idea. Looking at them on the wall now made Rewa feel proud of her work. She had received compliments for it all evening.

Rewa could see that the party planner had added some drapery and a few extra temporary touches here and there to suit the evening's occasion, and the place looked all together spectacular. There were lovely centerpieces on the tables, waiters in tuxedoes, and ushers in lovely gold dresses that made the event appear extravagant. *Hors' doves* and glasses of Champaign had been making the rounds non-stop since Rewa got there, and it was obvious that both chamber staff and guests were having a great time.

Chief Ralph Eke noticed her the minute he mounted the stage. He had specifically asked for her to be invited as he believed she deserved to be there, and he wanted to celebrate her for the effort she had put in. He had been astonished when he and a few other partners had taken a tour of his newly decorated building. Omorewa Ilo was clearly meticulous and had added a classy edge to every part of the building. She had placed an invisible stamp of exquisite quality on the place. It was completely transformed from the damp old structure he had purchased almost a year ago to something spectacular. In Ralph Eke's opinion, Omorewa Ilo definitely deserved to be here tonight.

What Ralph found when he toured the entire five floors of *Princes Place* was excellent work indeed. Omorewa Ilo had exceeded his expectation and gone way beyond his vision for the new place. He generally was not easy to please, and he knew it, but he had been unable to contain himself when Mrs. Atta and a few others at the chambers had taken him round. They could read in his eyes that he was beyond pleased with the designer's work. "*Excellent*" had been his response from the minute he walked into the reception of the new building. After the tour, Mrs. Atta breathed a sigh of relief and confessed that she had been apprehensive that he would disapprove of the renovations. Secretly though, she would have thought him *raving mad* if he had. Rewa was a *rock star* as far as she was concerned!

Ralph was well-traveled and also a member of the *International Bar Association.* He had quite a number of legal associates and clients outside the country and had visited a lot of Law firm buildings abroad. In his view, none of them matched the new *Princes Place* building. One kind of got the feeling of being transported to another world from the minute one stepped into the foyer downstairs. *Princes Place* was exquisite and looked like something out of a corporate Los Angeles magazine, even better, he thought.

Ralph had received compliments on the building since they moved in and knew he could not take any credit for it. He had only signed the cheque! It was Rewa who did the work and most definitely earned the accolade. It looked far more elegant and expensive than the sum they had paid her. She had really thought about the minutest detail. He found it amazing that someone as young and unassuming could pull off such tremendous work. He had definitely underestimated and misjudged her when they met in his office a few weeks back.

Rewa, of course, had come highly recommended by one of Ralph's friends at the golf club, *Kunle Wellington*. She had done up Kunle's office a few years back, and he had referred her to Ralph. Ralph knew Kunle had great taste, so he had not even bothered to look her up before he asked Mrs. Atta to give her the job. He had expected a good job, having seen Kunle's office but what Rewa delivered was an *exquisite* job.

Ralph had only recently found out that Rewa was the daughter of an older friend and client, *Chief Benjamin Ilo*. It really was a small world, he thought within himself. He had not made the connection between both their last names and wondered if he would have hired her had he known who she was earlier. The issue of a conflict of interest would have crossed his mind. He also wondered if she was aware of his relationship with her father. If she was, Rewa had not acted it. She had been highly professional from the beginning of the project till its end, according to Mrs. Atta. Chief Benjamin Ilo himself had also been sent an invitation to tonight's event but had sent a message that he would be out of the country.

Now, mounting the little stage that had been erected for the occasion, with his little speech in hand, Ralph Eke observed Rewa from the podium. She was having a conversation with one of the associates. She looked very different from the seemingly clumsy lady he met a few weeks ago. This evening, however, she looked every bit like the designer who put *Princes Place* together. He struggled to keep his mind on the task at hand and cleared his throat as he drew closer to the microphone.

Rewa wore a lovely black, floor-length lace dress. It was a *fit and flare* with long sleeves and a low back. It hugged her figure perfectly and suited the black tie event beautifully. Her hair was swept back in a sleek, tight knot that enhanced her facial features, making them more pronounced. Her make-up was light but perfectly applied, and she wore the pair of drop diamond earrings her mother had given her when she turned forty. She knew she looked great and had been sure to slip on a pair of comfortable black, high-heeled, strappy sandals as she had expected to do a bit of mingling tonight. The invitation card had read that there would be cocktails served before dinner. She had therefore come prepared.

Rewa wished she had some company with her, though, and discovered lately that she hated attending events such as these alone. Unfortunately, she could not think of anyone to accompany her tonight. Besides, it had been too much of a short notice to bring a *plus one*. She, however, had to admit that she had enjoyed the evening so far, regardless. The staff here at Prince's Chambers were friendly and made her feel like one of them. Rewa decided to give it another fifteen minutes and then take her leave.

"Distinguished ladies and gentlemen, it is an honor having you here at this great event, put together by our very dedicated staff here at *Princes Chambers*." Chief Ralph Eke began with the vote of thanks.

Rewa turned her head to see who was speaking on the microphone. She was standing in the far right-hand corner of the large room conversing with a member of staff and had a good view of the stage. She had not seen him all evening and had wondered about that. Mrs. Atta, who had welcomed her when she arrived, had mentioned something about her workaholic boss having popped in earlier and popped back to his office on the fourth floor to finish some work. "He isn't much of a *party person,* you see...he's far too *serious,*" she had whispered to Rewa. "He has these events purely for us, the staff," Mrs. Atta explained as she led Rewa in.

Rewa wondered when Chief Eke had sneaked back into the party. He looked rather dashing in his tuxedo. She observed that he still looked tired and was beginning to see that the aloofness she noticed on his face at their first meeting weeks back was probably just a part of his *natural* expression. The only difference this evening was that he managed a small smile as he spoke, and Rewa could see from where she stood that he had an immaculate set of teeth. Simply put, Rewa thought Chief Ralph Eke was a very good-looking man. *If only he wasn't so cocky,* she thought, remembering how irritated she had been at his quick dismissal of her *after* he had kept her waiting at their first meeting.

The room had hushed up as Chief Eke began speaking, and Rewa watched his staff as they gazed upon their *Head of Chambers* in admiration. He was clearly well respected by them.

"Hello, Rewa...?" A quiet male voice said behind her. Rewa turned and saw it was *Stephen,* Faith's newly wedded husband. He did not seem sure that she was the one. She could hardly blame him as they had only met once, at his wedding a few weeks ago. Besides, she thought, she looked rather different this evening in her elegant dress than she had at his wedding.

"*Yes!* Hi Stephen! *My God!* What are you doing here? You should still be on your honeymoon!" She responded quietly but excitedly, trying not to draw attention to them. They exchanged a small hug.

Stephen smiled and said, "I know, but I used to work here at *Prince's* many *moons* ago. I got an invite and was *summoned* to attend." He smiled at Rewa. *Of course,* Rewa thought silently. That was the connection. She remembered now that Faith had mentioned him being a lawyer. She felt it uncanny that he had worked at Princes too.

"How's my friend, *your wife*? I'm surprised she let you out. I mean, it's been what? Five minutes since your wedding?" They both laughed at her comment. Stephen was a great guy, and Rewa believed Faith had found her *soul mate* in him. They were a perfect match for each other, and he worshipped the ground Faith walked on. In his short speech at their wedding reception, he had said he considered himself blessed to have found Faith. Rewa knew her friend felt the exact same way about her new husband. They had both found true love. They chatted in hushed tones for a few minutes until Rewa suddenly heard her name mentioned.

"I would like everyone to please give a round of applause to Ms. Omorewa Ilo for the tremendous work she put into this building. Ladies and Gentlemen, you would agree that we are in a splendidly decorated building. Please come up for recognition Ms. Ilo," Chief Eke said. He put the microphone down and himself joined in the riotous applause.

Rewa was in total shock and felt utterly disoriented as the applause started and grew louder. She had gotten distracted by Stephen and had not heard any of Chief Eke's speech. Now, she was being beckoned to come up the stage by Mrs. Atta, who stood at the foot of it. She could see an usher standing by Chief Eke, holding a large bouquet of flowers, clearly intending to present her with them. Mrs. Atta walked up to Rewa and more or less tugged at her arm to snap her out of her shock. Rewa had not in any way expected the special acknowledgment and wished she had been forewarned.

She walked the short distance back to the stage with Mrs. Atta and climbed the short steps gracefully. She told herself, *Okay, get a grip, girl, play it cool.*

Chief Eke stopped clapping, picked the microphone up again, and said, "Ms. Ilo, on behalf of all of us here at *Prince's Chambers*, I present to you a token in appreciation of the incredible work you did here. Thank you." He took the bouquet off the usher and handed her the flowers and the microphone, indicating that she said something to the crowd.

Composing herself quickly, Rewa took the microphone from her host and said,

"*Wow*!" She started breathlessly, "I wasn't expecting this at all. I want to use the opportunity to thank everyone here at *Princes'* for the support, patience, and accommodation given to my staff and me from the inception of this project to its completion. I'm glad that you are pleased with the finished work. The pleasure was all mine, actually. Thank you for these." She said, indicating the flowers, "Thank you all." The crowd applauded again as Rewa handed the microphone back to Chief Eke and descended the stage. *Great time to leave,* she thought within herself.

* * * *

"*My Goodness! Rewa!* You looked absolutely *gorgeous* in the photo! Omosede exclaimed excitedly. She more or less threw the tabloid magazine at Rewa, who was rousing from sleep. She wondered if it had been a good idea to give her immediate younger sister a spare key to the flat. *'Sede',* as she was fondly called by their entire family, had mentioned that she would drop by this morning to take her sister out for breakfast at *'Dr. Robert's Cafe'* but Rewa had not thought it would be this early. She squinted, took a lazy look at her bedside clock, and realized it was past nine in the morning. She had not heard her sister come into the flat, let alone into her bedroom.

Sede moved to the window and drew the curtains open noisily. The bright morning sun was almost blinding. It was so like Sede to be the *drama queen*. She was the most boisterous of the Ilo sisters and had a knack for being rather tactless, or like she often said, it wasn't being *'tactless'*, but being *'down to earth'*.

Rewa grunted and pulled a pillow over her head as if to shut out the light and interruption to her sleep but Sede plumped on the bed carelessly, jolting her again out of her stupor. Grabbing the magazine again, Sede thrust it in her sister's face. "Look at it! Do you realize how many phone calls I've received already this morning over your appearance in *Scope*?" She asked her sister animatedly. "Why didn't you tell me? And then, you're in the picture with *Chief Ralph Eke*! Freaking unbelievable, sis! When did all this happen? Didn't even *know* you knew the guy!" Sede asked her sister frantically, not caring that she was still drowsy from sleep.

Rewa was not sure if it was the fact that she had been asleep that made her sister's voice seem so irritably loud. She loved her and would do anything for her, but right now, she wanted to throttle her for disturbing her sleep. She had actually forgotten they were going out for breakfast and, at the minute, was not looking forward to it. She took the magazine her sister extended to her and sat up instantly the minute she saw what Sede was talking about.

All sleepiness out the window, Rewa looked at the tabloid paper, and her eyes seemed like they would pop right out of their sockets. The picture of her receiving the bouquet of flowers from Ralph Eke at the commissioning of *Princes' Place* last week was sprawled across the front page of *Scope* magazine with the caption

'Chief Ralph Eke's new love interest'

"*What*?" Rewa shrieked in horror. The picture told a story that one did not need to read. The Usher who initially held the bouquet of flowers before Chief Eke presented them to her had been cleverly cut out of the picture. Ralph Eke was smiling down at her in a way that could be deemed *'lovingly',* and she, in turn, appeared to be gazing up into his eyes with nothing but pure affection. Rewa was beginning to wonder if it was the same event she had attended. She suddenly panicked, with a look of sheer horror sweeping over her swollen sleep face.

"What would his wife think?" Was all she could manage, looking at Sede in a frightened manner. Sede herself seemed rather confused by Rewa's question.

"*His wife*? What *wife*?" She asked Rewa in return. "He is a *widower* sister, *dearie*. He doesn't *have* a wife! She died like a million years ago...he's *only* the most *eligible bachelor* in the country! What rock have you been living under, Sis? Don't you read the social pages?" Sede asked in an exaggerated, befuddled manner. "Didn't he tell you? How can you date him and not know that?" Sede asked with an expression of disbelief.

"You don't get it...I am *not dating* him!" Rewa yelled in response to her sister, still in utter shock. "Well, that's certainly not what Scope's alleging...*So?* I want to hear it all, every last detail! How did you meet him?" She asked her sister excitedly.

CHAPTER THIRTEEN

"I Don't think she's ready for that kind of relationship or any, bro." Adia said sympathetically as she handed her brother a glass of lemonade. She smiled as the confused expression on Earl's face deepened.

It was Adia's response to Earl's puzzled explanation of the car situation with Labake and how she had insisted on repaying him for having her car towed and fixed by his mechanic. He could not understand why she was so insistent on reimbursing him for the car repairs. He had paid *Kevin* the mechanic in full the day after her car was towed. Labake had nevertheless paid Kevin the money when he delivered the car back to her, even after Kevin had mentioned to her that Earl had settled the bill. She had politely asked Kevin to refund the money to Earl.

Adia and Earl were seated on the back porch, overlooking the small lovely garden of the home Adia shared with Kwame and their two daughters. Kwame was on his way home from work, and Earl and Adia waited for him to arrive before supper was served. In the meantime, they sat on the shaded back deck of the house, overlooking its beautiful garden and having some lemonade.

The weather was beautiful, and though the sun was about to set, the air was cool and crisp with a hint of fresh soil, suggesting it was about to rain or perhaps that it was raining elsewhere in Accra. It was a rather tranquil and relaxing atmosphere out there on the deck, but Earl could not say he was enjoying any of it as his mind was on Labake and the events that transpired between them just a few days ago.

"Believe me, sis. I could tell she wasn't interested. I only want to be friends with her...at the moment anyway. Why is she so bent on keeping me at arm's length?" Earl asked his sister, still clearly confused and hoping somehow that her answer would shed some more light on Labake's aloofness.

"I really don't know the details, but I know she was in quite an abusive marriage. Think she's trying to get past it and is understandably being cautious," Adia replied, settling into the loveseat made out of raffia, opposite her brother. She knew it was hard for him to understand, but it was hard for her to offer a better explanation as she did not know Labake that well and Kwame had not said much about her or her past either. All Adia knew was that Labake was the sister of a friend. She was not sure if even Kwame knew the precise nature of abuse Labake had suffered in her marriage. All they knew was that she had fled her home country for fear of losing her life at the hands of her husband.

"So she *was* married...I see..." Earl trailed off as realization set in. "That explains it. I was beginning to feel paranoid, thinking it was something about me in particular. I wonder what he did to her," Earl said with a slight frown. "She's so closed off and distant. I mean, she's polite enough but definitely not inviting. It's as if she just wants to be left alone," he finished with a concerned look on his face now. "Well, I have no intentions of doing that," he said in a determined and almost inaudible tone of voice. It was clear Earl was thinking out loud as he said it so quietly Adia had to read his lips to get what he said.

"I see you've taken a fancy to her then," Adia smiled at her brother, who stared into space with a stern expression, deep in thought. She knew Earl so well. He had the kindest, most generous, and most compassionate heart. She also knew he had a penchant for projects, fixing things and people too. He was always trying to help make things better for everyone, sometimes even to his own detriment. Unfortunately, he could not in *every* case, and she had hoped he learned that over the years. She also knew that her brother was driven and stubborn. When he set his mind on something, he just never gave up on it easily. She hoped Labake would be one of his successes.

"I advise that you be sensitive and tread carefully though, bro. She's fragile. The last thing you want to do is frighten her away," Adia advised gently. She gave Earl a knowing look.

Earl himself had not been too lucky in love, and his kindness had been taken for granted on more than one occasion. Adia had always teased that he was too much of a *nice* guy, making him appear boring to the *type* of women he had fallen for in the past. They ended up taking advantage of him and moving on once they had their fill.

Earl smiled at his sister and said, "I know what you're thinking. Labake is *not* one of my many *projects* Addy. My heart just really went out to her the first time I met her, you know, she struck a chord, and I feel the need to be there for her if she would let me..." He trailed off again, even more determined to give it a shot now.

Adia smiled at Earl just as Kwame joined them on the deck. He greeted his wife with a kiss and bear-hugged his '*favorite brother-*

in-law' as he referred to Earl. Kwame and Earl were quite chummy and had always been. They had been in college together, and Kwame met Adia through Earl while in school.

As Kwame made himself comfortable next to his wife on the loveseat, Adia poured him a glass of lemonade and said,

"Your brother-in-law here has taken quite a *shine* to Labake...he's obviously been beaten by the *love bug*". She teased.

Earl laughed and said, "I *haven't taken a shine* to her. I simply want to be her friend...there's a difference".

"Ah, I see," Kwame said, giving Earl an exaggerated wink. "High time someone in Accra caught your attention, bro. We'd begun to wonder about you, haven't we, Honey?" He asked Adia playfully, clearly joining her in teasing his friend of many years.

"Only trouble is, I'm not sure Labake would be interested..." Kwame supplied. "She's in Accra to lay low for a while. She was in a bad marriage, you see. Her husband was a real piece of work, apparently.Poor thing; she was in a pretty bad way when she arrived here. She's come to get away from it all and perhaps build a new life for herself and her daughter. I feel she's slightly better now, but she understandably will have some trust issues and may not be open to your *friendship*. Think you've chosen the wrong one to take a *'shine'* to, Bro." Kwame finished and took a sip of his drink.

Earl pondered on what Kwame said for a moment and then said, "Well, there's no harm in trying. I wonder what he did to her. In what way was the husband abusive to her?" Earl inquired of Kwame, trying to get a better picture of the situation with Labake before he embarked on his mission to get closer to her.

"Honestly, bro, I don't have a lot of detail. But then, what difference does it make? *Abuse is abuse,* and no one should be forced to live with any form of it," Kwame replied with a slight undertone in his voice. Clearly remembering the abuse he and his brother had suffered growing up. Adia reached out and stroked her husband's thigh at that moment. She knew it was a rather touchy subject for him.

"Labake's sister, Laide, is an old colleague and a good friend of mine," Kwame further explained to Earl. "She mentioned that her sister was in a bit of trouble and had to leave Nigeria in a hurry. She couldn't risk Labake and Ella staying with her in the *Republic of Benin,* where she lives, and suspected it would be the first place the estranged husband would look. She wanted them somewhere else, where they couldn't easily be found. She asked for my help in settling them here, in Ghana, and I obliged. They are good people, really...Labake just fell into the wrong hands. I never asked for the details of the marriage, bro, so you'd have to get them off her if you can. I imagine she'd need some time and patience, though. All the best with it, buddy," Kwame concluded with a smile that said *I'd rather you than me*.

Kwame understood perfectly how *time and patience* would be a major factor his friend would need to embark on the *herculean* task of tackling a victim of abuse like Labake. Though he did not have the facts, he knew the effects of abuse too well. His own father had been an alcoholic and a man who talked with his fist. Kwame and his older brother, Kojo, had watched their mother being battered by their father almost to death several times. She had finally mustered up the courage to leave him one day when they were teenagers.

Their mother herself had struggled to make a new life for herself and her two sons but had eventually died of cancer barely two years after leaving their father. She had never forgiven her husband, and neither had Kwame. He had not seen or heard from his father till this day and was not even certain he was still alive. He wished his mother had left him earlier; she would at least have had much more time to enjoy some peace in her life before she passed.

Earl was willing to leave the conversation on Labake for now. However, he was even more determined to unravel the mystery that was shrouded around her. His *modus operandi* was going to be to take it slowly, but his main goal was to bring her out of her shell. He did not think it was healthy to leave her to her own devices and was going to take it upon himself to at least try. She needed to experience new things and new people to help forge ahead with her new life. He knew it too well himself; he was never one to let a nasty experience stop him from trying again. He hoped he could get Labake to see that too.

* * * *

Labake stirred the rickety Toyota into Kwame's driveway. Ella, as usual, bounced up and down in the back seat, excited at the prospect of having a *sleepover* with Kwame's young daughters. Labake wished she was as excited as her daughter was. She had never liked the idea of *sleepovers* as she was nervous about her daughter spending time away from home, in someone else's care. It was too late to get out of it now as it had all been pre-arranged a week ago when Adia had invited Ella over. The children were on summer vacation, and Labake was running out of ideas on how to keep Ella occupied during the entire two-month school holiday.

The Hotel was organizing a *Holiday Summer Camp* program for children, and Labake had enrolled Ella in it, but it was not starting till the following week. She had planned to take a few days off work to spend time with her boisterous daughter till camp started. Ella was a bright child and needed to be stimulated even *during* holidays as her father always said. Until Adia's *sleepover* invitation, Labake had wondered how to achieve that during the few days before summer camp began.

Labake often worried if Ella was indeed being *well stimulated.* She was such an intelligent child, and Vince had insisted that they learn different ways to keep her engaged. Labake did try to do just that and sometimes wondered if he would approve of her way with their daughter now. She felt an overwhelming need to prove she was capable of raising her child properly in the absence of her father. She tried to balance the amount of television Ella watched and was glad she had an avid interest in reading. She had re-read her small collection of books over and over again, and Labake made a mental note to visit the children's bookstore to get her a new set of books and other reading essentials. In fact, she was going to do just that after she dropped her off at Kwame's, she told herself.

Labake did not like the idea of her daughter spending five nights away from their home. She knew Vince would never have allowed it. She had politely declined at first when Adia had mentioned it in Church last Sunday. Unfortunately, Ella had overheard the conversation and had thrown tantrums until they got home, begging her mother to let her go for the sleepover.

"I want my daddy!" Ella had yelled at her mother, crying when they got home from church. She said that usually, when she wanted her way on anything, knowing her mother just melted each time she did. Labake knew she had to find a way to stop Ella from using the '*I want my daddy*' weapon as a manipulative device. She, however, could not help the feeling of guilt that overwhelmed her each time the child mentioned her father.

Labake still carried a lot of guilt for depriving her daughter of her father and still sometimes felt it was selfish of her to do so. The last thing she wanted was for Ella to grow up without her father, just as she and Laide had. After all, Vince had never hurt his daughter, not even once. He adored her and even wanted more kids, though he was aware of the health risks to Labake. She was the one Vince had hurt, so why did Ella have to suffer for her own pain? It was a question Labake turned over and over in her mind, amongst others. It just sometimes seemed unfair to the poor child in her view, but she could not see that she had any other options other than going back to Vince. The thought of what he would do to her if she did was unimaginable. Labake shuddered, thinking about it.

After her tantrum, Ella had sulked and looked miserable by her mother's refusal to let her go for the *sleepover*. Labake eventually gave in when she could not take it any longer, and Ella finally got her way. Labake knew it was weak of her to let Ella manipulate her into changing her mind, but that familiar feeling of guilt just gnawed at her. She rang Adia up the following morning to find out if the invitation was still open.

So, here they were, in the old rickety car, outside Kwame's house as Labake prepared to give Ella a *pep* talk before they went indoors.

"Now remember our conversation and what you promised mummy you would do while you're at Nana's house, Ella," Labake said as she parked the car in front of the house.

"What's *con-ve-sa-shon* mummy?" Ella asked intelligently. Labake sometimes forgot she was only seven years old and did not quite understand the big words yet.

"It is *con-ver-sa-tion,* and it means two or more people talking with each other. So I was asking if you remembered what you and mummy talked about before we left home," Labake explained patiently again.

"Yes, Mummy. I promised to be a good girl and to be polite to everyone," Ella replied cleverly.

"Good girl. I also said you should remember to calm down because you know you get very easily excitable sometimes. If you behave yourself at Nana's house this time, there will be more *sleepovers* after this one. Understood?" Labake was happy she remembered to add that last bit as an incentive to keep her daughter from being too hyperactive while at Kwame's.

Looking out of the window distractedly now, Ella asked as her mum opened the passenger door to let her out of the back seat, "What's *exsaiteble* mummy?"

Labake rolled her eyes and sighed. "It's *excitable*. Remember I told you what it meant just the other day? Try and see if you can remember," she said to her daughter. Ella, who loved a challenge, stepped out of the car and stood by the car door for a moment instead of running up to the house, trying to remember what *'excitable'* meant. After a few seconds, pleased to have remembered, she said excitedly,

"O! I remember now, mummy...it's when I jump up and down because I can't wait to do something..." She looked up at her mother for approval as Labake reached for the overnight bag with her things in it.

"*Good girl*!" You're such a clever girl. Well done, baby," Labake affirmed and grabbed her hand. "My daddy said I was clever like him," Ella responded innocuously, hopping up and down as they walked to the entrance of Kwame's house together.

Labake stiffened at the comment. She was pleased Ella still remembered her father even after all this time and talked about him once in a while, but it always made Labake feel sad when she did.

Ella had been nearly six when they left and was going to be eight in a few months. She was growing up so fast, and it frightened Labake that she would have to explain the real truth about why she could not see her father soon.

Sighing, Labake knocked on the front door, and within seconds, it swung open.

"Hi, guys!" Adia said, smiling at Labake and Ella. "The girls have been excited at the prospects of a *sleepover*, and they're upstairs in the playroom, Ella. Will you go join them, *sweet pea*?" She asked Ella, who did not wait to be asked a second time. She immediately bundled up the stairs in search of her friends. "See you soon, darling," Labake called after her, but Ella was gone before she could complete the sentence.

Labake smiled at Adia. "Thank you for the invitation again, Adia. Her things are in here," she said, handing her Ella's overnight bag.

"Please come in, Labake, join us for supper. We're having it on the back deck, outside." Labake looked passed Adia to the back of the house, through the open front door hesitantly. She just wanted to leave so she could catch the bookstore before it closed for the day. She was not much of a small talker either; it just was not a *strong suit* of hers. At the same time, she did not want to seem rude, and it did not look like Adia was going to take no for an answer anyway as she all but dragged her into the house.

"Er...If it's not too much trouble...I was hoping to catch the children's bookshop before they closed..." She explained distractedly in a low unsure tone as Adia shut the door behind them.

"*Trouble*? No trouble at all! There's plenty of food and Earl's here too. Come on outside," Adia said, leading the way to the back of the house.

Labake stiffened again at the knowledge that Earl was there too. She wished Adia had mentioned that just before she shut the door, she would have *stressed* her need to get to the children's bookshop. She had been so distracted by Ella and her questions outside that she had not noticed Earl's sleek, black car parked in the driveway along with the others. Perhaps she would have been better prepared to decline Adia's invitation to supper.

Reluctantly, Labake followed Adia to the back porch, where a table with a variety of lovely-looking dishes was spread. The table, with candles and lamps lit everywhere, looked beautiful, and the atmosphere was warm and welcoming. Labake felt herself begin to relax a bit. Kwame and a surprised Earl both put their forks down and got to their feet as Adia and Labake approached.

Neither Earl nor Kwame knew that Adia had intentionally failed to mention that Labake was dropping Ella off for a *sleepover* tonight. She had also deliberately informed Labake of Earl's presence *after* she had agreed to join them for supper. Adia could not explain why but she wanted Earl's and Labake's meeting tonight to be the *coincidence* it was *set up* to be. Besides, she also wanted to get to know Labake better, particularly now that she knew her brother was interested in her. Earl had talked about her all evening without even realizing it, causing Adia and Kwame to exchange several knowing looks with one another each time he did. It was clear Labake had made quite the impression on him.

Adia and Labake had never really had a proper discussion, as Labake always seemed uneasy around people. She made a point of keeping to herself a lot and was always on her guard. Adia deemed it necessary now to get to know her better. She thought a *friendship* between Earl and Labake would do them both good and decided to play *cupid* by planning this evening. She was at least going to set the ball rolling!

Earl tried to get over his surprise as he rose with Kwame. It had been over a month since he mentioned his interest in Labake. However, he had not had much luck with her as she would not make herself available to go out with him or to even have a proper chat with him on the phone. She had made excuses the two times Earl had rung her up, inviting her out, but he was not discouraged by her refusal. He planned to keep asking until she ran out of excuses and agreed to have a meal with him, but he had resolved to give her some extra time.

"Hello, Labake," Kwame greeted first. "Good to see you." Silently, he thought it uncanny that Labake walked in just moments after they had spoken about her. He had asked Earl if he had been able to convince her to go out on a date with him, and Earl had said he was confident he would eventually. Kwame was aware Ella had a sleepover with his girls, but it had skipped his mind that it was tonight. He, therefore, did not mention it during the conversation with Earl prior to Labake's entry. He gave his wife a slightly puzzled look and instantly understood what was going on when she smiled at him sweetly. It was obvious Adia had planned the evening to somehow include her brother and Labake. He knew his wife too well and now understood she had something up her sleeve.

Kwame took a look at his brother-in-law at that moment. Earl was also in the dark about Labake's visit tonight as he appeared pleasantly surprised to see her and grinned at her like a *Cheshire cat*. Kwame recognized that expression on Earl's face. They had been friends for a long time and knew one another quite well. *He's definitely been bitten by the love bug*. He mused silently.

"Labake just dropped Ella off for a sleepover with the girls, and I invited her to join us for supper," Adia explained, a tad too simple, looking at her brother. She, like Kwame, had also noted Earl's slight puzzled but pleased expression at Labake's sudden appearance. It seemed as though his evening had just taken a more Interesting turn. She mused secretly.

"Hey, Labake," Earl said, holding out a hand to her for a gentle shake. Recovering quickly from his surprise at seeing her there, literally moments after they had discussed her.

"Great to have you, Labake. Please sit. We only just started," Adia said, setting a place for her directly opposite Earl. It was a four-sitter round table, creating a cozy and intimate feel. The air was filled with pleasant fragrances from flowers in the garden. It was getting dark, and the temperature had dropped ever so slightly. It was a perfect evening to have an outdoor meal, Labake thought within herself as she joined them. She gave Earl a small smile and took the seat offered to her by Adia.

Labake had been hungry before she got there as she had not had anything to eat since breakfast. It had been a really busy day for her at the hotel, and there had been no time to stop for lunch. She had, however, suddenly lost her appetite. She hated it when her plans changed without her input or preparation. It made her feel like she had given up control of her life to yet another person, allowing them to dictate her boundaries just as Vince had. In this case, it was Adia who had taken over the reins of control without her input, and Labake did not like the feeling one bit.

The one thing she enjoyed since her escape from Vince was the freedom to make her own plans and decisions. It was new at first, but she had grown used to it and loved it. She had vowed never to put herself in a position where she lost the power to make her own decisions *ever* again. She was aware of her new liberty to be spontaneous and perhaps change her plans on a whim, but she still struggled with that. She loved making her own plans and carrying them all out without any other person's influence, and she was going to keep it that way. It made her feel safe, secure, and in control of things.

Labake and Earl had not seen each other since her car broke down. She felt awkward now and was unsure what to say to him, especially after insisting on repaying him for her car repairs when she did not need to. She had also blown him off the two times he had attempted to ask her out for a meal. She hoped he did not consider her rude or ungrateful for her insistence on paying for the repairs on her car. She just did not want to feel indebted to him or anyone at that.

"I bet Ella is thrilled about the *sleepover*," Earl said. Attempting to break the ice as he sensed Labake's discomfort.

Amidst what he now knew to be pain and extreme caution in her eyes, Earl thought Labake was one of the most naturally beautiful women he had seen. She did not have any make-up on, and apart from the faint scar at the top right corner of her brow, she had such flawless beauty. She was tall, slim, and shapely where it mattered. She had on a simple knee-length floral print dress. Her hair was in a loose, untidy knot at her nape, and to him, she could have passed for an innocent teenager though he judged her to be in her mid to late twenties.

Earl had noted the slight limp in Labake's step when she walked to the table. It was not something he had noticed prior to this evening. He observed it did not affect her graceful movement, though. Sitting at the table watching her, he wondered what her *real* story was. She was like a puzzle he *needed* to unravel.

"You should have seen the way she bolted for the stairs when I told her the girls were in the playroom," Adia answered before Labake could. She passed a bowl of *wache* to Labake as she spoke. Labake spooned a bit of it onto her plate but did not feel hungry anymore.

"How's life at the hotel Labake?" Kwame asked, "I hear it is being taken over by some German company."

"That's the rumor going round but we haven't heard anything from management," Labake answered softly, thinking news did travel fast. There was talk of the hotel being sold going around lately, and the entire staff at the hotel had their ears to the ground. Labake thought there had to be some credence to the rumors if Kwame knew of it already. After all, *The Dolphin Hotel* was currently owned by his elder brother, Kojo. He, therefore, had some accurate insider information though he did not let on that he knew anything for sure.

Labake had initially worried about the hotel being sold. She had wondered what would happen to her job if the new owners decided they wanted to employ new staff. She, however, felt better equipped than she had when she first started. She had developed some administrative skills, amongst others, to help secure another job if she needed to. She was in a far better place than she had been when she newly arrived in Accra, penniless, jobless, and without any work experience whatsoever. Not to add confused and emotionally distressed. She now drew some confidence from the experience she had acquired at the hotel. If anything unexpected happened, she was hopeful it would help her find another job easily.

Labake had also been prudent in her spending. She had not exactly enjoyed an extravagant life with Vince. Though he made far more than an adequate income and could afford to run their home without any financial assistance from her, he kept a tight rein on every penny he gave her. Perhaps just so he could control her even more, Labake thought. He had bought her stuff only when *he* believed she needed them. This helped her now and made it easier to remain frugal in her new life.

Another factor that had helped her save some money was the free accommodation she enjoyed as a staff of the hotel. She had managed to put some money away for a rainy day. It was not much, but it would tide her and Ella over, long enough to find alternative accommodation and another job if the need arose. Her sister Laide also sent her some extra money monthly, *just to help out,* she would say. Though Labake had assured her many times that she did not need to, Laide sent the money anyway, and Labake felt forever indebted to her for all the support she had rendered her since she left Vince.

"Let's keep our fingers crossed that the new Management retains the current staff. They more often than not like to hire fresh people," Adia said without thinking and then covered her mouth in embarrassment when she realized what implication that would have on Labake's job.

"*Oops*...I'm sorry, Labake...I was thinking aloud," Adia said apologetically.

"Don't apologize, Adia...it's what we've all thought about at the hotel. It's usual, isn't it...for new management to bring in their own people. It isn't something I haven't considered," Labake said graciously. She gave Adia a reassuring smile.

"Not necessarily," Earl said. "Sometimes, new Management is quite happy with the results of the present staff and therefore happy to carry on business as usual. Besides, they'd need a lot of the old staff to train the new ones and may just consider it unnecessary...*especially* if the old staff has performed well." Labake knew he added that for her benefit and thought it sweet of him to try and reassure her.

"Well, let's hope that's the case here. Though I've also heard of companies who have it written into the *Contract of Sale* that the old staff be retained by the new management for a certain period...who knows what could happen?" Kwame said, passing a bowl of salad to Labake. "Whatever happens, there are loads of other places to work in Accra," he concluded on a positive note. Changing the topic, he asked,

"Speaking of Accra, how are you finding it here, Labake? It's been almost two years since you got here, isn't it?"

Labake knew her hosts were being polite and trying to include her in the general conversation, but she wished they would move on to another topic. She hated being the center of attention.

"Very well, thank you, Kwame. Though I must say, in between settling Ella in school and working at the hotel, I haven't seen a lot of it. It's been busy...but peaceful," Labake said and wished she had not added that last comment as all eyes at the table turned to her at that moment. It was as though they were thinking, *that's understandable; we're well aware you didn't have any peace in your past life.* Or was that her being paranoid again? She wondered.

"Er, I could show you around town this weekend if you like?" Earl said gently with a hopeful look in his eyes.

"Now that's an idea!" Adia said a bit too excitedly. "You still remember your way around town, don't you, bro?" She asked her brother with a wink.

Everyone at the table but Labake burst into laughter, causing Labake to wonder why. She was aware Earl had recently relocated to Accra from Canada. Adia had mentioned that when she introduced him to her at Nana's birthday party a few months back, but Labake did not get the joke.

"Of course, *I do know* my way around town. I grew up here, remember. I'll be more than willing to give you a tour around the city, Labake. Tomorrow is Saturday, and with Ella being here with the girls, could I pick you up at about noon if you aren't busy?" Earl asked Labake again.

That was the last thing Labake wanted, but she felt her hands were tied. All eyes around the table were on her again, waiting for her response.

"Er...I may have to work tomorrow. I'm not sure..." Labake trailed off. It was happening again; that familiar feeling of panic she experienced when it felt she was losing control of her plans suddenly threatened to overwhelm her again.

"I'll ring you to confirm in the morning...if that's alright," Earl concluded before she could come out with an outright *no*.

* * * *

Labake had a lot on her mind she needed to discuss with Laide. First was her worry about Ella growing up without her father, and then there was the issue of Earl, who just did not seem to get the idea that she wanted to be left alone. The first thing she did once she got home after dinner at Kwame's was to ring her sister up. After listening to her patiently, Laide said,

"As far as this guy is concerned...*Earl,* did you say his name is? I think it may be a great idea for you to foster some kind of friendship with him. I mean, how could it possibly hurt, especially if he's Kwame's brother-in-law? Besides, it would be good for Ella too...she needs a father figure in..."

"*Laide*!" Labake cut her sister off in mid-sentence. "She *has* a father! That's the last thing I want from him or anyone else for that matter!" She screamed into the phone.

Sensing her sister's response was out of fear and what Laide suspected to be naivety, Laide said patiently,

"Calm down, Labake. It's unfortunate that you've had a raw deal and haven't experienced what it means to *really* live. I mean, that brute of a husband married you way before you became a woman and controlled your very existence to the point that you never fully blossomed into the woman you could have," Laide paused to let what she was saying sink in and then continued.

"This is why I believe you *need* therapy. You need to seek some sort of professional counseling. You've been through a lot and need some help in dealing with your mind. It's been almost two years since you left the savage you were married to, and in a way, he still controls your *every* thought. So much so that you're not mentally ready to move forward and truly enjoy your new-found freedom. Your mind is so closed to the thought that you're still quite young. You have your whole life ahead of you, and it and that of Ella's must continue. It's time to drop all that mental baggage and experience something new, sis...*real life*. It's a *new* beginning, a *new* chapter of your life...turn the page and embrace it. Vince was your *past*, and you moved on physically from him. It's now time for you to move on *mentally* too...this is why I'm taking it upon myself to book you some help. *Dr. Stella Davis* will be perfect. It's her area of specialty, and her practice, thankfully, is in Accra," Laide concluded in that tone of voice that made Labake know she had no choice in the matter.

Laide did not bother mentioning to Labake how Doctor Stella had helped her through her own childhood baggage. Though the process had been long and difficult, she was a lot better now. She still spoke to Doctor Stella via telephone whenever she needed to.

"I don't need to see a *shrink* Laide. I'm doing just fine. The trouble is..."Labake started but got cut off by her sister.

"Trust me, Labake, we all need a *shrink* at some point in our lives...*you* most certainly *do* need to speak to someone, and I insist that you accept the help I'm offering, or I'll travel to Ghana and drag you to your appointments myself if I have to! It would do you a world of good. I'll ring Dr. Stella and get back to you with the date and time of your first appointment," Laide said and hung the phone up without waiting for a response from her sister.

CHAPTER FOURTEEN

Rewa's phone had not stopped ringing since her appearance with Chief Ralph Eke on the cover of the famous tabloid, *Scope*. Almost everyone she knew, even friends she had lost touch with, rang to enquire about her *relationship* with the most *eligible widower* in the country. She was tired of explaining that the headline on the cover of the tabloid and the picture were two different things that did not belong together. In the end, she had refused to take calls from unfamiliar numbers. She'd had enough of it and just wanted to bury her head and make it all go away.

Omorien, her youngest sister, had finally had her second baby. It was a boy, and everyone in the family was excited and planning a trip to Texas for the *Baby Dedication* in about five weeks. Rewa was busy at work, and though she planned to join the rest of her family on the trip to Texas, she was worried she would not find the time to get away as soon as she hoped. She had not prepared for the type of business *Princes Place* had brought her. She was inundated with quite a number of new design projects and was having some difficulty coping with the number of concurrent projects she had running at the moment. One of which included doing up the interiors of four judges' inner chambers at the Courthouse on the Island.

Finally, she had decided to take on a couple of *trainee* decorators as she could not keep up with the workload. She eventually settled for a young man, *David,* and a lady, *Vera,* who already had remarkable training portfolios. They followed her to meetings, instruction-taking stages, and everything else so she could show them the ropes. This made her even busier. She knew it would pay off in the long run and that hiring the new staff was progress. She expected her workload to ease up within a few weeks when she could take some time off to visit her sister and latest nephew in The States.

Today being the last Sunday of the month, Rewa was having lunch with her parents and her sister Omosede's family, which included her husband *Larry* and their two daughters, *Lilly* and *Rose,* who were six and eight, respectively. They were seated around the grand Ilo dining table, and lunch had been served. Chief Ilo had made this a tradition since all his girls left home. They all had lunch together on the last Sunday of each month to touch base and bond as a family. It also gave him a chance to see his grandchildren too.

Rewa usually did not look forward to these lunches as she knew the subject of her being unmarried somehow *always* crept up into the conversation. She was not in the best of moods today as she was under pressure from work, and she hoped the topic of her single status would not come up today. She particularly found it embarrassing that such matters were discussed while her brother-in-law, Larry, was present. After all, it was not his or anyone else's business.

"So, I see you're an *acquaintance* of Ralph Eke," Chief Ilo began, directing his comment to his eldest daughter. He smiled and gave Rewa a knowing look.

"Not you as well, daddy," Rewa said in a withdrawn manner, rolling her eyes. She did not miss the look her parents exchanged at that moment, and she could see that Sede was in on it too. Feeling slightly ambushed, she said, "Why do people believe *everything* they read? What has Sede been saying?" Rewa asked accusatorily, giving her sister a dirty look.

Omosede was the rumormonger in the family. If you want information on anyone in the Ilo clan, just ask Sede. If she did not know, then no other information was *kosher*. Rewa suspected that her father's comment and the funny look her parent's just exchanged at her response had something to do with information her younger sister had shared with them.

"*Me?* Why me? I haven't needed to say anything; the whole country *except you* reads *Scope,* Sis," Omosede said defensively, but Rewa knew her sister too well. She knew Sede was the closest to her parents and would have been the one to show them the offending tabloid magazine of her with Ralph Eke. She also knew her father did not have the time to *buy,* not to mention *read* any tabloid magazine, and her mother, though a socialite herself, was more interested in TV gossip shows. Therefore, it fell on Sede to be the one to have briefed her parents about the trending rumor about her and Chief Ralph Eke.

"Well, I am *not* Chief Eke's *acquaintance* or *love interest* in any way. I just happened to have decorated his new building," Rewa explained to her family, who had all stopped eating at this point, waiting for more information on the subject, including Larry, who normally just acted like he was a part of the furniture at the Ilo

Sunday lunches. In truth, however, he picked up *everything* that was said and shared it with Rien's husband in Texas. Rewa wondered if her own husband, if she ever managed to marry one, would be invited to the *brothers-in-law clique,* which, at the time being, consisted of both her sisters' husbands - *Larry* and *Bode*.

"You just did his building up, and he *presented* you with flowers...*publicly*? That wasn't what the paper said, dear," Mrs. Ilo said, clearly disappointed. It was obviously not what she hoped to hear from her eldest daughter. She had always known Rewa to be quite private and the most secretive of her three girls, so it just seemed as though Rewa was trying to hide this new relationship with the *big-time* lawyer. *Why*? Mrs. Ilo failed to understand.

Rewa could feel her anger begin to grow. It was almost as if she had to *prove* she was not lying to her parents about the article in *Scope*. She could not handle being the subject of discussion today and hoped to successfully keep a lid on her rising temper.

"Well, sorry to disappoint you, *mother,* but that was *all* it was. He gave the flowers to me in appreciation for the work I did on his building *at the commissioning* of the said building. Why would I lie about that?" She asked, looking first at her mother and then round the silent table. Sensing the tension that was about to erupt, everyone instinctively began eating again.

"I'm not saying you're lying, dear. It's just that the picture was rather...suggestive, and they do say *there's no smoke without fire*. It was quite convincing too, and we just thought perhaps... " Mrs. Ilo was saying.

Rewa did not wait for her mother to finish her sentence. She dragged her chair back noisily on the marbled floor of her parents' ostentatiously decorated dining room and said to them politely, "I have a lot to do tomorrow. Can I please be excused?" It was more a statement than a question.

Sensing his daughter's anger, Chief Ilo cleared his throat and said gently, "Don't leave on account of what is being discussed, *baby girl*. We're just anxious to know if anything er...romantic...is happening in your life. We were excited and hopeful that something *was* going on between you and Ralph. As a matter of fact, I know him very well, he is a good man, and if anything was to develop between you two, then your mother and I would be very pleased." Chief Ilo never wanted to upset any of his girls. He knew Rewa's single state was a touchy subject for her and wished now that he had not brought it up in the first place.

"That's *exactly* the point, Daddy! Absolutely *NOTHING* is developing between Chief Eke and me! He is just or *WAS* just a client and nothing more...a *satisfied* client who decided to show his appreciation by giving me flowers for the work I did for him. *Nothing more*! The tabloid just made it seem more than it was. Again I ask, why is it that even the most enlightened and educated people believe *everything* they read?" Rewa asked, glaring at her father in annoyance. Then she continued when no one answered.

"If you don't mind, I have to leave now." Without waiting for approval this time, Rewa picked her bag up and left her parents' house angrily.

Outside, she fumbled with her car keys for a minute just because she was extremely upset. As she got behind the wheel, her phone began to ring. As it was an unfamiliar number, she ignored it and drove out of the Ilo mansion. She was angry at everyone in her family at that point. She always felt terribly misunderstood by them. Why did she always have to be the subject of discussion at the Sunday dinners? Surely there was a lot more going on within the family than her single status. Her youngest sister Rien just had a baby. Why could they not discuss that or perhaps their impending trip to Texas? She wondered angrily.

Fuming, Rewa drove to her office, not caring that it was a Sunday. She did not want to go home and had quite a bit of work to do anyways at the office. She had samples to order online and emails to send to track some furniture and window treatment she was expecting from Dubai.

As she parked her car outside her office building and alighted from it, she noticed a black SUV parked near the gates, and one of the security guards was speaking with its driver. It was weird as she was sure the building was empty. She wondered what anyone could possibly want on a Sunday afternoon at an office complex downtown. Perhaps the person was lost and needed directions, she thought.

Rewa walked past the jeep without looking into it to see who its occupant was. Just as she was about to walk through the gates, she turned back to see a man alight from the SUV and the security guard beckoning to her animatedly to walk back to the jeep. Rewa's heart skipped a beat when she saw who it was. Chief Ralph Eke waived to her briefly as if to get her attention. He began walking towards her, and Rewa could not understand why but she swiftly straightened the dress she had on. She was not looking bad, seeing as she had gone to her parents' straight from church and therefore looked nicer than she felt in the short red dress she had on. *What could he possibly be doing here on a Sunday*? She wondered.

"Hi Rewa, how are you doing?" He said with that familiar bored look on his face. Rewa noticed that, as usual, his greeting was not paired with a smile. He looked nice and casual in a black linen shirt and blue denim pants, though it appeared as though he had not even tried to make an effort with his appearance.

"Hello, Chief Eke..." Rewa said. It was a greeting that sounded more like a question. Ralph watched her reaction. He knew she would wonder what he was doing there. He thought she looked nice in the red dress, but her expression was not a friendly one; it was more curious, if anything, he observed.

"I'm sure you're wondering what I'm doing here on a Sunday, but I've tried ringing you since last week and even earlier today but you haven't answered your phone. I happened to drive by on my way to the chambers and noticed your board sign. I wanted to know if you were in town, seeing as you weren't answering your phone, so I decided to inquire of the security guards...it's uncanny that you're here too," Ralph Eke explained, studying Rewa's face as he spoke.

"Oh really?" That was all Rewa could manage. She did not know what to do with that piece of information. She stood there for a moment, just looking at him. Then she asked politely. "Can I help you with anything, Chief Eke?"

"*Ralph,* please, call me Ralph," he said. She was so professional, he thought. He liked that a lot as it was not often one met professional people in these parts of the world.

"Yes, I hope you can, actually. I have another project I'm hoping you'd be able to help me with, but I'm going out of the country tomorrow...I might as well let you know what I want before I leave, just to give you some time to think about it while I'm away. Is there anywhere we can talk?" Ralph asked, suggesting that he did not want to carry on the conversation outside.

"Yes, of course. Please follow me, Chief...er Ralph." Rewa stuttered and led the way into the building and her office on the first floor.

Ralph Eke watched Rewa as she walked briskly in front of him. She carried herself with an air of coolness. Gone was the *klutz* he had believed her to be on the day she had dropped her papers on his office floor at their first meeting. He had concluded that she was not just confident; she was a highly intelligent and extremely gifted lady. That much he had garnered from the excellent job she had done at *Princes Place*. He did not know why but he found himself wondering what it was that made her tick. She did not seem to care in the slightest about who he was. Most women flirted with him from the get-go but not her, he observed. He liked that about her. He could definitely work with that, he mused silently.

"Can I just ask why you haven't answered your phone in the last few days?" Ralph asked once he was seated in one of the chairs opposite Rewa's desk in her very nicely decorated office. She had all sorts of sample materials in the far corner of the room. Her desk was piled high with paperwork, and he could tell she was a hard worker just because she was even there on a Sunday. He would never have mentioned it, but Ralph Eke was really impressed with the pretty lady before whom he now sat.

Rewa cracked a small sheepish smile. Not one to lie, she decided to come clean about the true reason for not answering her calls. She had not recognized Ralph Eke's number as she did not have it saved on her cell phone. She had never needed to ring him personally when she worked on *Princes place*. Her main contact person on that project had been Mrs. Atta.

After Rewa explained about their appearance on the front page of *Scope* and how her phone had rang non-stop, Ralph smiled and said someone had mentioned it to him, but he had not actually seen the magazine himself. He waived it off as irrelevant and got down to business. He explained that he had recently purchased a block of flats in the United Kingdom and needed Rewa to do it up.

"I see, thank you, Ralph, for the offer, but *residential* interiors aren't my thing. I do offices and business premises mainly. I can, however, recommend..." Rewa started, but before she could finish, Ralph interjected.

"Are you saying you *never* do residential properties *at all*?" He asked, cutting her off in mid-sentence with a raised eyebrow.

How rude Rewa thought within her, she wondered who he thought he was.

He had such an arrogant air about him. She was glad she did not have to be nice to him as she no longer considered him a client. She was going to turn him down no matter what she concluded, just to prove a point that he could not always have what he wanted, as Mrs. Atta had said about him.

"I have done them in the past, but..." Rewa tried to answer but again got cut off by a clearly impatient Ralph when he said,

"Then that settles it." He rose to his feet as if to suggest the meeting was over. "I would like you to do the job...that's if you can squeeze it into your busy schedule. My Personal Assistant will be in touch with the details on Monday. I will be back from my trip by the weekend, and you can let me know when you'd be able to travel out to Surrey to inspect the place and perhaps start work on it. Thank you, Rewa, do enjoy the rest of the day," Ralph Eke said and left Rewa's office before she could even respond.

Rewa swiftly got to her feet, mouth opened in perplexity, just as Ralph Eke shut the door behind himself softly. *What had just happened?* She was never usually lost for words. Had Ralph Eke just bossed her around in *her own* office? *Just who exactly did this man think he was? How dare he think he could order me around? The effrontery!* It seemed to have slipped his mind that she was not on his payroll - at least not anymore. *How dare he come here unannounced and again on a Sunday and issue out orders to me?*

Rewa decided she *was* really having a bad day now. First, her family, and now Ralph Eke! To think he was the reason she had stormed out of her parents' house in anger just an hour ago. She was highly irritated and wondered if she would be able to do any work now.

What was it about Ralph Eke that irked her? He seemed to always leave her feeling inadequate and *put-in-her-place* each time she interacted with him. He had simply brushed off the tabloid story that had caused her so much grief as if it was insignificant, and had even told her to pay it no attention. The more she thought about him, the angrier she got. She could not remember the last time *anyone* got under her skin this way.

Rewa hated being disrespected, especially by a man. What was even more unsettling was that she could not exactly say he *had* actually disrespected her as he really had not said anything rude to her, except his rude interruptions. It was also the manner in which he spoke to her. He was authoritative in a slightly subtle manner, in a way that made it impossible to call him out. *Well, he isn't my boss,* Rewa thought. *So he could take his offer and do whatever he wanted with it.*

After an hour of trying but failing to focus on what needed doing, Rewa decided to pack it all in and go home. She'd had enough for one day.

* * * *

The following morning, on his flight to Cape Town, Ralph Eke's thoughts drifted to Omorewa Ilo. He found her rather fascinating and could not explain why he felt drawn to her. He knew he liked her work ethic and creativity, but he also knew there was more. He was not easily drawn to anyone and was not much of a *people person*. He most definitely was not much of a *ladies' man,* either. He had decided to stay single after his wife passed away over seventeen years ago, to the displeasure of a lot of his family and friends who had tried countless times to match-make him with a number of different ladies. They believed he needed the stability a wife brought into a man's life, but he had declined, preferring to remain single.

As far as Ralph was concerned, it was hard to find a lady who liked you just for you and nothing more. Far too many women these days were only after one thing, *money*. So many of them were *gold-diggers,* and the last thing Ralph needed was to be with someone who had ulterior motives. Besides, he was not sure he had the patience or capacity to deal with the type of drama a woman would bring into his present lifestyle. He believed he was far too old and way too busy for all that. He knew it was perhaps a selfish reason not to open himself up to a meaningful relationship, but he could not help the way he felt.

Ralph had married his late wife Trisha, just as they both graduated from Law School. They had been in love till she died of a rare form of cancer. Though they had been together for a short time, he felt he would always be indebted to her. She had given him a wonderful marital experience and, of course, his twenty-two-year-old son *Israel,* who now lived in the United Kingdom.

Ralph had brought Israel up alone since he was five years old. While he acknowledged that he could not have done it without the help of his sister and late mother, he had refused to take another wife just so his son could have the benefit of being raised by a man and a woman. He had not believed that then and still did not believe it now that a child was more balanced if raised by both parents. They had done okay by themselves for the most part, and Israel had turned out just fine as both his aunt and grandmother had provided all the love and warmth he could ever have needed from his mother. His maternal grandparents were also hugely supportive and helped raise him too. Like Israel, they both lived in the United Kingdom and were very much a part of both Israel's and Ralph's lives.

Ralph wondered now why he was thinking the way he was. He had believed that he would remain and die a widower and had never even considered re-marrying again. He was not sure if his present thoughts were because he missed the company of a woman in his life. He was a very busy person and had a lot to fill his life, mostly his work. He had grown accustomed to being by himself and was not quite sure he would ever trade his present freedom for a relationship. Of course, he'd had a fling or two since Trisha, but he was not looking for anything permanent. He was not even sure that he remembered how to *woo* a lady anymore as the truth was, women these days did not make a man *chase* them. A lot of them tended to be easy and a bit too keen to give themselves freely to men without any or little persuasion or resistance. Whatever happened to the concept of *wooing*? Did it even still exist? Ralph wondered.

Even the ladies at his church were not any different. They all just wanted to get married without considering life after the marriage itself and its attendant issues. He usually just smiled when he noticed a lady was doing all she could to flirt with him or get his attention. It was one of the reasons he had taken the decision to remain single and celibate. Ralph remembered the last lady he had dated and how she had made sexual innuendos towards him. He had been disappointed because she was supposed to be a minister in her church. He shook his head now and thought it a shame that things were not different even in church.

Ralph's late wife, Trisha, had been *drama-free,* which had been his initial attraction to her. They had never had any issues in the years they were together as Trisha, like him, had been peace-loving. They had lived together in love and harmony till she got ill. Ralph had done his best to keep her around for much longer, but the cancer eventually got the better of her. They had traveled all over the world in search of a cure to no avail, their efforts had all been futile because of the rarity of the type of cancer Trisha had, and it had spread like wildfire far too quickly.

It had taken Ralph a considerable amount of time to come to terms with Trisha's death, and he had only managed to pull himself together because of his son, Israel, who had been quite young at the time and needed him. Ralph was grateful that he had Israel and was quite proud of the *father-son* bond they shared though they did not live in the same country anymore. They spoke on the phone quite often, and when he could find the time, Ralph visited the UK a lot so that they could spend time together.

Ralph needed Rewa to do the new apartments he had recently acquired in the United Kingdom. He could not think of anyone else, and he was not going to accept *no* as an answer either. Besides, he could not explain why but he needed a reason to have her around. He perceived she would be difficult about it, but he kind of admired that about her. She did not seem like a *pushover* and did not seem to care about who he was, a fact that further drew her to him. He looked forward to working with her again as he knew for sure he would.

CHAPTER FIFTEEN

It was unavoidable. Her sessions with Dr. Stella Davis had been fully booked and paid for by Laide. Labake knew she could not refuse to go now, seeing as Laide had threatened to come to Accra and drag her to the sessions herself if she had to. She sighed now as she sat in Dr. Stella's reception room, waiting patiently to see the shrink. That annoying feeling of losing control began to gnaw at her yet again. She found herself doing something she had not planned to do of her own volition. She did not feel like she needed to air her dirty laundry out in public, least of all to a total stranger. How was that supposed to help her in any way? Labake wondered. She just needed to be left alone, but it seemed no one could understand that.

There was Earl, also breathing down her neck to take her out, which he had eventually succeeded in doing. Labake felt he had backed her right into a corner and that she could not refuse, especially as Kwame and Adia were both expecting her to humor him and go out on a tour of Accra with him. That, again, was something she had not felt she needed. She had lived in Accra for almost two years now anyway; going on a tour of the city was unnecessary in Labake's view.

To her amazement, however, she had actually enjoyed herself with Earl. It had started out awkwardly at first, as she had been terribly anxious that morning and had a panic attack. She had not had any in the last eighteen months and had believed them to have gone forever until the morning of her outing with Earl. She was beginning to understand now that feeling overwhelmingly nervous was the obvious trigger of the attacks. There perhaps was also a level of fear and trepidation in the mix as well. The attack had lasted about five minutes, and Labake was thankful that she had been alone when it happened. Poor Ella would have been terrified if she had witnessed her mother wheezing and gasping for air.

Earl had picked Labake up at the hotel, and again because she was not trying to get too familiar with him, she met him downstairs at the entrance of the Staff Quarters. Once she was settled in his car and they were on their way, Earl's hand had accidentally brushed her thigh as he put the car in reverse to back out of the parking lot, and Labake flinched. It was as though he had touched her with a hot iron rod or something similar. It had been hugely awkward, with Earl apologizing profusely at her reaction. Earl had decided within him never to touch her without warning and hoped she did not think he had done it intentionally.

It was not till about another forty minutes or so before Labake began to relax again with her companion. He made light conversation in his very soft way of speaking whilst showing her the sights, and she found she even forgot herself sometimes and laughed at his jokes. She found him quite funny and liked the fact that he teased her a lot too. It was odd, but Labake found that somewhat enjoyable and wondered why she did.

When the tour of the city was over and Earl drove Labake back to the hotel, she politely thanked him for his time before she alighted from the car and bade him a good evening to his dismay. He hoped she would at least let him walk her to her door, but she had declined and said that it was not necessary. Earl had not made a fuss about it. Instead, he thanked her in return for allowing him to take her around town and bade her goodbye.

Now that wasn't so bad, Labake had mused within herself as she walked up the stairs to her apartment. She was relieved it had gone smoothly but particularly that it was over. Earl Tetteh seemed like a very sensitive gentleman, and she'd had a great afternoon, but she hoped he would leave her alone from here on. She had taken Laide's advice and hoped she was satisfied too. She said that much to her later that evening when Laide rang her up to find out how her outing with Earl had gone. "It was nice...really nice, better than I envisaged," Labake confided in her sister shyly.

"Ms. Labake, the Doctor will see you now," the receptionist said, bringing Labake back to the present.

Dr. Stella's clinic was very nicely decorated. It was located in downtown Accra which suggested she was quite successful at what she did. When Labake walked into her office, she was surprised to find a lady who could not have been more than a few years older than Laide, her older sister. Dr. Stella rose from her desk and greeted Labake with a reassuring smile. She was a petite lady, smartly dressed with short cropped hair and a pair of glasses on her oval-shaped face.

"Nice to meet you, Mrs. Ebodo. Please have a seat." Labake cringed at the way the Doctor had addressed her. It had been some time since anyone referred to her as *Mrs. Ebodo*. Even at work, she was simply known as *Labake*. Doctor Stella's skilled and trained eye noted Labake's slight reaction to her name. She gestured to the leather sofa in the corner of the room.

The place had been set up nicely, Labake observed silently. There was a small coffee table with various types of magazines on it. Labake also noted that there was what appeared to be a voice recorder on the table as well as two large, lit perfumed candles on the table too. Labake presumed the latter were there to help put the patient at ease, but it did not seem to be having any effect on her at that moment.

Dr. Stella herself took the chair opposite Labake and asked, "Would you like anything to drink...*Labake*? I hope I can call you that." She asked politely, smiling at her new patient.

Labake declined the drink and said, "Please, call me Labake." Relieved that Dr. Stella had asked.

Usually, Dr. Stella would attempt to first gauge what was going on within a new patient's mind from their exterior before they even began speaking. She suspected from the way Labake carried herself and averted her gaze that she had confidence issues. What she was unsure of was what it was born out of.

All she knew about the bulk of her patients at the very beginning of their sessions was whatever they filled in on a basic online form, after which payment for the sessions was made. Her receptionist would then download the forms and ring the prospective patient with an appointment date and time. Therefore, Dr. Stella often did not know anything else about why a patient was in her office. She preferred it that way, as it was a blank canvas on which she could evaluate the patient and then draw her conclusions based on what she perceived to be the problem.

Dr. Stella was aware that in Labake's case, the form filling, appointment, and payment process had all been made on her behalf by her sister, Laide, who was one of her old patients. Laide had not said much to her about Labake or whatever she needed to see her about. She had just mentioned that she needed to book her sister some sessions as she believed Labake was in dire need of them.

Dr. Stella Silently compared Labake to her sister and could hardly tell they were related. There was no major physical resemblance between them. For one, Laide appeared a lot more confident from their first meeting. She had mentioned in their sessions that she had a younger sister and talked a lot about their childhood. Dr. Stella, therefore, had some knowledge of Labake's background but was ready to crack on as to the real reason why she was there.

Very gently, Dr. Stella said, "Before we begin, I must inform you that our sessions will be recorded for filing purposes only." That said, the doctor pushed a button on the device when Labake indicated by a slight lifting of a shoulder that she did not mind and said softly but professionally, "Why are you here, Labake?" She flipped the page of her notepad and gave her newest patient her full attention.

* * * *

"Hello Labake, Earl here. How are you and Ella doing?" *What did he want now?* Labake wondered. *Why won't he just let me be?* "Hello," she responded quietly. "We're both doing well, thank you. How are you?" She asked politely in return.

"I'm good, very good, thank you. I'm taking Nana and Akua on a picnic at the beach tomorrow and wondered if you girls would like to tag along," Earl said. He paused and waited for Labake's reaction. Though he tried to sound as casual as possible, he suspected she would decline and then added, "Actually, I'm only trying to be gentlemanly here. I should warn you that I don't plan to take no for an answer."

Labake heard the humor in his voice and decided to surprise him by saying she and Ella would love to join them on the picnic. She was not sure why she agreed. Perhaps therapy with Dr. Stella *was* having a positive impact after all. She was also looking for something to keep Ella busy till school resumed the following Monday. Summer camp was over, and Ella seemed bored already. Labake thought a picnic would be great to occupy her, if only for a day. Slightly stunned by Labake's response, Earl said, "Great! We'll pick you guys up at around noon time tomorrow then. See you soon."

Earl was surprised at how easily Labake had agreed to the picnic. He had expected her to give an excuse as to why they could not come just the way she had each time he invited her out. She had, however, managed to pleasantly shock him by her immediate willingness to come out with them. Could it have anything to do with the girls being present? He wondered.

Earl remembered their first outing and how it had gone, especially after his hands had accidentally brushed against her thigh. He had decided to be gentle with her. He spoke softly and realized she began to relax a bit more while he gave her a brief history of the country and the people of Ghana. He made sure not to touch her again or make her do anything without seeking her approval first. He also got her involved in the decision-making process on where to go first. That put Labake slightly more at ease with him, he had observed. She did not initiate any conversations and did more listening than talking. Earl had also tried his best not to ask her too many personal questions as he sensed she was not ready for that. He talked mainly about Accra and himself and some of the places he had been on his travels.

They had stopped for drinks and some beef pies along the way and eaten them in the car as Earl had not wanted to *rock the boat* by taking Labake for a proper meal in a restaurant. He suspected doing so would make her uneasy and perhaps suggest they were on a date of sorts. No, he was going to take it nice and easy with her. He believed he had made some headway so far, as she appeared to have dropped her guard, be it slightly. He was not prepared to mess things up by undoing the little he had managed to accomplish with her. He was not going to rush it either, as he sensed it would frighten her and likely send her in the opposite direction from him. It was a chance he simply was unwilling to take.

Earl had studied Labake some more in the three hours they had spent together that afternoon. He watched her mannerisms and reactions to places and even to some of his jokes and comments. He knew he needed her to trust him, he also needed to put her at ease and help her learn to relax around him, but more importantly, he needed to take it slowly if he was ever to have a chance at being her friend. *Time and patience* were what Kwame had suggested, and Earl decided he had a lot of both to give her.

The picnic was just another excuse to see Labake again. Though Earl loved his nieces and took them out from time to time, he really needed to see Labake again. He did not want too much of a time lapse between them after their tour of Accra. He did not want to give her a reason to retreat into her shell. He wanted to build on the little rapport they had established, just from that one successful outing they had.

* * * *

The following day, an excited Ella got up bright and early, thrilled at the prospects of a picnic with her friends. Labake now realized she had made a mistake in telling Ella about the picnic last night when she put her to bed. She had hoped for a lie-in this morning before the picnic as it was her first full Saturday off work after a busy week. She wished she could have at least another hour in bed, but Ella had other plans as usual. She ran into her mother's bedroom, jumping up and down her bed and yelling, "*Wakey, wakey* mummy!" She said, "We're going on a picnic, remember!" Her voice seemed louder than normal to Labake, who picked up a pillow and covered her head with it. "*Mummy*!" Ella giggled, attempting to pull the pillow out of her mother's grip.

"Alright, alright," Labake said groggily, "Let's have breakfast first. The picnic isn't until another few hours, but you can go get your swimwear and something pretty to wear from your closet in the time being." She hoped that would distract Ella and buy her another fifteen minutes of sleep. It did, as Ella bounced off her mother's bed and raced to her own bedroom in search of a picnic outfit.

A few hours later, Labake and Earl watched the girls from a safe distance as they played with a ball on the beach. It was awkward that they had their swimsuits on but were nowhere near the water. They did not seem to mind either, as they appeared to be having a great time from the delightful giggling and laughing sounds they made.

Earl and Labake were seated on a beach towel under a large palm tree, watching the girls as they made light conversation. Labake, though cautious still, was more relaxed with Earl than she was before. He had an easy personality and always had a great story or joke to tell. She sat comfortably with him, unaware of the sight they presented to the on-looker. They looked like a married couple on a picnic with their three daughters. She was also unaware of the effect she had on Earl. He stopped talking for a while and observed her through his sunglasses. She was a ravishing young woman, he thought within himself, and the fact that she was not even conscious of it made Labake all the more intriguing to him.

Labake had on a short, floral beach dress that was conservative but still had enough sex appeal for someone as modest as she was. She also had a pair of sunglasses on and a wide-brimmed straw hat that Ella had insisted she bring along. A large matching scarf draped over her shoulders as she was aware her dress was short and cut rather low at the back. The scarf served the dual purpose of concealing the scars on her bare back and slightly exposed thighs.

The scars were sustained from Vince's belt buckle on numerous occasions. They were long healed but still quite visible. The dress was the only appropriate thing Labake had to wear for the picnic and she had thought hard before deciding to wear it. She finally settled for it when she found the large matching scarf, which she now clutched tightly around her shoulders.

Earl watched Labake silently for a while. He could tell she was relaxed as she made more effort to make general conversation this time, unlike the previous time they had been out together. She had said very little, if anything at all, though she politely laughed at his jokes. Today was, however, different, and Earl was happy that they seemed to be making some progress. He decided on the spur of the moment to go for it and let her know how he really felt about her.

"Labake, I have something I'd like to say to you. I hope and pray it won't be my undoing and that perhaps somehow, you'd understand what I'm about to say frightens me...quite a bit, for fear that you may not want to hear it." Labake's curiosity got the better of her, and before she knew it, she asked what it was. She hoped she had not acted in a way that offended him in any way. She still could not read people very well, particularly the opposite sex. She looked at Earl through her sunglasses with concern.

"I've tried to give you some time as you have more or less made it clear you aren't interested in any sort of relationship...but I'd like to put it out there from the on-set that I like you...a lot. I won't put any pressure on you to like me back, but I want you to know that I want to be there for you and Ella. Now I know that..." Earl stopped mid-sentence when he suddenly realized Labake had begun trembling. She got to her feet abruptly, and as she did, the scarf around her shoulders slipped to the mat they were sitting on, revealing her scarred back. Earl's jaw dropped, and his mouth hung open at the sight of it. Her bare back was covered with angry-looking scars that though healed, were gruesome to look at. He momentarily forgot what he had been saying and was unable to disguise the horror on his face at what he was looking at.

Seeing Earl's reaction to her back, Labake bent quickly to retrieve the scarf from the mat and jumped when Earl got to his feet and reached out to touch her. He was horrified by what he had just seen and could not control himself from asking, "*My God!* Labake! Did he do that...who...did that to you?" Out of shock, he stuttered as he realized he had been about to reveal his knowledge of her abusive past. She had not mentioned it to him and he did not want her to know he had discussed her with Kwame and Adia; not at this stage anyway. His mouth still hung open, and it was obvious he was totally unprepared for what he was now summing up about her past. *Her husband most certainly was a maniac!* Earl thought in horror.

Though she did not respond, it was clear, from her reaction, what the answer was to Earl. It was a confirmation that Labake *was* a survivor of *domestic* violence, and God only knew what else, Earl realized.

Labake looked like a frightened puppy at that moment. Hands still trembling, she shakily replaced the scarf on her shoulders and turned away from Earl. She was thankful for the sunglasses she had on. She did not want Earl to see the fear in her eyes. She was suddenly overcome by a strong need to run. Her heart had started pounding wildly, and her entire body shook uncontrollably. Looking away, she said in a breathless whisper, "I'd like to leave now, please...if you don't mind."

Earl did not say another word. He stood there for a moment in sheer perplexity and watched as Labake walked towards the girls to let them know it was time to leave. He was in horrified shock. He had never seen anything as gruesome as the scars on Labake's back, not in real life. How could any human being do that to another? He wondered as he bent to gather their picnic things. He was sad that the girls' fun was short-lived, but the mood, his inclusive, was now ruined and what was worse was the knowledge that *he* had ruined it by coming clean about his feelings for Labake too soon.

They drove in silence from the beach to the hotel, with just the girls chattering in the back seat. Labake sat rigidly in the passenger's seat till Earl pulled into the parking lot at the hotel staff quarters. "Thank you for the picnic," she said quietly, averting his gaze. She bade Nana and Akua goodbye and said, "Come on, Ella." Ella grumbled and sulked, not wanting to leave her friends yet, but she did as she was told, sensing her mother was not in any mood to placate her.

"Can I ring you later?" Earl asked Labake softly, and Labake gave a slight nod in response. "Promise me you will answer when I do." She repeated the nod and shut the car door.

Later that evening, after Labake put Ella to bed, she thought about all Earl had said and her reaction to him. Why had she reacted so vehemently? Dr. Stella had mentioned during one of their sessions that most people had a *'fight or flight'* reaction to danger, but Labake found she only ever experienced the *flight* bit each time she *felt* endangered. When was she ever going to stay and fight? She wondered. Perhaps something really was *broken* within her, she thought now. Perhaps she did need *mending*.

Labake was ashamed that Earl had seen her scarred back, and she was not too pleased he appeared to know about her past. His initial question about her back made it obvious he knew something about it, and she wondered if Adia or Kwame had said something to him about her marriage. She knew neither of them knew the half of it as Labake had never talked to either of them about her past. However, she knew her sister Laide had mentioned what her circumstances were when she asked Kwame for his help in settling her and Ella in Accra. Kwame was therefore aware Labake was in hiding from her husband, and of course, one did not go into hiding from a husband except one's life was in danger, so Kwame was aware she had been in an abusive marriage. Labake now wondered how much Laide had told him and how much he, in turn, had said to Earl.

Thinking about Earl now, Labake sighed and wondered what had frightened her about his revelation. He was not trying to force her into doing anything she did not want. He had only asked to be her friend! Surely that was not anything out of the ordinary to ask. Labake decided to bring it up with Dr. Stella on Wednesday when she had her fourth appointment.

Labake's first session with Dr. Stella had started rather slowly as she was not used to talking to anyone, least of all a stranger. By the second session, however, Labake was more relaxed. She was beginning to like and trust the Doctor and had managed to discuss her marriage and her fears for the future.

Her cell phone began to ring, and Labake was thankful it was Laide. After she narrated the whole picnic incident to her, Laide said,

"You see why you needed therapy? Your reaction to what this Earl guy said was rather odd. I just hope he isn't beginning to think you're a *weirdo*." Laide laughed. "He only wants to be your friend. You need to let him in, sis," Laide advised her sister. She really hoped that therapy would help Labake get over the emotional trauma of what she had been through with Vince. It was obvious her wounds ran deep.

"He appeared to know about the situation with Vince too. The first thing he asked was if *he* had inflicted the wounds on my back. Now I know you spoke to Kwame about my situation before we arrived in Accra. He clearly had to know...I wonder how much you told Kwame and how much he told Earl..." Labake asked her sister breathlessly. She'd had some time to think since putting Ella to bed, and the day's events just kept replaying in her head.

"Didn't really go into details with Kwame. I just said my sister was in a bit of trouble with her abusive husband, and she needed to get away from him... and that it had to be a place where you could lie low for a while, where there were no family ties or connections. He probably mentioned to this Earl chap who obviously put the pieces together considering your body language," Laide concluded, giggling. Labake thought about what her sister said and began to wonder if her *body language* did say far more than she wanted to about her marital experience. She certainly hoped not.

Later that evening, when Earl rang, he began by apologizing for making Labake feel uncomfortable at the beach earlier that day. "I need to let you know that it wasn't my intention to make you feel that way. Please let me say that I'm not sorry for putting it out there that I want to be in your life and Ella's too. Now, I suspect you may not be ready for anything more, but please let me be a friend, Labake. I don't intend to smother you or pester you in any way. I'd just like to be able to ring you and perhaps take you out whenever you can spare the time. Now that doesn't sound bad...does it?" He asked gently.

Labake was quiet for a moment. She was not quite sure how to answer Earl's question, particularly because she still did not feel ready for any friendship and was unsure she could manage one. Her life just seemed rather complicated at the moment, and she believed friendship with Earl, or anyone else, would further complicate it. She was *on the run,* for Pete's sake. She was not even sure how much longer she would be in Ghana or what the future held for her. It had been two years, and everything was still *up in the air*!

There was also Ella to think of. Labake did not want to confuse her by having a man around, one who was not her father. Besides, Labake had not had a friend since her school days years ago. She was not sure she even knew how to be anyone's friend; she had been by herself for too long as Vince had not encouraged any friendship with *anyone*. She also had not maintained the little friends she had from school. She had therefore led an isolated life since she was seventeen and did not quite know how to live a different one.

Labake knew she was also scared. Scared of something she was not quite sure of yet. She believed she did not have the freedom to accommodate a new relationship and was unwilling to take one on at the moment. All she wanted was to be left alone to live a life of obscurity with her daughter if that was possible.

"Er...hello, are you still there, Labake?" Earl asked with some humor in his voice.

Labake decided to be honest with him as she felt he deserved that much. Dr. Stella had said there came a time in one's life when one had to say things honestly. It was part of taking control of one's life and a way of building one's own self-respect. It was the *adult* thing to do.

"I...I feel as though you're asking too much of me at the moment, Earl..." It was the first time she had ever said those words to anybody. She took a deep, shaky breath and continued.

"I'm not sure...not sure I can be a friend...to you or anyone else at the moment. It's...it's just so complicated right now...there's a lot to think of...I'm sorry, but it would be selfish of me to take your offer of friendship and...and not give you friendship in return. I...I just have a lot going on at the moment...I couldn't possibly get anyone else involved...it's complicated, Earl, I'm so sorry, but I have to be honest with you..." Labake trailed off abruptly as if she had said too much. She held her breath and waited for an angry reaction or harsh words from Earl. It was what she was used to. She believed anger was the only reaction a person had when they could not get their way. Vince had taught her that much. Earl, however, said softly,

"Labake, I know you've been through so much. I mean, it's obvious from the way you carry yourself. I also know that we are all products of our experiences and that a bad experience can scar us for life sometimes if we let it. I know this because I've had a few bad relationships myself. So many...I shouldn't even want to ever try again, but I also know that sometimes, one needs a few bad experiences to help one learn and become better in future relationships. I hope this doesn't sound insensitive of me, particularly because I don't know your story, but all I'm asking for is friendship. I would like to be your friend. I understand that you feel being friends requires some retributive action on your part, but it doesn't...not in this case anyway. All I ask is that you give me a bit of latitude to *be* a friend to you, and if at any point you feel it isn't working for you or that you have had enough of me, then I promise to understand and not bother you again. Now, how does that sound?" Earl asked again, hoping this time for a more positive answer.

He is not going to leave it alone, Labake thought within and sighed. Instead of sounding angry like she expected, Earl sounded even softer. He spoke almost soothingly, and she was amazed by his reaction to all she had said. She thought it was quite an offer. She found herself saying. "Thank you, Earl. I'd need some time. Please give me some time to think about it. Thank you."

CHAPTER SIXTEEN

"Ms. Omorewa Ilo?" The female voice on the other end of the phone enquired.

"Yes, this is she," Rewa answered, hating the interruption to her work. She was deeply engrossed in what she was doing. She and Vera, her new trainee, were choosing fabrics for a client's home office. They had just found the perfect color when Rewa's cell phone began to ring.

"Hello, Ms. Ilo, my name is Yinka, I am Chief Ralph Eke's *Personal Assistant,* and he has asked me to ring you with regards to your conversation with him about his new UK property," the lady on the other end of the phone said and paused for some reaction from Rewa, but none was forthcoming.

After a moment, the realization set in for Rewa as she remembered her conversation with Ralph yesterday. He had said his PA would give her a call with details of his new project in the UK.

"Hello, Yinka," Rewa said simply, again irritated that Ralph Eke appeared to have ignored what she said and now planned to force her into a transaction she was unwilling to make. Why could he not accept that she wasn't interested in doing his UK property? He just always had to have it his way, Rewa thought.

"I have some documents prepared with regards to the project and would like to personally bring them over to you, so we can have a sit-down and discuss further details. I have also been asked to get a specific travel date to the UK from you...perhaps to enable you to go and inspect the property in question. This is in order for us to go ahead and make travel arrangements..."

Rewa interrupted her at that point. She had heard enough and was quite prepared to send Ralph a reply through his PA without any further thought on the subject. She was determined to refuse the contract to renovate Ralph Eke's new UK project. She believed he needed to know first that she was not prepared to break her policy of doing strictly corporate interiors, not *even* for him. Second, he could not *always* have his way. She had said as much to him when he came to her office *unannounced and on* a Sunday too, but he had obviously rudely ignored her refusal. Rewa tried to muster up a polite but firm tone of voice when she responded to Yinka, the PA.

"Yinka, please let the good Chief know that as much as I appreciate his confidence in my work, I, unfortunately, would be *unable* to handle this UK project. As I explained to him yesterday, I *do not* decorate residential properties. My business is *strictly* designing *commercial* and *business premises*. However, I have a couple of colleagues who do great work designing residential spaces that I can recommend and would be quite pleased to forward you their details," Rewa finished as politely as she could.

"O...er...I'm not sure Chief Eke is aware as he gave me clear instructions and details to forward to you...er... but I will pass your message on to him. Do have a good afternoon," Yinka said before she got off the phone.

Poor Yinka, Rewa mused. She was, however, pleased that she had stuck to her gun. She did not care who Chief Ralph Eke thought he was, but he was not going to give her the *run-around*, no matter what. She was not his employee and refused to be treated as such. She replaced her phone on her table and returned to what she had been doing without a second thought.

* * * *

"O Rien! Not you too!" Rewa moaned. She really needed someone on her side for a change. It was now apparent that somebody in the Ilo clan was working hard at bringing everyone up to speed about her *'new love affair'*. They had rung her youngest sister up in Texas about her *secret affair* with Ralph Eke, and Rien was ringing Rewa up to hear it from the *horse's mouth*.

"Sede really needs to stop spreading false tales...I'm so cross with her right..." Rewa continued.

Rewa was convinced it was her immediate younger sister Sede, who had shared it with Rien, the youngest Ilo sibling. That was the usual trend in their family. Someone hears something about another person in the family and promises to keep it a secret from everyone else within the family but then does not and swears the person to whom they divulge it, to secrecy. It was the price to pay for belonging to such a close-knit family, and Rewa was used to it. However, she was fed-up with this particular rumor making the rounds. She made up her mind to have strong words with Sede about it the minute she got off the phone with Rien.

"*Sede*? You've got it all wrong, sis. It was actually *Jas* who mentioned it to me...remember Jas, my old girlfriend from school? She apparently read it in the tabloids and sent me a Facebook message."

"*Facebook*? O no!" Rewa was mortified now. She felt like the whole world now believed the lie of her affair with Chief Ralph Eke.

What was she going to do about it now? Her *wrongly* perceived affair was now on the *world-wide-web*!

Rien chuckled at Rewa's response. She knew her eldest sister was not much of a social media person and knew she was clueless as to how it all worked.

"That isn't how it works, sis. Jas sent me a *personal* message on Facebook. She didn't *post* your alleged affair on the net," Rien said, laughing at her eldest sister. She deliberately did not include that she was sure by now that *Scope* Magazine had published the story on the net themselves and did not need Jas' help doing so. Rewa would have an aneurism if she mentioned that, Rien mused silently. Rewa was the most private of her sisters and, in some cases, probably the most naïve too, never mind the fact that she was the eldest.

"Jas mentioned she'd read somewhere that I was about to become the sister-in-law of one of the most eligible bachelors back home, and I was like, that's news to me! It wasn't Sede who leaked *your big news,* sis..." Rien teased her older sister, whom she loved so dearly. She secretly hoped it was true, though, that Rewa was involved with Ralph Eke as she could not wait for Rewa to find love and settle down. She was one of the greatest people Rien knew. She was loving, caring, and every bit the *mother hen* over her younger siblings. Rien believed she would make a great wife to the right man. She just prayed it would happen soon.

"Glad to hear it, but it hasn't been easy, you know...I feel as if everyone has believed a great big lie! He is *just a client* who showed his appreciation for the work I did on his building. The paparazzi certainly went to town *doctoring* the picture of him presenting me with flowers at the commissioning of the place. It's frustrating, to say the least!" Rewa whined to her youngest sister. Rien was usually the most sympathetic of her sisters, and Rewa loved her for it.

"So tell me, sis, I couldn't find any photos of him on the net. Is he good-looking? Is he your type? I mean, he's a chief...the picture I have in my head of a chief is someone *old* and *fat*!" Rien said, giggling excitedly. Her giggling became infectious, and Rewa could not help herself; she giggled too.

"*Dude!* I can't deny that he is handsome, though! He looks *anything* but the kind of chief you just described and the kind I also had in my head before I met him. He is the *proverbial tall, lean, dark, and handsome* guy every girl dreams of...only trouble is he is so cocky and obnoxious and a bit too used to having his own way. That, for me, is the most irritating quality a guy could possess. So, to answer your second question, sis, no, he definitely *isn't* my type *personality-wise* anyway." Rewa's giggles had now been replaced by a frown as she finished, remembering Ralph Eke's rude ways.

She then changed the subject and enquired about her new nephew. She could not wait to take a short break soon so she could join the rest of the family on a visit to Texas to meet him.

* * * *

A month later, Rewa was in the long line at Heathrow airport, waiting to go through immigration. As far as airline *fast tracks* were, this one was appalling, and she wondered now if it had been worth paying the extra sum for her class of travel. She had just arrived at *Heathrow* airport from Dallas after visiting her sister and adorable new nephew, *Anjola*. She was now in transit and her connecting flight home was not till another twelve hours. She, therefore, decided to leave the airport, go into town and check into a nearby hotel. She needed to rest for a while, freshen up and perhaps do a bit of shopping in London before she caught the next flight home. She was tired; the flight in from Dallas, Texas, had been ten long hours.

It was mid-August, and the weather was nice and warm though it was just about eight o'clock in the morning. Finally, after getting through immigration and on her way out of the airport, Rewa spotted Chief Ralph Eke, also on his way out of the busy airport. It appeared he had just arrived from somewhere too. She took a sharp breath and released it slowly when she realized a greeting was unavoidable, as he had seen her too. He was the last person she needed to see at that moment. She had not seen or heard from him since she sent him that message through his PA, declining to work on his UK project. She had been pleased that he had got it and perhaps decided to employ the services of another decorator.

Chief Eke was rather good-looking, Rewa thought, in a blue blazer over a white shirt and blue jeans. His hair looked greyer at the temple than she remembered, and he looked his usual resigned and tired self. This time, however, he managed a smile as he approached her. He had a brown leather pulley case in one hand and what appeared to be his passport wallet in the other.

"Hello, Rewa, fancy seeing you here," Ralph said. He seemed pleased to see her, which Rewa found awkward as he was usually withdrawn and aloof when they met. However, she tried to disguise what she really felt about seeing him there and then.

"Hello, Chief...Ralph," Rewa corrected herself. She just did not feel comfortable being in a *first-name* type of relationship with Ralph Eke. She wanted to keep it strictly professional and wondered why. Perhaps it had something to do with the rumors of their love affair. She self-consciously looked round now, as it suddenly dawned on her in that instant what type of picture they presented right there, in the arrival hall at Heathrow airport. They looked as though they had arrived on the same flight and were traveling together.

Ralph's smile deepened when he saw her expression. He knew what she was thinking but did not say anything as he was aware of how uncomfortable she was on the subject. Instead, he bent and took her small carry-on suitcase from her before she could say anything and gave her a nod in the direction of the exit doors, suggesting she follow him outside. Rewa followed his lead, her mouth agape again. She did not understand what he was doing but did not want to make a scene. The last thing she wanted was to draw any attention to them as she hoped no one who knew him would see them together again. After all, he was a public figure back home.

"Do you have a car picking you up?" Ralph asked as they got outside the bustling airport. It was the middle of summer, and there were children with parents all over the place.

"I'm planning to take a taxi, actually..." Rewa answered, a tad curtly. She looked around and could see a rank of black taxis across from where they stood. But before she could say anything else, Ralph said, "Come with me. I have a car waiting."

"Er...no...no thanks...I..." Rewa started but stopped abruptly as Ralph had started walking away, both their cases in hand, towards a sleek, black chauffeur-driven *Mercedes-Benz.*

The chauffeur, spotting Ralph, immediately jumped out of the car and loaded the trunk with both their cases before opening the passenger door for Rewa, who fumed. One could not tell if Ralph was aware of Rewa's anger at that moment, but once they were seated at the back of the car, he turned to her and asked with a half-smile,

"Where would you like to go, *madam*?" He asked in an exaggerated, humorous way.

How dare he think he could just whisk her away in his fly car? Rewa thought angrily. He was the most arrogant man she had ever met, and she had a good mind to put him in his place right there and then. He had not even asked her if she *needed* a ride. He had not thought about her plans; he had just assumed he could impose himself on her and *make* her follow him. Well, she was not having it!

"You really need to try listening to people and taking their views into consideration before you act. You didn't think you *needed* to ask *where* I was going or if I *was* going *anywhere*, did you?" Rewa said in a low tone, just so the driver could not hear what she was saying as she hated making a scene. She knew what she was saying did not make much sense, but in her anger, she had not quite planned on the delivery of what it was she was protesting about.

Ralph chuckled at her comment and asked, "Have you just told me off?" He found her anger rather amusing. "I mean, you *were* headed out of the airport when I saw you, so it was obvious to me that you *were leaving* to go *somewhere*. Who arrives at an airport just to stay there?" Ralph chuckled, emphasizing how silly that sounded, then continued. "All I did was offer you a lift out of the place. How is that a failure to *listen to people*?" He asked, smiling at her again, pretending not to know what the matter was.

His patronage annoyed Rewa even more, but she realized he was right. She had been going somewhere, but she refused to give in that easily. "That's exactly the point!" She insisted again in hushed tones. "You didn't exactly *offer* me a lift. You just *assumed* that I needed one from you!" She said through gritted teeth.

Ralph looked at her and shook his head, smiling still. She was an *enigma,* he thought within himself.

"Where to, sir?" The Caucasian driver asked. Ralph turned to Rewa again with a questioning look this time.

Rewa shifted in her seat uncomfortably, feeling rather silly now at her reaction. She hadn't pre-booked a room at any hotel as she had decided on the spur of the moment to leave the airport and check herself into a nearby one.

"I...I'm actually en route from Dallas. My connecting flight home isn't till later tonight, so I decided to check myself into a nearby hotel till it was time to leave. I haven't made any hotel reservations." She explained and then leaned towards the driver and asked, "Can you please take me to the nearest hotel? Any hotel close by would do, thank you."

"That won't be necessary," Ralph said. "You can come home with me, I have plenty of room, and when you're good and ready to return to the airport for your connecting flight, Warren will drive you, won't you, Warren?" Ralph asked the driver.

"I most definitely will, sir," Warren, the chauffeur, responded politely.

"Er...no thank you, I would rather check in to a nearby hotel if you don't mind...*please,*" Rewa answered, but Ralph waived her off, saying, "I insist. *Maida Vale,* please, Warren." He instructed the driver. His phone began to ring at that point, and he raised a finger in that annoying way of his as if to say, *'Give me a moment'*.

Rewa had her mouth open to protest again about going to Ralph's house but shut it at that point and fell back in her seat, sulking like a defiant teenager who had been refused something by a parent. She had a good mind to shout *'STOP THIS CAR AT ONCE*

AND LET ME OUT!' to Warren but realized how ridiculous she would look if she did. She sat back instead, fuming silently as Ralph carried on with his phone conversation.

Some forty minutes later, Warren drove up the driveway of one of the most charming two-story buildings Rewa had ever seen. It was a corner piece on a very secluded lane, and from the surrounding properties, one did get the strong impression that people who lived in the neighborhood were affluent. There were tall hedges around the property such that one could not quite catch a glimpse of the building itself until one drove through the small entry and up the driveway. It was an old *Tudor* style house with black beams on the walls and huge windows. The lawn was neatly mowed, and there were a couple of large oak trees on the far right side of the property. The house stood elegant and proud in the middle of the large expanse of land. It was magnificent.

Rewa's parents also owned a couple of grand houses here in the UK. However, they were unusually large with expensive, ornate furnishing. If she had planned this detour, she would have made arrangements to have the keys to one of them ready for her to pick up, but she had not, hence her plans to check into a nearby hotel from the airport. Her parents' houses were, however, nothing like this one. No, there was something different and unusually welcoming about this particular house. It was picturesque and made Rewa want to see more of it. The interior decorator in her leaped with pleasure and anticipation as she drank in her surroundings. It was spectacular, and she absolutely loved it. It was not as large and showy as her parents' ostentatious homes, but it was elegant in a very modest way.

"This is a lovely house," Rewa mumbled absent-mindedly, staring out of the car window as Warren pulled up in front of the house. She absorbed the breathtaking environment, momentarily forgetting her anger with her host for *dragging* her there, and could not wait to get indoors. She wondered what it looked like on the inside. She would have begged at that moment for an invitation indoors.

Ralph watched Rewa's every reaction as she took in her new environment. He could not explain why but he was pleased that she appeared to appreciate her surroundings. He usually could not care less what people thought about him or anything he owned. As grateful as he was for his numerous possessions and the fact that he could afford them, he never lost sight of the fact that they were just mere *chattel*. As far as he was concerned, they were material things, and he had said that to his son Israel many times. Ralph was proud too that he had raised Israel to understand that hard work did pay off and that it was not what a man owned that defined him as successful. *Character*, he had always said to his son, was far more important.

The double doors leading into the huge house swung open as they alighted from the car and a lady dressed in a black and white uniform came out to meet them. She clearly was the housekeeper, and Rewa judged her to be from The Philippines. She was followed by an older black gentleman, also in a uniform, and they both greeted Ralph warmly and carried their luggage in. *No wonder he was so spoiled,* Rewa thought. *He has a housekeeper and butler to wait on him hand and foot!* She hissed almost audibly.

Ralph made a hand gesture towards the door, inviting Rewa to walk in front of him into the house. Just as she had imagined, the large hallway they walked into was as enchanting as the exterior. There was a grand, curved staircase made out of wroth iron leading upstairs and an elaborate gold framed round table with a large bouquet of fresh flowers, in an equally large glass vase sitting on it, right in the middle of the hallway. The floors were laid with black and white tiles that reminded Rewa of a chess board. There was also a large chandelier hanging from the ceiling. It was simply exquisite. As a decorator, Rewa would not have changed a thing.

Ralph enquired about someone from *Manila*, the housekeeper. He introduced Rewa as his guest to her and asked for a room to be set up for her forthwith, after which he turned to Rewa and said, "You must be as hungry and tired as I am. What do you say we have breakfast, after which Manila will show you to your room?" It was the first time he had ever asked her anything, Rewa observed. He usually just gave orders. She mused silently.

"That would be nice, thank you. You have a lovely home," she said again as she walked further into the beautiful house.

Ralph had mentioned on their way from the airport that he had flown in that morning to attend his son's graduation ceremony from Medical School the following day. So he *does* have kids, she had thought within herself and wondered what type of father he was, given his obvious impatience with people.

"Thank you," he said in response to Rewa's compliment and said, "This way, please."

Rewa mused within herself as she noticed that Ralph Eke seemed to be making more of an effort at being a gentleman. Gone was the sarcastic-looking, bossy ex-client she was getting used to. She, however, did not say anything as she followed him into the equally spectacular dining room. There was an array of food displayed on the large oval-shaped table, and again, Ralph gestured for Rewa to sit down, and himself followed suit. Rewa noticed he did not sit at the head of the table. Instead, he sat across the table from her, observing her as she pleasantly took in her unfamiliar surroundings.

"Can I ask who decorated this house?" Rewa could not help asking as she sat to eat. The elderly gentleman who seemed like the butler waited on hand to see if they needed anything else till Ralph signaled that he left them alone.

"My late wife actually did a lot of it. She had a *flair...*" Ralph answered, spooning some scrambled eggs onto his plate. "Israel, my son described it as *'dated'* a while ago. He thinks it needs a *facelift*. Those were his exact words, by the way," he explained.

"And what do you think?" Rewa asked, buttering a slice of toast.

"I'm not sure. You're the decorator...do you think it requires a *facelift*?" He asked her playfully.

"Looks perfectly fine to me," Rewa answered. "It's *quaint*...and the interior fits the age and type of building it is. I was under the impression the property which needed renovating was in *Surrey* and not *Maida Vale*?" She asked before she could stop herself. They had not talked about her refusal to decorate Ralph's new property, and looking at him now, Rewa wished she had not brought it up.

Ralph chuckled and put his fork down. He studied Rewa in an amused way. She suddenly grew self-conscious in that instant and looked down at her plate. What was it about this guy that made her feel silly? She began to feel guilty at the way she had refused to decorate his latest acquisition, just to prove a point to him that she was not going to be bossed around.

"You mean the property you *stubbornly refused* to decorate?" Ralph asked her, smiling.

"I really don't do residential properties, especially when...when..." Rewa trailed off when she realized what she had been about to say.

"When what, Rewa?" Ralph asked. He was amused now and could see the defiance rising again from her disposition.

"...especially when the client is as arrogant and cocky as you are..." She just blurted it out without much thought. "There, I said it!" Rewa said and exhaled like a deflated hot air balloon. She had finally got it out.

Ralph's immediate reaction surprised her. He burst out laughing.

"Let *you* tell it," he said and laughed some more. Rewa was not sure how to react to his laughter.

"I see you think it's funny," she said, glaring at him now. "Besides, what do you mean by that?" She asked curiously.

"Well, if anyone is arrogant and cocky, it definitely isn't me. You seem to be the one with a *chip on your shoulder*. It's as though you *always* have a point to prove," Ralph gently explained as if he were talking to a petulant child, which made Rewa even angrier now.

"Of course, I *have a point to prove*...with pushy, condescending people like you, you can bet I have *a point to prove*. You just showed up at my office, *without an appointment,* and on a Sunday too, I might add, issuing orders without my input...just who exactly do you think you are? If my refusal to let you *force* me into doing something I don't want to makes me appear to have *a chip on my shoulder*, then so be it!" Rewa said defiantly. She put the piece of toast she was eating down, tossed the *napkin* on her lap onto the table angrily, and then looked at him. Struggling to control her temper, she said, "I thank you for your kind and generous hospitality. Now, if you don't mind, can I have my bag brought down, so I can be on my way, please?"

Ralph, sensing that she was now really vexed and about to leave, looked at her for a moment and said softly, "Relax, will you, Rewa. I was only teasing. I apologize if I have offended you in any way since we met or if I come across as *cocky and arrogant*. Please don't leave, finish your food and rest a while." It was a humble plea, one which made Rewa feel even sillier now. Perhaps she had read him all wrong. She hesitated for a bit, embarrassed by her rudeness and the calm way he had responded to it. She nodded in response, unable to speak as his humility *and* maturity had completely thrown her aback.

"*Great*! Can you also do me a favor and at least come and see the new place before you leave for the airport? We could take a drive to Surrey so that you can give me your opinion on what you think of the place. All this, of course, after you've had a chance to catch some rest.

Rewa nodded again, and they both ate in silence for a moment, and then Ralph, sensing her embarrassment, told her his plans for the new place. He explained that he had bought it for investment purposes. It was a block of four flats he wanted to renovate and rent out to holidaymakers who visited London.

She's something. Ralph thought after their meal when he got into the master bedroom. He had never had anyone speak to him the way Omorewa Ilo had, but instead of being irritated by it, he loved it! It endeared her to him in a strange way. Under her cool and calm exterior laid a feistiness that excited him. She definitely was no *shove-over,* and he had noticed it from their very first meeting. Ralph had seen the flash of anger in her eyes when he had ended their very first meeting abruptly. She had referred to him as *pushy, arrogant,* and *condescending* too. He grinned, thinking of all she had said at breakfast.

The truth was Ralph Eke was not used to being *told off* by anyone, particularly because of his position in society. Most people sucked up to him because of what they believed they could get from him, and a lot were sycophants, especially ladies. Omorewa Ilo's reaction had therefore caught and held his attention. She was special because she was not afraid to challenge him or say what she felt about him. He had not seen that in a woman in a long time. Her *spunk* was a quality he admired about her. He really was interested in getting to know her a bit more. She had sparked something within him, and he had now decided to play it coolly and turn on the charm. He decided he liked Omorewa Ilo; he liked her a lot. He wondered what her father, his client, Chief Benjamin Ilo, would have to say about them as an item.

* * * *

Rewa loved the room Manila had set up for her. It was beautiful in an understated way. Everything seemed new and fresh, and she had even put a bunch of fresh flowers on the nightstand which was fragrant and brightened up the place. More importantly, the bed was super comfortable; she observed as she lay in it.

Rewa wondered about Ralph Eke's late wife. It was obvious from the decor of the house that she had impeccable taste. Rewa had noticed a large gold framed portrait of a lady hanging on the wall as she and Manila ascended the stairs on her way to the guest room after breakfast. Rewa had asked who the lady in the photo was, and Manila said she was the late Mrs. Eke. She was beautiful, and Rewa wondered how old the portrait was.

Rewa's mind drifted back to her conversation with Ralph Eke at breakfast. First, she could not believe she was in his London home and had even agreed to go and inspect his Surrey property. She chided herself for being so rude to him in his own home after he had been kind to offer her a lift into town from the airport, fed her, and even offered her a lift back to the airport later.

Why had she reacted the way she had to him? Was it her pride or the fact that he got to her in a way that made her feel vulnerable and inadequate? Why was she so uptight lately? She made up her mind to start praying about her touchy attitude and to apologize to Ralph later, though she still strongly believed he deserved *some* if not all of what she had said to him. A part of her, however, felt she had overreacted just before she drifted off into a deep, sweet sleep in the lovely guest room of the beautiful *Tudor* style home in London owned by Chief Ralph Eke.

CHAPTER SEVENTEEN

More time had been what she had asked for, and Earl was trying really hard to be a gentleman and give her just that, but it was beginning to feel like one of the hardest things he ever had to do. It had been almost two weeks, and he wished he had asked for a specific day to check back for an answer. The silence was driving him crazy!

Earl was grateful for the distraction his new hotel project served in the meantime but his weekends and evenings had more or less suddenly become empty. He had been out with a couple of his old schoolmates a few times, but they were all married, and there were only so many outings one could have with married folks, they all stayed home with their wives and kids eventually. So, in the meantime, Earl waited patiently for an answer from Labake as to whether or not she would let him be her friend. He was going to give it a few more days, after which he planned to give her a call.

Earl's mind drifted again and again to the incident at the beach the other day, particularly Labake's reaction to his offer of friendship and the ugly scars on her back. No wonder she was as closed off as she was, he thought. He had been alarmed when he saw them and wondered what else her husband had done to her. It was obvious he had not only broken the skin on her back, but he had also broken her mentally and psychologically. How could anyone be capable of doing that to another? Earl wondered. He believed only a savage animal could have done that, and this further made it a matter of importance for him to remain in Labake's life somehow.

He believed Labake needed to be *nursed* back to living the type of life she deserved and that she needed some protection. What or who from, he was not quite sure, but Earl just could not imagine leaving her to herself. He needed to make things better for her as she had clearly been through hell in her marriage, and strangely enough, he felt it behooved him to make things right for both her and Ella.

* * * *

"So Labake, how is friendship with Earl going?" Dr. Stella asked gently. She had formed a particular fondness for Labake and had come to understand that she displayed all the symptoms of *Battered Woman Syndrome*. In Labake's case, it ran so deeply and had almost completely eroded her natural ability to think the way a well-adjusted, adult woman should. She had been with her abusive husband since her teenage years and had thus been conditioned by him to think, reason, and behave a certain way. He had more or less raised her before she even became a young adult. As a result, it was a challenge to determine her real personality had she not been subjected to the abuse in the first place.

Their sessions were improving in the sense that Labake was able to talk about her feelings and emotions a bit more openly than she had at their first few meetings. What was even more amazing was that she did not even need to be prompted most times. Once she sat, Labake would usually just get to whatever was on her mind. On very few occasions, though, she would be quiet and would almost need to be cajoled into talking.

Dr. Stella believed Labake to be on the mend, slowly but surely. In most cases, she tried to let her patients confront and accept their past in such a way that it had little or no influence on their future. She gave them coping skills to manage and accept the past, present, and future as separate life occurrences. The aim was to help them form and develop new patterns, all with a view to setting new perspectives and outlooks for the future.

Labake sighed at Dr. Stella's question. Earl had come up in their sessions a few weeks ago when Dr. Stella asked if there were any male figures in her life presently. Labake had said no at the time as she had not even considered Earl to be a part of her life. However, she further asked if any man had expressed an interest in her since her separation from her husband. Labake had slowly nodded and mentioned Earl but had swiftly and firmly stated her disinterest in pursuing any relationship with anyone at this time. Dr. Stella had noted it and moved on. She, however, brought it up at every session since then in an attempt to get Labake to talk about it. She was fully aware that Labake still felt as though she was doing something wrong by entertaining any sort of friendship with Earl. It was as if she believed she was betraying her husband by even talking to him.

Though Earl had kept his word and had not pushed for anything stronger between them, his *'putting it out there'* that he had more than a platonic friendship in mind made it harder for Labake to fully let go with him, no matter how hard she tried. She wondered now if she would ever be able to fully let go with *any* man at all, as it just seemed impossible to her. When she mentioned this to Dr. Stella, she posed another question to Labake.

"Why do you think you may not be able to fully let go with Earl or any other man Labake?" Dr. Stella had an idea why Labake felt this way, but she needed her to talk through the particular emotion she was feeling at that minute.

"I guess I really am beginning to see why I do need counseling...it's as if something within me...a radar, if you like, is broken and needs fixing...I just don't know how to let go with Earl or anyone...I feel like I'm incapable of trusting *anyone,* let alone *feeling* anything for anyone. It's almost as if I'm doing something wrong by just even talking to Earl. I don't know...I'm stuck..." Labake trailed off as was her custom. Dr. Stella observed she never fully completed a sentence. She would start talking when prompted by a question and was able to articulate exactly what she was feeling in so many ways but would then stop mid-sentence as though she suddenly felt she had said too much.

"Why Labake? Why do you feel *stuck*?" Dr. Stella prodded. She needed Labake to try and find the reasons for the way she felt by herself, and though her session was almost over, Dr. Stella refused to break the chain of this particular conversation as she knew it was pivotal to Labake's therapy.

"I'm not sure. I feel so guilty about a lot of things...as though I'm doing something wrong. I find myself still questioning *everything* I do...with Ella, Earl...just *everything*...!" Dr. Stella could see the frustration in Labake's gait, though she could not quite see her eyes because she stared into space. It was obvious she struggled to find the right expression for the exact emotion she seemed to be contending with within. She also appeared to be processing her thoughts as she spoke.

Dr. Stella was quite pleased that Labake was making such progress. She was like a wounded, caged animal who needed to escape and find the freedom to live. Her apparent struggle at that moment was proof that she now realized she needed to help herself in order to finally get on the road to recovery. However, *Recovery* perhaps was not even what Labake needed, Dr. Stella concluded as she quietly observed her patient. Labake's real personality had never really surfaced, given the stage of life when her abuse started and the length of time it had gone on. The plan was for her to develop a path to self-discovery and then perhaps start building from there. Dr. Stella was determined to help her get there.

"...wondering if he would approve and what he'd do if he didn't. Even after all this time away from him...he still has the upper hand...he's still in control..." Labake continued without any prompting from the doctor, who knew *he* was her abusive husband. She said it in a whisper as if she had found the solution. Realization seemed to have finally set in, and she suddenly broke down in that instant and began to cry. It was the first time she had since starting therapy over two months ago. It was as if admitting Vince still controlled her every move, even after all this time, made her realize how much of him she still carried within her.

"...he was right after all...right when he said I was nothing without him...that I couldn't survive...or make it on my own without him..." Labake sobbed as she spoke, eyes and nose dripping. She felt pathetic and hopeless as she spoke.

"What else did Vince say to you, Labake?" Dr. Stella asked, passing the box of tissues she kept on the coffee table to Labake as the tears kept flowing. She needed Labake to spit it all out in the hope that she would realize how awkward it sounded and perhaps get her angry with the lies her husband had fed her during her time with him. Anger was great emotion in times like these. Dr. Stella needed Labake to feel angry as it had a way of bringing out the courage most people were not aware they possessed.

"*What else*, Labake?" She urged gently.

"...that I was good for nothing, useless to myself and everyone...I couldn't amount to anything...he brought me out of the slums and...and that...that I'd return there without him," Labake shuddered violently as the tears continued.

It was heart-wrenching, but Dr. Stella knew these were tears that she had bottled up for years. She sat silently for a moment, observing her patient as she sobbed. She felt compassion for this young woman who had been through hell and back. She had never seen Labake this way in the two months since she began her therapy sessions. No, Labake was not one to ever let her vulnerability show. She had been trained and pre-conditioned to bear all things herself. For Dr. Stella, this was great progress in her therapy.

"...and was he right, Labake? Do you believe these things Vince said to you to be true?" Labake looked up at Dr. Stella at that point. Her eyes and tear-stained face were reddened, and she looked vulnerable as she blew into the tissue in her hands and shook her head the way a child would. It was as if realization dawned on her again as she processed what the doctor had asked her.

"How long has it been since you left Vince, Labake? Have you or Ella been ill even once since you left him? Have you not fed and clothed both of you in almost three years since leaving Vince? Have you not stood on your own two feet and taken decisions for yourself and your child *all by yourself* after all this time? Have you not proved Vince wrong? Can't you see that you have done exactly what he said you couldn't in the last three years? Can you not see that all he said to you were lies, Labake? Lies to control your mind and make you feel powerless to help yourself?" Dr. Stella asked softly. She watched Labake's reaction as she asked each question. She needed Labake to see how simple the answers were to each of them.

With tears finally subsiding, Labake looked at Dr. Stella steadily for a moment and exhaled deeply. She then said simply,

"He lied…I do see…I proved him wrong. Vince was wrong…I am not useless without him…I see that now. Thank you, Dr. Stella…thank you." It was barely a whisper, but it was a great revelation.

Dr. Stella knew at that moment that Labake got it. She saw a flicker in her eyes, something she had not seen in them in the ten weeks since they started their sessions. It was enough for her today. She believed there was hope yet for Labake and that she was going to be alright in the long run.

As she drove back to work that afternoon, Labake thought about all Dr. Stella had said and began to feel as if she had been deceived by Vince. He had succeeded in *brainwashing* her into believing she was incapable of doing anything right or succeeding at anything without him. He had sold her a lie, and she had foolishly bought it. It was beginning to dawn on her that he had tricked her into believing so many falsities about herself. She thought about all the lies he had fed her and made her believe and was now beginning to see how evil her husband had been.

* * * *

It had taken almost three weeks for Labake to decide what her answer to Earl was going to be. She had listened to her sister, Laide, and had decided to take Dr. Stella's advice as well. They had both thought friendship with Earl could not do any harm so long as she drew boundaries that she was comfortable with, and Labake had finally begun to warm up to the idea.

She had dragged her feet on the issue and could not bring herself to tell him until he lost his patience and rang her up one Friday evening. He had been forceful about the demanding way in which he had enquired about her decision, but Labake had not minded and, in fact, thought it rather cute in a weird way that he appeared to be a bit frustrated when he asked.

"Look, Labake, I have tried my best to give you the time you requested, but I'm sorry, I can't keep waiting to hear from you. I need to know your decision, but I must warn you that I'm not prepared to take no for an answer, especially as I have..." Labake cut him off by chuckling at what he was saying. She was amused at how frustrated he sounded. Was he really that *friendless?* She mused.

Earl, on the other hand, was pleasantly surprised that Labake found what he said amusing. He paused momentarily, not quite sure how to respond to her chuckle.

"I won't mind us being friends, Earl," Labake said simply, which threw Earl off even further. He was suddenly tongue-tied as he had not expected that answer from her.

"However,I ask that you be patient as I suspect I may not be as good a friend to you in return...and would therefore need some time and understanding from you. We could start slowly...as I do have a tendency to...to clam up at times when I feel...when I feel like things are getting a bit too... perhaps a bit too much..." Labake continued but stopped mid-sentence again as if she was expecting a negative reaction from Earl.

Dr. Stella had said honesty was the best policy and had encouraged her to always speak her mind and be forthright with whatever it was she was feeling. That was not something Labake was used to; she kept her feelings bottled up and sometimes did not even know how she felt about anything. Vince had never asked for her thoughts or feelings on anything, and sharing them was never an option. She was learning to say what she felt emotionally and to give an opinion as and when she deemed it necessary, so long as it concerned *her*, *her* daughter, and what *she* was thinking. Those had been Dr. Stella's exact words.

Earl was amazed at what Labake said to him and was rather stupefied by the words she spoke. It was the longest sentence she had ever made to him, and he was glad he had called instead of waiting any further.

"I totally...totally agree that we should take it slow. Please let me know whenever you feel like things are getting a bit...too much...*friend*." Earl mimicked Labake's exact words with some humor in his voice. He was happy she caught his humor as they both laughed at the term *'friend'*.

Labake was beginning to believe Earl was even more affable than she had first thought. He was so different from her husband. He was agreeable and treated her respectfully, even when she expected him to respond to her in anger. She had not quite seen him upset yet, but something within her sensed he was not the volatile type. Then she remembered that Vince had not appeared so either, in the beginning. He had been quite amiable when they had first met. He had appeared very easygoing and had treated her with what she had believed to be love and kindness at the time. *Ha*! If only that had been true.

Vince had turned out to be quite the opposite of what he had led Labake and her family to believe. He had turned into a monster rather quickly, and Labake had wondered many times if he was even mentally stable. He had been immensely unreasonable and irrational, flipping his cool at the slightest instance. No explanation was ever enough to keep him from giving her a beating, especially once his mind was made up. He had always misjudged and misunderstood her every action, even when she had done something nice for him. In the end, she had given up trying to explain herself and the reasons behind her every action as he never accepted them as true anyway. Somewhere in his head, Labake believed Vince had seen her as the adversary and treated her as such *all* the time.

Thinking about it now, Labake could not remember Vince ever apologizing to her about anything in the years she had been with him. Not even for the pregnancies she lost as a result of his violence. He had never spoken to her softly or tenderly but had treated her with disdain as if she had been a great disappointment to him.

Dr. Stella, however, made her realize that Vince had treated her that way so he could manipulate and control her behavior. He had dominated absolutely every aspect of her being, and she had enabled him by showing absolutely no resistance and conforming to his every wish in an attempt to please him. Unfortunately, she had never succeeded at that. In fact, he made her feel as if she had gotten worse as their years together went by. Vince had made her feel worthless and inadequate. He had not only made her feel like a waste of space but he had also said it to her over and over again. Labake vowed she was never going to give anyone that kind of control over her life *ever* again.

CHAPTER EIGHTEEN

Chief Benjamin Ilo shifted uncomfortably in his chair. He had wisely asked his Personal Assistant to hold all calls today and also asked him to inform the guards at the gate outside that he would not be receiving any guests today. He needed time to think as he had a lot on his mind. He was at his desk in his study and desperately needed some *alone* time for a change. He had said as much to *Philomena*, his wife of forty-four years. He didn't want any interruptions, even by her.

Mena, as he called her, and his three daughters had received the fright of their lives a year and a half ago when he had suffered an angina. Mena had found him herself on the floor of the den, clutching his chest and gasping for breath. She believed it was sheer providence that had made her walk into the den at the exact time she had. It was what had saved her dearly beloved *Benny's* life, as she fondly referred to him. Since then, she was known to pop her head in through the door every now and again, just to ensure he was alright.

Chief Ilo loved his wife beyond words and knew he was the *king of her castle* too, but the last thing he needed today was her fretfulness. To his relief, she had bid him farewell and left for a party with her bosom friend *Mrs. Thomas* a few minutes ago, leaving the fragrance of her strong perfume in her wake, permeating the entire house. He was sure, however, that she had left strict instructions with the resident steward, Emeka, to keep an eye on him as Moses, the PA, had been sent home early today.

Chief Ilo got out of his chair and walked to the large window which overlooked the other side of the mansion he had built several years before. However, he could not appreciate the beautiful, well-tended garden Mena was so proud of. His mind was on a far more pressing issue, one he had kept to himself for over twenty-eight years and had even completely forgotten about until he had that ugly dream again, overnight. It had been at least a couple of years since he last had it, and now he wondered what had caused it to haunt his sleep again.

He turned back to his large desk and reached for his pills and the glass of water next to them. The last thing he needed was another episode as he could already feel the pressure building up in his chest. Until the angina, Benjamin Ilo had believed himself to be quite healthy, and except for his small pot belly, he was not bad looking for a sixty-nine-year-old man. Mena had, however, put him on a strict diet of seafood, fruits, and vegetables since the angina, causing a marked reduction in his waistline. He did not care much for the restricted diet, but he appreciated his shrinking tummy.

"We can't afford to take any chances, *Benny*. You could have died!" Mena had said when she explained his new diet. Benjamin knew she was reacting out of fear but also knew not to argue with her once her mind was made up. He had now resigned himself to a far healthier lifestyle than he was used to, and Mena was pleased he had embraced the new diet without any major complaint.

Benjamin Ilo swallowed the pills with some water and sat down behind the large ornate desk again. The television was on, but he was not watching it; he was far too distracted to even notice it. He closed his eyes and leaned back into the leather-bound swivel chair. He could still see Iyabo's angry face in his mind's eye as she screamed how unhappy she was with him, swearing and spitting endless curses at him. It had been such a vivid dream, one he did not think he could forget in a hurry.

Benjamin Ilo knew it was time to do what he should have done many years ago. It was time to right the one wrong which had haunted him all these years, though he had deliberately ignored it and even forgotten about it at some point. It had been so many years ago, but he knew he had to go in search of her. He did not quite know how to go about his search and was not entirely sure where to begin or whom to confide in. He only trusted a handful of people in his life and they were all within his family. He, however, knew he could not let any of them in on his predicament yet.

Initially, Benjamin Ilo had worried about how Mena and the girls would react when they found out. He was quite aware that he would have to brace himself up for some reaction when they did, but he had decided to climb that bridge when he got to it. It was inevitable, and they would eventually find out that there was a strong possibility that they had a stepchild and younger half-sibling, respectively, out there, somewhere.

Suffering an angina some eighteen months ago had been the rude shock that brought Benjamin Ilo to the realization that no man was promised the next day. That near-death experience, coupled with the nightmare he had, made it all the more paramount that he found Iyabo as soon as possible. What his wife and daughters would think was the least of his worries at the moment, he was suddenly overcome by a strong need to do the right thing.

What Benjamin Ilo found even more worrying about the dream was how clear it was that even after all this time, Iyabo still bore some animosity towards him. He could not blame her, though. After all, he had denied the pregnancy she had claimed was his some twenty-eight years ago. He was ashamed of himself and of the fact that he had left her and never looked back. How could he have done that to her? He had daughters, for crying out loud. If any man did that to any of his girls, he would castrate him! He chided himself silently.

At some point, Benjamin Ilo had not believed that Iyabo's pregnancy was truly his. He had believed that getting pregnant was a ploy by Iyabo to entrap him. He had, of course, also worried that Mena would be shattered first by his illicit affair, second with someone of Iyabo's caliber, and third, and worst still, that the affair had produced an illegitimate child! He was sure that she would have left him and that his girls would have been devastated by the whole sordid affair.

He had believed Iyabo to be a *gold-digger* who probably was uncertain of the paternity of the child but had settled for him only because he was affluent. Thinking back now, she had never given him a reason to believe she had other lovers, but he had chosen to believe she did as it had been convenient to do so at the time. How cowardly he was to have done that to her.

His immediate reaction after Iyabo disclosed her pregnancy had been to insist she got rid of it the following day. He had threatened never to see her again if she did not. Of course, she had cried and begged to keep their love child, claiming she loved him and did not intend to bother him or affect his marriage in any way. She had been quite prepared to keep their affair and child secret if only he would let her keep the pregnancy. He had vehemently refused and had reached inside his pocket, brought out a wad of cash, and dropped it on the bed he had just vacated, insisting she had an abortion the following day. It was at that point he walked out of her room and out of her life in anger and what he now knew to be cowardice too. That was the last time he had seen Iyabo, on her knees, pleading with him not to go, some twenty-eight years before now.

Thinking back now, Chief Ilo could only attribute his reaction at the time to the fact that he had been much younger and foolish. He wished now that he had handled the situation differently. It was his biggest regret in life so far, and he was suddenly consumed by the need to make things right.

Iyabo had claimed to be over three months pregnant at the time. He had never visited her again and had assumed she did have the abortion. He had never even bothered to confirm that she had. He wondered now what the odds were that she had kept the pregnancy and had the baby. She had never come looking for him and had never contacted him to date, making him conclude it was probable she had terminated the pregnancy as he had instructed her to. Besides, Iyabo had been so malleable and virtually worshipped the ground he walked on; she did whatever he told her to do without question. Chief Ilo knew now that he had taken advantage of that fact.

Suddenly, a thought crept into Chief Ilo's mind. What if Iyabo *had* kept the pregnancy and had a baby boy? His eyes brightened, and the corners of his lips curved into a small smile at the thought. Then he would have an *heir apparent* to his vast empire, an *Ilo* to carry on the family name. He had hoped that he would have a male child when he and Mena were younger, but there had been complications with his last daughter, Omorien's birth, and they had both agreed to stop trying for a son after her birth. He had decided he did not want to ever again put his dear wife through the rigors of childbirth. He, however, now toyed with the idea that he could have a son somewhere, out there in the world, and the thought warmed his belly to no end. Now, he *had* to find Iyabo and ask for her forgiveness for the way he had treated her. He also needed to confirm if he did have a child with her.

If he did have a child by Iyabo, he definitely wanted to meet and perhaps introduce him or her to the rest of his family. He never wanted his wife or daughters to find out any other way if he died suddenly. If he did have an illegitimate child by Iyabo, he was also quite prepared to compensate her financially for the trouble of bringing the child up alone and without his support. He hoped now that she had kept the pregnancy and had the child, though he knew it would affect his family one way or another.

Chief Ilo knew he needed help in trying to locate Iyabo and that whatever help he got in trying to find her would have to be as discreet as possible as he did not want anyone finding out yet. The tabloids would have a field day with the story, and he could just see the headlines now,

'CHIEF BENJAMIN ILOS SECRET LOVE CHILD'

It would have such a horrendous impact on his image and on his family, particularly his darling, Mena, if it ever came out that he had a love child by an illiterate woman, a complete nobody from the wrong side of town too. He could never have that leaked. Therefore, he had to manage the situation as delicately as possible.

He did not know how or when it started, but as far as Benjamin Ilo could remember, people of all sexes and ages lined up outside his home and office building, soliciting financial aid from him. Everyone in society knew he was a kind-hearted philanthropist and that he never turned anyone away without rendering them help, one way or another. He counted it a privilege to give to the needy and considered it his way of giving something back to society. In fact, he had set up a special fund exclusively for this purpose, and that was how he had met Iyabo in the first place.

She was one of the numerous people who waited in line to see him at his office for financial help. He had judged her to be in her early twenties at the time. She was a single parent to a two-year-old daughter whom she had with a man who refused to acknowledge the child. She had brought the emaciated child with her at the time, claiming she was unable to take care of her as she had no money for food. She was illiterate and had no formal education whatsoever. She was a bag of bones herself and looked rather ill at the time of their first meeting. Chief Ilo had felt compassion for her and had been quite prepared to send her away with some money for food, but she had declined. She said she cooked well and just needed some money to start a small food hawking business.

Chief Ilo had been quite moved by her story and impressed by her specific request. She was aware of her gift and knew it could be a source of livelihood for herself and her daughter. He had given her money for food to eat in the interim and more to start the business.

Iyabo had further impressed him when she returned a year later to thank him and share her small success with him. She was making a steady income from the sale of the food she cooked and had become quite popular in the locality where she lived. She had brought him a cheap bottle of wine which she had painstakingly wrapped as a gift to show her appreciation for his help. She looked a lot better than he could remember and had gained a few pounds since their first meeting. In fact, he had been unable to recognize her until she introduced herself. They had got talking, and one thing had led to another without any deliberate intention on either of their parts. They began an affair that lasted a few months.

What had drawn Chief Ilo to Iyabo was the fact that she had not been looking for a mere *hand-out* from him. Instead, she had found her talent and hashed out a plan to turn it into a sustainable business. That suggested to him that she was not lazy as most of the other people he helped were but had an industrious side to her. She had also returned to show her appreciation for the money she received from him. Most people he helped never returned with an update. They showed their profuse appreciation once he handed them the money but never came back to share their success stories with him, not to mention bringing him a gift. These were factors that caused Iyabo to receive and hold his attention and, perhaps, endeared her to him in the beginning.

The fact that Iyabo was now *easy on the eyes* did not help the situation and was also a factor in Chief Ilo having an affair with her, not-withstanding that she could not read or write. She was pretty, extremely neat and tidy, and an excellent cook. She also knew how to look after a man, as she had whenever he visited her in the room she lived in with her young daughter. She tended to his *every* need while they were together and was extremely obedient and respectful to him. She never argued with him, did as she was told, and treated him like royalty. Iyabo worshipped him with her body and everything she had without question, and he loved how she made him feel.

Chief Ilo knew he had no *real* feelings for Iyabo and never pretended he did. It just was not that type of relationship, and he was not with her for anything else but her complete adoration of him. He was quite aware she would have done *anything* for him, just like a dog would for its master. It was somewhat depraved of him, and he eventually came to his senses after a couple of months. He tried to call it off with her as he knew there would only ever be one woman for him, and that was his wife, whom he truly, deeply loved. He was, however, hooked on Iyabo and still could not explain why even now, years after. Perhaps he was *that* hooked on Iyabo's lavish affection for him and how she did it without expecting anything in return from him. She never asked anything of him except for his initial help in starting her food business. Her falling pregnant had been the factor that had jolted him back to his senses and had made him end it with her as abruptly as it had started.

Chief Ilo had only ever had one other affair since his marriage to Philomena. That had, however, been in the earlier days of his marriage when his wife had traveled to the United Kingdom to deliver their first daughter, and it had not lasted more than a month. Somehow, the affair with Iyabo had carried on for far longer than it should have.

It had been a rather clandestine relationship and involved him visiting her in the shack of a room she lived in once or twice a week when he could spare the time, usually in the early evenings. He had been quite careful and discrete about his visits to Iyabo. Even *Wahid*, his main driver, had been unaware of it. He would usually drive himself to the slums, have a great meal cooked by Iyabo, and, of course, have wild sex with her. They never really talked, and he gave her money from time to time for her upkeep and general wellbeing. Today, he wondered what it was that kept him going back to her.

Benjamin Ilo had never allowed Iyabo to visit him at the office again after she returned to show her appreciation for the money he had given her. He had told her never to come to his office when they started seeing each other as he did not want to raise any suspicions or be seen in public with her. Iyabo had complied and never came to his office after that, even after he stopped visiting her when she disclosed that she was pregnant. This was a fact that had made it easier for him to forget about her and her pregnancy.

* * * *

Rewa could not quite believe she had yielded to Ralph Eke's wish. He had somehow succeeded in having his way yet again and had managed to get a commitment from her to decorate his newly acquired apartment building in *Surrey, England*. Rewa was uncertain how it had happened, but contracts had been signed and exchanged, and the deed was done. Here she was now, six weeks later, in Surrey, supervising the project. The weather was great for a September and perfect for the extensive work she needed to do. Schools had resumed for the year, making the streets slightly lighter and the delivery of supplies to the site a lot easier during business hours.

As she needed to be close to the site, Rewa was lodged at a nearby *Air BnB*. Her parents' London homes were too far a commute to the site. Ralph had offered his own home for her to stay for the entire duration of the project, which Rewa hoped would be five months. He had also made his car and driver available to her whenever and wherever she needed to go, but Rewa had declined, preferring to do her own thing. She did not need to be waited on by his entire staff. She was a big girl and was quite capable of sorting herself out, and she had said as much to him to his utmost amazement.

Rewa had cleared her schedule as much as possible back home and was in contact with her interns via social media. Her plan was to travel back and forth as often as she had to, just to keep up with all other jobs scheduled for completion back home too. She had lined up all the professional workers she could lay her hands on here in Surrey to help aid the speedy completion of the project. So far, everything was going to plan, and she prayed it stayed that way with little or no hiccups.

Ralph had traveled back home because of his work, but they already had two very comprehensive meetings. Rewa was now fully sure of what her brief was and was ready to start work a week after their second meeting, which was a fortnight ago. They were also in touch via phone and social media if she needed further clarification on anything. This time, there were no go-betweens like Mrs. Atta to pass information through to Ralph, except for the odd communications with Yinka, Ralph's Personal Assistant.

Rewa remembered how rude she had been to Ralph after he gave her the lift from the airport and offered her a room in his home weeks before and smiled. Of course, she now knew why she had reacted to him that way in the first place. Hemust have thought she was the most ill-mannered person he had ever met as she had insulted him *in* his own home.

After breakfast, on that faithful morning when she had bumped into Ralph Eke at Heathrow airport and had been whisked away to his lovely home in *Maida Vale*, Rewa had taken a nap in the room Manila, Ralph's house-keeper, had prepared for her. She had slept like a baby for three hours, after which she had a shower and put on some fresh clothes which she had brought along in her carry-on luggage. The room had been so comfortable, and she felt refreshed and re-energized to face a trip into town and then back to the airport for the final leg of her journey home.

Ralph was seated in the library, reading the papers. He wanted to be ready when Rewa came back downstairs after her nap so that they could take the trip to Surrey. He needed to show her his new apartment building. He thought it best to seize the moment now that Rewa was here and had finally agreed to see the place. He did not want to give her the chance to change her mind.

"Rested?" Ralph asked when she knocked on the door which was ajar and stepped into the large room. Manila had mentioned that Chief Eke was in the library at the end of a long hallway just behind the elegant staircase. Rewa had wandered down the hallway in search of her host, still taking in the exquisite beauty of his London home. There was an array of family pictures on the walls and a couple of chandeliers hanging from the ceiling. The entire house made one feel as though its owner was quite important.

The library itself had a wall of different books and some leather-bound ones too. There were four armchairs at the center of the room, one of which Ralph sat in. There was a coffee table with a few more books on them too. On the other side was a large desk, and again, like the other rooms she had been in, there were a couple of bouquets of fresh flowers on the desk and coffee table, making Rewa wonder how often Manila changed them. All in all, just like the other rooms in the house, Rewa thought the library was rather enchanting.

Ralph placed the newspaper he was reading on the table, took off his glasses, uncrossed his outstretched legs, and rose from his chair. He gave her an appreciative look and managed a small but reluctant smile.

Rewa had on a large grey cardigan over a pair of blue jeans and low-heeled, knee-length rider's boots. Her make-up was light, and her hair was freshly combed, framing her beautiful face. She was quite the looker Ralph thought within himself but said instead,

"I wondered if you would be rested enough to get up in time for our visit to Surrey." He did not wait for a response from Rewa but reached for his sweater on the chair and asked, "Ready to go check this place out?"

Rewa's attraction for Ralph Eke suddenly hit home at that moment as she watched his movement. She realized that her weird attitude towards him from the moment they first met was a result of a strong subconscious attraction she had for him! She found this sudden realization rather unsettling. *Well*, she thought again, *he most certainly can't find that out*! Not for half a second!

Ralph unknowingly looked rather dapper in a pair of faded grey jeans and a matching tee shirt. *How was he a chief?* Rewa wondered. His tall, lean frame made him look like a Hollywood actor. There was also a boyish quality to him too that she found appealing, and his salt and pepper sideburns just made him look all the more attractive. Rewa finally spoke after observing him for a moment

"Er..." Rewa began, clearing her throat. "I feel like I owe you an apology for my behavior earlier. I guess I can only blame it on the long-distance flight...I get a bit testy when I've been in the air for too long, I'm guessing. Please forgive me," she finished, trying to make light of the situation. She gave him a small coy smile. Feeling slightly embarrassed, she looked away and around the library and said, without waiting for a response from him, "I'm ready to go when you are." What was wrong with her? Why did she suddenly feel all giddy? *Get a grip, girl!* She chided herself.

Ralph looked at her for a short moment. He was even further amazed by this feisty, fire-cracker of a lady, he could not explain it, but he found her endearing still. She knew who she was and was not going to allow anyone to take her for granted, but at the same time, she knew when she erred and was able to ask for forgiveness when she needed to. He liked that about her but did not say anything about it. Instead, he said,

"I'm the one who should be apologizing, particularly if I come across as *cocky* or *condescending* in any way. I guess I still need that refresher course on *'how to be a people person',* as someone pointed out to me a few years ago. That being said, let's get out of here before you change your mind." Ralph said, laughing with her and leading the way outside, to the car.

This was an entirely different man from the one Rewa had met a few months back. Ralph Eke had been extremely polite to her on the ride to surrey and as they inspected his block of flats. He was almost *chivalrous,* Rewa thought, or perhaps it was all in her mind; she laughed now. He had treated her like she wanted to be treated by a man, with the utmost respect.

They exchanged a few ideas and discussed some of Ralph's plans for the place. Later, he treated Rewa to a lovely Thai meal in *West-End's Soho* at a busy but nice fancy restaurant. She had insisted on paying for her share of the meal after the bill was brought to the table, but he had flat out refused, wondering within himself who this lady was!

Ralph was used to women taking advantage of him and all he offered. Yes, he was used to taking the average lady out to a restaurant and her ordering the most expensive meal on the menu and then *assuming* and *expecting* he would pay for it. Not that he ever minded paying as he could not even imagine asking a lady to pay for a meal she had eaten with him. It was not because he was a chauvinist or egocentric; he just believed it was inappropriate, and a man *always* picked up the tab in his day.

Rewa was, however, one of the more unusual types. She was different, Ralph observed. She was a proud, single lady who did not only demand that you treated her properly but who was also ready to accept full responsibility for herself. It was almost as if she let you know from the start that she was not going to tolerate any disrespect from anyone and most certainly was not going to give anyone a reason to disrespect her. He liked that about her. In fact, he found it refreshing that ladies like Rewa still existed. He had given up looking for a lady of her caliber long ago.

As she still had some time to kill before her flight home that evening, Rewa mentioned she wanted to walk around the shops after their meal, and Ralph willingly obliged and walked with her. He enjoyed her company a lot and wanted to spend more time getting to know her. Walking with her had felt so right for him, and he struggled to restrain himself from reaching for her hand and holding it in his as they walked down the busy streets of Soho. They chatted easily as they walked, and Rewa found him quite an interesting companion too. They seemed to agree on a lot of things and had the same views on a number of subjects. It was uncanny that they also seemed to have similar taste in objects they saw in the shop windows.

After they had walked for a while, a man whom Ralph introduced as an old friend recognized him and stopped to say hello. Rewa found it amazing that people even recognized Ralph, thousands of miles away from home. She watched in silence as he conversed with his friend for a moment, then began to realize she had misjudged him. Ralph Eke was not the cocky, condescending man she had concluded he was.

On the contrary, he was quite a humble person. He did not rub his fame or status in anyone's face or make any special demands, forcing people to acknowledge him or who he was. In fact, he was quite the opposite. It was as though he tried to blend in, and Rewa saw that in the way he was dressed and in everything he said and did. He was extremely polite to the waiter who served them at the restaurant, leaving her a rather generous tip. He was polite to Warren, the driver, Manila, and the rest of his staff at the house in Maida Vale too. He also instinctively took Rewa's little purchases from her and carried all the shopping bags in his hands as they walked and talked. How had she read him so wrongly? Rewa wondered at that moment.

After an hour of walking and shopping, Ralph and Rewa walked back to the restaurant where the driver was parked and headed back to Ralph's house in Maida Vale. It had been a refreshing time spent together for both of them, and they got to know each other a bit more and perhaps even called a silent truce of sorts between them. Hence Rewa's decision to oblige Ralph Eke and agree to decorate his block of apartments.

Both Rewa and Ralph had been blissfully unaware of the type of picture they painted to the innocent bystander all day. They looked perfect together, *Josh* thought. He was the *paparazzo* who had followed them since their arrival at Heathrow airport that morning. Lurking discreetly in the bushes outside Chief Ralph Eke's London home had certainly not been in vain. It had paid off beautifully, and he had more than enough material to sell to the tabloids for weeks to come.

CHAPTER NINETEEN

Vince frowned at the interruption to his little snooze. He wondered who could be blowing up his phone. He winced as he made to get off the couch. He had the world's biggest *hangover*. He looked around his untidy living room for where he had left his cell phone. It rang exceptionally loudly to him, but for some reason, he could not figure out what direction the sound was coming from.

He staggered up to his suit jacket, which lay shapelessly on the coffee table, where he had discarded it on his return home from work. He kicked a few empty beer cans out of his way to retrieve the offending phone from his pocket. He had to squint to read who it was on the screen, blinking a couple of times when he realized who it was. It was his friend, *Humphrey,* who worked with the *State Security Service*. Vince wondered what he wanted as he had not heard anything from him in almost four months. He cleared his throat and tried to sound as sober as he could when he answered.

"O boy, how you dey?" Vince asked Humphrey in *pidgin*. His voice did not sound as good as he wanted it to, so he gave up trying as he did not think he could do any better.

"I dey. You dey sleep?" Humphrey asked his friend. It was seven-fifty-three in the evening. He did not expect Vince to be asleep at that time.

"I'm tired, man. I had a couple of beers and just crashed on the sofa," Vince replied, feeling he did not need to pretend he had not been asleep when he clearly had been. The only thing that was untrue about his answer was the number of beers he had actually had. He could not even count how many he'd had since his return from work as there were quite a number of squashed cans all over the place from God only knew how many days.

"We have a lead on your wife," Humphrey said, getting straight to the point. He heard Vince take a sharp breath and continued.

"Apparently, there was a trace of her having crossed the border at *Seme* almost three years ago. Her passport and that of your daughter's were scanned at the immigration desk there. Do you know by any chance if she perhaps has ties to anyone out there?" Humphrey asked.

He was pleased to have some news about his friend's wife and daughter as the trail had gone cold for too long. He was only worried that it had taken them far too long to find anything. Three years was a long time; Labake and Ella could be anywhere on the globe at the moment, and they'd had a good head start to travel anywhere in the world. The Republic of Benin, though a small country, was also a hub from which many world destinations were accessible by either air or sea. It was *something,* but Humphrey was not going to hold his breath in the hope that Labake would be found. In fact, he made a mental note to remind Vince of this too, before he ended the call.

Vince shouted, "*Finally*! *Some* news! I was beginning to wonder if their existence was a figment of my imagination! I mean, how could a woman and child just disappear without a trace? That's great news, buddy! I have absolutely no idea of anyone she may have links to in the *Republic of Benin*, and she doesn't have any other family I know of except her sister. How did we miss this vital piece of information, though? Why didn't we check the border earlier? How about CCTVs at the border? Surely they should have recordings of them and how they left the place," Vince asked his friend a barrage of questions, excited at some news. It was as if the alcohol had suddenly evaporated from his system.

"We *did* check the border, but honestly, I don't know how nothing turned up until now, almost three years after the fact. As for any CCTV coverage, they only show cars coming in and out through the border and not actual immigrants themselves. Most times, travelers hand their passports to illegal facilitators or touts at the border for stamping on their behalf. They pay them a sum in order to get through the stamping stage as speedily as possible. The touts, in turn, pay the immigration officers to expedite the process. Passports are therefore stamped sometimes without the officials actually viewing the holders of such passports physically. The place isn't just rowdy mate; corruption is rife in its structure and systems," Humphrey explained to Vince, who listened to every word he spoke avidly.

"Back then, there were hardly any clear structures in place, and passports were stamped at the point of entry as opposed to being electronically scanned as they are now. Some passports even slipped through the cracks and weren't processed at all in those days. Things are, however, a lot better now with the new *Comptroller General* and the new *e-passport* requirements. There are also more CCTVs in place now and a lot more orderliness in processing travel documentation. Especially as they must go through scanning and what have you. Unfortunately, change has come rather too late in this instance. It isn't much, but at least we have something to go on in locating your wife and child. At this point, however, there's still work to be done in tracking them down, considering it's been over three years since they've been gone...they could be anywhere by now, but my guys are still digging. I'll keep you posted if anything else comes up, buddy," Humphrey concluded.

"*Yes*! That's great news, my friend! At least we have something to go on...it's better than no information at all! Thank you, thank you!" Vince said excitedly, trying to absorb and process the news all at once. His hope had been spiked by *some* news, and he was beginning to come back alive again as he had all but lost any hope of ever seeing his little girl again. He had already missed three years of her life as she would be nine soon. He gritted his teeth and squeezed his palm shut tightly, hitting the arm of the sofa over and over again till he lost all feeling in it. There would be hell to pay if he ever found Labake, he promised himself.

Vince had drunk himself to madness in the last three years. He was completely lost, not knowing where his wife and child were or what to do about their sudden disappearance. He was also on the verge of losing his job as his personal life now affected his performance at work. He was unable to concentrate or stay sober and had *hangovers* every day on the job for the last couple of years at least.

He had also been short and irritable with his associates and colleagues and already had a couple of meetings with *Mr. Singh*, his annoying boss, about his behavior and performance. He had recently received a letter from the *Human Resources* Department informing him that he was now being placed on a three-month probationary period, within which he needed to literally *get his act together*. Of course, this had not helped his drinking but rather worsened it. He was angry and frustrated, and drinking himself to death seemed the only solution.

His mother had come to see him every weekend, along with her pastors from church. She believed he needed some *spiritual intervention* and was miserable about her son's current lifestyle and her lost grandchild. Vigils were being held at her house every Friday night, all with the view to getting Ella back.

Vince thought of ringing *Mama* now and giving her the good news but then thought against it. He did not want her to resume calling him every day to enquire about any further news. She had done that in the first year of Labake and Ella's sudden disappearance, and it had almost driven him over the brink. No, he was going to avoid telling his mother anything yet.

Vince's mind drifted to Labake again for a second. Where could she be? He wondered again. Who had given her the idea to leave and helped her with her plans? He had to admit that fleeing the country via *The Republic of Benin* was ingenious as he would never have thought she was capable of hashing out such a plan! He, however, knew it was a matter of time before he caught up with her, and when he did, she was going to pay very dearly for the pain she had caused him. He assured himself again, gritting his teeth as he opened another can of beer.

* * * *

It was a Friday evening, and Ella was spending the weekend again with Kwame's daughters. Labake had summoned up some courage to invite Earl over for supper. It had been a month since her meltdown during her therapy session with Dr. Stella, who had encouraged this evening's event and nearly two weeks since she had *agreed* to be Earl's *friend.* Dr. Stella had challenged Labake to invite Earl over for a meal. "Let's see how you cope with that, particularly by yourself and in your own space," she had said to Labake with instructions for her to write down every single emotion she had, leading up to Earl's visit.

Of course, Earl himself was not aware that he was a part of Labake's therapy. He was not even aware she *was* in therapy. He had been pleasantly stunned when Labake invited him over for *a meal this Friday...if you like...* had been her exact words. That was a few days before, while they chatted on the phone. It was Earl's new custom to ring her up every evening since she agreed to accept his friendship. They would talk about both their days and generally got to learn bits and pieces about one another. They had been out a couple of times for ice cream with Ella and his nieces since their *new friendship* began but had never been alone, by themselves.

Tonight, however, was different, as Earl and Labake were going to be alone without the girls. It was also the first time Earl would be visiting the apartment Labake shared with her daughter. She had always made a point of saying her goodbyes downstairs, in the parking lot, each time he dropped them off after an outing. Earl had gotten used to it and never even suggested coming up to the apartment. He had believed he would one day be invited up to the apartment when Labake was good and ready. He was never going to compel her to do anything she did not want to or impose himself on her in any way. He was happy she had invited him over tonight, of her own volition.

Earl was proud of the level of progress he and Labake had made. Her guard was coming down slowly but steadily, revealing a highly intelligent lady. Earl particularly loved the fact that she laughed at his jokes and could take a few of them too. He loved teasing and making her laugh and just loved the sound of her laughter. He thought it sounded like a teenage girl's, actually. The more time he spent with her, the more he fell for her. She was a lot more comfortable with him now and did not seem as afraid as she had been in the beginning. She had been like a caged bird needing to be freed so it could flap its wings, fly and thrive. Earl believed they both enjoyed one another's company and could not wait for their evening together.

Labake, on the other hand, was a nervous wreck as she planned and cooked the main meal for the evening. Initially, she had worried that Earl would consider her invitation rather forward of her, but he had been a great sport about it and said, "I thought you'd never ask! I wondered if your cooking was really that bad." He had teased. It was one of the things Labake liked about him. He would tease her and was never afraid to be *goofy* or silly with her. She liked that a lot as it reminded her of her childhood. She and Laide had teased each other all the time, and she had been cheeky herself once upon a time.

At seven o'clock that evening, when Labake let Earl into the apartment, he smiled at her warmly as he sensed she needed a bit of encouragement. He could see she was nervous and rather self-conscious of the fact that they were alone. He handed her the small fruit basket he had picked up on his way as he had not wanted to come empty-handed. Labake received it reluctantly with a shy smile and said, "Thank you. You didn't have to." She was pleasantly surprised at the gesture. The basket consisted of a large bunch of bananas, a large bunch of red grapes, some nectarines, oranges, and a large pineapple. Labake thought it was a generous gift and the first anyone had ever given her, asides from the books and hair clips Vince had given her before they were married.

Earl did not pay Labake any compliments on her appearance for fear of making her even more uneasy, but she looked great to him. He knew she would not have made any effort about her looks, at least not on his account. It was not her style, but she looked rather fetching in the simple long kaftan she had on. Her arms were bare, and Earl pretended he did not notice the scar on her left arm. He was happy that she did not feel the need to conceal it. Her hair was let down and fell to her shoulders, framing her naturally beautiful face. It was the first time Earl had seen her hair down, as she usually wore it in a bun. It was jet black, thick, long, and shone in the warm glow of the lamp that was on in the small apartment.

Labake smiled nervously at Earl as she shut the door. She desperately tried to hide her nerves and hoped she was doing a good job of it.

"The food smells nice already," Earl said, looking around the tiny but tidy apartment. He took the seat Labake offered on the slightly battered three-sitter sofa in the living room. There was a kitchenette in the not-too-far corner, and Earl could see the shelf in the other corner with an array of books he was sure were Ella's proud collection. There were a few toys neatly arranged on the shelf, and immediately, Earl could tell from the layout of the place that Labake was extremely organized. It was not much, but it was clean and tidy, and with the nice aroma coming from the kitchenette, it smelt homely in a way that appealed to his senses.

"Would you like a drink? I've got water and some fruit juice...if you like?" Labake asked politely but almost hesitantly. She wished she had a wider variety of drinks to offer her guest and kicked herself for not getting some other things.

"I'll have some water, please. Thank you," Earl answered, and Labake moved swiftly to get him a glass of water. Earl noticed the limp in her step again, though it was barely obvious when she walked.

Labake began to feel awkward again as she did not know how to start a conversation, given the *odd* circumstance. Except for Vince's friends, she had never hosted a guest of her own, and even that was far from hosting; she just did what her husband ordered her to do, to make his friends comfortable. She was, however, good at taking orders, and that was one thing she had certainly learned in the years she had been with Vince. He gave an order, and she did his bidding without any questions, and even then, she was still unable to please him.

"So, generally, Labake, how different would you say Accra is compared to any other place you've been?" Earl asked from where he sat, breaking the ice. He sensed that Labake was still uncomfortable, and from the sigh she let out, it was apparent that she was indeed grateful for his question.

"I...I guess I can only compare it to my home country," she answered, handing him a glass of water. "I mean, I can't say that I've been to a lot of places...so there isn't much to compare it with..." She trailed off and contemplated sitting on the sofa next to him as it was the only sitting in the tiny space apart from the small dining table with two single chairs near the kitchenette. Earl moved a bit more to the edge of the couch, giving her more than enough room to sit on the long sofa. Labake sat on the other edge of the sofa, turning to face Earl.

"Really? I guess I should ask where you have traveled to then," Earl continued. Labake could tell he was being friendly and wondered now why she had said what she had. She was still uncomfortable talking about her past, but she knew it could not be avoided now.

"Well, we did travel to the UK once...I mean...myself and my...my..." Labake started to explain before she thought of what she was saying. She trailed off again in that familiar way that Earl had grown accustomed to, but this time, he did not help her by changing the subject. He waited for her to finish, knowing exactly what she had been about to say. He waited, but Labake just looked away and got to her feet abruptly. "Excuse me..." She said to Earl, "I should turn the oven off..." It was as if she had said too much again. She felt both stupid and embarrassed at the same time and was beginning to feel that having Earl over for dinner was a terrible idea.

Earl totally understood what it was that had just happened; he could read Labake better now. She never discussed her past with him, and he had never pried, not wanting to scare her away. He believed that when the time was right and she felt more comfortable with him, perhaps she would open up a bit more with him. In the meantime, he sat on the sofa and watched her move to the kitchenette like a robot. Even with the slight limp, he observed that Labake was quick on her feet.

As Labake opened the oven door to check its content, she remembered her very first trip to the United Kingdom with Vince. It had been her first and absolute worst trip ever. It was Vince's youngest brother Sebastian's wedding, and they had traveled to London for the occasion.

Ella had been about two years old, and *Mama*, Vince's mother, had agreed to look after her in the five days they would be away, seeing as she was not able to attend the wedding herself. She'd had *hip replacement* surgery two months before and was still recovering from it. Of course, she would not have had to lift a finger to care for her granddaughter by herself. Mama had a number of housemaids to do the job for her.

The trip had been a horrible nightmare for Labake from start to finish. Vince believed he had done her a favor by taking her along on *the trip of a lifetime* and reminded her of it each time he got upset with her during their stay. He had complained about one thing or the other right from the time they checked in at the airport. She was too slow, she was the dumbest person he ever knew, she did not fill the departure forms correctly, she had failed to pack his favorite jacket, and the list went on and on. The worst thing was that she had been air sick and thrown up on board the flight, thereby causing him some embarrassment. He had been livid and yelled at her on the plane several times, and that, in turn, caused them to receive stares from other passengers seated around them.

Labake had not known at the time that she had been pregnant a third time, and what she had assumed to be air sickness had actually been morning sickness. When they eventually arrived at Sebastian's London flat, where they were staying for the entire duration of their visit, Vince accused Labake of flirting with the cab driver who had brought them from the airport.

Labake was thankful Sebastian had been home when they arrived at his flat that evening, as he had been her saving grace. Vince had locked the guest room door the minute they entered and whipped her with his belt. It was as though she had committed too many atrocities from the moment they checked in at the airline counter, and he could not wait to teach her yet another lesson. Sebastian had broken into the guest room to rescue Labake from his brother when he heard her crying and pleading with Vince to stop.

It was amazing that Labake had not lost the pregnancy on that trip, as Vince had beaten her badly one more time before they returned home for something else Labake could not quite remember now. She had eventually lost the pregnancy a week after they returned home, and she had not even known she had been pregnant. It was confirmed at the hospital that she had been about eleven weeks pregnant.

The doctors had been unable to ascertain why she had miscarried, but Labake had her suspicions. Vince went utterly crazy when he beat her. No part of her body was spared once he started. He punched, kicked, and even choked her a couple of times during their stay in London. Unfortunately, the baby had died within her for only God knew how long, and the complications from that had been another one of her near-death experiences that had caused the Doctors to advise her never to attempt having any more babies in the future.

"Where did you just go, Labake?" Earl asked, causing Labake to jump back to the present. She did not realize he had followed her. She took a swift startled step backwards, struggling to bring all of herself back to the present. It had been a split minute, and she did not even remember bringing the steaming casserole dish out of the oven and onto the kitchen counter. The oven door was, however, still open, and Labake subconsciously bent to shut it in order to disguise how far she had traveled back into her past and also to mask how startled she was.

"I called out to you several times, but you didn't answer. I had to come closer to see if you were alright...are you alright, Labake?" Earl asked her softly. He was concerned; she looked like she had just seen a ghost.

Labake was not sure if it was what he said or how he said it that quickly put her mind at ease. She gave him a half smile, hoping to reassure him that she was alright, and said, "Dinner is ready. Please take a seat at the table." She picked up the dish, indicating she was ready to follow him out of the tiny kitchenette to the small dining area.

Earl stood there for a moment but decided to do as she asked. He sat at the table that Labake had set and decided to make light of the situation by asking,

"It smells great! What are we having? I'm famished!" He said, rubbing both his hands together excitedly. Labake smiled and brought the hot casserole dish to the table. "I hope you like goat meat. It's goat casserole with rice," she stated, hoping he would enjoy it. She was yet to find someone who did not, though. It was one of the best dishes she made, and she was able to make quite a few very well. She had somehow inherited her late mother's cooking skills.

"Yummy! I *love* goat meat. I mean, I've heard of lamb casserole, but *goat* certainly sounds fabulous!" Earl said.

"Let's hope you feel the same way after you've had a bite," Labake teased. Grateful that the air had changed for the better, and the night seemed to be taking on a different turn from its initial one.

An hour later, after the meal had been eaten and the dinner plates cleared, Earl took his seat on the sofa, feeling sated. He thoroughly enjoyed the meal Labake made and, in fact, had a second helping too. A fact that pleased his hostess tremendously. She had promised to do him a takeaway pack with the leftovers and offered him some coffee. She made herself a cup too, and they sat comfortably on the battered sofa again, making light conversation.

Labake found she really did enjoy Earl's company. He was easy to talk to and deftly changed the topic when he sensed it was not something she wanted to discuss. Earl, however, decided to seize the moment again and take things a bit further. He could not help it but needed her to know how special he thought she was. He decided to throw caution to the wind and go for it *again*. He hoped for a better result from the beach incident. He hoped their continued friendship since then would somehow have put her at ease with him, at least enough for him to broach the subject again.

"Labake, I know you may not be ready to hear what I am about to say, but I feel led to go ahead and say it again anyway. I don't want you to take it the wrong way, and I definitely don't want you to run off in the opposite direction...I mean, the last thing I want is a repeat of what happened at the beach the other time...which I accept full responsibility for as I didn't plan to say what I did at the time I did...it just came out..." He paused for effect as Labake smiled shyly again, remembering the incident at the beach and her *Knee jerk* reaction to what Earl had said.

"I need you to know, however, that I am not out to make you do anything you're unwilling to do. I believe that exercising one's free will is of utmost importance in matters of the heart." Earl paused again for some reaction from Labake. He tried to be extremely cautious as he did not want to frighten her again.

Labake took a sip of her coffee and braced herself for what Earl was about to say. Surprisingly, she found she was not nervous or agitated in any way by what she perceived he was going to say. Perhaps it was the soothing warmth of the coffee or the soft way he spoke. Labake indicated that she was all ears, and Earl continued.

"You see, Labake, like I mentioned the other time, I have been in horrible relationships myself in the past. I have been used and taken advantage of and therefore understand the need to err on the side of caution when it comes to deciding who to give one's heart. I have also suffered heartbreak as well, but... what I feel for you transcends all I have ever felt in the past - the *good, the bad, and the ugly*. I'm drawn to you in ways I have never been to anyone. I love being around you and Ella too. Now I know you aren't ready for anything stronger between us, but I want you to at least consider it. You don't have to give me an answer right away. I'm willing to start something deeper with you, even if it's on your terms. You dictate the pace, and I promise to honor and respect whatever you decide. All I ask is that you at least consider it. I just want to be there for you. I feel the need to make things better for you, to have you experience a different type of relationship, one that is positive and affirming, one that..."

This time it was Earl who trailed off when Labake put her coffee cup down on the stool next to the sofa and rose slowly. She walked to the bay window of the apartment. It overlooked the parking lot of the Staff Quarters. There was not much to see, but she needed to put some distance between herself and Earl as she could not bring herself to look at him at that moment. She felt vulnerable, and tears welled up in her eyes for reasons she could not quite place, but she knew she could not let Earl see them. Was it what he said that moved her so or the tender manner in which he said it to her? She wondered briefly.

Earl sat quietly for a moment, watching Labake. He wondered now if she was going to ask him to leave. Perhaps he had said too much. She just stood rigidly, looking out of the window with her back to him. He wondered what she was thinking. He decided to wait it out and see if she said anything.

After what seemed a moment, Labake said in a very low voice; it was almost a whisper. "I can't, Earl, you're asking too much of me...I'm still married for one...I can't give you what you want, and I don't want to hurt you. I'm *bereft*...incapable of giving what you require. I don't have the capacity to accommodate you or any kind of relationship at the moment...at least, not the type you want...or deserve. You don't know me...you don't know what you're asking...it's really complicated. My life is...*really* complicated..." she trailed off again.

Earl's heart went out to Labake in that instant. Her voice, though low and barely audible, was anguished. It was riddled with pain, and though she spoke in hushed tones, he could hear her pain very loudly. He rose from the couch but stood where he was. He did not want to frighten her by moving any closer.

"Labake, I know you're still married *on paper,* but you have lived separately from your husband for some years now...if you filed for divorce at this stage, you'd get it just based on that. If you don't try, you'll never know what it is you're missing out on or if it would be worthwhile or not. Would you rather wonder for the rest of your life if we could have made something of this relationship? There comes a time in a person's life when they just take the plunge and jump in. You can't plan every single aspect of life. What's the worst that could happen? After all, you've been through...not that I know the details, but from what I perceive, you've been through hell and back...you survived it too!" Earl spoke in an even softer tone than before, standing there, looking at Labake's rigid back.

Labake turned at that moment, and Earl could see the tears glistening on her cheeks. She looked defeated when she dropped her arms to her side and spread them. "Look at me, Earl. There's nothing here for you, can't you see? I have nothing, *absolutely* nothing left to give you or anyone. I don't even know how to give anything to anyone. This is *who* I am!" Labake cried.

Earl took a step towards her, and Labake suddenly froze, raising her arms as if to ward off what she perceived to be a blow from him.

At that moment, she looked frightened, and the look of raw fear in her eyes stopped Earl dead in his tracks.

"What...what did you think I was going to do?" This time it was Earl who looked stupefied like he had seen a ghost. Did she think he was going to hurt her? He suddenly wondered.

"Did you...did you think I was going to hit you, Labake? *Did you?*" He stuttered, searching her eyes as he asked her. It was as if his life depended on her answer. Face ashen, Earl dropped his hands to his sides and took a step backwards.

"I would *never*, could *never ever* hurt you like that or in any way Labake, I promise you, please don't ever think I could. You don't have to be afraid of me...*ever,* Labake," it was a whisper, but Labake heard every word. Embarrassed by her reaction, Labake turned her back to Earl and faced the window again, struggling to calm her racing heart. Suddenly she heard Earl say,

"I'm sorry I frightened you, Labake. Thank you for dinner. Enjoy the rest of your evening." He then turned and let himself out of Labake's apartment quietly.

CHAPTER TWENTY

It had been a series of back and forth, but Chief Ralph Eke's four flats in Surrey, United Kingdom, had now been completely transformed, and all four flats were fabulous. Rewa sighed as she let herself into her apartment in *Crossway Estate*. She was relieved that it was over and that there had not been any major hitches in the completion except for the Albanian painter she had hired and had to fire because he just did not have an understanding of deadlines or timing. He had been contracted to paint the interior of the last apartment but had dragged his feet until Rewa had decided she'd had enough. She had replaced him with *James*, whose work ethic was the complete and extreme opposite and who had completed the job in record time. Rewa had decided to keep his details on record for any future jobs in the United Kingdom.

The keys to the flats had been handed over to the Estate agent as Ralph had instructed, two days after they both took a tour of the newly renovated block of flats. Again, Ralph was an extremely satisfied client and had approved all of Rewa's ideas and suggestions on the project. They had worked closely during the renovation process, though he had given her a free hand to do what she thought was best. He was amazed that all her plans and suggestions had come to fruition beautifully. Rewa was particularly pleased that there had been no need for an extension this time; the project was done and delivered a few days before the stipulated date.

This was Rewa's third job in the United Kingdom. Her last two had also been completed without any hitches, but they had been commercial properties and, therefore, more familiar and under her control. This was her first residential project outside the country, and she was glad it was done and, more importantly, that her client was a *happy camper* about it too.

"I'm not usually easy to please, but I think you really do get me. You should change your policy to include dwelling spaces. This is amazing...spectacular even. I must say I'm very pleased with the work you've put in again, Rewa. Thank you," Ralph had said as they viewed the last apartment together.

Rewa had smiled in response. She was pleased that he was happy with the work and was quite aware that he would not have pretended to like it if he did not. It had taken all of four and a half months, and Rewa was glad to be back home in time for Christmas. It had been a really busy project for her, and she had traveled home a total of seven times from its beginning to its completion.

Except for one last project, which she was finishing the following week, Rewa was quite ready to close for the year. She was tired and needed a break to recoup. She excitedly looked forward to the holidays this year, particularly as Rien, her youngest sister, was coming home with her family from the United States, and plans were underway for everyone to spend the entire period at the Ilo mansion. It was the first time Rewa was going to be sleeping over at her parents' since moving out, and it was also the first time they would all be under the same roof for the holidays here in the country. Usually, they all met up in one of their parent's homes in the UK. This year, however, Mrs. Ilo had decided to go a different route as she did not think the winter would be good for her and her husband. "Your father and I are getting on in years, you know, dear. The weather here would do us both good," She had explained to Rewa a few days earlier.

The last project for the year, which Rewa was planning to finish next week, involved decorating a staff room at one of the most prestigious schools in the country. Work had started and been on for about six weeks, and Rewa's intern, Vera, had done a good job handling it and the irate school proprietress while Rewa was away. She had also assured Rewa that all was in line with their timing, so they would complete before Christmas as the school wanted the place ready by the New Year.

Rewa was quite pleased with Vera's work as an intern. She was professional and highly driven. She had the same keen eye for detail as Rewa, and they worked brilliantly together. Rewa believed she had more than what was required to go professional. Unfortunately, she could not say the same thing for David, the other intern she had hired. He, on the other hand, was not as driven and had moved on to pursue a career in music. Rewa believed it was a better career choice for him as he was crazy about music and always had his headphones on, even at work! She was relieved but knew she had to look into hiring another intern to replace him in the New Year. The business was growing, and she was not able to handle things by herself anymore, and having Vera was not enough either.

As she dropped her bags and began to undress, Rewa's cell phone started ringing; it was Faith. They had not really had time for a good chat in quite some time as they were both very busy. Faith with her new husband, Stephen, and Rewa with the London project she had been working on.

"Are you home, dude?" Faith asked without a greeting.

"Yes, I just got in from London. What's...up, girl?" Rewa asked, yawning.

"You need to put your TV on and go to channel 2 T hat celebrity show *Star Parade* is on, and guess what? You're on it too! Why didn't you tell me, girl?" Faith asked excitedly.

"What? Tell you what, girl?" Rewa asked, reaching for the TV remote on her nightstand with a bit of apprehension. She flicked to the channel Faith had mentioned and, for a second, was not quite sure what she saw. Then she focused intently on the pictures and the words at the bottom of the screen *'Big time lawyer, Chief Ralph Eke, steps out with his new love interest on the streets of London. Are wedding bells soon to ring?'*

Rewa's mouth hung open for a moment as the realization of what she was watching dawned on her. She saw different photos of herself with Ralph outside the airport at Heathrow, at dinner in Soho, and in front of his UK home as they arrived from the airport too. There were several other photos being flashed on the screen. There was even one of them as they arrived at Ralph's newly decorated block of flats in Surrey, along with the caption she had just read. Rewa was horrified, and all she could mumble finally was, "I can't believe this." It frightened her that she and Ralph had clearly been followed by photographers all through that first day when they had both arrived in the UK and over the past few weeks, during the renovations in Surrey, and neither she nor Ralph had been aware of it.

"Hello...*dude*, are you there? Can you see what I see? What's going on? Apparently, the tabloids have been talking about it for the last one week! Hasn't anyone mentioned it to you? Stephen also mentioned seeing you at Chief Eke's party a while back and how you'd done his new offices up, but I see there's more to your *relationship* with the chief...been keeping some secrets, haven't you, *dude*? So, come on, it's out, so *out* with it!" Faith ranted, jumping to the wrong conclusion already.

Rewa wondered how she was going to convince Faith too that her relationship with Ralph was a phantom one, made up by the tabloids. She had not even been able to convince her own family that what existed between her and Ralph was purely business!

She wondered if Sede's silence on the subject was due to her reaction at the last Sunday lunch with their parents. Sede would usually have alerted her of all the extra pictures and rumors making the rounds, but she had not this time. *Why?* Rewa wondered. She decided to find out later but had Faith to deal with in the meantime.

* * * *

The following Monday, Rewa was rejuvenated by the time she got to work. She had spent the entire weekend in bed and had slept like a baby. She had not realized how exhausted she was. She took some messages off *Imeh*, the office receptionist, and had a brief meeting with Vera before she settled behind her desk. Just as she began to gather her thoughts on what she needed to do first, Imeh knocked on her door and came in again with an unusually large bouquet of beautiful flowers and an attractive gift bag.

"This just arrived for you, Ma'am," Imeh said, placing the flowers and gift bag carefully on her desk. The fragrance from the flowers instantly pervaded her small office.

Rewa mumbled a distracted *thank You* to Imeh, wondering who the items were from. It was not her birthday, and as far as she knew, she did not have any suitors or admirers at the moment. She rummaged around the flowers for a card or note but did not find any. She reached for the gift bag and found a handsomely wrapped box with a small card attached to it. The card simply read,

> ***Thanks for accepting to do the job and for doing a wonderful job indeed. Please accept the little gift as a token of my appreciation. Warmest Regards, Ralph.***

Rewa's eyes widened in surprise. Did he intend to give her gifts *every* time she completed some job for him? She reached for the wrapped box and opened it. Her jaw dropped when she found the silver, antique *Christian Dior* watch they had both admired in a shop window the evening he had taken her out for a meal in Soho. The watch had caught her attention in the shop window as they walked down the busy street that evening, about six months ago. Rewa had stopped to admire it and said she thought it was a lovely piece, and Ralph had agreed.

Rewa was amazed that Ralph had noted the watch and gone ahead to purchase it for her. How had he remembered the exact watch or the exact store even? Surely it was far too expensive a gift to give one's decorator? She was pleasantly surprised that he had taken time out of his busy schedule and gone to the trouble of locating and buying her the watch, but she knew she could not accept it. She had merely provided him with a service which he had paid for, handsomely too. She was not expecting any extra remuneration.

Besides, she was well able to buy herself the watch if she had wanted to, but it had not been on her shopping list that evening.

Moreover, she had too many watches for one person and had no intentions of adding to her collection any time soon, though she thought the watch to be a beauty. Rewa believed it was way too extravagant a gift to receive from a client. Even the flowers were a huge bunch, she thought. Ralph certainly did not do things in small measures, she mused. She could not remember the last time a man gave her a gift or if she had ever received one at all. She thought it extremely sweet of him, though.

Rewa carefully wrapped the gift back and decided to give Chief Eke a ring to say *thanks*, but *no thanks*. If only the tabloids could see this, she thought within her. Ralph clearly did not care what they thought. He had clearly ordered the flowers, purchased the watch, and sent them to her through the florist, she assumed, with both their names on it as sender and receiver. What if it had fallen into the wrong hands? Rewa suddenly thought. She was mortified by the thought. In her mind's eye, she could just see the watch and flowers sprawled across her TV screen and in *scope* magazine again. She really was becoming paranoid; she hissed at the thought.

Rewa took a moment to think of what to do and how to respond to the gift. She knew she had to return it but now pondered on how to do that without appearing rude. It was a rather kind and generous gesture, and she wanted to be as polite as she could when she returned the gift. She picked up her phone and started to dial Ralph's number but then thought against it. She replaced the phone on her desk and thought hard about her next move. She then decided to send it back to the Chief through Imeh with a politely worded note.

> *'The pleasure was all mine, Ralph. Thank you for your custom, the beautiful flowers, and the very generous gift.*

Unfortunately, I can't accept the gift as I merely did the job you paid me to do. I, however, appreciate the kind gesture. Much Regards, Omorewa Ilo'.

Rewa read the note again and squashed it in her palm. It just did not seem polite enough. She decided to hold off returning the gift until she was sure how to go about it politely. She was going to sleep on it so that she did not do the wrong thing.

Why was it so hard for her to accept a simple gift of appreciation from a satisfied client? Was it because it was from *Ralph Eke* and the fact that she was attracted to him? She had received many gifts from satisfied clients before; why was this different? Perhaps it was because *this* gift could hardly be described as *simple*. It was a rather expensive one that *she* particularly liked. Again, was that not a good thing? That it had been something *she* specifically liked? Or was it the interference of the tabloids that made her so cautious? She was uncertain about what her reservations were. She just knew she could not accept Ralph's gift.

Rewa sighed and forced herself to get on with the business of the day, pushing every thought of Ralph Eke and his gift to the back of her mind.

* * * *

Ralph sat behind his new large desk in his new office on the fourth floor of *Princes Place*. He had been in meetings all morning and was glad they were over. He needed a breather and decided to take a moment to himself. He mentioned to Yinka that he needed some time before the next item on his agenda for today. His thoughts drifted to Omorewa Ilo as they had many times since they bumped into each other at Heathrow airport over six months ago.

He wondered what it was about her that he found difficult to shake off. Was it her feistiness or *spunk*? He was still unsure but knew he had not felt this way about a woman in a long time.

Ralph wondered again if it would be deemed a conflict of interest if he decided to ask her out on a date. After all, her father was not just a good friend; he was also one of his clients. He handled most of Chief Benjamin Ilo's legal issues, including his probate affairs. He had not mentioned any of it to Rewa as he only recently began considering a deeper relationship with her. However, he was aware that it was professionally unethical for him to discuss his clients with anyone.

What would Benjamin Ilo think of him dating his daughter? Ralph further pondered. Would he approve of a relationship between them? He frowned as he realized he was *putting the cart before the horse*. He was not even sure that Rewa would consider dating him. One thing he was certain of, though, was that he could not get her out of his thoughts.

Ralph had remembered the antique watch Rewa liked from the Soho shop window and decided to purchase it as a gift for her without much thought. He believed she deserved it and was quite pleased that he remembered the exact watch. He had searched for it, ordered it online, and had it delivered to his London home. It was then picked up by one of his associates, who had been on holiday in the UK, and brought home to him.

He had been rather surprised when Rewa returned the watch. He thought she was unbelievable! He had been surprised but thinking on it now; he really should not have been. It was so like her to *prove a point*, he mused. She had attached a polite note with the returned watch, saying she was glad he was pleased with her work but that the gift was unnecessary. She had added that she hoped he did not think it rude of her but that she could not accept it. She had returned it the morning after she received it through one of her employees.

Ralph suddenly decided to invite Rewa out. He spontaneously seized the moment, picked up his cell phone, and dialed her number. He did not know what had come over him but knew he was not going to let her dismiss his interest in her. He just was not one to take *no* for an answer and was quite determined to get to know her, one way or another. She answered it on the third ring.

"Hi Rewa, how are you doing?" Ralph asked as though they were old friends.

"Hello...Ralph, I'm doing well...thank you. How are you?" Rewa answered politely but cautiously, trying to figure out from his tone if he was upset by her returning his gift.

"I'm good too," Ralph responded and paused momentarily.

"I have to say thank you again for the flowers and...er the gift. I hope you don't think it was impolite of me to send..." Rewa started but got cut off by Ralph when he said,

"Don't worry about it. I'm actually ringing to invite you for drinks or dinner, perhaps tomorrow evening?"

"Oh...er..." Was all Rewa could manage. He had completely thrown her off course by his interruption and dismissal of her apology. *Just who did he think he was? Why was he so rude?* She wondered. The least he could have done was let her finish her statement, she thought angrily.

On the other hand, she thought again. She had not bothered to pick up the phone to ring him and show some appreciation for the rather *generous* gift he had bought her, and here he was, asking her out for a meal. *Who is this guy?* Rewa wondered. He was full of surprises. He should at least be offended by what she was now sure was *her* apparent rudeness in returning the watch, but he was not! Rewa secretly found that admirable and mature of Ralph Eke. She suddenly decided at that moment that his dismissal of her apology before she even finished it was a big tick in his favor and all traces of anger disappeared. She cleared her throat and said,

"Alright, tomorrow evening is fine, Ralph. Thank you."

This time it was Ralph who was thrown off course by Rewa's answer. He had expected her to turn him down, but instead, she had surprised him by agreeing to an outing with him.

"*Great!* Where should I pick you up?" He asked.

That was a tricky one, Rewa thought, as she was not quite sure she wanted him to come to her flat. She also did not want him to pick her up from work for some strange reason. Was she trying to avoid them being seen together? Why was he not bothered by that? Another public outing would *really* get the tabloids going again, but Ralph seemed unperturbed by that. Reluctantly, she said.

"*Flat C. Ten, Crossway Estate.*"

"Super. I'll pick you up at seven-thirty tomorrow then. *Italian* perhaps?" Ralph asked, and Rewa said Italian food was great. After she hung up, she smiled at the thought of going out with *Chief Ralph Eke* again and, strangely, looked forward to it.

* * * *

It had been difficult getting any information about Iyabo, but Chief Benjamin Ilo had now received word that she had died a few years back. He was deeply saddened by the news and now understood why she had haunted his dreams in recent times. Perhaps her spirit could not rest till he did right by her, he thought.

He shook his head as though attempting to shake off the feeling of paranoia that threatened to engulf him at that moment.

Chief Ilo was, however, all the more consumed by the need to find the young daughter she had brought with her at their first meeting. He estimated her to be in her early thirties now, but as he had no names to go by, it was even harder to find her. He hoped she was alive and well and that he was not just grasping at the wind in search of a ghost.

The nightmares were even more vivid and persistent now. In the last one, Iyabo had a mini version of him in her palm and threatened to squeeze him to death if he did not do right by her. Chief Ilo had been awakened by the dream, drenched in his sweat, in his cool, air-conditioned bedroom. His abrupt jolt from sleep had awakened Mena, his wife too, and as usual, she had fussed around him, whipping the blood pressure monitor out and taking his blood pressure reading. She had refused to go back to sleep until she was sure the reading showed he was alright and insisted on taking him to the doctor first thing in the morning.

Chief Ilo, however, knew his blood pressure was fine as he had increased the dosage lately, seeing as he was rather anxious about his *secret*. He had no one to confide in but had been forced to mention it to his friend, the Director General of *The National Intelligence Agency*. He had first asked for his help in locating Iyabo and, now, her daughter. He had also requested that the highest level of confidentiality be employed in their search. He did not reveal the full reason for his search to his friend, and *Alhaji Bala Nassir* had not asked. All he knew was that he owed Chief Ilo a favor and was keen to repay it. In fact, he counted it an honor to be of assistance to the Chief and was glad his team had been able to get some information on Iyabo. He had assured Chief Ilo that they would find her daughter too.

Chief Ilo, through his many influential connections, had helped secure Alhaji Bala Nassir's son, *Rufai's* first job at the *National Petroleum Commission.* Alhaji was grateful to him and had been thorough in his search for Iyabo. He had explained the sensitive nature of the search to his men too. Chief Ilo was a very important personality in society. Therefore, the highest and utmost level of discretion had been employed in handling the entire operation covertly.

Alhaji Bala had deployed his best men on the job, using every governmental agency and resource within his grip to help a good friend. He had stopped at nothing and spared no expense in ensuring that they dug out as much information as they could on Iyabo and, subsequently, her daughter *Maria*. In fact, he had tagged the entire exercise, *operation urgent,* and had himself kept abreast of the operation from start to finish.

It had taken a lot to track her down, but after another three months of searching, Iyabo's daughter was found within the employment of the *Ministry of Foreign Affairs*. Chief Ilo had been overjoyed to receive some news about her. He knew his friend, Alhaji Bala, had used every resource at his disposal to find her and had promised his team some *private* remuneration if they found her. Of course, he had kept his promise and rewarded them handsomely.

Chief Ilo had garnered so far that Iyabode's daughter's name was *Maria Olaide Jacobs,* and she lived and worked at the High Commission in *Port Novo,* Republic of Benin. He, however, had not been able to establish if she had any other siblings by her mother. He knew if she did, there was a strong possibility that the sibling was his biological child. So far, there was absolutely no information on that. He was, therefore, left with no other option but to contact her.

Armed with the relevant information, Chief Ilo now planned his next move. He considered paying Maria Olaide Joseph a visit in person at The Republic of Benin as he did not think a phone call would be appropriate, considering the nature of his visit.

* * * *

The following evening, at exactly eighteen minutes after seven o'clock in the evening, Ralph Eke drove into *Crossway Estate*. *Chike*, his personal driver, had been given the evening off, seeing as he lived on the other side of town and there was rush hour traffic in the city at this time. Ralph had left the office earlier than usual because of his date with Rewa. He wanted to make a good impression by being punctual as he suspected it would put him in Rewa's good books. He was aware she was big on being respected and treated properly. He was not about to blow it again and risk being called *arrogant* or *condescending*. He smiled, remembering Rewa's gutsy outburst at the dining table in his London home.

It had been a rather busy day for Ralph. He had made appearances in two different courts, one of which was the *Federal High Court*. He had met with a potentially new client, received a new brief that afternoon, and had a lot of paper work to sort out on it, amongst other things. To say he was exhausted was putting it mildly, but it had not stopped him from looking forward to the evening and his date with Rewa. He was in the mood for some great company and some good food as he had skipped lunch due to all the meetings he had.

The guards at the gate rang Rewa up before they gave him access into the estate, so she knew he was here. Ralph remembered that he had visited *Crossway Estate* once before. An associate of his had lived here. He wondered if he still did as he parked the car near apartment building number ten and alighted from it. He looked round the open estate and thought it was a lovely place to live.

Ralph checked his watch and entered the building, looking out for *Flat C,* which was Rewa's. It was on the ground floor and was located on the left side of the main entrance. He straightened his jacket and was glad that *Bonnyface*, his Steward at the house, had remembered to pack him a change of shirt for his date tonight. He loved a crisp, clean shirt. He had freshened up at the office and changed into it before leaving to get Rewa.

When the doorbell chimed, Rewa gave herself another look in her bedroom mirror. She looked round for her clutch purse and then shook her head when she saw the pile of outfits she had tried on but discarded on the armchair beside the bed. It had taken her a good hour after her return from work to decide on a suitable *ensemble* for her date with Ralph. He had not mentioned anything about work or if he had another business proposition for her. She therefore assumed and *hoped* it was a proper date. She *fancied* him like crazy and really did want to get to know him a bit more.

Rewa was still amazed that Ralph wanted anything to do with her. She had treated him with nothing but rudeness since their first meeting and had even returned the rather expensive gift he had bought her without much consideration for what he could possibly think of her manners. He had surprised her when he asked her out on a date instead of being cross with her. Rewa was impressed that he had been mature enough, too, not to bring it up. In fact, she found him all the more attractive for how he had handled her returning the gift.

She smoothed down the navy blue, satin pencil dress she had on and hoped it was not too obvious she had gone out of her way to make an effort in her appearance tonight. It was her first time wearing the dress since she bought it, and it hugged her in all the right places. It was midi length and showed her delicately shaped ankles beautifully. She settled for a pair of bright green high-heeled sandals and loved the slight sway in her hips when she walked. Her make-up was light and airy as usual, and she had her hair in a simple loose ponytail.

At the door, she took in a sharp, deep breath and opened it. She loved the appreciative look Ralph gave her when he saw her and thought he looked good in the casual sports jacket, white shirt, and grey slacks he had on. He looked and smelt fabulous, Rewa thought.

"Hi Rewa, you look great. Ready?" Ralph said simply, offering her his arm as she stepped into the hall way. Rewa noticed he had not smiled at her. He, however, had a polite look on his face as he greeted her. Again she noted that he looked slightly aloof and tired. She was beginning to understand that this look was part and parcel of him and concluded that his smiles were a rare commodity, she mused silently.

"Hi Ralph, thank you. You don't look bad yourself," Rewa responded as she shut the door and took the arm he offered her. They walked arm in arm as Ralph led her outside to the car. "Do you realize that's the nicest thing you ever said to me?" Ralph said as they got to the car. A corner of his lips curved into a half smile as he said it. Rewa decided to humor him as she realized he was trying to break the ice by teasing her.

"Hmmm, let's see...there was that time I seem to remember apologizing for my rude behavior in England...that, I think, was nicer," Rewa said and smiled as she got into the car. Ralph actually laughed at her remark as he shut the car door after she was settled in the front seat. He then strode to the driver's side and slipped behind the wheels.

"You mean the day you *attempted* an apology to me in London? I agree. That was much nicer than the compliment." Ralph said, now smiling at his companion before starting the engine of the sleek, silver Mercedes. *Wow*! He had finally cracked a full smile, Rewa thought. In fact, he had actually laughed at her joke. It was going to be a lovely evening, she concluded.

"You should do that more often, you know...it suits you," Rewa said.

"Do what?" Ralph asked, giving her a quick, curious look.

"Smile more. Noticed your smiles are rather few and quite far between...a *rare commodity*," she teased him back. This time, Ralph did laugh.

"Really? I wasn't aware anyone was *keeping record*..." He said, laughing one more time. The sound of his laughter was like music to Rewa's ears. It was so male and rich in quality. She absolutely loved it. He then asked how her day had been, and she launched into the story of the irate client she had dealt with that afternoon.

They carried on chatting for most of the ride to the Italian restaurant, where Rewa was transported to *Firenze* the minute they walked in. The place was packed with foreigners, and the décor reminded her of a trip she had taken with some of her friends from university to Tuscany and Florence. The smell of pasta and pizza carried through the original home-style Italian restaurant that Rewa noticed had no signage outside the building. She wondered about that when they drove into the premises.

"How did you find this place?" Rewa asked Ralph as they were led to a table. A rotund, pot-bellied, middle-aged Italian man came over to say hello to Ralph in his very strong Italian accent. It was obvious that Ralph was somewhat of a regular at the place from the warm greetings he exchanged with the man who was introduced as Vincenzo *'or Vinnie for short'*. Ralph and Vinnie chorused the last bit when Ralph introduced him to Rewa as the owner. They both laughed heartily, and Rewa smiled, concluding it was a private joke between them.

CHAPTER TWENTY-ONE

Labake had not heard from Earl in almost ten days. She was beginning to feel he had finally lost interest in her, now that he knew just how *damaged* she was. Her reaction to him when he came for dinner at her apartment the other night had probably scared him off, she thought. Perhaps it was for the better, she sighed. Perhaps she was too damaged to even consider a platonic friendship with any man.

It had been too soon to think she could invite Earl into her life, and she said as much to Dr. Stella at her next session. Dr. Stella, however, assured her that inviting Earl over for a meal and the events of that evening were all baby steps she had taken in the right direction. She said she was quite happy with the turnout of events with Earl and Labake the other night. Labake, on the other hand, was surprised Dr. Stella was pleased as she believed her evening with Earl had been a colossal disaster! Dr. Stella insisted that Labake was on the right track and making progress, but Labake could not see how. She was convinced she had ruined their last evening together and Earl was now clearly put off by it.

Labake was surprised that instead of the relief she expected to feel from Earl's recent distance, she had the weirdest feeling that someone was missing from her day-to-day life. She had not realized how accustomed she had grown to their evening phone conversations and all of his quips and deep insight into a lot of things. She missed hearing his voice, and even Ella had once asked if Uncle Earl had traveled. Labake had said he was probably busy as she had not known how to answer her daughter. She just hoped Ella would grow used to his absence. The last thing she needed was to have to explain *why* Uncle Earl was not going to be in their lives anymore. Ella had only just begun to understand her father's absence; adding Earl's to the mix would be way too much for the poor child, Labake thought sadly.

When Labake had mentioned how she was rather surprised that she missed Earl to Dr. Stella, the doctor had smiled warmly. She said that was a great turning point in her therapy as it showed she had opened up her heart, albeit narrowly, to let someone in at last. Labake was unsure that she had but was quite pleased with the idea of making *some* progress. Any type of progress would do; she just wanted to feel a bit more normal, whatever *normal* was.

Laide had clapped excitedly when her sister confessed how she missed Earl. "That's just great!" She had exclaimed. "Perhaps you should take it upon yourself to give him a ring to see how he's doing," Laide had encouraged. She loved the fact that Labake missed Earl and was beginning to believe he really was a great guy though she had never met him or spoken to him. She also loved the fact that he was Kwame's old friend and brother-in-law too. Any friend of Kwame's was definitely a friend of hers, Laide mused silently as she trusted Kwame and knew Earl would be a good person just by affiliation.

Unlike Dr. Stella, though, Laide had been sad after Labake gave her details of her evening with Earl at her flat and how it had ended.

She knew within her that Earl was good for her sister and needed him back in her life desperately. Labake seemed a changed person since she had let him in. She giggled more, her cheekiness seemed to have returned, and she sounded a lot better and chattier on the phone each time they spoke. There was no doubt that the Labake Laide had known growing up was beginning to peep through the fragile and confused shell of a person she had picked up at the *Seme* border nearly three years ago. It had been a long process, but there was suddenly light at the end of the tunnel Laide beamed now as she spoke to her sister.

"Er, I don't know about that, sis," Labake said hesitantly at Laide's suggestion that she make the first move to contact Earl. "I'm not sure I can or even want to. I don't want to appear too forward or as if I *need* him in my life to function...especially when I know I can't give him what he wants either," she concluded sadly.

That was the simple truth in her mind. Ringing Earl now would be saying she wanted more from the relationship when she was unsure of what she wanted from their friendship. Labake thought it better that the relationship ended the way it had. Besides, Earl had seen the *real* her, the side of her that was damaged, and had perhaps realized he could not handle it. She was only slightly saddened by that but knew she would get over it with time. She had gotten over far worse.

* * * *

Contrary to what Labake thought, Earl rang her up just as she walked into her flat a fortnight later. She had barely managed to drop her grocery shopping on the kitchen counter when her cell phone began to ring. Ella had disappeared into her bed room when they got in, under her mother's instructions to go and wash up for bed.

Labake rummaged around her large hand bag for her cell phone. She could not explain why but she was pleased to see Earl's name flashing on the screen when she found it. She hesitated for a moment before answering it, wondering what it was he wanted. She had not heard from him in over four weeks and was beginning to accept that she probably never would again.

"Hello," Labake answered simply. She was breathless as her heart had begun beating excitedly. She hoped Earl could not hear it in her voice.

"Hi, Labake. Earl here. How are you and Ella doing?" He asked in his usual soft way. Labake paused for a bit, wondering why he felt the need to introduce himself. Did he think she had deleted his number off her phone already? Then again, she was not quite sure how she was to react to him or his question. While she was glad he had reached out to her, she was also slightly irritated that he had switched her off for almost a month and seemed to be switching her back on now that he felt ready. She decided to play it coolly and maturely by stating simply again,

"We're both well, thank you. How are you?" She asked politely.

Earl let out a sigh and said, "Can you spare a few minutes to talk? I'm downstairs in my car."

Instinctively, Labake moved to the bay window overlooking the car park and could see Earl's car. The tail lights were on. She hesitated for another few seconds and then said, "Let me see to Ella, and I'll be down in a few minutes." It was a breathless response again, and she tried to steady her nerves. It was weird, but she was nervous and excited at the same time that Earl was there. Why did she feel this way? She wondered.

She self-consciously smoothed her dress down and went in search of Ella, who had changed into her PJs and was already dozing off in bed. They'd had supper already while out grocery shopping. Ella had nearly worn Labake out, begging her to get her some pizza. Labake had given in, and they'd had some pizza at a nearby pizzeria. Ella had her fill of it, and Labake could tell that she was now tired. She had fallen asleep on the drive back home from the superstore. It was already eight thirty-six pm, and Labake was not surprised she was tired as it was past her bedtime anyway. Ella roused from her snooze as her mother came into her small room.

"Brush your teeth, darling?" Labake asked Ella, who yawned and nodded as her mother sat on her bed and tucked her in.

"Good girl. Let's pray then," Labake said, stroking her daughter's braided hair. She loved her so much and wondered how she could ever live without her. Ella was fast asleep before her mother ended the prayer. Smiling, Labake got up gently, gave her a kiss, and turned off her bed side lamp. She shut the door to Ella's room gently, checked her reflection in the small mirror on the wall by Ella's room, and went down to the parking lot to meet Earl.

Labake wondered why she was suddenly particular about her appearance; she had never been in the past. Trying to make a good impression on Earl was the least of her worries. She wondered now what had happened to change that. She really must have missed him, she told herself. It was awkward, but she looked forward to seeing him at that moment.

Earl watched her through the rear view mirror as she walked to the passenger door. He indicated that she came in and sat in the passenger seat next to him. Labake hesitated for a moment and then obliged. She looked at him for a short while after she was seated. Neither of them spoke at first; they just sat there, staring at each other. Labake was first to look away, after which Earl began to speak softly. Again, it was a tone of voice that Labake found soothing and one she had missed far more than she realized.

"I've missed you Labake...*dreadfully*...and Ella too...I tried to stay away but couldn't. I felt I needed to give you some space...I'm still uncertain why. I guess I felt like I was forcing you to do something you weren't prepared for...I never want to be *that guy* Labake but seeing the fear in your eyes when you thought I would hit you made me feel like a *bully*...I suppose I was of the opinion that you or even both of us needed a breather, some time to think and perhaps process things a little more without any pressure, particularly from me to you. I'm sorry, but I couldn't stay away much longer...I...want you to know, Labake, that I would *never* hurt you..."

Labake suddenly began to speak as if Earl had not been saying anything. Earl stopped mid-sentence to hear what she had to say. He had to strain his ears to hear her, though, as she spoke in a whisper. She stared out of the car window as she began, and to Earl, it was as if she was speaking to someone else.

"Ella's father...my husband, beat me. He beat me for the six and a half years I was with him, almost every week...sometimes two or three times a week...except when he was away. He was cruel...mean, and spoke with his fist. He raped and violated me constantly...even when I was pregnant." Labake paused for a bit. Both her lips and hands trembled in unison as she spoke, forcing her to shut her eyes, willing them to stop. When they did not, she stuttered even more as she continued.

"I lost...lost three babies as a result of the beatings...*three*." Labake paused for a bit, opened her eyes momentarily and looked down at her trembling, tightly interwoven fingers subconsciously, then closed them again. Earl watched her silently and was not quite sure what to make of her disposition at that moment. It was as though she was ashamed or perhaps felt guilty for her loss. She seemed lost in deep thought for a bit, and then she continued.

"I was advised by the doctors not to have any more babies as I nearly died...after the last miscarriage. I can't have any more kids...not that I wanted any more...anymore with him. He threatened that if I left, I would never...never see Ella again...I knew he meant it. So I stayed and bore it until...until I couldn't anymore...I didn't plan it...I was so...so, so afraid. Without planning or much thought, I just took Ella and ran one day...after he went away on a trip. *I ran*...I was afraid he'd find us...*God*, I was petrified! I've been on the run...in hiding for almost three years now...and I'm still afraid...been afraid for so long..." Labake trailed off into silence, as was her custom.

She opened her eyes again after a moment and turned in the passenger seat to face Earl, who looked at her with nothing but raw compassion.

"So, you see, Earl, it's far more complex than you know. I don't want you to feel sorry for me or to get you involved in any way...that's not why I'm telling you this...it's so you know *I am broken* in ways you may never understand. I'm not free or have the liberty to even *be* in a relationship. I'm still unsure about the future, uncertain about what I'm going to do with myself or my daughter...it's all up in the air. I can't even make *any* long-term plans..."

Labake stopped talking in that instant as a lump had formed in her throat, and tears slowly rolled down her cheeks. She looked at Earl in frustration as if willing him to understand.

"Can I...can I please give you a hug?" Earl said in a soothing tone, unsure of what else to say. He felt a strong urge to hold her and make her feel better somehow. He did not wait for a response from Labake. He stretched out his hands and, ever so gently, enveloped her in a warm, tight embrace.

Another strange emotion went through Labake in that instant, one she was unfamiliar with. Oddly, she found Earl's response and gesture immensely reassuring at that moment. She could not keep herself from melting into his warm, strong arms as she began to sob quietly. Earl rubbed Labake's back soothingly, holding on to her tightly. It was the closest they had ever come, and they both felt good and consoled by the warmth their closeness drew.

Labake, for the first time in her adult life, felt safe and secure just by that singular gesture from Earl. It was inexplicable, but she suddenly felt an overwhelming sense of peace, as though she belonged in his arms. Earl, on the other hand, was so overcome with emotion. He was deeply moved by what Labake had just shared. He caught a tear as it almost dropped off his face and into her hair. He had been right all along; Labake *had* been to hell and back.

After what seemed a moment, when the tears subsided, Labake looked up at Earl sheepishly. In that instant, Earl found he could not help himself, and without much thought, he bent his head and claimed her lips in a warm, gentle, but hungry kiss. It was as if Labake had been expecting it; she yielded to his lips and responded hungrily too. Something strange was happening to her that she could not quite explain. She suddenly did not feel as ashamed or as scared as she had been in the past. In that instant, all she wanted to do was stay right there, in Earl's arms forever! She responded to his kiss just as hungrily too. She had never been kissed this way before, and it was unbelievably pleasurable. Was it the smell of his cologne that mesmerized her so? Labake was not sure. All she knew at that moment was that something had come over her, causing her to experience things she had never felt before. What was even more intriguing was that she desperately wanted more of it.

Vince had been the first and only man Labake had ever been with, and he had forced himself on her right from the beginning. Labake's very first sexual experience had been nothing *magical* like the description in the romantic novels she had read as a teenager. Vince had manipulated her into having sex with him one evening when she had visited his studio flat. She had been reluctant to as she had not expected him to make a pass at her. When she resisted, he had used blackmail, playing on her inexperience and naiveté. He had insisted that her unwillingness to have sex with him was proof she did not love him the way he loved her. "All couples in love, *make* love, Labake. Do you love me?" Vince had asked, and when she nodded shyly, he said, "Prove it."

He had not cared that she had no experience nor even tried to make it special for her. He had pushed her down on his bed and had his wicked way with her. He had been extremely rough and had taken and given nothing in return. Labake had not known it at the time, but she now knew that her first sexual experience with Vince had been tantamount to *rape* as she never consented to consummating their relationship. Unfortunately, that had set the tone for their marriage. In the six years she had been with him, sex with Vince had *always* been forceful, rough, dominating, and demeaning, and until now, Labake had believed sex with her husband to be *normal*. She had decided long ago that sexual desire and love making, as described in the various romantic novels she read in the past, were all fairytales that never really happened in reality. She was unaware that sex was to be enjoyed by *both* parties.

After that first experience, sex with Vince had grown more difficult as he had never had the patience to teach her or to ensure she enjoyed their time together. Falling pregnant with Ella had made things even worse. Labake had been ill throughout the pregnancy, and Vince wanted sex every time, not caring that it was physically inconvenient due to Labake's ill health and size too. He had forced her to yield to his advances and more or less pounced on her as and when he pleased. In fact, Ella was delivered prematurely, some nine weeks before she was expected, due to Vince's constant violation of Labake.

What Labake now shared with Earl was different from what she had ever experienced before. Vince had been impatient and frustrated with her lack of experience in the months following their marriage. He gave her orders on how to pleasure him and punished her when she failed to do what he wanted satisfactorily. It always had to be the way Vince wanted it, never mind the discomfort it caused her.

Labake remembered one experience she had when she had been about six months pregnant with Ella. Vince had an insatiably high sexual libido and wanted sex almost every morning and night. Oft times, after he was done, Labake had difficulty walking. She would be sore all over for days and never had time to heal from her husband's violent sexual ways.

On this particular evening, Vince had wanted sex so badly and, as was usual, had been frustrated by Labake's inability to please him for her lack of experience. He had instructed her on what to do to give him the pleasure he sought, and while they were at it, in his usual impatient manner, he slapped her across the face in frustration, *in the very act.* He was inside her and slapped her again and again, claiming she was useless. That had not stopped him from pounding away at her, though; in fact, Labake believed he was aroused by it. He had pinned her down with his weight making it difficult for her to escape. She had laid there, crying out as she tried to shield her face with her arms from the slaps, which only served to annoy Vince further.

When he had finally reached his peak and got off her, Labake had a split lip, a bloody nose, and two swollen cheeks. She had been in pain for days after that and had vowed never to let it happen again. She figured if she followed his instructions as accurately as she could, as and when he dished them out, she would never have to experience that again. She was wrong, though, as it happened many times more after that.

Labake had never had such a strong sexual pull towards anyone in her life as she now had with Earl. It was as though something had taken over her body, rendering her powerless and unable to control it. She drank him in and yearned for more, as did Earl. It took every last shred of will power for him to draw away slowly. He searched Labake's eyes as she opened them slowly for any signs of trepidation, fear, or even shock, but there were none. If anything, she seemed dazed and perhaps even drunk. Earl bent his head again and kissed her once more. This time, slowly and Labake responded and yielded to him unabashedly again. It was magnetic, kinetic, a pull, a force. It was wholesome and simply magical, Labake thought. It awakened her body in a rather pleasurable but unfamiliar way.

* * * *

Vincent Ebodo fumed silently as he watched his wife in the arms of a total stranger. He tried to calm himself down by taking short, sharp breaths as he watched Labake and the man she was with in disbelief. Before long, he could see the steam from his flaring nostrils begin to cover the car windshield. It took everything in him to keep him from marching to the sleek black car, yanking the door open, dragging his estranged wife out of it, and pummeling her to death.

The more he watched them from his rental car, the more enraged he got. He had to look away at some point, as he had seen enough. She had never responded to him in such a way, not in the entire six years they had been together. He had always known Labake was a *slut*! To think he had now caught her in the very act, with another man, after almost three years of searching for her. His suspicions had been right all along! It was true that she *had* run off with another man! He could not quite see the *bastard's* face as his head was turned away from the car window, but Vince clearly saw how entangled Labake was in his embrace.

After nearly three years of searching for his wife and daughter, Vince could not believe his eyes as he drove through the opened gates of *Dolphin Hotel's* Staff quarters in Accra. Seeing Labake walk out of the building and walk towards the sleek black jaguar, just as he discreetly parked the rental, was nothing short of a miracle. He had not even needed to wait, ask around or confirm if indeed his source was right as to her exact whereabouts. She had just strolled out of the building in the nick of time! It was as if fate had decided to spare him the added delay.

For a moment, Vince almost did not recognize her as she seemed to have added a bit of weight. Her walk also seemed unfamiliar. Had it not been for the slight limp, he would have sworn that it was not Labake. It was strange, but he thought she looked a lot better than he remembered. Vince had decided to park his rental car a good distance away from the few other cars in the lot and had turned off the head lights and engine of the car so he would not be noticed. He had watched as Labake bent to peer into the car window in a rather *suggestive* manner, just the way a *harlot* would do, and watched as the strange man in it beckoned for her to get into the car. He had also wondered what they were talking about as he tried to figure out what the relationship was between them. He had been utterly and unpleasantly shocked when the fellow had bent to kiss his wife. *His wife!* He hissed and shifted angrily in his car seat as he turned to watch them again.

Vince was enraged and again struggled to contain the urge to go over to the black jaguar and drag Labake out of this stranger's arms. He, however, decided to wait it out patiently. He had to catch her alone first. He wondered where Ella was as there had been no trace of her since his arrival over thirty minutes ago. Perhaps she was indoors, he thought.

Well, *'The patient dog eats the fattest bone',* he encouraged himself and decided to wait before he sprang into action. He reached for the cool metal inside his jacket and stroked the butt of the *Glock* almost lovingly in anticipation. She was going to pay dearly, he assured himself again. He had a plan but was not entirely sure how he was going to carry it out, given how easily Labake had appeared. He needed to think and re-strategize. Yes, he was going to lay low here and rehash his plans to get his daughter back and out of this *God-forsaken* country. He told himself as he continued to watch Labake and Earl from his rental car.

CHAPTER TWENTY-TWO

Ralph Eke and Omorewa Ilo spoke with each other on the phone almost every evening since their meal together at *Vincenzo's*. It had been a lovely date, and it was beginning to dawn on Rewa that there was a possibility Ralph was interested in her *romantically*. The thought of that being real warmed her inner parts a great deal. She was a lot happier these days, and life suddenly seemed more colorful to her. She wondered if the way she felt had anything to do with the tabloids going wild about a *relationship* between her and Ralph that did not even exist yet. Ralph did not mention the latest news making the rounds about their perceived relationship on their date, and she had decided not to bring it up either.

Rewa was amazed by the different side of Ralph she had experienced on the evening they spent together. He had been extremely courteous to her and had treated her with nothing but respect. Since that evening, she looked forward to his calls and enjoyed their phone conversations a lot. She found he had a dry sense of humor that appealed to her immensely, and she enjoyed the way the relationship was going, though she was unsure if she could call it that at the moment. He had not exactly asked her for anything more serious or even defined what type of relationship theirs was. Therefore, she decided to put him in the *friend zone* until something on towards happened and showed he belonged elsewhere.

Rewa was beginning to fall for Ralph too and hoped he would speed things along. However, she managed her expectations and made room for the fact that he may not be interested in anything but a simple friendship with her. She had enough experience about expecting too much from a prospective suitor who later turned out not to want anything more serious. She'd had her fingers burnt a few times to know better. Rewa yearned for another outing with Ralph, but he did not ask for one yet. He, however, rang her up every evening, and they chatted and talked about themselves and their day.

Rewa caught herself day dreaming a lot recently. She had already begun to imagine what it would be like to be Ralph Eke's girlfriend and, perhaps, even his wife! She would often mouth the name *Omorewa Eke* to herself, sometimes to see if her forename and his last name had a nice ring together, then she would laugh and mutter *Get a grip, girl* to herself. It was not the first time she had paired her name with a prospective suitor's. It never really ended up the way she hoped. She decided to patiently wait it out and not jinx this *budding* romance with Ralph too early by pairing their names together before time. She really hoped whatever it was that was developing between them blossomed into something lasting and beautiful.

* * * *

Omorewa Ilo put some lip gloss on her lips and examined her reflection in the mirror. She was pleased with what she saw. She slipped on a pair of pumps and gave herself a final look. The primrose-colored top and the dark, skinny leather pants she had on were simple but would have to do, she told herself. Her gaze shifted to the pile of clothes she had tried on and discarded on her bed yet again. Turning back to the mirror, she hissed. Why did she have to do this every time she met with Ralph? She always seemed unsure of her wardrobe each time they had plans to meet.

Tonight was particularly special as she was going to be meeting Israel, Ralph's twenty-three-year-old son. Rewa knew this was why she felt slightly nervous. She hoped Israel liked her and that she made a good first impression. She knew no one else was as important to Ralph and, in a way, felt as though Ralph needed Israel's approval of her before he took their relationship any further. Rewa smiled, put a pair of loop earrings on, and shook out her long hair so that it bounced and hung loosely around her face. She looked exactly how she intended this evening - *young, fresh-faced with a hint of swag*.

All three of them were having dinner at Ralph's house. He had sent a car and driver for her, and both were waiting outside her flat to take her to his home on the Island. It was her first visit to Ralph's home here in the city, and though she would not have minded driving herself, Ralph had insisted on sending a car for her.

Rewa grabbed a bottle of wine from the rack in the kitchen and headed out to the sleek black *Toyota Land cruiser* jeep. She was both nervous and excited at the prospect of meeting a member of Ralph's family and prayed it went well. The driver swiftly came out of the vehicle and opened the back seat door to let her in as she approached. She smiled at him in appreciation. Ralph had rung her up earlier with the driver's name and a description of the car she was to identify when she came out of her building. *Dele*, the driver, was quite professional and did not utter another word to her.

Some thirty minutes later, Dele drove through the gates of a newly built, very modern, two-story building in one of the more popular gated communities on the island. Just like his London home, it was breathtaking! Not that Rewa expected anything less. She was beginning to understand that everything about Ralph Eke was large and extravagant but quite unlike her parent's properties. His were subtle and understated in a way. It was obvious he certainly had great taste, and as the tires of the luxurious car crunched up the gravel-filled grounds of the premises, Rewa found herself once again wondering what the beautiful white house looked like indoors. In the meantime, she took in every detail of the exterior.

There was a patch of lawn at the front of the property that was neatly mowed, and there were large terracotta pots of green plants lining the front of the building. The gabled roof was dark and shingled, contrasting tastefully against the white exterior walls of the building. The windows formed part of the landscape in a way, and they were unusually tall and narrow. One could only imagine what the place looked like in the day time as it had become dark by the time Rewa arrived.

Dele came round to get the door for Rewa and helped her alight from the high vehicle. He walked in front of her, leading her to the large double doors at the entrance. He rang the doorbell, and a moment later, the door swung open, revealing someone who was the spitting image of Ralph, save for his slightly lighter complexion and age. Rewa instantly knew who he was. His eyes were warm as he gave her a reluctant smile. *Aha!* Rewa thought he had that same look as his father; it was a resigned but present look. She immediately recognized that no harm was meant by it; it was just an *Eke thing,* she mused silently.

"You must be Ms. Ilo...? I'm Israel," he said warmly in an accent that was mostly British, and Rewa returned the smile, taking the hand he offered and shaking it. "Hello Israel, a pleasure to meet you. Please call me Rewa."

"How about *Aunty* Rewa?" Israel asked, smiling coyly now. Rewa knew she loved him the instant he said that. She smiled at him but did not respond. She was impressed by his manners. Ralph had clearly done a good job of raising him, she thought, or how else would he know that in this part of the world, young people referred to adults much older than them as *Aunty* or *uncle*? It just showed good manners, and Rewa was pleased that Israel had some.

"Come on in, *Aunty*. Dad's in the den," Israel said politely.

Rewa stepped into the contemporary, elegant hallway of Ralph's Lagos home. The entire house smelt of leather, and there was no mistaking the owner was male. It was a beautifully decorated place. The walls were white inside too, and there were white and black picture frames on the walls. The floor was made out of what seemed like dark brown oak. There was recess lighting in the high ceiling and a large dark brown wooden bench not too far from the front doors. It was simple in a very extravagant way.

Ralph came out from nowhere at this point. Smiling at her, he said,

"Hi there, I see you've met Israel. *Izzy*, meet *Ms. Omorewa Ilo. She* will be joining us for dinner," Ralph stated simply. He bent and gave Rewa a warm hug, leaving her mesmerized by the fragrance of his cologne and wanting to hold on tightly to his lean body.

"We've met," Israel said, rolling his eyes fondly at his father. Rewa could tell they had quite a close *father-son* relationship despite the fact that they did not live in the same country. Ralph had mentioned that Israel had decided to stay back in the United Kingdom after his degree and was even starting a job soon in one of the teaching hospitals in Manchester. Israel was home on holiday and was going to be returning to the UK soon.

Rewa smiled at him and returned the hug. She drew away reluctantly and handed Ralph the bottle of wine she had brought along and said, "This is for you. Thanks for inviting me."

Ralph took the bottle of *Prosecco* from her and smiled. "Thank you, Rewa. Come on in, and thanks for honoring the invite. How was the ride over?" He asked, taking her hand and leading her past a few other turnings into what seemed to be the living room. He smiled at her again when he watched her assess her surroundings distractedly as they walked into the beautifully decorated room. It was different from the other large, more formal sitting room they had passed by, just off the hall way. This space had a more *lived-in* look. There were two large, worn leather sofas in here, and one of the largest flat screen TVs Rewa ever saw in a dwelling house hung on the wall with a tennis match showing on it. Ralph reached for the TV's remote control and lowered its volume, gesturing for Rewa to take a seat on one of the sofas.

Rewa looked around the room, which itself followed what seemed to be the general theme of the house – wooden floors, recess lighting, and black and white picture frames on the walls. Except for the grey walls, the living room looked just like the rest of what she had seen of the house already, elegant but rather *male*. There was a large green plant in the corner and a large, white, shaggy rug in the middle of the room with a large glass coffee table on it. There was no doubt that the owner of this space was a man, Rewa thought again and smiled.

"The trip wasn't bad at all. Traffic is usually lighter around this time, anyway. I must say, you have a lovely home," Rewa answered. It was obvious that this was the more comfortable room for her host. She noticed the different games, consoles and electronic gadgets on the coffee table. There was also a pool table in the background near the window, a gaming machine and a guitar on its stand on the other side of the room. There was a mini-bar too, and Ralph walked up to it and opened the mini fridge attached to it. "Thank you...most people who visit think it's *too masculine*. Dinner should be served in about fifteen minutes. What can I get you to drink in the meantime? A soda, juice, water? Think we should have some freshly squeezed juices here, somewhere..." Ralph said, digging deeper into the refrigerator.

"Water's fine, thank you," Rewa responded, watching her host from where she sat. It amazed her that he could appear so relaxed. He had mentioned in one of their phone conversations how much of a *homebody* he was. He did not go out a lot except when he had to. She knew he was a very busy man, and he had said that he was not much of a *social butterfly*. That explained why there were no pictures of him on-line when she had attempted to do some snooping on him before their first meeting.

One could never tell he was a *chief* from just watching him at that moment. He had on a simple white tee shirt and a pair of ripped-washed denim pants. He certainly had not dressed for the occasion, and Rewa was thankful that she had also gone the casual route. Not only did he not look like a chief, but Ralph Eke also looked nothing like the serious, extremely successful, Senior Advocate he was! Save for the tired, resigned look that Rewa now knew to be just his natural facial expression, he looked really laid back and relaxed, walking barefooted towards her with a glass and bottle of water in his hands. He set both down on the side table near Rewa and proceeded to open and pour some of the water into the glass for her.

"How are you even *a chief*?" Rewa suddenly asked, thinking aloud. Ralph smiled and sat beside her, tucking a knee under another on the large leather sofa. He picked his glass of water up from the coffee table, lifted it to her as if to say *cheers,* and drank from it. Then he cleared his throat and said.

"The title is an inherited one and was actually conferred on my late father. It passed to me, being his only son, when he died. Apparently, it's the tradition where we come from. The title has passed from generation to generation, and on my passing, it falls on Izzy...now, imagine *him* as a chief!" Ralph laughed just as Israel joined them at that moment and asked curiously. "Imagine *who* as a chief?" He had overheard the last bit of his father's comment.

"I was just explaining the chieftaincy thing to Rewa. How you're the next chief in line once I'm done!" Ralph burst out again in that rich laughter that did something pleasant to Rewa each time she heard it. Israel rolled his eyes again at his father and picked up one of the cell phones on the table. He seemed totally unperturbed by what his father said.

"I never really think about the title or even remember it... it's more honourary, if anything. Not to worry, buddy, you won't either!" Ralph added. Rewa smiled at what Ralph said and at Israel's reaction to it. They appeared to have a rather easy relationship and looked more like friends or brothers, even as opposed to father and son. Israel had popped some ear phones on and begun typing away on his phone; he had clearly zoned out of the conversation.

"So what if Israel never has a son? What then happens to the title?" Rewa asked inquisitively.

"Well, so far, it hasn't happened, but I guess it would move to one of his cousins who is male," Ralph answered.

"Not sure *Dozie* would be happy about that...he'd be horrified, actually!" Israel said in response to his father's comment. Suddenly both he and Ralph burst into laughter. Rewa laughed too, though she did not know what the joke was. The sound of father and son's laughter made her chuckle, and she suddenly found herself warming up some more to them. Ralph then explained that Dozie was his fifteen-year-old nephew, whom everyone in the family referred to as a nerd because of his rather bookish ways. Rewa, Ralph, and Israel all laughed again when Rewa tried imagining a fifteen-year-old nerd being ceremoniously installed as a chief.

When the laughter died down, Ralph turned to Rewa and asked, "So, as a decorator, do you think the house is *too masculine*?"

Rewa looked round the large room again and shrugged before she said, "Whatever floats your boat, I guess...your house should be a reflection of who you are."

"That's exactly what I said when aunt...what's her name again, dad? Er...Aunt *Viv*... when *Aunt Viv* came round and went on about it!" Israel chimed in, his eyes now back on his phone as he spoke.

One of Rewa's brows went up at the *Aunt Viv* comment. She wondered if Aunt Viv was an ex-girlfriend of Ralph's but said nothing about it. Ralph saw her expression and explained that Aunt Viv was a friend of the family who had visited several times and always complained about the *deco* of the place. "It is too white, black, and grey, she would say," Ralph finished just as a man in his fifties, in a white uniform, came in and announced that dinner was served.

Ralph and Israel led Rewa into the dining room, just further up the hall, where a spread of all kinds of delectable-looking dishes had been laid. The lovely aroma of food made Rewa's tummy rumble, and she took the seat that Ralph pulled out for her in clear anticipation. She had not had much to eat since breakfast that morning. Rewa's seat was right next to Ralph's at the head of the table, and Israel took the seat on the other side of it, next to his father, so that he and Rewa were sitting directly across from one another.

The dining was just like the rest of the house but with a few silver accents here and there. The table was made out of fabricated silver and was claw-footed, and so were the chairs, which had black velvet cushions on them for comfort. There were lit candle sticks on the wall, offering an additional glow to the room. It was a handsome room but had a cold, almost *Goth* feel to it. Rewa observed but, again, said nothing about it.

"Congratulations, Israel, on your graduation. I hear you'd be starting work soon. Are you looking forward to it?" Rewa asked Israel, who smiled coyly at her and concluded he liked his father's new *girlfriend.* Of course, *the old* guy had not said anything about that yet, but Israel knew his father too well. He knew he would never invite her over to dinner if he was not planning on making her his girlfriend. In fact, Rewa was the first lady to be invited over that he knew of; then again, the tabloids had mentioned the relationship brewing between Rewa and his father. It seemed there was some truth to this particular piece of gossip. Israel mused.

Israel usually kept abreast with information in his home country though he did not live here anymore. Both he and his father were quite used to the tabloids and the different stories they concocted about his father, so much so they never even talked about them. His father had yet to say anything to him about Ms. Ilo, but Israel had a gut feeling that the *old guy* liked her a lot. He could tell from the way he kept smiling at her. He was going to tease him about it later after she left.

"Thank you, Aunty. I *am* looking forward to starting work. I'm just not sure about moving to Manchester," Israel started as Ralph spooned some pounded yam on to his plate, listening to the conversation between his son and Omorewa Ilo. He strongly felt that Rewa was the one for him and could see that even *Izzy* approved of her as he was not usually this chatty with people. Ralph watched them silently for a moment as he filled his plate and decided he would make his next move, never mind that she was the daughter of his friend and, more importantly, his client. He had held back for a while, contemplating it. He, however, knew what he had to do. He wanted Omorewa Ilo in his life, and he was going to have her in it, no matter what.

CHAPTER TWENTY-THREE

Once the sleek, black jaguar went past his rented car, Vince sprung out of the car and hurried up the stairs as discreetly as he could after Labake. He needed to know what exact apartment she was headed to, so he could execute his plan accurately. He was relieved to see that her lover had not followed her in but had given her a rather long parting kiss before he left. Vince had been unable to get a clear visual of the driver of the *jag* as he drove by. It had been too far and too dark for him to make out the stranger who had just been all over his wife in a passionate kiss. *How dare he?* He fumed silently.

When he had established which apartment Labake's was, Vince returned to his rental car again. He did not want to be seen by anyone; if he was seen, he needed it to be by as few people as possible if he could manage it. Thankfully, the staff quarters of *Dolphin Hotel* was quiet. Apart from the two ladies who had walked past him as he returned to the rental, he had not seen anyone else and was almost certain no one had seen him either. The two ladies had been too deeply engrossed in whatever it was they had been discussing to even notice the stranger they had just walked by.

Now, all he had to do was wait another hour or so. He needed the place to be as quiet as possible, just so there were no unwanted interruptions, after which he would execute his plan and take what was rightfully his. It had been over three years, but he was glad the day had finally arrived. He had not been able to think or focus on anything else in the last few years. He felt Labake had cheated him out of three years with his daughter, and that was unforgivable in his view. Those were years he could never recover.

Labake was going to pay very dearly for the grief she had caused him. In fact, the thought of what he would do to her when he eventually did find her was all that had kept him going in the last three years. Vince gritted his teeth and squeezed his fist at the thought of it. He had been totally consumed with locating her whereabouts and getting his daughter, in particular, back home with him, where she belonged. That was all he cared about, and he just hoped Ella was in the apartment with Labake.

Vince's mind drifted back to the day he finally received news of his wife and daughter's exact location; it was as if he had won a billion dollars. He had not been able to believe it at first. He had all but lost hope of ever finding them. The trail had gone cold again after Humphrey mentioned that there was a trace of Labake at the Seme Boarder. Another seven months had gone by before Labake was finally found in Accra, Ghana. Vince was extremely grateful to Humphrey, his friend at the *State Security Headquarters,* and his team. He could not have found his family without them.

Once traces of Labake had been detected at the border in Seme, both hers and Ella's passport details had been forwarded to the ports of other neighboring West African countries. Humphrey and his crew thought it necessary to enquire if they had passed through any of them elsewhere. Language barriers, different rules and procedures, and, of course, a lot of bureaucracy had made it a rather long and arduous task to receive any information through the varying systems of these other countries. They all had varying practices and their own means of dishing out human travel information and documentation. This had therefore required a lot of time and patience.

Of course, ECOWAS rules were present to help ease the transference of information back and forth between the different West African dominions, but in developing countries, processes were much slower, regardless of the presence of international rules. Eventually, evidence of Labake having entered Ghana with Ella emerged, and there was none to suggest they had left in the last couple of years at least. It had been a lot easier to trace further where exactly in Ghana they were, after all that.

Vince had all but lost faith in the Security and Intelligence agencies until Humphrey had linked up with a colleague of his who was a high-ranking official at the *National Intelligence Agency*. Vince felt a huge sense of self-worth in having buddies in *high places* who were willing and had indeed gone out of their way to use resources at their disposal to help find his *runaway* wife. He vowed never to look down on the ability of these agencies to do their jobs. It had taken longer than expected, but they had come through for him in the end.

Humphrey had further set up some officers from his office in readiness to send them to Ghana. They were to liaise with the Security forces there to have Labake extradited and returned home with Ella to face kid-napping charges. Vince had, however, declined. The last thing he needed was the whole country knowing how weak he had been as a husband, such that his wife was able to abscond with his child for almost four years! No, he could not risk that. He was going to handle it himself and knew exactly what he needed to do.

Vince had told very few people about the disappearance of his wife and child, especially after that *bastard* of a neighbor of his, *Olakunle,* had blamed him for it. He frowned now, thinking about their conversation. Apparently, Deji Olakunle was Vince's neighbor within *Crossway Estate*. They had met for the first time one evening at *Stella's Bar*, which was a local drinking spot round the corner from their estate. Deji, who also had problems with his own wife and had been *drunk as a skunk* that evening, believed he had all the answers to Vince's marital issues.

After Vince lamented about his ungrateful wife running off with his daughter, Deji had accused Vince of being the probable cause of his wife's disappearance. According to him, *no woman ever left a man who was good to her*. What Vince found most annoying was that Deji was a complete stranger whom he had barely spent a minute with and who knew absolutely nothing about him or his marriage! *The effrontery*! Vince thought angrily now. However, he learned his lesson and kept mute about his issues after that. He smiled and told anyone who enquired about Labake and Ella that he had sent them abroad for some time. It was too embarrassing to tell anyone that his wife had absconded *with* his child! Thankfully, that was all about to change soon, he told himself.

Vince had explained to Humphrey that he would handle his family's return home himself. He'd had enough time to make his plans, had mulled over them all this time, and had perfected the skills needed to carry them out. Humphrey had offered him names of agents posted in Ghana and officials at the High Commission in Accra, should he need them. He had also warned him to be extremely careful as different rules applied here. Vince had again assured him that he knew what he was to do and promised to get in touch after he had successfully achieved his aim.

Vince had once dated a Ghanaian girl for over a year and had been to Accra several times in the past, he was not exactly a tour guide of the city, but he had a fair knowledge of it, especially with the help of the *GPS*. Once he arrived by air, he rented a car at the airport and checked himself into a hotel not too far from *The Dolphin*. He did not get a return ticket home as he knew he would be driving back home from Ghana *with* his daughter at least.

So, here he was in Accra, parked outside the hotel staff quarters where Labake lived, and everything was going perfectly according to plan. Spotting her when she came out of the building and walked towards the black *jag* earlier was like the cream on the cake. It had further convinced Vince that the *elements* were in agreement with him.

At a few minutes past midnight, Vince got out of the car and sprinted into the Staff Quarters of *Dolphin Hotel* with the small bag he had packed full of all kinds of tools and gadgets. He took a cursory look around the building and smiled before he went in. It was just the way he had hoped it would be. Apart from the outdoor lamps that were on, the place was dark and quiet, with no one coming or going. Finally, he was going to get what was rightfully his.

* * * *

"There's a Chief Ilo on the phone for you, Laide. Should I put him through?" Jean Paul, one of the switchboard operatives at the High Commission, said over the phone to Laide. An eyebrow went up when she heard the unfamiliar name. A *chief*? She was not sure she knew any chief. "Thanks, Jean Paul. Please put him through," she said hesitantly as she swiveled round her desk and sat up. She was certain there was a mix-up somehow, but she was not going to waste any time discussing that with Jean Paul.

"Good Morning, am I through to *Maria Olaide Joseph*? The elderly male voice on the other end of the phone asked. It was not a mistake then, Laide thought within herself. The call *was* actually for her, and whoever it was knew her full name. Her attention peaked at that moment, and she straightened her shoulders in anticipation of what was to come.

"Yes, this is she," Laide responded, waiting for a proper introduction.

The Chief cleared his throat and began speaking, "I'm sorry to intrude on your day like this. My name is Chief Benjamin Ilo. Er...if you don't mind me asking, are you the daughter of *Iyabode Makanjuola,* please?" Chief Ilo paused for an answer and continued when Laide confirmed she was. "I used to know your late mother, *Iyabode*. In fact, I only just learned days ago of her passing a few years back. I was...still am so sorry to hear that and have been trying to find you for some time now...I remember she brought you with her to see me years back...when you were a little girl."

Chief Ilo paused again and continued when Laide did not respond to any of what he had said.

"I just arrived in *Port Novo* and was hoping to have a sit down with you to discuss something rather...rather personal to me...and perhaps...your late mother. I'm staying at the *Grande` Hotel du Lac.* Now I'm aware that this may sound strange as you don't know me, but I have some vital information to pass on to you...about your mother...and myself. I plan to return home the day after tomorrow. Would you please meet me at the Hotel restaurant sometime today... if possible?"

Laide thought the Chief sounded nervous but extremely polite. He was clearly from her home country; she could tell from his accent. She wondered who he was, his connection to her mother, and more importantly, what exactly it was he wanted to discuss with her. She also wondered if it was safe to meet with him.

There was very little chance now that there was a mix-up somewhere. She knew for sure that she was exactly whom the Chief wanted to speak to as he knew not only her full name but also her late mother's name. He had also said he even met her as a little girl. How had he found her, she wondered now? She had left home quite a number of years ago. Her first posting had been a brief one in Tanzania, before Lisbon, Portugal, and then here in Port Novo, Benin. Apart from her sister Labake, she barely kept in touch with anyone back home, especially since her mother's death. So how had the chief found her?

"Can we not discuss whatever it is you have to say to me over the phone...sir?" Laide asked. She needed to have an idea of what it was he wanted to tell her and to see if it was worth her putting in an appearance at all.

"I'm afraid it isn't a matter I'd like to discuss over the phone, dear. I am a bit of a public figure back home. As I said, it is a rather private and very personal matter and I am aware that your office records a lot of phone conversations...I won't want our discussion to fall into the wrong hands...or ears, I should say...if you get my meaning. I'd rather speak to you in person if you can spare the time."

Laide figured that what the Chief had to say to her, the *important* and very *private* information he needed to give her, was vital if he came all the way to Port Novo to share it with her. She could not remember her mother ever mentioning any Chief. Her curiosity grew stronger, and she decided to meet with him at the popular five-star hotel in a couple of hours' time. She finished work at three-thirty pm anyway, and the hotel was just round the corner from the building that housed the High Commission. She would get one of the attachés to walk with her and remain discreet as she met with the chief. This was just the usual protocol here at the High Commission. As an official of the Foreign Mission, you did not go anywhere without facilitators or accompanying personnel.

Laide, however, decided to do some research on the chief before she met with him later that afternoon. She had written his full name down when he introduced himself at the beginning of the call and would at least *google* him. He sounded educated and polished. There was bound to be some information about him on the *World Wide Web,* especially as he had referred to himself as a *public figure* back home. She also decided to give her sister Labake a ring to find out if their late mother ever mentioned knowing a Chief in the years before she passed. Labake had spent more time with *Maami* as they both referred to their mother and also had a much closer bond with her than Laide did. Laide hoped she would have some information about this Chief Ilo.

* * * *

A couple of hours later, Laide spotted the chief the minute she entered the restaurant within *Grande` Hotel du lac*. She had been here several times for lunch with her colleagues. It was a nice place, and the food was superb. The Chief stuck out in the *not-so-busy* restaurant like a sore thumb, especially because he was alone at his table and looked quite different in the particular type of traditional wear he had on. It was a different style from that worn by the men here, in *The Republic of Benin,* and there was a regal and perhaps wealthy quality to the chief, just from his appearance.

Laide thought he looked slightly pensive and had his eyes fixed on the entrance when she and *Ola,* the attaché, walked into the restaurant. Once Laide gave the signal, Ola moved to the other side of the large room and took a seat. He maintained a good distance but kept a discrete and watchful eye on Laide from where he sat. That was the training he had received on the job, and he was good at it.

When Laide got to the table, she stretched her hand out to the Chief a bit hesitantly and tried to gauge the type of person he was now that they were face to face. She had not been able to speak to Labake on the phone as planned, but she had done some digging and found that Chief Benjamin Ilo was an extremely wealthy *VIP* back home in Nigeria. He, however, did not look like any of the pictures she found on the internet. He looked smaller, and his eyes seemed to dance a bit, perhaps out of nerves, when he realized she was the one he had been waiting to meet. Why did he seem so nervous? Laide wondered.

"Good afternoon, sir. I'm Olaide Joseph," Laide stated simply. The Chief rose slowly from his seat and took the hand she offered. He looked genuinely happy to see her, and Laide again wondered why.

"You're welcome, my dear. I'm Benjamin Ilo. Please have a seat. Would you like anything to eat or drink?" Chief Ilo asked, but Laide declined. She needed him to get to the bottom of why they were there as quickly as possible so she could be on her way.

"Right, let me first start by saying again that I'm sorry for the loss of your mother. She was a good person," Chief Ilo started, and Laide nodded hurriedly as if to say, *okay, please move on*. Her look was unflinching. She did not know the man or why he was there and wished he would dispense with the formalities and get to the reason why he needed to see her already.

"Can I ask, at this stage, if you have any siblings by your mother...younger perhaps?" The chief further enquired. His eyes narrowed as though he was trying to find the truth out through Laide's reaction to his question. Laide hesitated, her eyes narrowed slightly too at his question and body language at that moment. If he knew her mother as much as he claimed he did, why did he not know that she had two daughters?

"Er...yes, I do. I have a younger sister," Laide spoke reluctantly as all she came to do was listen to whatever *he* wanted to get off *his* chest. She was not here to provide vital information about herself to a complete stranger. She just needed to hear what *he* had to say. She was not planning to draw him her family tree.

"Would she be in her late...twenties?" The chief inquired slowly. His shrewd eyes were fixed on hers, and they seemed earnest, almost desperate even, Laide observed.

"Yes," Laide responded, refusing to supply Labake's exact age. She saw the immediate look of strained relief on the chief's face and heard the sharp intake of breath when he heard her answer. He slowly took a few sips of the glass of water on the table. It seemed to Laide that he had trouble swallowing the liquid. She decided to wait patiently for him to say something more.

"Well, my dear...not to beat about the bush, there's a strong possibility that your sister is my...is my biological...is my child," Chief Ilo said and waited for what he said to sink in. Laide blinked a couple of times as she processed what she had just heard.

"What?" Laide asked in a low tone. She was suddenly slightly confused. What exactly was the Chief saying to her? She asked again. "Sorry...can you repeat that, please?"

"You see, your mother and I...we...we had an affair some twenty-nine...twenty-eight years ago...it was brief...well...not quite, it lasted almost a year. I was married...still am... with a family of my own at the time...It was the first time I ever cheated on my...my wife and I regretted it...still do till this day...I...do not regret your sister, of course, but I regret the way I handled the whole affair after...after..." Chief Ilo stuttered and paused for a bit, struggling to find the right words to make Laide understand. He could not quite make out what the expression on her face was at that moment as she stared at him blankly. He then continued.

"You see, I had helped your mother start her small cooking business. I gave her some money when she came to ask for my help and...and long story short, one thing led to another...we started this affair. I tried to break it off several times but couldn't...Iyabo was a good person, and I guess I...I felt sorry for her. It wasn't supposed to happen, but she fell pregnant, and I lost my mind thinking about myself and how my wife would react and then...my girls...how it would affect them. It was selfish of me, and I can only blame it on my foolishness at the time. I insisted your mother terminated the pregnancy and knew I had to stop seeing her at that point...it was just all wrong. I refused to see her after she told me of the pregnancy and assumed she had the abortion as I never heard from her again after that," Chief Ilo finished awkwardly. He looked uneasy and perhaps ashamed of his story.

Laide looked away in that instant as she became overwhelmed with emotion. Though she did not remember a lot of her early years and certainly did not remember seeing the chief with her mother, she remembered *Maami* being pregnant with Labake and how she had struggled after her birth. There had been complications with Labake's delivery, and *Maami* had fallen ill due to an infection she had contracted after Labake's birth. She had almost died as she was unable to afford better healthcare.

In fact, Laide remembered their neighbors at the time, running in and out of the one room they lived in on the day Labake was born. Labake had been delivered at home by a traditional midwife who lacked proper training. *Maami* had cried out in pain for quite some time, causing a small crowd of neighbors to gather outside the doorway of their room. Laide remembered feeling frightened and confused by what was happening as no one had explained to her that she was about to become a big sister.

At some point on that fateful day, there had been utter pandemonium as rumors flew about the place that *Iya Laide,* as everyone referred to *Maami,* had died. Laide had spent a full week with *Iya Jide,* a neighbor and close friend of *Maami,* while *Maami* recovered. A week later, however, she developed further complications and had to be rushed to the general hospital, where she had to have a hysterectomy. This last detail, Laide and Labake had only discovered as young adults when *Maami* had told them the story of Labake's birth. She had never once mentioned Labake's father and had fallen silent each time Labake asked about him.

A tear slipped down Laide's face at what *Maami* had been through, how she had struggled to bring them up by herself in circumstances that could be deemed *abject* poverty. It saddened her to think Labake had been fathered by a billionaire who had impregnated their mother and ran off to his cushy life without a thought until now, almost thirty years after the fact and six years after *Maami's* death.

Laide then remembered her father's ill-treatment of *Maami* when he had resurfaced again in their lives a couple of years after Labake's birth. He had helped *Maami* restart the small cooking business again but had been mean to her, resenting the fact that she'd had another child by another man in his two-year absence. He had beaten her too, the few times when he had bothered to put in an appearance until he also eventually took off and never came back.

At least Chief Ilo had the excuse of not knowing *Maami* had *not* terminated the pregnancy as he instructed her to. He could be applauded for coming back in search of the child he was not even sure he had, albeit twenty-eight years late, Laide thought. The same, however, could not be said of her own father, who *knew* of her existence but had walked out of her life regardless. Laide had not seen or heard from her father in almost thirty years, and she had absolutely no plans of searching for him either.

She thought about Labake now. Her once sweet and intelligent sister and all she had also been through at the hands of her abusive husband. She wondered what her sister's life would have been like had Chief Ilo stepped up and been the father he should have been to her. If indeed he *was* her father.

These were the reasons why Laide had sworn never to marry. As far as she was concerned, no man was worth the trouble they brought. Her own father was enough proof, and so was Vince, Labake's abusive husband and now this Chief who had shirked his responsibilities years ago. The two women she knew and held dear, including herself, had all been treated badly by the men they had been acquainted with at various points in their lives.

Laide shook her head and turned to face Chief Ilo, who had grown silent watching her. He could tell she was deeply emotional and had seen the different emotions pass through her eyes.

"Why now? After all this time? Why have you come looking for the child you *abandoned* years ago?" Laide asked him with hot eyes.

Chief Ilo shifted uncomfortably in his seat at the question. He had expected some negative reaction from Maria Olaide Joseph and knew he deserved it, but he had come prepared to appeal to her too. She held all the aces in him gaining any access to her sister, the daughter whom, by his calculations, he was now sure was his. He, therefore, needed Maria to see things from his perspective.

"My dear, I'm not expecting you to understand why I did what I did as there's absolutely no excuse for it. People, however, do make mistakes...regrettable mistakes in life. I have no real regrets in my life except this one. The truth is that I honestly did believe your mother had the abortion as I told her to...I never heard from her again after that. She knew my office but never got in touch, even after she had the child...I know I said she was never to come to the office, but...one would expect that...that she would have, considering the child..." Chief Ilo had gone red in the face, his eyes watered, making it look like he was about to cry. He caught the tear that slipped quickly with his handkerchief, cleared his throat and continued.

"I, however, can't say I blame her for staying away... I don't hold it against her, not in any way. As I said, I was young and acted foolishly. It was selfish of me, but I was also worried that I'd lose my family if it ever came out that I hadn't only had an affair but that I'd fathered a child outside my marriage too." Chief Ilo swallowed hard and paused again before continuing.

"In answer to your question, I had a heart scare recently and would have died if it wasn't for God's intervention. I was in a coma for three days...while I was in a coma, and even after I came out of it, I've had repeated visions and dreams of your mother and she...she wasn't happy with me in them...after all these years, I wondered why but eventually put two and two together. I figured that the reason I kept having these recurring nightmares was probably because we...Iyabode and I, still had some unfinished business between us. It was why I decided to begin my search for her and have been looking for her for almost two years now. I eventually found out that she had died...I felt terrible to hear that. The next thing was to begin looking for you as I knew for sure that she had you. I was thankful when something came up on you after about another year or so of looking. My heart scare made me even more determined to look for your mother. I wouldn't want to die without finding out if I had a child with her...I would also want my family to know about her if anything happened to me. I believe God is giving me a second chance to put things right; indeed, it's been a long time coming. I'm quite ready to face whatever consequence comes of it."

That last bit the Chief said with apparent vehemence, Laide observed, and it made her feel almost sorry for him at that moment. He had searched for *Maami* for two years and spent another year looking for her once he discovered *Maami* had passed away. That revelation somehow made Laide feel slightly better.

Perhaps having a father would somehow help Labake, Laide thought silently. Surely this was an opportunity out of her current situation. She could perhaps come out of hiding and return home, considering the chief's position in society. Laide found herself now desperately hoping Chief Ilo *was* Labake's father. He could perhaps offer her some protection from that *brute* of a husband of hers, at least. He was clearly an influential man and had found her against all the odds. She just had to look for a way to convince Labake and was not even sure how she would receive this new development or if she was even ready for it, considering all she had been through.

Laide squared her shoulders and cleared her throat before saying, "Well, as you would understand, sir, this is a rather...*complex* situation...to say the least, and there isn't any *real* proof that you *are* my sister's biological father...I mean, how can you...*we* be sure of that?" Laide asked. She silently hoped for some reassurance from him that he *was* Labake's father, and she was glad that he at least appeared desperate to be.

Chief Ilo dipped his hand in his pocket and pulled out an envelope. He laid it on the table and pushed it to Laide. "This is a sample of my hair and some cash to cover the cost of DNA testing. Please use both to disperse any doubts you or your sister may have. I am convinced that your sister *is* my child, but I know you, and perhaps her, may need some convincing. I suspected the issue of having a DNA test might come up and therefore came prepared. Would it be possible...can you at least tell me her name and where she is? Is she here in *Port Novo* too?" Chief Ilo asked with a glimmer of hope in his eyes.

He had got to be kidding, Laide thought. She had no plans of telling him anything until she was sure and until she spoke to Labake. She, however, did not think this was a matter to be discussed on the phone. She was going to have to pay her sister a visit in neighboring Ghana this weekend or perhaps wait till Ella was on holiday in a couple of weeks, as Labake and Ella were planning on visiting her here in Port Novo.

Ella! Laide had almost forgotten about her niece and wondered what Chief Ilo's reaction would be to having a granddaughter too. Laide knew now that there was a lot to discuss still, far more than the Chief was aware of.

"I hope you understand, sir...that I don't feel comfortable sharing any more private information with you...not at this stage anyway. I would need to sleep on all we've discussed and...of course, figure out a way to explain it all to my sister too...see if she would be willing to...to hear from you. As you can imagine, it's a lot to take in...even I am struggling to process it all. I'll need some time to think about all we've discussed but will, however, be in touch...soon, sir," Laide said politely to Chief Ilo.

She was known to be the stronger of the two sisters in character and emotions too. She had strong views about men, especially because of all she had experienced as a child. She hated the patriarchal nature of the African societies she had lived in, first as a child and now as an adult and was quite known to stand up for herself where necessary, particularly if she believed she was being treated unfairly *by a man*. A colleague once described her as a *feminist,* and she had, in turn, called him a *chauvinist*. He had laughed about it, but Laide had meant it deep down within her.

While she did not approve of Chief Ilo's treatment of *Maami* – his abandonment of her and Labake all these years, Laide was raised by an extremely respectful mother. She had taught her girls some deep values, including honouring the elderly. Laide did not care much for the Chief. She had, however, treated him cautiously but politely throughout their discussion, which lasted forty-five minutes. After all, she thought within herself, he was *allegedly* her sister's father, and she was not going to deviate from the training she had received from her late mother just because he had dealt carelessly with her family.

"Thank you, Maria...er...Olaide...thank you so much for coming to see me. This is my business card; of course, you know where I am. Like I said, I'll be here till the day after tomorrow if you need to get in touch before then," Chief Ilo said appreciatively and got to his feet when Laide did. She observed that Chief Ilo wasn't a very tall man, but looking at him closely now, Laide thought she saw a slight resemblance to her sister. If he was indeed Labake's father, then Labake had clearly got her height from *Maami*, she mused silently.

She picked up the complimentary card and envelope with the cheque and DNA sample in it, gave the Chief a slight courtesy, and left the restaurant, which was now filling up with late lunchtime patrons. Ola, the attaché from the High Commission, followed her out, discreetly.

CHAPTER TWENTY-FOUR

"So, what did you think of Rewa then?" Ralph asked Israel the morning after Rewa's visit. Being a Sunday, Ralph and Israel were on the drive home from church. Ralph thought it a perfect time to bring the subject of Rewa up. He had thought about it all night and decided Israel's approval of her was quite important to him.

Israel was a part of the reason Ralph had refused to date seriously when Israel was younger. He had not wanted any distractions or interference raising him. He also did not want to confuse him, as Israel did not exactly have an easy time after his mother's death. He had been five and quite attached to his mother when she died. He had also had some difficulty talking about her after her death. Bringing another woman on the scene would not have been such a great idea.

It had taken Israel some time to begin to adjust and come to terms with his mother's death. Ralph had done his best to be there for his son as much as he could though he had been quite busy with his career. He had grieved the loss of his wife by burying himself in it. His mother and older sister had helped provide the female support a boy could need, and till this day, Israel was quite close to his grandmother, whom he called *gramps*, Ralph's sister, *Didi,* and her boys, who were also about Israel's age.

Israel was however a grown man now, and Ralph was proud of the man he had become. He was reasonable, responsible, and quite well-rounded for someone who had been raised by a rather busy father. Ralph also had his late wife's family to thank for that too. They had been a huge support in the early days, and he could not take all of the credit for how well his son turned out.

Israel had left his father and Rewa to themselves after dinner last night and gone out with his cousins. Ralph was not even aware of the time Israel got back in last night as he had gone straight to bed when he returned home from dropping Rewa off at her flat. It had been such a great evening, and he wondered what Israel thought of their dinner guest last night.

"You like her a lot, don't you, *Father*?" Israel smiled and gave his father a quick wink as he drove them home. He referred to Ralph as *Father* when he wanted to be cheeky, but most times, he called him *dad*. He had nothing but love and respect for his father. They had butted heads a lot when he was a teenager, but they had weathered the storm of those years and remained quite close still. Ralph had learned a long time ago to trust the training he had given his son, and Israel had earned his respect too, being the responsible young man he was.

"Actually, son, I do…I *really* do," Ralph responded, ignoring the cheeky look his son had just given him. "She's great, actually," he added. He felt good admitting his affection for Rewa, and it was almost as if he had now admitted it to himself too.

"She's different, isn't she?" Israel said with his eyes still on the road as he maneuvered the car on to the bridge.

"*Different*? How so?" Ralph asked, keen to understand what his son meant.

"You know...different from the last two you dated...even *Aunt Viv*," Israel explained to his father.

Aunt Viv had been his mother's old friend, and Israel had known her most of his life. She had a major attraction to Ralph even before her friend's death, but he had avoided her advances, and Israel teased Ralph about her all the time. They both thought *Aunt Viv* was overbearing and had a strong opinion on *everything*. She had tried everything to get Ralph's attention, but he avoided her like the plague as she just was not his type, and even if she was, Ralph knew he could not date his late wife's friend; it just seemed ethically wrong to him.

"*Viv*? Are you kidding? Rewa's *nothing* like Viv, and you know it!" Ralph quipped, causing both he and Israel to burst out in laughter.

"I know, dad, only joking. I really do like your new girlfriend. She seems fun and interesting. Seems very er... how do you say? Er... *level-headed*. That's it; she seems pretty level-headed," Israel concluded.

Ralph laughed at Israel's comment and said, "She's not *my girlfriend...yet*." He smiled, remembering the conversation they'd had in the car when they arrived at her apartment last night and smiled. "But she will be...soon. As per her being *level-headed*, well, let's just say the jury's still out on that one son. She's quite *serious-minded,* but trust me, she can be quite spunky or perhaps feisty too...and I find that somewhat attractive about her," Ralph concluded,

Israel took his eyes off the road briefly and glanced at his father. "Seems to me she's the perfect match for you then, *Father*." He did not say anything further on the subject, but he smiled, thinking Chief Ralph Eke *had* finally been bitten by the *love bug,* and he was happy for him; it had been a long time coming.

* * * *

Rewa was having such a beautiful morning. She hummed the song *'Great is thy faithfulness'* as she dressed up for work. The sky seemed so bright this morning, and everything seemed to be going beautifully well. She had a feeling it was going to be a glorious day and could not even tell why. All she knew was that her life seemed to have found new meaning in the last few weeks, and she suspected it had a lot to do with *Chief Ralph Eke*.

She smiled just thinking about him. It was all she did lately, day dreaming about Ralph, what could be and what she hoped would be. She had already started praying about him, too, trying to be spiritual and real about her prayer points. She liked him a lot and prayed it worked out between them - if it was the will of God for them both.

Rewa remembered her evening with Ralph and Israel the other night. She particularly remembered and replayed the entire conversation they had in his car, outside her apartment building, when he dropped her off that night. She was so excited and wished she had someone to discuss Ralph with. She, however, knew she had to be wiser this time. She was going to manage her situation with him as sensibly as she could. Her first inclination would usually have been to ring Faith up or even one of her sisters, but because of the delicate nature of the situation and the recent interference of the tabloids, Rewa knew her relationship with Ralph had to be handled as carefully as possible. So in the meantime, she kept quiet about it and prayed about it instead.

The conversation had been light as Ralph drove her home that evening. He had spoken a lot about Israel and his achievements and how proud he was of him. He had also mentioned that Rewa's father was a great friend and client of his, to which Rewa had been slightly surprised. Her father had also mentioned that Ralph was a friend, but Rewa had not realized they had any business dealings together, though she knew her father engaged the services of a couple of other attorneys too. She wondered what her parents would think now if anything did happen between herself and Ralph, considering how vehemently she had denied that they were in a relationship at the family lunch a few months back. However, she decided to give it little thought for the time being.

She and Ralph had also talked about the tabloids and the different stories making the rounds about their *budding romance,* but Ralph had swept it away again, stating he was used to it and usually did not pay them any attention.

Just before she bade him good night and moved to alight from his car, Ralph had reached out and held Rewa's hand and said.

"They think we're an item anyway. Why don't we just do it?" Ralph had asked Rewa, who was not quite sure she heard him right, and said, "Excuse me?"

Ralph had then said, "I can't deny that I'm attracted to you, Rewa. I think I've been since the moment you walked into my office, the first day we met and you dropped your papers all over my floor..." That bit, he said with a cheeky grin on his face. Rewa was not quite sure how to react to what he was saying as it was completely unexpected at that moment. All she knew was that her heart had started beating faster, and she felt he could hear it. She had not realized she had held her breath for so long until she saw that he was waiting for a response from her. When none came, as she could not speak for some reason, Ralph continued.

"I know it's been a bit *topsy-turvy* between us, and we didn't quite get off to a great start...but we could give dating a try. I must, however, warn you that I'm a little rusty on the dating scene but with a little patience...I guess I could..."

Rewa suddenly chuckled, stopping Ralph in his tracks. He saw the amused look in her pretty eyes and then said, "Well, at least you think I'm funny...I'm trying to be serious here..." Rewa just loved the lost, self-conscious expression on Ralph's face at that moment; she thought it was priceless. It was the first time she had ever seen him appear to be out of his depth as he seemed to struggle with finding the right words to say to her.

"I must say, your lines are pretty *whack...rusty* doesn't quite describe it," Rewa said playfully, finally finding her voice. He was like a self-conscious schoolboy who lacked any self-confidence in asking a girl out. At that moment, all she wanted to do was give him a reassuring hug.

"Thanks...for the *observation,* but you know what I'm trying to say...haven't done this in a long, long time..." Ralph said, and Rewa chuckled again and replied, "It's obvious." He certainly did not appear cocky now, she thought and found him and what he struggled to say rather endearing.

"So? What say you?" Ralph asked Rewa, who just sat and studied her companion as one would a puzzle.

"*What say me*? About what?" She asked, having been in deep thought.

"What say you about *us* dating...going steady, going out or whatever they call it these days?" Ralph enquired impatiently.

"I see you're quite the *romantic*," Rewa said sarcastically, but what she really wanted to do was scream *yes!* She however knew she could not; she needed some time. She could not quite believe it was happening. Chief Ralph Eke was asking her out! *The most eligible widower* in town, as her sister, Sede, had referred to him months back.

Rewa was thrilled and wanted to scream *Thank you Jesus!* Instead, she had played it cool and asked Ralph to give her some time to think about it first. He had walked her to her apartment door, and Rewa bade him goodnight. When she got into her apartment, she shut the door and got on her knees. Pumping her fist in the air, she shrieked, *"Thank you Jesus!"* It was going to be a great Christmas after all; she could just sense it!

* * * *

"I knew it!" Sede suddenly shrieked. "Your reaction that afternoon suggested there was more to your relationship with *Chief* Ralph Eke! You should have seen her, Rien; she bolted the minute the topic was raised at that *very awkward* family lunch." Sede finished dramatically. Rewa noticed that she overstretched Ralph's traditional title too. Gosh! She loved her sister very much, but she could throttle her at that moment. Rewa thought within her. Sede *always* had to be the *drama queen* in *every* situation.

Christmas was in a few days, and all three girls were at Rewa's apartment, having lunch. Rien had arrived with her family from Texas a few days before, and the girls had thought it would be nice to catch up at Rewa's, especially as Rien wanted to see Rewa's new apartment. All three sisters were seated around Rewa's small dining table, eating except Rewa, who bounced her newest nephew, *Anjola,* on her lap. His sister was at the Ilo residence with Rien's husband. Rewa had just revealed her new relationship with Ralph to them, and she *had* expected some drama from her middle sister in particular.

Rien smiled at Rewa and said, "That's some great news, sis! I'm really chuffed for you." Rewa smiled her appreciation and held the hand Rien stretched out across the table to her. She could not help it; she grinned coyly from ear to ear, like a Cheshire cat. She found herself smiling a lot recently. To say she was happy was an understatement; she was ecstatic!

"Slow your rolls, girl," Rewa said to Sede, rolling her eyes at her. "We hadn't actually started dating at that point. I was just his decorator...dating is quite a new development that started justa week ago! I wasn't going to say anything yet, but I noticed another picture of Ralph and me having dinner at *Island Place* the other day in the tabloids again. I knew no one would believe there wasn't anything more going on between us after seeing that photo," Rewa explained to both her sisters.

That had been the night she decided to accept to date Ralph exclusively, the night they had become an *official* couple. He had asked again if they could give the tabloids something *real* to talk about, and she had smiled shyly at him and said, "Why not." It had been Ralph who had smiled like a Cheshire cat that evening when she accepted. He had leaned over the table and given her a quick kiss on the lips. Rewa was sure someone had seen it and taken a photo, but she was not about to say anything about the kiss to her sisters.

After she gave her sisters the full story, Sede began to drum on the dining table, chorusing *Rewa has a boyfriend,* and Rien got to her feet and danced to Sede's beat, singing along happily too. Rewa laughed and gave her nephew a cuddle saying, "I guess *Aunty Rewa* really *does have a boyfriend."* To which all three girls laughed heartily.

"How's it been so far? Have you told the folks it's official between you guys? Do you think you'll get married? Have you met his son?" Sede suddenly began to ask animatedly. She was like an excited child over a brand-new toy.

"Hey, girl! One question at a time!" Rewa said to her, chuckling. She knew both her sisters were happy about her news. It had been something they'd prayed about for so long.

"How's it going, sis? Do you really like him? The last time we spoke, you thought he was a bit...arrogant?" Rien asked, needing some reassurance that Rewa was truly happy.

"Are you kidding right now, Rien? I mean, look at her...she's having a blast! She hasn't stopped smiling since we got here!" Sede provided, giving her baby sister an exaggerated look of disbelief.

"She's right, Rien. I *am* having a blast! I've fallen for Ralph so badly that I feel as if I have to reel myself in at times! I thought he was cocky and condescending, but he really is none of those things. He's actually a sweet guy...really," Rewa said, putting Rien's mind at ease.

"So, here's the real question, sis...when are we meeting him?" Rien further enquired of her eldest sister, clapping her hands and rubbing them together excitedly.

"*Nah,* Rien, the *real* big question is, how was your first kiss? Sede interjected before Rewa could answer Rien's question.

"*Sede*!!!" Both Rewa and Rien exclaimed at the same time with an embarrassed look on both their faces. Everyone in the family knew Rewa to be the more private and perhaps even *secretive* sister. It was a wonder she had even told them as much as she had already.

"*What*???" Sede asked, looking at both her sisters as though they were from another planet. "I mean, I *assume* you *have* had your first kiss...or haven't you?" She asked Rewa pointedly. On a different day, Rewa would have been cross with Sede's direct intrusion on her privacy, but that was the *Pre-Ralph* Rewa. These days, hardly anything got her angry. She smiled sweetly at both her sisters and said, "Sorry, sis, I don't intend to *kiss and tell*."

"*Spoilsport*. That sounds like an admission, actually. That's enough for me," Sede said, sticking her tongue out and rolling her eyes at her elder sister.

Rewa smiled at her sister and stuck her own tongue out at her, too, remembering the first real kiss she and Ralph had shared. It had been one evening after another lovely outing. Rewa had invited him in when he dropped her at her apartment. They had just had a lovely meal at one of the nice restaurants in town, and the evening was still young. Neither Ralph nor Rewa were willing to end the evening in a hurry. If this was how it felt to have a *mature,* romantic relationship, then she really had been *missing out* all these years, Rewa thought as she got some water out of her refrigerator for both of them.

She had a warm, fuzzy feeling in her stomach each time she was with Ralph and her heart just seemed to beat slightly faster. She had yearned to be kissed by him since their first outing in Soho months back and had wondered when or if at all he would make a move. He had planted a quick peck on her lips a couple of nights before to seal their relationship, but it had been just that, a quick peck. Rewa wanted more; she wanted to feel his lips on hers and believed they both had a huge sexual attraction for one another. They were both Christians and believed that sex outside marriage was completely off the table, but Rewa knew she would not mind the odd kiss here and there. She had been celibate for some time now anyway, and she planned to remain so until her wedding night.

Ralph rose off the couch to help her with the tray of water and glasses when Rewa came out of the kitchen. He took them off her and set the tray down on the coffee table. He then silently drew her to him in an embrace. His eyes were fastened on hers, and Rewa noticed his usual expression of aloofness intensify at that moment, confirming to her again that it really was his natural facial expression. She had noticed that his son Israel had the very same look too.

"I'm going to kiss you now...can I please kiss you now?" Ralph whispered in a voice laced with desire. Rewa giggled at his warning and said, "Was that a statement or a question?" She asked flirtatiously. She was amused by Ralph's question; she wanted to burst into laughter at how proper he was but knew it would ruin the moment. Suddenly, she felt like a secondary school girl as she shut her eyes, and tilted her head up to him, pursing her lips in anticipation.

Ralph smiled and bent to claim her lips properly for the first time. It was slow at first, but then it got deeper and stronger. Before she knew it, Rewa felt drunk, and the room began to sway a little. It was as though she was caught in slow motion. It had to be the most beautiful kiss she had ever experienced in her adult life, Rewa thought now, remembering it.

"Hey, sis! You're about to start drooling, you know...what? Remembering your first kiss with Ralph?" Sede asked, jolting Rewa back to the present.

"Can we even call him that? He's a lot older than us, Sede," Rien supplied with a slightly worried expression on her face.

Rewa smiled and said, "You guys are amazing...didn't expect such excitement *and* questions! *Phew!* Talk about a *grilling*! Not to worry, Rien, Ralph is quite liberal-minded. I bet he wouldn't care what you called him. As for you, Sede, I only have an *eye roll* in response to your rather *intrusive* and *nosey* questions." Rewa rose from the table, handed her nephew back to his mother, and began clearing the dishes.

CHAPTER TWENTY-FIVE

Vince picked at the door lock to Labake's apartment as quietly and patiently as he could. He had studied all kinds of locks in the last few weeks and found that there was hardly any lock that could not be compromised. All one needed was time and skill. Suddenly, he heard the click he was waiting for and almost shuddered in relief, but instead of the door opening all the way, it had a chain on it, preventing a full opening. He cursed under his breath, irritated by the unexpected chain on the door. He looked around again, hoping he did not have any spectators, and put the tool bag he was carrying down again as gently as possible. He rummaged through it for the mini cutter he had brought along just as a second thought. He was thankful he had listened to his gut and brought it. The chain attaching the door to the frame came undone with one swift hand movement on the instrument.

Vince took a sharp breath and quietly entered the tiny, darkened living room. He had checked for any noise or movement through the door before he began to pick the lock. He did not hear a TV or anything like that on and was almost certain Labake and whoever else was an occupant of the apartment had retired for the night. Adrenalin had begun pumping, and the effects of the *weed* he had smoked before he left the hotel had also kicked in. He smoked some weed every now and again to keep focused and had picked up the habit again after leaving University when Mr. Singh became his boss some eight years ago.

Vince looked every part the house burglar in the attire he had chosen to wear in executing his plan. He wore a dark hooded sweatshirt with a pair of matching joggers with a baseball hat which he now revealed after pulling back the hood of his sweatshirt. He moved the flashlight he had brought around the small living space and stopped dead in his tracks when he thought he heard a muffled voice towards the back of the apartment. He walked slowly towards it in his *trainers* and stood as still as possible, listening to Labake's conversation with the voice he now recognized to be Laide's, her sister's.

He was relieved to hear it was a phone conversation but lost his temper when he heard Labake describe the kiss she had exchanged with the stranger in the *Jag*. He listened and heard how she suddenly broke down in tears because she was still married to him but was *in love* with the stranger he now garnered was named *Earl*. His nostrils began to flair. He had always known she was a little *slut* and was even more convinced it *was* this Earl of a character who had helped her run away from him. How long had she known and dated him? Vince wondered.

Thinking about Labake with Earl some more suddenly shot his temper up and made him lose his cool completely. It had not been his exact intention to crash into the room the way he had. His temper got the better of him as he listened to the phone conversation between his wife and her sister. It had already got his imagination going, and then to hear himself being described as *over* by Laide had further foiled his entire plan.

* * * *

"Guess what, sis?" Labake asked her sister, Laide, excitedly over the phone. As was their usual custom before they both turned in for the night, Labake and Laide spoke every evening since Labake and Ella's arrival in Accra. Labake lay on her chest, legs up, ankles crossed, on her bed, in a pink tank top and matching cotton shorts as she spoke excitedly into the phone to her elder sister. The only source of lighting in the small room was a bedside lamp.

Out of habit, she left her room door slightly ajar in case Ella came into her room in the middle of the night, as she was known to do sometimes. Her cell phone was on speaker as she spoke to Laide, another habit she had formed. With Ella asleep, apart from the hum of the air conditioner, the apartment felt somewhat quiet but listening to Laide's voice via her phone speaker did not make Labake feel so alone.

Labake had already filled Laide in on how Earl had rung her up out of the blue after some three weeks of silence. She explained how she had been so happy to hear from him, how she had not realized how much she missed him and how she went downstairs to meet him at the car park, at his request. Laide could hear the excitement in her sister's voice, which became infectious as she began to feel excited too. It had been a long time since she heard Labake sound the way she did now. She was grateful that things were becoming better for her sister and that a bit of her old self seemed to be returning. The way she giggled reminded Laide of their earlier years as children. It really was a joy to hear Labake this way.

"What?" Laide asked enthusiastically, smiling in anticipation of what Labake was so excited about.

"He kissed me!" Labake blurted out shyly but excitedly still. Conscious that Ella was asleep in the next room, she desperately tried to keep her voice as low as possible. The walls were rather thin in the apartment, and Ella was a light sleeper. The last thing Labake needed was to awaken her or have her overhear the conversation between herself and Laide.

"*Kissed you?* Where? How? Was it a peck on the cheek? On the lips or a proper kiss...as in, lips locked?" Laide asked yearning for details and deliberately trying to make her sister blush. She was thoroughly enjoying the news Labake shared with her and had hoped for months now that she would give in to Earl's advances in time. She was elated that it was happening much sooner than she had envisaged!

Labake giggled and said, "*Yes*! It was the latter! Like *three* times!" Struggling to contain her excitement but unable to. "*Really*? Tell me all about it, and don't leave a single detail out!" Laide said, now even more exhilarated with Labake's news. Labake gave her an exact rundown of things said and done by Earl when she joined him in his car earlier.

"It was really nice and...and...it felt different...you know. Not like anything...I've ever felt. I almost didn't want him to stop and was powerless to resist him too, as I really wanted him to..." Labake further explained to Laide and trailed off when she realized what she had been about to say.

She paused for a moment, and Laide immediately sensed what Labake was feeling.

"Labake? Are you there?" Laide enquired when her sister suddenly fell silent.

"Yes...yes, I am. It just suddenly feels like I did the wrong thing...what was I thinking? I didn't stop him...I even enjoyed it...I'm married...*still* married to...to Vince! *God*! What have I done? *Adultery*...I've committed *adultery,* Laide! What was I thinking? The worst of it is I...I think I'm falling in love with Earl...but I'm *married...still married* to Vince. That's a bad thing, Laide? *It's a sin!*" Labake said in an almost hysterical manner and suddenly broke down in tears. "Why is it so complicated? Why is my life so complicated, Laide?" Labake asked her sister in frustration. In her head, being married to Vince was a real weight that just seemed to get more burdensome, even after all this time away from him.

Laide felt sad for her sister as she began to sob. She hated that the thought of Vince still seemed to set Labake back, particularly when something good like what she shared with Earl happened. The thought that Vince, in a way, still dominated her sister despite being thousands of miles away, and even after all this time, angered Laide. Or was Labake still so damaged that she psychologically felt the need to sabotage a romantic relationship with Earl just so she could somehow keep Vince in view? Laide had read somewhere that sometimes, domestic violence had far-reaching effects on its victims, such that even when they were no longer exposed to the violence or a threat of it, the victim still felt trapped in their minds. Could this be what was happening with her sister?

"Labake, when will you stop feeling sorry for yourself? It's high time you woke up and smelt the coffee! Yes, you've been through a terrible experience, but you're past it now! It's time to move on and stop making references to the past! In fact, being with Earl is a sure way to move on and *forget* the past. Your past life is over! *Vince* is over! It's you, Ella, and Earl now, if you would let him love you. When will you get that...?"

Suddenly, Laide heard a bang on the other end of the phone. It was like something crashing against a wall, and then she heard Labake scream. It was a blood-curdling sound, causing Laide to instinctively jump off her bed and yell into her phone, "Labake! Labake!! Labake!!! What's the matter? Labake! Can you hear me? Labake!!!" Laide cried into the phone. She was alarmed and wondered what was going on with her sister, thousands of miles away in Accra. Her heart began to pound, and she began to feel slightly giddy. She paused for a bit to see if she could hear anything else through her phone. Then Laide heard what she thought was a familiar male voice on the phone but could not quite remember whose it was until he spoke to her directly, through Labake's phone. The blood drained from her face when recognition dawned, and she heard Vince's voice next on the phone. She felt both confused and perplexed at the same time as she tried to work out what exactly was happening at that moment.

"So you think *I'm over,* do you, Laide? *You think I'm over*? Well, I am not!!! How long did you think she could hide from me?" Vince yelled into the phone at Laide, who still wondered if she had actually heard right or if she was imagining things. She heard Labake screaming and shouting in the background and suddenly heard Ella crying loudly too, as Vince cursed at her mother before the phone suddenly went dead.

* * * *

Vince pulled out the *Glock* and crashed into Labake's bedroom unexpectedly, causing her to leap out of her position on the bed with a frightened look on her already tear-stained face. The look of sheer fear on her face was priceless, Vince thought. It gave him an inexplicable rush of pleasure. His next thought was to kill her there and then. Just kill her and take his daughter, whom he was not even sure was in the apartment yet. He, however, resisted the urge to shoot Labake at that point. Killing Labake now was too simple a way for her to die. He needed her to pay for the hurt she caused him, and he was going to enjoy every minute he spent torturing her. He was going to make her life miserable first, such that she would wish she had not done what she had. Besides, he needed to know where Ella was, and killing Labake would not help him if Ella was not in the apartment. He chided himself for not looking around the small closet of an apartment for his daughter first before he followed Labake's voice.

Initially, Labake did not recognize her estranged husband as she scrambled for the extreme corner of the bed, against the wall. She cried out again in fear and could not quite comprehend what was going on. *Was she being burgled? Oh God! Ella is in the other room! Had he seen her? Did she leave the front door unlocked? How had the stranger got in? Wait a minute; there was something strangely familiar about those eyes.* She blinked twice as if to clear a blur in her vision and recognized who it was. This was no stranger, she thought in utter panic; it was *Vince*! He had found her, just as he always promised he would if she ever left him. This was the day she had dreaded most in the last three years. It had finally arrived. He had said she could not run from him as he would catch up with her, and he finally had.

He looked different, leaner, and meaner. He looked like the monster he was, Labake thought, her heart beating wildly. She feared that Vince was going to kill her and she was going to die, leaving her daughter. Who would help her now? Then she saw the gun and screamed louder. It was all over now, she thought; he was here to kill her. Her mind froze for a bit as she watched Vince cautiously. The memories all came rushing back now. The *flight or fight* emotion within her resurfaced again. In a matter of seconds, she was living her nightmare, transposed back to *Crossway Estate*, trapped in the most unpleasant situation ever, one that was once her life and had now come to haunt her here in Accra, thousands of miles away. She was her husband's prey again.

Labake tried to focus and willed herself to think. What was her plan? It was foolish of her not to have one, knowing this day would come. How would she stay alive in her present circumstance *for* her daughter? Labake wondered as she watched the familiar evil glint in Vince's eyes. He looked as though the sight of her pleased him and angered him at the same time...which was it? She tried to gauge silently in trepidation.

Labake screamed as Vince reached for her and struck her with the butt of the gun. He took her cell phone off the bed where she had thrown it when she first saw him and spoke into it to Laide. When he was done, he threw the cheap phone against the wall, crashing it into tiny small pieces. He reached for Labake again, causing her to scramble out of his grip like a wild animal. He grabbed her ankle, dragged her off the bed, and began spitting out curses at her as he angrily dealt her repeated blows to the head. Labake screamed and cried out as Vince beat her. They were vicious blows that made her sound like a wounded animal at some point as she gurgled and cried out, still struggling wildly to break free from her husband's grip.

Suddenly, Labake swooned, causing the small room to seem as though it had turned on its head and whirl around as she began to pass out. There was blood everywhere, on Vince's fist, on the bed, and on the wall too. Vince found he could not get a grip on his anger.

He wanted her to hurt badly and feel the pain she had caused him all this while.

"Where is my child?" Vince yelled at Labake as her eyes rolled back in their socket. He left her momentarily and yelled, "Ella! Ella!!" His breathing was labored from pummeling his wife as he struggled to gain some composure, enough to at least complete his mission. He turned for the door and saw his daughter in her pajamas, clutching a stuffed bear, clearly transfixed, confused, and afraid at what she was witnessing. Her mother's cries had awakened her, and she stood there, clearly in shock.

Suddenly, as though jolted, Ella screamed and ran to her mother, making a beeline to avoid the stranger who reached for her. She did not appear to recognize her father or even his voice as she had never seen or heard him like that before. She had been too young to remember the incident at her grandmother's house years before when her father had first attacked her mother with her in the same room.

Vince was shattered that Ella appeared frightened of him and herself began screaming, "Mummy! Mummmmy!!" She cried earnestly, tugging at her mother, who lay bloodied on the floor by the bed. Labake stirred and slowly came to at Ella's screaming and nudging.

"Ella...*Princess*...it's me, daddy...*your* daddy *Princess*...don't you remember me?" Vince asked his daughter, trying to soften his tone of voice though his eyes were still wild with rage.

Ella shook her father's hands off and pulled her mother's arm instead, urging her to get off the floor. Suddenly, ignoring the immense pain in her head and the accompanying fuzzy feeling that came with it, Labake scrambled off the floor, again like a wounded animal, her primal instincts in top gear. She grabbed her daughter, backing further into the room, away from Vince, who stood for a moment himself, confused by Ella's reaction to him. He had not expected this reaction nor anticipated it from his *princess*. In fact, his entire plan was going contrary to his intentions.

Vince then pointed the gun at Labake, who shrieked and turned Ella's face into her belly. She was unaware of how much Ella had seen, but she knew it could not be good. In spite of all Vince had done and what he was doing at that moment, the last thing she wanted was for the poor child to remember her father in that manner, not because Vince deserved any protection on her part but for Ella's sake. She did not want her daughter tainted by the horrendous picture of what was happening in that instance. It was, however, too late as Ella had seen far too much already. The side of her mother's head dripped with blood, and her left eye was beginning to swell. Her upper and lower lips were split and beginning to swell too. There was blood running from her nose and the corner of her mouth.

Labake's entire face seemed to have become a shade of purple and red, and she had to shake her pounding head as if to ward off the cloud of unconsciousness that threatened to envelop her again and again. She struggled to stand and stay up as she clutched her whimpering child to her belly, trying to keep focused with one eye on Vince. She felt so helpless and could not think of what to do. She had not uttered a single word to Vince and had never really been able to. She was terrified and wondered why it was a struggle for her to keep her eyes open. She felt as though she needed to lie down but could not. *I need to stay awake for Ella,* she told herself over and over again in her mind as her eyes threatened to close and she felt her knees buckle. *God, please help us!* She thought within her.

"I see you've managed to turn my own daughter against me," Vince began with a snarl on his face. His eyes were even wilder now, and he looked dangerously evil at that moment. Labake felt as though the nightmares she'd had of him chasing her with a murderous look in his eyes were now being replayed in real time. Her heart beat wildly, and in a way, the sound of it kept her from slipping into oblivion as it rang in her ears. Labake maintained her grip on Ella's head, clutching it to her belly so she could not turn it.

"The way I see it, you have two options," Vince continued as Ella whimpered and Labake cowered silently in the corner of the room, struggling still to stay conscious.

"You can get a bag, pack a few things and your passports and return home without me having to get the *Ghanaian* police involved...as I hope you're smart enough to know, kidnapping is a crime in every country," Vince continued in a dangerously quiet voice. Labake blinked twice, trying to comprehend what he was saying. Was he here to take her back home as his wife? To carry on as if the last three years did not happen? She wondered.

"...or I shoot you dead, here and now, and your miserable, worthless life would be over. Either way, I leave Accra *with* my daughter, whom I came for. I could tell the police that I was aggrieved and claim some psychological breakdown for having not seen my only child in the last three years. All I have to say is I was provoked by that, and it led me to kill my estranged wife, who ran away with my daughter to another *freaking* country! Three years, I've missed *three years* of her life! You did that...*you*!" Vince had begun to yell as he spoke. It was as if the gravity of what Labake had done dawned on him even more as he spoke the words. Again his anger got the better of him, and he fired the gun at Labake, causing Ella to scream as her mother slumped.

CHAPTER TWENTY-SIX

"I *Want* my mummy!" Ella yelled at her father, who clumsily tried to shove her into the back seat of his rental car. He hoped no one would come out of any of the other apartments as a result of the kafuffle. Ella screamed, cried, and fought against Vince from the moment he got her out of the apartment, all the way down to the discreetly parked rental. He began to think he should have brought something along to make her unconscious while he got her away from her mother. He had not anticipated any of this.

"I want my Mummy...MUMMMMMY!!!" She yelled at the top of her voice, as one crying out for help. She bit her father's arm and kicked him in the shin, making it difficult for Vince to put her in the car. Vince winced in pain and panicked. His entire plan was coming apart right before his eyes! His temper had gotten the better of him and was ruining everything.

He *had* planned to threaten Labake with the gun and also planned to threaten to hand her over to the authorities for kidnapping if she refused to come back home with him. He had actually believed it would be that easy. He had thought Ella would be much more compliant and *want* to come back home with him, but that was so far from the case. Instead, she bellowed at the top of her voice, kicking and screaming, awakening the entire building.

Vince desperately tried to think of a way to keep his daughter quiet and thought he might need to knock her out as he struggled to bundle her into the car again. Ella bit his arm again, and he lost it this time, instinctively hitting her across the face. Rather than keep her quiet, the poor child wailed louder and fought even harder to break free from her father. Under different circumstances, Vince thought he would have been proud of the level of resistance his little girl put up, but at present, he wished she would cooperate with him *and* his general plan.

One or two lights came on in the building, and Vince saw someone running towards him in the corner of his eye. It was *Kofi*, who worked as a chef in the hotel kitchen. "*Hey*! What do you think you're doing? *Hey...*" Kofi said as he got closer and saw Ella struggling with Vince. He reached for Vince's arm and pulled it to try and get his attention. Vince got even angrier by the interruption. He turned to Kofi and struck him in the face as it was too late to reach for the gun. The sudden blow caused Kofi to stagger backwards. Ella cried louder for her mother as Vince reached for the gun and pointed it at Kofi, who struggled to comprehend what was happening. He recognized Ella instantly but was unsure who the man in black was. All he knew was he appeared to be kidnapping the poor child, a colleague's daughter. When Kofi saw the flashing steel of the gun, he stepped back with both hands raised and decided to reassure Ella instead.

"That's alright, Ella. It'll be alright, dear...what do you think you're doing, Mr?" Kofi asked again. He still had his hands in the air. "Where is her mother?" He asked Vince, who stepped away from the car, enough to cause Kofi to step even further away from him.

"All you need to know is that *I am her father,* and I've come to take her home. Now, mind your business and walk away, or else..." Vince said to Kofi in a menacing way. Kofi looked from Vince to Ella as if waiting for the child to confirm if what Vince had said was true. "Where's your mummy Ella?" Kofi asked Ella, who pointed up towards their flat but kept crying. "Do not talk to my child!" Vince yelled at Kofi, breathing heavily and wielding the gun at him. Once he saw Kofi maintained his distance, he turned to Ella again and attempted to put her in the car again. In that instant, Ella bit her father's wrist, very hard this time, causing him to wince in pain. She yanked his arm off hers and ran towards the building.

Mrs. Asumadu, the Head House Keeper of the hotel, was awakened from sleep suddenly. She thought she heard a loud bang and wondered what had caused the noise. She lived on the top floor too, in the apartment next to Labake's immediate neighbor *Acho,* who was away on training in Senegal. The noise had been so loud Mrs. Asumadu had heard it through the wall she shared with Acho. Alarmed that something terrible was happening on the premises, she had peered through the bay window and saw someone running towards the stairs. After a moment, she had quietly cracked open her front door and seen from the communal veranda, which led to the exit of the building, a man with Ella near the car park and the gun pointed by Vince at Kofi, who had his hands up in the air. What was going on? She wondered. Immediately, Rose Asumadu crept back indoors and rang her husband, *Lance Asumadu,* who was head of security at the Hotel and happened to be on duty that evening.

"There's something going on here, dear! A man is pointing a gun at Chef Kofi and struggling with Ella...Labake's little girl...they're all downstairs at the car park. Please ring the police...hurry! I'm scared!" She whispered to Lance, who asked a few more questions before springing to action.

The hotel was on a direct link to the local police and even had a few policemen stationed within the premises just so hotel patrons felt at ease. There had been a few armed robbery incidents in hotels around Accra recently. As a precaution, the management had therefore requested a few officers to be stationed within the hotel grounds.

"Take it easy, Man. You could hurt someone!" Kofi yelled at Vince as he swore under his breath and went after Ella, who had managed to scramble into the building. Kofi thought to go after them at first but changed his mind and decided to go back into his apartment on the ground floor, to get his phone instead. He needed to alert security at the main gate before things got out of hand.

Just then, Vince turned and saw Kofi running purposefully into the building. He became frantic and felt as though everything was going against his original plan. He panicked and fired the gun at Kofi, believing he was going to get some help or perhaps a weapon of his own. However, he missed and was stunned that he had and that Kofi was getting away. He fired the gun again and caught him just under the neck this time.

Vince saw Kofi crumble to the floor and derived some satisfaction from it. Kofi was a distraction, and Vince could not have him alerting anyone else. If he could just get Ella, he could still carry on with his plan, he thought within himself. He turned and continued after his daughter, hurrying up the stairs, taking them two steps at a time. He suddenly froze when he heard the sirens in the distance; they sounded closer and closer. *The police?* Who had alerted them already? He wondered. He then contemplated continuing with his plan by fetching Ella or leaving her, getting back to the rental car, and making a quick exit.

Vince was aware he had killed two people at that point. There was no explaining to the police how his wife had kidnapped his daughter three years ago and how he had come back for her. He was now a bonafide murderer and attempted kidnapper himself, and there was no escaping the law if he was caught at that point. He had killed Labake and the nosey neighbor who just would not let things be. He now had blood on his hands. How had it all gone so wrong? He wondered again in frustration. He decided he needed to get Ella now that he had shot and killed her mother.

As Vince took a further step towards the apartment, he heard police boots coming up the stairs behind him. He turned with the gun still in his hand and heard, "Police! Drop your weapon...*now*!" Vince stood rooted to the spot for a moment, gun in hand, pointed to at least five uniformed policemen, all armored up in bullet vests and helmets and armed with bigger guns, lined up all the way down the stairs.

God! How many of them were there? He wondered, thinking he really had messed things up. *I must look like a thief caught in the very act of robbery,* he thought within himself and shook his head slowly. Well, he was here for one thing, and he had to achieve it, police or not. This was his last thought as he fired his gun at the police.

* * * *

Labake's index finger suddenly moved and became still again, causing her sister, Laide, to jump to her feet, where she sat a few meters away. She moved to her sister's bedside as quickly as she could and said softly, "Labake...Labake, can you hear me?" Labake did not respond, her eyes were shut, and she just lay in the hospital bed lifelessly. She had been comatose for seventeen days now, and Laide prayed she would come out of it. Except for the quiet beep from the machines, indicating she was still alive, Labake looked dead.

Though she'd had a blood transfusion to make up for the copious amount of blood she had lost from the bullet wound she received from Vince's gun, Labake still looked deathly pale, and Laide was worried about her. The surgeon who had operated on her to dislodge the bullet and fix the damage done to her chest had said it was a miracle she was still alive. The bullet had narrowly missed her heart but had pierced through and lodged in a lung, almost collapsing it. A rib had been removed by the surgeons so that they could get to the bullet.

The surgeon, *Dr. Laye,* had seen from the X-rays that all of Labake's ribs had been broken and healed from past wounds. They had enquired if she had ever been in an auto crash or something similar before. Laide had explained that Labake was a victim of domestic violence. She had struggled to overcome the shock of discovering that her sister had been beaten that badly. She felt sadder now that she had been unaware of the extent of violence Labake had suffered at Vince's hand prior to her arrival in Accra. Hitherto, Labake had not mentioned how badly Vince had hurt her; it just was not her way to complain.

Laide was thankful that Labake had been found at the time she had, on the night of the incident with Vince. She prayed earnestly that she would survive her husband's violence yet again and be all right in the long run. Labake and Ella were all the family she had. She could not imagine life without either of them.

Vince had really done it this time. She frowned as she stood, watching her baby sister. Apart from the major issues with her lungs, Labake also had some swelling in her brain from the repeated blows Vince had dealt her to the head before he shot her. *The guy was a maniac!* Laide hissed again. The police had concluded he had come to Accra to kill Labake and then steal Ella back home with him. How could he have expected that to happen? What had been his plan? Laide wondered now. She concluded that Vince was mentally ill and her poor sister had lived with him for over six years. She hoped that Labake lived to tell her full story one day.

Laide remembered the revolting feeling of panic she had when Labake's phone went dead seventeen days ago after Vince had interrupted their conversation. She had been delirious with sudden fear and confusion at first, wondering what was going on. Laide had forced herself to try and remain calm so she could think about what next to do to help her sister, who was thousands of miles away in Ghana.

She had immediately rang Kwame when she realized what was going on. She had asked him to please ring the police. In a panicked state, she explained how she believed her sister's violent husband had found her, and she was uncertain what he would do to her. Kwame had done just that and arrived at the hotel within minutes. According to him, what he had seen on arrival was only best imagined. There was blood everywhere, from the top of the stairs of the hotel Staff Quarters to Labake's apartment. Of course, Labake had been found unconscious, in a pool of her own blood, in her bedroom.

Unfortunately, Ella had seen it all. She had witnessed her father beat and fire his gun at her mother and seen her mother's unconscious body, covered in blood. She had also seen the blood everywhere, on the sheets, walls, and floor of her mother's bedroom. She had been the first at the scene in the apartment after her father shot her mother and the only witness to what exactly happened. The housekeeper, Mrs. Asumadu, had managed to tear her away from her mother's side and take her out of the small apartment. Ella had screamed out of fear when she ran up to the apartment and found her mother in the state she was.

Vince had been shot dead during the crossfire between him and the police. He had shot at them, and they had no choice but to shoot him. He had died instantly from a single bullet to the head. By the time Kwame got to the scene, Vince's lifeless body was sprawled at the bottom of the stairway, where it had fallen as the police waited for both the forensics and ballistics unit's arrival. Kwame had managed to make it into the apartment after explaining who he was and how he was related to its occupants. Laide was thankful for Kwame's help again and felt she would forever be indebted to him.

It had been really late when the sordid affair started, but Laide had also rung one or two of her own colleagues at work and explained that she had a family emergency to attend to in Accra and therefore needed some time off work. She took the next available flight out of Benin to Accra to be with her sister and niece.

That was seventeen days ago, and Laide had not envisaged the situation would necessitate her staying this long, but there was no way she was leaving Labake's side until she was sure she was okay. Besides, Ella needed her too. The poor child had been catatonic as a result of the traumatic experience she had been through and had nearly become an orphan in one night. She needed a family member around to look after her. Laide had managed to get Ella to talk about it, and she had in her own way. She was still clearly in shock, but Laide knew she would be alright with time. She had ensured she started school almost immediately, so she did not miss a lot of it and just to get her back into as familiar a routine as possible. It seemed to have helped too, as she had begun to speak a bit more about the shooting incident.

Laide had asked for some extra time off work from her line manager. She mentioned how her sister had been shot and now lay comatose in the hospital. She explained that she needed the extra time to care for her and her niece. She, however, had not bothered to go into the gory details of *how* Labake had been shot but was aware that the news of her shooting had spread like wildfire. The whole of *West Africa* had read of the incident as it was in the papers, and of course, social media had played its usual role in *trending* the story. *Mr. Gyang* had been very understanding and asked her to take all the time she needed.

Everyone was talking about the *Nigerian* man who had attempted to kill his estranged wife and kidnap his young daughter in Ghana. Laide sighed, just thinking about it. The papers had given all kinds of scenarios about the incident, and not one had even come close to the truth. One of the papers had even said that Labake had run off to Ghana to be with her lover, a married man. If only they knew the real story, Laide sighed again as she watched her sister.

Suddenly she remembered her meeting with Chief Ilo the afternoon before Labake's incident with Vince. She had not even had a chance to discuss it with Labake yet. She had planned to do so when Labake and Ella visited her in Benin during the holidays, but that had all changed now. She hoped her sister would come out of the coma and get better soon, so she could tell her. Laide thought it would be sad too if Chief Ilo never got a chance to meet the daughter whose whereabouts he had only just discovered.

Then there was the DNA test Laide had done while here in the hospital. She had taken a sample of Labake's hair and the sample Chief Ilo had given her to the hospital laboratory for both to be tested. The results were not out yet, though. They had said it would take at least ten days. The cheque Chief Ilo had given Laide had been more than sufficient to cover the cost of the test, but she had not used it. She planned to send it back to him someday, along with the test results, when they came back. Laide wondered again what Labake's reaction would be when she found out there was the possibility of her having a father who was alive and wanted to meet her.

There was a small knock on the door, and Laide turned to see Earl walk in quietly with yet another bouquet of flowers. She recognized the worried look in his eyes immediately. He did not speak but gave her a reassuring hug. She watched Earl silently for a moment as he moved to the bed where Labake lay lifelessly. Laide had felt his genuine love for her sister from the very first day she met him. She knew he worried just the way she did. He had mentioned that he had been with Labake earlier, on the day Vince shot her. He said he wished he had never left her that evening.

Laide had met Earl by Labake's bedside when she arrived at the hospital in Accra. He had also been at the scene of the incident at the Hotel Staff Quarters. He introduced himself to Laide and had seen Laide's slightly raised eyebrow when he mentioned his name. They had exchanged a brief hug and had taken turns by Labake's bedside to look after Ella in the last seventeen days. They had talked a lot, and Laide was comfortable with Earl and his relationship with her niece too. She had also seen the way Ella responded to him; he was like the father she deserved, Laide thought. Earl was kind and patient with Ella; he bought her books to distract her and keep her mind off her mother and encouraged her to make *get well soon* cards for her too.

Earl also brought bunches of flowers to Labake's hospital room every single day since she had been there. The entire room was full of them and smelt like a garden. Laide had teased him about it and watched as he held Labake's hands and talked to her when he thought no one else was present in the hospital room. Laide had secretly listened to him talk to her and pray for her while she stood behind the door a couple of times.

Laide had not meant to eavesdrop on Earl but had gone to the bathroom and stopped outside the door on her way back to Labake's room when she heard him talking. He promised he would never leave Labake alone, how if she came back to him, he would give her the type of love and life she deserved, how he wanted to marry her, be a father to Ella, and be there for them both. Laide had rested in the knowledge that if Labake pulled through, Earl would fulfill his promises to her. All that was needed now was for her to come out of the coma. She thought all three of them would make a nice family.

One eye on Labake's still form, Earl distractedly lay the new bunch of flowers next to the others he brought in the last few days. As his attention was on Labake, he accidentally knocked one of the glass vases off the table, causing it to fall and shatter into pieces on the tiled hospital floor. One was not quite sure if it was the noise of the smashed flower vase that caused Labake to stir in that instant and begin to cough profusely. Her eyes were still shut as she coughed and whizzed, struggling to breathe. She coughed a few more times, turning her head from side to side repeatedly.

Laide panicked and instinctively pressed the red button by the side of the bed, alerting the nurses of what appeared to be an emergency. Earl, on the other hand, hearing Labake struggle, shot up from where he was crouched down, picking up pieces of broken glass off the floor, and sprinted to the door to get some help.

A moment later, Earl came back in with a doctor and nurse, who ushered both Earl and Laide out of the room as they attended to Labake. "Why wouldn't she stop coughing?" Laide asked Earl, who had begun pacing back and forth outside Labake's hospital room. Earl did not answer but suddenly stopped pacing and asked, "How was she today?" He looked deathly pale himself, Laide noticed and could tell he was just as worried as she was.

"She was just the same, really. Except..." Laide started, then suddenly remembered that Labake's finger had twitched a moment ago.

"Except what?" Earl asked.

"Her finger, the index one...it moved about thirty minutes ago...that's a good sign, isn't it, Earl?" Laide asked nervously. She needed some assurance that her sister would be alright, and Earl sensed it. He decided to be a man about the whole thing and be there for Laide too. He moved to the bench where Laide sat and crouched down in front of her. He took her hands and looked into her frightened eyes, and said,

"Of course it is! She hasn't moved in seventeen days, and now she's coughing! It's only a matter of time now before she comes round. She'll be alright. I just know it...Labake's a fighter." Earl smiled at Laide reassuringly and hoped he had managed to convince her. He also prayed silently that all he just said would indeed happen.

At that moment, Adia, Kwame's wife, came in with Ella, and Ella rushed into her Aunt's arms. Laide hugged and held on to her tightly. She prayed for both their sakes that Labake came out of the coma in one piece. Ella moved to Earl after a short while, and he picked her off the floor and hugged her warmly too.

Laide smiled at Adia and said, "Thank you for keeping her. Don't know what we'd have done without your help." Laide was indeed grateful to Kwame and his entire family. She did not want Ella coming to the hospital every time and did not want her returning to the scene of the crime where her mother was shot. Laide had therefore asked if she could stay with Kwame and his family, and they had happily obliged, seeing as Ella was friends with their girls and was used to staying with them during the holidays.

Adia sat next to Laide on the bench and said, "It's our absolute pleasure. How's Labake doing?" She asked, concern written all over her face. Laide filled her in on the latest details as nurses and doctors came and went from Labake's hospital room.

An hour later, the doctor came out of the room and explained that they had to give Labake some new medication and put her on another ventilator as she had trouble breathing. She was stabilized at that point but needed to rest. Her lung was not functioning as well as they had hoped, and they were currently trying to avoid an infection in that area too. He assured them that they were doing everything to make her comfortable and were keeping a close eye on her. With the new medicine, they expected to see some signs of improvement within the next few days.

"Is she conscious? I mean, did she open her eyes?" Laide asked the doctor, and he said she did but was asleep now as she was under some heavy medication.

"Can we go in and see her?" Earl asked the doctor. Ella was still in his arms, comfortably resting her head on his shoulders. Her thumb was in her mouth. Laide noted that she had started sucking her thumb since the ordeal with her parents and knew it had something to do with her witnessing everything that had happened.

The doctor said they could see Labake briefly but needed to be as quiet as possible so Labake could get the rest she needed. Laide heaved a sigh of relief and thanked the doctor as all four of them proceeded to go into Labake's hospital room.

CHAPTER TWENTY-SEVEN

Earl gave *Denton*, the foreman, a few new instructions and bade him a happy weekend. Apart from a few minor hiccups, the new hotel building construction was going as well as could be expected. It had been nine weeks since they started, and they were at the final stages of foundation laying.

It was getting busier as they progressed, and Earl could not say it had been the easiest of starts for him. There had been a delay in receiving planning permission from the authorities, causing a delay in the original commencement date. That, coupled with the added pressure of Labake's shooting, had taken a real toll on him. Particularly when she had been comatose. He remembered the dread that consumed him each time he walked into the hospital, not knowing if she would be alive when he got to her room or if she would even pull through at all.

There had been major setbacks to Labake's recovery, particularly her time in hospital. In fact, she had been declared dead on two different occasions but had somehow miraculously come back both times. That she was alive today was a miracle! Earl sighed now, remembering.

Earl had feared Labake dead when Kwame rang him up very early on that unfortunate morning. *'Labake's in trouble,'* Kwame had simply stated on the phone to him, and he had not needed to hear anything more. He scrambled out of bed immediately, threw on some clothes, and drove to *Dolphin* Hotel in a panicked frenzy. Labake's unconscious, bloodied body was being carried out on a stretcher into the waiting ambulance just as he arrived. Her head seemed twice its size, and both her eyes were swollen shut. To say he was horrified at the sight of her would be an understatement. He had grown ashen with grief, seeing her in that condition. He was convinced she could not make it.

Of course there had been utter pandemonium at the Hotel Staff Quarters as it seemed the entire staff had gathered around the small car park in shock. There had never been any drama like that on the premises. It was apparent that a lot of staff in residence were worried for both Labake and Kofi. Labake was known and described to the police to be polite and quiet, keeping to herself a lot. Her daughter Ella, of course, was more popular seeing as she was a boisterous child. A lot of the staff at the hotel were baffled that anyone would want to hurt Labake since they had no idea of her past. The police also tried to piece together what role Kofi, one of the chefs at the hotel kitchen, had played in the incident. Why had Vince shot him too? His neck had been supported by a cast, and he was also being taken to the hospital when Earl got to Dolphin Hotel. Like Labake, he was also unconscious.

Thankfully, Kofi had made it out of his coma sooner than Labake and had explained all that he had witnessed that morning to the police. Kofi had mentioned how Ella had saved the day as she had put up quite a fight with her father, causing a major delay in Vince's getaway. Had she not broken free from her father and run back to the apartment, the story of events that morning would be a different one, he had explained.

When Earl got there, Ella was being checked by one of the paramedics and was crying uncontrollably. The poor child had seen the whole thing and was clearly in shock. She had broken free and leaped into Earl's arms the minute she saw him. In turn, he had held her tightly, attempting to soothe her but failing to as he was yet to overcome the terrifying shock of what had happened himself.

When Earl remembered how close he came to losing Labake, he cringed. He was so grateful to God for sparing her life and giving him a second chance to prove his love for her. He felt an immense sense of guilt for having left her on the evening of the shooting incident. It was later revealed through the Hotel's strategically placed CCTV cameras that Labake's crazy husband had been at the staff quarters for quite some time. He had sat discreetly in his car, watching him and Labake from a distance on the evening he nearly killed her. Earl had not even noticed Vince's rental car when he drove by it on his way out of the hotel that evening.

How had he not sensed that something terrible was going to happen that evening? Earl asked himself again and again. He was usually quite sensitive. He had been so excited about the *unplanned* kiss he and Labake had shared and the fact that she had yielded to him and kissed him back that he had driven out of the hotel on a major *high*. The thought that he would lose her after they attained such a huge milestone frightened Earl to no end. It had been a major breakthrough for him in their relationship after everything he had done to make her feel safe with him.

Earl shook his head, remembering those dark days after Labake's shooting. He turned off the lights to his site office, a porter cabin temporarily erected on the proposed hotel site, and headed for his car. He had been sick with worry in the seventeen days Labake had been comatose. He felt rather guilty for having left her alone for three weeks prior to the shooting incident, though they had made up on the night she had almost been killed. He had promised himself and God never to take her for granted if she survived.

Earl knew he would have never fully gotten over it had Labake not come through. He loved her so much and felt even more convinced that she was the one for him. He found her resilience, even after all she had been through with that maniac of a husband, remarkable. She never complained, never felt sorry for herself; she just kept pushing through it all. Earl believed he needed Labake to be his fully. By God, he was going to ensure she had the life she deserved.

* * * *

Labake shifted uncomfortably on the new sofa Laide, her sister, newly purchased. What she really wanted to do was to get up and go to work again. Her instructions were either to lay in her bed with some magazines or on the new sofa, in front of the television. Labake wished Laide would stop fussing and waiting on her hand and foot. She needed things to get back to normal again if they ever could and she would give anything to be able to go get Ella from school again, but Laide would not let her. "But I'm fine now, Laide, honestly. The infection has cleared, and I'm not coughing or wheezing anymore...apart from the slight cold, I feel great, sis!" Labake had assured her elder sister, but she was not having it.

"Besides, you've taken far too much time off work...you've done more than enough, sis...I'm not exactly handicapped, you know...really, I feel just great!" Labake added as Laide set the tray of tea and fruit salad down on the new coffee table next to her sister.

Labake tried to sound as gingerly as she could but deep down, she knew she did not feel so. She was tired a lot, and she just wanted to go back to sleep even after she had been in bed for so long. She felt guilty that her sister had more or less given up her own life to care for her and Ella. She did not think it was fair, and Labake prayed for the strength to begin to feel more like her old self again. She desperately wanted to regain the independence she had struggled to achieve since her escape from Vince and did not want even her health to get in the way. She needed some normalcy back in her life. Though the thought of things returning to the way they were seemed ridiculous at this point. *How could they?* Labake wondered now.

Her husband had attempted to *kill* her and now had been killed himself. She was officially a widow and was free of Vince physically anyway, but why did she feel so guilty still? He had almost succeeded in taking her out for good and had almost destroyed their daughter in the process by making her witness things she should not have at her tender age. So why did she feel responsible for his death? Vince had done her wrong from the minute she had married him and had caused her a lot of pain, loss, and torment. He had more or less destroyed every shred of her personality, rendering her almost useless to herself or anyone, so why did she carry this guilt of his death with her? She found herself thinking he would still be alive had she not run off with his child, and the thought of that did not make her feel free in any way.

The nightmares had returned, and Labake woke up in fright each time she fell asleep. The last one had been even more frightening than the one before. Vince had been dragging her with him into an open, freshly dug grave, telling her she was going to be buried with him too. Labake had woken up screaming the new house down, causing Laide to rush to her room in fear. Thankfully, Ella had been with Kwame's girls that weekend and had not been awakened by her mother's screaming.

Labake still jumped at the slightest sound, particularly at night, and had been put on tranquilizers to help her sleep through the night. They were not much help as she was still awakened by the nightmares and oftentimes was scared to go back to sleep. When would it all end? She wondered. Was she always going to be a *freak*? One who had dark nights and was always scared of even her own shadow? What was *her normal* ever going to be? She wondered but was suddenly jolted from her thoughts when Laide spoke in response to her earlier complaints.

"Remember what the doctor said, Labake. You're to have plenty of rest and not do anything strenuous...that's exactly what it's going to be, my dear. You almost *died*! In fact, you *did* die, *twice* I might add! I'm not taking any chances, and I refuse to be the one to raise *your* child! So quit whining and relax. Besides, I'm now officially on leave from work, decided to take an extra month as leave...we *were* meant to be on holiday in *The Gambia,* remember? Before that brute showed up and nearly killed you," Laide responded, unperturbed by her sister's complaining.

She sat on the other end of the sectional sofa she had recently purchased for the new house, watching her beloved sister, who lay on the end of it. If Labake only knew what it was that troubled her in the minute, Laide sighed. They had all been through a terribly rough ordeal in the last couple of months, and Laide could not thank God enough for sparing her sister's life. She was glad Vince was dead and could breathe easier, knowing he would not be a threat to her sister and niece anymore. She, however, had something just as difficult, if not more, to reveal to Labake. She was nervous that it would be another hard pill for her to swallow, given all she had been through in her life.

Laide had kept the issue of Labake's paternity to herself for the last three months. She had hoped and prayed that Labake would live to learn of her father's existence and the fact that he had come looking for her after all this time. Laide had since determined that there was a ninety-nine percent chance that Chief Ilo *was* Labake's biological father, the DNA test she had conducted at the hospital had emerged positive.

Laide had tried to gauge if her sister was well enough to handle the news. She was just about coming to grips with suddenly becoming a widow and still struggled to get over recent traumatic events. Laide certainly was cautious about adding to it by telling her of the father she never even knew existed.

Laide had searched for an alternative accommodation in the city for Labake to recuperate. She did not think returning to the apartment within the Staff Quarters at *Dolphin Hotel* would be ideal for Labake or Ella. The place was flooded with bad memories of the night Vince almost killed her, and the last thing Laide wanted was for either Labake or Ella to keep reliving the horrible incident by being back there. It would have been far too much for both mother and child, Laide thought. Besides, the place would have been too small for all three of them as she knew she needed to spend some more time here in Accra till Labake got back on her feet.

Laide had been glad when Earl helped find the new bungalow through a real estate buddy of his. It was in a nicely secluded part of town, not too far away from the hotel and far away from the *paparazzi*. They still bothered them from time to time, hoping to catch a glimpse of *the lady who had survived her husband's brutal attack*. Laide had purchased some furniture to make the place comfortable, packed up Labake's and Ella's few belongings, and moved them into the new place. She looked around the living room now and was pleased with what they had accomplished before Labake came home from the hospital.

Labake had insisted on returning to work at the hotel when she fully recovered, though everyone there now knew a bit more about her past than she wished. However, she loved working there and was glad that her new home was not far from it or Ella's school too. She was thankful for the quietness she now enjoyed after so many visits from a lot of well-wishers. She appreciated them all but had looked forward to some silence.

The police had come and gone from the hospital and even the new place, still piecing together the final details of Labake's shooting and Vince's eventual death. Vince's family had also been contacted and informed of his death, and his brothers had been to Accra to take his body back home. They had not bothered to contact Labake or to even enquire about their niece, but Labake had not expected they would.

Labake's colleagues from the hotel, including top management, had come and gone from both the hospital and the new place for days too. Some were still trying to get over the shock of the whole incident, some wanted to talk about it, whilst others just came and sat quietly out of empathy. They all wished her well and a speedy recovery. Labake was particularly grateful to Kwame's brother Kojo, who owned the *Dolphin Hotel*. He had settled her hospital bills and even insisted that the Hotel Kitchen prepare and send daily meals to her new home until she fully recovered and returned to work.

Never had there been such drama within the hotel's Staff Quarters, and Labake was sad that she took center stage in the very first one. She had heard different versions of her own story making the rounds there. One of the hilarious ones she heard was that she had been married to a man who made a living as a hired assassin. The rumors, as outrageous as they were, did not bother Labake too much, but she was pleased she did not have to live in the staff quarters anymore. She was not sure she wanted to see the place ever again, and thankfully, she did not have to in order to carry out her duties at the hotel.

"What did you want to discuss with me, sis?" Labake suddenly asked, remembering Laide had mentioned earlier that there were some things she needed to talk to her about. She watched as Laide shifted uncomfortably before she put her own tea mug on the coffee table. Labake's eyes narrowed slightly. She knew Laide was never nervous about anything but something about her countenance at that moment bothered her a bit. Why was her sister acting strangely? She had caught her watching her weirdly these past few days, and Labake wondered if there was something negative about her health that Laide needed to speak to her about. Had the doctors mentioned anything to her about the infection she had suffered? She wondered as she scrutinized Laide's face in anticipation.

Laide sat up. She saw the pensive look on Labake's face and prayed she would be able to swallow what she was about to tell her. Perhaps it was too soon for Labake to handle, she wondered now, wishing she had not said anything about needing to speak to her earlier that morning.

"Erm...I need you to er..." Laide stuttered as she tried to get the words out but realized she was unprepared and did not quite know how to form a sentence to ease the blow of what she was about to reveal to her sister.

"You're scaring me, Laide. What is it? Is it the infection? Am I still ill?" Labake asked worriedly.

"*Ill?* Oh no, sis, it isn't that at all..." Laide hurriedly put her sister at ease. "Er...a few months ago...almost four actually, I received a phone call at work from someone, a man from back home...a Chief...*Chief Benjamin Ilo*. He asked to meet with me. He said he was an old acquaintance of...of *Maami* and had something he urgently needed to discuss about her," Laide started, looking straight into Labake's eyes. She looked pale and rather anxious as she listened intently to what Laide was saying to her.

"Did *Maami* ever mention the name to you? I mean, does it sound familiar at all?" Laide asked when Labake remained silent. She watched as Labake shook her head silently, indicating she had never heard their mother mention the name before. Labake and her mother had been quite close, especially in the years before her marriage to Vince. *Maami* had shared a lot of stories with her, and Labake had known all her mother's friends too, but the name Laide had just mentioned did not ring any bells whatsoever.

"Anyway, I reluctantly went to see him...he was staying at a hotel just round the corner from the High Commission. Apparently, he'd been searching for *Maami* for quite some time but had learned a while back that she'd passed...passed away. He said he remembered that she had a daughter...me...and had hired a private investigator to look for me or anyone who knew me. It had taken him a couple of years, seeing he didn't have any personal details...but he finally found me..." Laide paused again, searching for the words to try and finish. She looked away from her sister's prying eyes for a moment, then got off her end of the sofa and slowly moved over to the other end where Labake lay. She sat next to her, reached for her cold hands, and held them for a moment.

"What is it, sis?" Labake asked, "What did he want with you? Did *Maami* owe him some money or what?" She asked Laide, urging her to say what it was that she needed to say.

"He...he said he'd helped *Maami* start her food business and...and they'd had a brief affair for almost a year and...and *Maami* had fallen pregnant," Laide paused again, hoping she would not need to say anymore and that Labake would fill in the blanks herself, but she did not. Labake maintained the worried look on her face instead and waited for Laide to get to the crux of the matter, totally oblivious to the fact that she was being told the story of her birth and paternity.

"Yes?" Labake asked Laide, more consumed by Laide's weird behavior as opposed to what she was trying so hard to share with her.

"He'd insisted she had an abortion as he was happily married with kids of his own...but *Maami* sort of disappeared from his life, and he hadn't bothered to search for her...he wanted to know if I had any siblings born after me..." Laide paused now and held her sister's eyes, watching as the realization of what she had not fully spelled out now sunk in.

"*What...?* Are you saying...no...are you saying...is he...is he *my father*?" Labake asked, shaking her head as though she was trying to loosen the piece of information she had just garnered from her head. She clearly struggled to grapple with it. Her already pale face now looked completely drained of any color as she suddenly turned paper white. Both her eyes seemed like they would pop out of their sockets. It was the one time in almost four years that Laide saw such a profound reaction from her sister.

Labake suddenly sat up, removed her hands from her sister's, and shakily got off the sofa. She swooned a bit, causing Laide to jump up and grab her to keep her from falling, but Labake held out her hand, indicating she was alright.

"How long...how long have you known?" She asked Laide, holding one side of her head as a dull ache began, threatening to become a humongous one.

"Sit down, Labake...please. You don't look good at all, sis," Laide said softly.

"How long? *Four* months you said, you've known all this time?" Labake asked, ignoring her sister's concern.

"I was going to tell you when you and Ella came over to Port Novo for our trip to *The Gambia,* but then...then the shooting happened, and the right time just never came...you were in a coma for nearly three weeks, all I cared about was that you survived," Laide explained patiently.

Labake considered what her sister said for a moment and then asked, "But how sure are we that he...that he *is*...my father?"

"He left me a sample of his hair in case there were any doubts in our minds, and we wanted to carry out DNA tests. He also left some money to pay for the test, though he was convinced that you *were* his child, given your age, I guess...I had the sample tested against yours while you were in the hospital." Laide got up and reached for the DNA test results in her handbag. She had carried it around in her purse for weeks, scared that someone might stumble across it if she hid it elsewhere. She handed the envelope to Labake, who took it with trembling hands, opened it, and read it. She paced back and forth slowly and then turned to Laide and said,

"But why now...after all this time? What does he want? I don't have any money, and I certainly am not giving him any of my organs or bodily parts...I mean, why now? Where's he been all this while?" Labake asked, glaring at her sister.

"He says he wasn't aware of your existence as he assumed *Maami* had terminated the pregnancy like he'd instructed her to...he also blamed it on his foolishness at the time and his fear that his family would be destroyed. He mentioned having a heart scare a short while ago and how he would never want to die without verifying if he had a kid elsewhere. Apparently, he'd been haunted by dreams of *Maami*...and he just had to find out why, after all these years," Laide paused, watching Labake very carefully as she processed everything she was being told, then continued.

"He wants to meet you... he's hoping that you would want to meet him too. Oh, and guess what? He doesn't need *anything* from you...I *googled* him. Let's just say you're the kid of a *multi-billionaire,*" Laide said, trying but failing to make light of the situation as Labake sent her a look that indicated she was not in the mood for jokes.

Suddenly, Labake felt overwhelmed by everything Laide had just revealed to her. She began to cough uncontrollably, clutching at her chest and wheezing as she struggled to breathe. "I can...can't breathe...*help me*!" She said with difficulty. Laide moved swiftly to help her, but it was too late as Labake crashed into her, causing both of them to fall to the floor.

"Labake! Labake!! Can you hear me? Labake!" Laide cried, holding her sister's now unconscious body.

CHAPTER TWENTY-EIGHT

After another nine days in the hospital, Labake was back home again, this time on even stronger medication. Laide had rushed her back to the hospital after she collapsed when Laide revealed who her biological father was. Apparently, her immune system had been badly compromised by the first infection she had contracted, and she had to be put back on the ventilator to help her breathe properly again. The doctors had prescribed a stronger dose of antibiotics, and they seemed to be working as the bouts of wheezing and breathlessness she experienced had now stopped.

Now Labake lay in bed, thinking about her life. She had not said another word to Laide about Chief Ilo and did not feel she needed to. She thought about it a lot in the hospital and still did not quite know how to handle this new piece of information. What was it about her life that seemed to always make it extra complicated? To think she had been rather clueless about life in general as a child, totally unaware of the hand it would deal her in the future. How was she to know that her life would be this difficult when she became an adult?

Labake thought about her childhood for a moment. It had not been perfect, but they'd had some peace, albeit intermittently. Except for the times when Laide's father came back into their lives, she and Laide had generally experienced a great childhood. *Maami* had been a great parent to them, and they had found real love in her. She had been both father and mother to them and had poured herself into them. She trained them well and taught them good manners and hard work. She also taught them to be kind and accepting of others but also how to look after themselves and be independent – at least until Vince came along and eroded every sense of that away from her.

They did not have a lot, to begin with, but the quality of their lives had certainly improved when *Maami* started the canteen. She made enough money to put Laide through university and had been quite prepared to do the same for her until Vince came again and stole that dream from her.

Labake now had to admit that watching *Maami* get beaten by Laide's father had certainly damaged something in both her and her sister. It affected them in two extremely different ways. Laide had more or less become a *feminist*, extremely opposed to the idea that she needed a man at all, not to mention one who dominated her very existence. On the other hand, like their mother, she had allowed and tolerated both mental and physical abuse from the men they had been in relationships with. Labake now realized that one way or the other, both she and her sister were victims of domestic violence.

She sighed now when she remembered how *Maami* had been beaten by *Daddy* and the many times she and Laide had witnessed it, terrified that something really bad would happen afterward. It had been too much for young children their age to go or even grow through. Dr. Stella had mentioned there was a possibility that somewhere in her subconscious, she had seen violence as the norm between a man and a woman. She said it was probably why she had thought it acceptable and even endured it for as long as she had with Vince.

Labake regretted Vince's death, especially for her daughter's sake, and still bore some guilt for it, but she was tired of it all. She just needed time alone to think and be rid of all the dramas her life had somehow evoked. Vince's death had made her really begin to think about hers and Ella's future. She had begun to think, for example, about where they would live and settle down. Would they remain in Ghana, return to her home country or even move to Port Novo, where she could be closer to her sister? These were all the thoughts that plagued her mind until this sudden interference by Chief Ilo. It felt like an intrusion into her life, one she did not welcome or appreciate. She had believed herself to be ready to pick up the pieces again and face the future with Ella, but now she had the issue of her paternity to deal with, along with her current health problems. *When would it all stop?* Labake wondered.

Thinking about all Laide had said about this Chief Ilo and the DNA test that had proved indeed that she was *ninety-nine point nine percent* his daughter, Labake shut her eyes. It had been a few days, but she still reeled from the shocking revelation that she actually *had* a father all this time. Labake was aware from an early age that *daddy* was not her biological father, though *Maami* had never mentioned it. She had heard *Daddy* accuse *Maami* several times of being a loose woman because she had run off and had a child with another man in his absence. He had referred to Labake as *that bastard child* many times. She had, however, been too young in her earlier years to realize he was referring to her. Much later, it had become clearer that she and Laide were actually half-siblings, fathered by different men.

Labake had overheard a conversation between a couple of neighbors one evening in the backyard of the communal house they lived in at the time. *Iya Taju* and *Mama Nkechi* spoke at the water pump in hushed tones, but Labake heard every word. She had been on her way to fetch some water from the pump herself when she stumbled on the conversation between them and stopped just outside the backdoor to listen quietly.

Maami had just taken a beating from *daddy,* and the entire building, as usual, had been involved in breaking down their room door *again* to rescue *her. Daddy* had this knack for driving both Laide and Labake out of the room when he was ready to pounce on *Maami* for whatever reason. He would then lock the room door to avoid any interference from anyone. Labake and Laide would sit huddled together outside the room door in fear, listening to their mother cry out and plead with daddy to stop.

"How is *Iya Laide* doing now?" *Mama Nkechi* had inquired of *Iya Taju* as she waited her turn to fill her bucket.

"You know the younger one isn't his child. I think that's why the beatings have got worse since he returned," *Iya Taju* had responded. She was the main gossip in the building, and everyone came to her when they needed some piece of information about the other residents.

"*Really*? Laide and Labake have *different* fathers?" *Mama Nkechi* had further inquired. Clearly, this was the first time she was hearing it.

"Yes, *Iya Laide* got pregnant again after Laide's father disappeared for some time...apparently, he went back to his wife. I don't know who Labake's dad is, but I suspect it is one man who used to visit in that nice *five-o-five* car...but again, who knows?" *Iya Taju* had supplied.

Labake had been about six or seven years old at the time, and though she had not seen their facial expressions, she knew for sure her entire family was the subject of that conversation between the two women, particularly as *Mama Nkechi* had spelled all their names out, albeit in a *loud* whisper.

Labake never mentioned what she had overheard to her mother but had been curious enough to ask *Maami* a year later who her father was. *Maami* had asked who told her *daddy* was not her real father, and Labake mentioned hearing *daddy* refer to her as *that bastard child*. *Maami* had hissed and changed the subject. She had never given Labake an answer that day or the other two times she had asked her again.

In fact, *Maami* had never mentioned anything to her about her paternity. Perhaps she had been trying to keep the confidence of the chief, seeing as he instructed her to terminate the pregnancy. Knowing *Maami* and how she avoided confronting anyone, Labake now suspected that *Maami* had not wanted to raise her hopes by mentioning this Chief Ilo as her father. Perhaps to avoid her going about telling everyone who her *real* father was. *Maami* had kept a low profile; she never wanted to make any trouble for or with anyone. Labake concluded this was why her mother had never had a conversation with her about it.

The thought that she would never have the opportunity to discuss the situation with her mother or even have a proper conversation with her about the circumstances of her birth saddened Labake to no end. She had so many questions and was even sadder that she had to get the information from an entire stranger who had now been confirmed by DNA to be her biological father. Before now, all she knew about her father, from what Iya Taju had said, was that he drove a nice *five-o-five* car.

Labake did not quite know what or how to feel about Chief Ilo. Where had he been all her life? Laide had explained his reasons for his absence all these years, but why had he come looking for her now, years after *Maami* passed? He had asked her to terminate the pregnancy; why could he not just *let sleeping dogs lie*? She was doing just fine and no longer missed the absence of a father in her life. So why had he not just stayed away?

Then Labake thought about how wretched *Maami* had been and how she struggled at different times. Where was her *billionaire* father at those times? He had given *Maami* some money to start her small food business, taken advantage of her, got her pregnant, and disappeared, leaving her to raise his child by herself! How could she ever forgive that? He had not even bothered to find out if she indeed terminated the pregnancy. He just walked right out of her life! *Typical selfish man,* Labake thought. As far as she was concerned, what the chief did was even worse than what *daddy* did. At least *daddy* had accepted Laide and acknowledged her as his child, though he had been a beast like Vince and also eventually shirked his responsibility by leaving her too. Laide at least knew who spawned her. She knew whose child she was, even if she did not presently have a relationship with him.

There and then, Labake decided she did not want a relationship with her biological father. Besides, she suspected it would involve a new load of drama, and she just could not handle anymore.

Then there was Earl. The man who had changed her general view of men by his gentle and kind ways. He had somewhat managed to convince her that not *all* men were monsters, and she had grown used to having him around, and so had Ella. He had been there for her since they first met and through all of the mayhem Vince had brought with him to Accra. Labake appreciated all of that and had slowly begun to let her guard down with him, trust him and perhaps even fall in love with him. All of this, of course, before Vince stormed back into her life. She, however, was not so sure about pursuing a relationship with him anymore. She had too much on her plate right now and was having difficulty focusing on anything else but gaining her health back, making plans for the future, and coming to terms with her paternity issues. She felt she could not accommodate a relationship with Earl now; the timing just seemed wrong.

Something about all that had happened with Vince made her want to pull away from Earl. She could not help it, but she had withdrawn right back into her shell since Vince's death and was now back to wanting to be left alone with her daughter. She had avoided Earl since her return home again from the hospital and had not taken any of his calls either. Labake did not want to seem ungrateful for his support since the shooting. She could also imagine how strange her recent actions probably seemed to him. She just needed time to be away from every other thing or person that required something of her and hoped he understood that.

Labake's thoughts were suddenly interrupted when Laide knocked on her bedroom door and asked if she could enter. Labake asked her to come in and indicated that she sit next to her on the bed. "Feeling okay, sis?" Laide asked. She had dropped everything to be there for Labake and Ella since the shooting and had taken good care of them both. Before the school holidays, Laide had dropped Ella off at school and picked her up whilst her mother recuperated. She had gone way beyond the call of an elder sister and had been a mother, nurse, caregiver, and everything else to her younger sister and niece.

Labake was grateful to Laide and owed a lot to her for her help during her *crisis*. She loved having her sister around but also knew she would have to return to Port Novo soon. She desperately hoped for a quick, full recovery just so Laide could return to work, not that Laide worried about it that much. She had taken a long leave from work, believing her first priority was her sister's wellbeing. She needed to ensure Labake felt better and strong enough to handle things on her own and was even beginning to consider traveling back with both her and Ella to Port Novo so that she could keep a closer eye on them.

Laide saw the intense look on Labake's face and waited for her to respond to her question. She intentionally refused to bring the issue of her paternity up for fear that it would trigger another relapse in her health. She sensed it was on Labake's mind a lot as she seemed quieter and appeared to be somewhat withdrawn. Laide had decided to give her some time to process it all and decide what she wanted to do about her biological father. She had said as much to Chief Ilo the other day when he rang to enquire about Labake.

Of course, Labake was unaware that Laide and chief Ilo were in contact or that he had been anxious about her condition since learning of her attack by Vince. Laide had felt the need to mention the incident to him just so he was aware that Labake had been in hospital and was unable to deal with the issue of her paternity just yet. She had not shared any further details about Labake's life with Chief Ilo as she felt it was not her place to do so. It was entirely up to Labake how much information she shared with her father if she decided to even have anything to do with him at all.

"I'm alright, sis...just thinking about stuff..." Labake responded. Laide noticed she seemed resigned as she moved to sit up in the bed. Laide got up and helped prop some pillows against the headboard to make her comfortable.

"Okay...do you want to share your thoughts with me...now...or would you rather talk about them another time?" Laide prodded her gently. She did not want to pry or force her to speak when she was not ready to.

Labake looked away for a moment and then said, "I've been thinking about...about the Chief, Earl...and just *everything*. Her voice was hoarse as she spoke. She coughed a couple of times in an attempt to clear her throat. Laide passed her the glass of water by the bedside and asked, "What about them, sis?" She watched as Labake took a few sips of water and held the glass in both her hands.

"Well, I've decided I don't want a relationship with the chief," Labake stated categorically. "I wasn't aware of his existence and have survived without him...why would I want to bring him into our lives now? What purpose would that serve? I don't need him or anything from him, and I wish he hadn't come looking, wish he had left things the way they were...I mean, what role could he possibly play in our lives now? How do I become a daughter to a father at this age? How do I explain his absence from our lives to *my* daughter? I mean, *where has he been all this time*? He's carried on with his cushy life and family while *Maami* toiled day and night, raising us... what gives him the right to think he can just burst into our lives now? It seems as though he was *forced* to come looking *because* of his heart scare...if he hadn't had a scare, he wouldn't have bothered...it's *convenient* for him to do so now...well, it isn't for me!" Labake said vehemently, nostrils flaring as she began to cough profusely again.

Laide jumped off the bed and moved to pour Labake another glass of water. She then sat closer to her on the bed and rubbed her back gently as she drank the water. When the coughing subsided, Laide began to speak.

"Your anger is understandable, Labake. Perhaps you need some more time to think about it. Whatever you decide, don't deprive yourself of a relationship with your father, sis. Let's take our eyes off what he did or didn't do momentarily and look at the circumstances for a bit. That was then, and this is now...an opportunity for both of you to get acquainted...what should the situation be, going forward?

I know what it must feel like, at least I have an idea, given *daddy's* sudden disappearance from our lives...*my* life. I know how hurt I was by that and how I kept it all bottled up inside. It was one of the reasons why I began seeing Dr. Stella. I was so angry with *daddy*. The rejection I felt fuelled my anger towards him and perhaps men generally. I closed myself off from any male relationships and decided I never wanted to be married, given all we were exposed to as young girls. *Daddy's* inhumane treatment of *Maami*, the way *Maami* let him get away with it, how he acted as though I didn't exist, and all the names he called you.

It was all unfair, and I realized I held so much rage and bitterness within me. It left me cold and emotionless on the one hand and then like a raging bull, waiting to charge at the slightest provocation, on the other. But I got tired of it...I didn't want to be that person, Labake. Why would I let my father's wrong behavior during my childhood continue to affect my future as an adult? It's too much a price to pay, Labake. I no longer wanted to be a victim of my childhood. I wanted to live and experience new things and a new way of living. I needed to rid myself of the way I'd conditioned myself to think. I knew I wasn't going to be able to forget entirely all the wrong things that happened, but I needed to see it for what it was and unlearn all that I'd seen and begin to learn newer ways to foster relationships, whether they be work-related, romantic, or whatever.

It's time for us to live, Labake. Yes, through no fault of ours, we didn't have *normal* lives growing up, but we can do better now and create the kind of life we desire, God helping us. Would you rather continue in bitterness, knowing you have a father out there, yet refusing to relate with him? Surely that's too much of an added burden to carry on your shoulders.

As for how to be a daughter to a father, these are some of the new ways of living we need to learn! You don't have to do anything really; just meet with him and be yourself, taking each day as it comes. As for Ella, she doesn't need much of an explanation...she'd love the idea of having a Granddad...and as for Earl, you need to sit down with him and have a conversation. He needs to know what's going on with you...you owe him that much. He doesn't deserve to be treated the way you've treated him recently. He's been there through it all. Just speak to him and stop avoiding him. Ask him for some more time or let him know you're no longer interested in a relationship with him...whatever...just have that conversation," Laide finished.

She observed Labake for a moment. She had not said a word or reacted to anything Laide said. She just sat there, motionless, staring into space. Laide sighed deeply and decided to leave the room in search of Ella, so they could finish the puzzle they had been working on earlier. She figured she had given her sister a lot to think about.

CHAPTER TWENTY-NINE

It was another twelve days before Labake began to feel more like herself again. She had completed the prescribed course of antibiotics and was breathing better now. The bouts of coughing and wheezing had stopped *permanently* this time, she hoped, and she generally felt better. At her last visit to the hospital a couple of days ago, the doctors ran some more tests and finally gave her a clean bill of health. However, they had instructed that she took things easy, did not engage in any laborious tasks or routines, and just generally got a lot of rest.

Labake was relieved that the infection had cleared and that she felt more like her old self again. She felt good emotionally too, and was not as depressed as she had been since the shooting. It was as though she now had a clearer head and a better sense of direction. She also felt more in control of her life again as things had settled down to a degree. Her energy level had also received a spike, and she was ready to carry on with the business of living again.

Even Laide mentioned that something appeared different about Labake. She had prayed earnestly that Labake would snap out of the *funk* she was in, if not for herself, but for Ella's sake. The poor child could not understand why her mother was cranky and lay in bed all day. Ella had even referred to her mother as *anti-social*. It was a new term she had learned, and she had put it to use rather aptly, Laide thought. Hearing what her daughter said to her aunt had made Labake decide to put in more of an effort with her as she did not want to be remembered by her child as the *anti-social* mother.

Labake believed the reason for her newly improved mood and general countenance was because she had a clearer direction on what she needed to do about all the issues of her life which had overwhelmed her in the past few weeks. First, she had decided to remain in Ghana in the interim. She did not feel up to the task of having to pack herself and Ella up again to resettle in Port Novo or another new country. It was too soon, and neither she nor Ella deserved to give up the few friends they had made here. Besides, she loved her job at the hotel, the pay was decent enough, and despite all the drama that had taken place there with Vince, Labake knew she wanted to go back to work at *The Dolphin Hotel*. She was, however, glad she did not have to live there anymore. Laide had leased the new place for two years, and the rent was not too bad; Labake knew she could afford to renew the lease when it expired. She had quite a bit of money saved up and did not live extravagantly. If she carried on the way she had, she and Ella would do just fine here.

Labake had also decided to meet with Chief Ilo, her biological father. She was going to do it just as a *ticking-of-the-box* exercise. It was going to be purely a formality as she had already decided she was not interested in a relationship with him, and that was her final decision on the subject. She had thought long and hard about all Laide had said days ago and had decided to meet him just once, and that was going to be it. Laide had set up the meeting, and Chief Ilo was flying into Accra to meet with Labake in a couple of days.

Labake heaved an unsteady sigh and looked at the clock. Earl was on his way over, and it was going to be their first meeting since she left the hospital the second time. She had avoided him, refusing to see him, particularly because she had been overwhelmed by the shooting incident and everything else. Again, she had heeded Laide's advice to have a sit-down with him and had sent him a text the other day which had simply read;

> *HI EARL, I HOPE YOU'RE DOING WELL. CAN YOU PLEASE COME OVER SOMETIME SOON SO WE CAN TALK? YOU PICK A DAY AND TIME. THANKS.*

He had responded a few minutes later, saying he would come over today at three. Labake felt slightly nervous about their meeting this afternoon as she not only felt bad for the way she treated him but was also unsure about her relationship with him. Laide had said, "Just tell him how you feel, sis...make him understand that you haven't meant to hurt him but that you've been going through stuff...I bet he'll understand." She'd decided to take Ella out for some ice cream to give Labake and Earl some privacy and also because Labake did not want to further confuse Ella by bringing him back into their lives after a few weeks of his *forced* absence.

Ella was just about getting over the trauma she had faced, seeing her father in the worst light ever and then losing him too. This was perhaps another reason Labake had second thoughts about her relationship with Earl. She needed Ella to heal and hopefully come to terms with things before she even began to think about bringing another man on the scene. Ella loved Earl and had asked about him a number of times. Earl had been there for her when Labake was in the hospital. He and Laide had taken turns looking after her all through the hospital visits too.

The doorbell rang, and Labake got off the sofa, straightened the *kente* dress she had on, and went to let Earl in. She sighed shakily and opened the front door slowly. Earl stood at the door for a moment. He had a bunch of flowers and a *Grillo Grotto* paper bag in his hands. He knew she loved everything on the menu at *Grillo Grotto*. It was her favorite sandwich bar in the city. Labake thought it sweet that even after her refusal to see him all this time, he still came bearing gifts.

Earl smiled at her now, raised the bag up, and said, "I stopped at your favorite spot and got grilled chicken sandwiches for everybody!" He watched her for a while and observed she looked even thinner than the last time he saw her. Her eyes looked slightly hollow, but she still looked as beautiful, even without any makeup on. It was hard to believe she was almost thirty years old. She looked like a teenager, Earl thought. He also noticed that her eyes seemed to have turned sad again. They had improved before the shooting, but now, the sparkle in them seemed to have disappeared again. *Why*? He wondered. One would think she would be happier, considering her crazy husband, who had stalked and haunted her all this time, was no longer a threat to her or Ella. She was free of him, and he could not hurt her anymore. So why did she look unhappy? Earl wondered.

Labake smiled at him shyly and said, "Thank you." Her stomach was tied up in knots at the moment, the last thing she needed was a grilled chicken sandwich, but she remained mute about it. Instead, she stepped out of his way so he could come into the house. Her heart began to beat slightly faster as he walked past her into the living room. Something about seeing him after all this time and that faint but familiar hint of his cologne excited her, causing the butterflies to begin fluttering in her belly again. *Focus! That's not the reason you asked him over*. She cautioned herself silently.

When he sat on the sofa, Labake asked, "Would you like me to put that on a plate and perhaps fetch you a drink?" It was what she needed to distract them both and buy herself some time to think about what she needed to say to him.

"That would be nice, thank you. I won't mind some water, please. Where are Laide and Ella?" Earl asked. The house sounded far too quiet if Ella was in it.

"They er...popped out for some ice cream..." Labake explained on her way to the kitchen. She stuttered a bit as she was unsure if her explanation sounded odd and if he noticed that Laide and Ella were absent because they needed some privacy. Earl was a sensitive man. He was able to read beyond what was said.

"Aren't you having any? I got one for Laide and Ella too?" Earl asked when Labake set the tray of sandwiches and water on the coffee table.

"Not at the minute, thanks. I had lunch already..." Labake answered.

Earl asked if she was feeling better as he was aware she had been rushed back to the hospital a few weeks ago. When Labake nodded that she was fine, he said, "You actually do look better, I must say." They made small talk while Earl ate, and as it was not exactly her forte, Labake struggled to keep the conversation going, particularly because her mind was on the real reason why she had invited him over.

When he was done eating and the tray had been cleared, Labake began pensively. "Er...the reason why I asked you...you over was that I..." Why could she not just spit it out? She chided herself, but before she could continue, Earl said, "Labake, can I say something before you start? I've had stuff on my mind that I've wanted to say to you." Labake nodded and fell silent at that moment.

"I know you've been through a lot recently. I also know that things probably got a lot more complicated with the...shooting and all. I want you to know that I understand...honestly, I really do. When I think about all that happened..." Earl trailed off for a moment and looked away as tears had formed in his eyes. Labake watched him closely, unsure of what to make of what he was saying or where he was going with it. She decided to wait and hear him out. She sat so still and almost forgot to breathe.

Earl wiped the tear that threatened to drop from his eyes and turned back to Labake. It was obvious that he was emotional when he continued. "When I think about the experience of going into the hospital each evening after the shooting, when you were in a coma and how you gave up...*twice*...how we almost lost you...I...I feel blessed and grateful that you came back to me...to us. Labake, it's early days, I know, it's probably too soon, but I need you to say you'll marry me...I've had enough time to think about it. I don't want to wait any longer. I love you. I love Ella as if she were my kid..." Earl stopped for a moment and got the ring box out of his pocket. He knelt in front of Labake, reached for her left hand, and held it. "Let me love you, look after you...I know with time, you'll probably feel the same way about me...say you'll marry me Labake...please." The look in his eyes was as tender as cotton when he finished.

Labake was beyond astonished at what Earl was saying to her, so much so that her mouth hung open. How could he be proposing to her after weeks of her being *incommunicado*? He was supposed to be mad with anger that she had deliberately refused to see him, take his calls, or even respond to any of his messages. *Why wasn't he?* It appeared none of what she had done had dissuaded him from wanting to be with her. Labake found that baffling as she was used to angrier responses, but here she was instead looking into Earl's hopeful, amber eyes, having listened to him practically beg her to marry him. What was it about her that appealed to him this much? She wondered. She was broken and damaged, and had not even shown him any kindness in return. She also came with a child, a responsibility most men shied away from, so what was it exactly?

Labake shut her eyes for a few seconds and gently removed her hand from Earl's. "Please get up, Earl. I need you to get up and sit down...please," Labake started softly when Earl finally sat back down. "I'm surprised that you're even still interested in me, given...given the way I've treated you in the last few weeks. I'm sorry...so sorry for that, Earl...you deserve a lot better. I've been...I've been rather confused and overwhelmed since...since everything. There's been a lot to think about...I've recently come close to death...actually did die like you mentioned but somehow...thankfully, came back. I've recently become widowed, recently seem to have my life back, and also...recently discovered...I *have* a *biological father*."

Earl's brows went up when he heard about Labake's latest discovery, but he remained silent as he watched Labake now rise from the sofa. She stood there for a moment, arms wrapped around herself as if she suddenly felt cold. "So you see, Earl, there's just too much going on in my life right now...you're a great man, kind, caring, loving, and sweet but...I simply can't marry you...it just won't work given my current frame of mind. There's a lot to think about...I'm sorry..." Labake trailed off breathlessly, looking rather desperate.

Earl leaned back on the sofa and studied Labake for a moment. It was hard to tell what he was thinking as he looked as though he was in deep thought. After what seemed a moment, he said, "I'd hoped your answer would be different...but I guess it is what it is, and I must respect your decision. I wish you and Ella well, Labake. I'll see myself out. Have a good evening." That said, Earl rose up, hesitated a bit, and then proceeded to leave Labake's home. Labake, on the other hand, was surprised that he had not made it any harder, but she remained rooted to the spot where she was and watched Earl walk right out of her life.

* * * *

Chief Ilo took another pill from the bottle. His hand shook slightly as he turned the lid. He slipped the pill into his mouth and took a sip of water. The flight into Accra on his private jet had been quick and hitch-free. Moses, his Personal Assistant, was with him and now rode in the passenger seat in front, next to the driver who had picked them up from the airport.

They were on their way to see the daughter he had never met. Her sister, Olaide, had sent him Omolabake's address a couple of days ago, and Chief Ilo was nervous but happy the day had finally arrived. He was nervous because it had taken Labake a few months to agree to meet with him, and he was not quite sure how she would receive him. He, however, knew it was unavoidable now; he would not have put it off any longer, even if he could. It was what he had wanted since discovering over a year ago that she existed.

Of course, neither Moses nor the Ghanaian driver whom Chief Ilo's good friend, David Kuruma, had arranged to drive him around here in Accra, knew the purpose of his visit, and he intended to keep it that way. The last thing he needed was the story leaking before he had the time to reveal his big secret to his family.

Benjamin Ilo had plans to tell his wife and daughters about Omolabake after his meeting with her in person. He, of course, also had hopes of introducing them too. This would be after he *dropped the bomb* of her existence on them and after the dust eventually settled. He realized now that Omolabake herself would have to be willing to meet the rest of the family too. He only prayed the dust did settle as easily as possible, though he was quite ready to face whatever consequence came as a result of his revelation.

Chief Ilo's plan was to do it after the Christmas Holidays, seeing as his daughter Omorien, who lived in the United States, would also be present, as she was in town, on holiday with her family. He told himself it had to be done once and for all. He was tired of the secret. He hoped his wife, in particular, would forgive him as he needed her in his corner. The girls were older and had all fled the nest anyway, but he had Mena to live with. Right now, however, he focused on the task at hand – meeting Omolabake, his youngest daughter, for the very first time.

Benjamin Ilo remembered how helpless and hopeless he had felt when Olaide revealed that Omolabake was the victim in the news, which had recently exploded all over the country. He had read the story of the disgruntled husband who had traveled from Nigeria to Ghana in search of his estranged wife and daughter. The tabloids had said the husband had killed the wife but had also died in the crossfire with the police. Chief Ilo had even discussed it with Mena, unbeknownst to him that the wife in question was his own illegitimate child whom he had been searching for. Of course, at the time, he had not known Omolabake's name and so could not have had any idea who she was.

He had wanted to jump on the plane and travel immediately to Ghana once he found out, but Olaide had told him not to because

Omolabake was in a coma, and she thought the timing was wrong. He had prayed that she would pull through as he could not imagine her dying without him meeting her. He also remembered her mother, Iyabo's face, in the dreams he had and knew he needed Omolabake to survive the vicious attack by her husband. The *psycho* whom she had married was lucky he had been killed by the police. Had he made it alive, Chief Ilo knew he would have taken it upon himself to ensure he was extradited back to Nigeria to face the full wrath of the law. He gritted his teeth just thinking about it now.

The car turned into a small *cul de sac* in what appeared to be a quiet area of town named *Roman Ridge.* Omolabake clearly appeared to have done fairly well for herself if she lived in an area like this, Chief Ilo thought as he peered out of the car window. It seemed peaceful, and the surrounding buildings were equally impressive too. Chief Ilo himself owned two homes in the Airport area of Accra. He purchased them purely for investment purposes and had a general idea of the city himself. He, Mena, and his girls had come on several weekend *get-aways* to Accra when they were younger, and they all loved it here.

Chief Ilo realized he would be visiting Accra more often now that he had a child who lived here. His heart did a quick lurch when he realized he had put the cart before the horse. He was not even sure that Labake wanted a relationship with him at all. She had been reluctant to meet with him, and he could not say he blamed her. After all, he had not been there for her since her birth, and he had treated her mother rather badly when he walked out of her life, knowing she was pregnant with his child.

The driver parked in front of the address Olaide had sent Chief Ilo. Moses got out of the car and came to help Chief Ilo as he alighted from the car. Chief Ilo observed that the house was an old one, but it looked well taken care of. He wondered if it was a rental or owned by Omolabake as he proceeded slowly to the front door. Moses had returned to wait in the car with the driver. Chief Ilo rang the doorbell with some trepidation; moments later, Olaide swung open the door and smiled at him.

"Hello, Sir, nice to meet you again...I hope it wasn't too difficult to locate the address," She greeted. Chief Ilo returned the smile nervously and said, "How are you my dear? It's nice to see you too...again. No, it wasn't difficult to find the place with the *GPS*...it was a breeze actually."

Chief Ilo felt a little more comfortable with Laide now. They had struck up some sort of bond over the past few months, especially after Omolabake's shooting incident. They had spoken every day while she was in the hospital, and Olaide had come to see that her initial opinion of him was wrong as Chief Ilo seemed caring and genuinely concerned about Labake's progress. She had decided to *cut him some slack* and deal a little more kindly with him.

Laide opened the door wider and said, "Please come in, Sir, and have a seat. I'll go fetch Labake. In the meantime, would you like a drink? We've got some fruit juice or water and also have some food prepared...if you'd like anything to eat."

Chief Ilo looked round the spacious but sparsely furnished living room. There was nothing much to it, apart from the large sectional sofa, which appeared new. Everything else seemed dated, he thought. He had always had a keen eye for interiors. The place, however, smelt homely as he could smell the aroma of food the minute he walked in.

"Some water would be fine, dear, thank you," The Chief responded and leaned back into the sofa pensively.

Moments later, a young, tall, slender lady came out from what appeared to be a hallway and walked slowly towards Chief Ilo, and he immediately knew who she was. He rose from the sofa, his eyes fixed on hers and stood for a moment. It was unmistakably Omolabake, his *never before seen* child. She was beautiful and bore an uncanny resemblance to *Omosede*, his second daughter. In fact, he thought they could have passed for twins, except 'Sede was slightly older and shorter. Sede, out of his three girls, bore the closest resemblance to him. His other two daughters, on the other hand, looked more like their mother.

Chief Ilo studied Labake as she drew closer. He noticed the slight limp in her step and tried to interpret the expression on her face but could not. She had that familiar blank look his first daughter, Omorewa, usually had when she was not trying to be friendly. Omolabake seemed to also look like Rewa, his first daughter at that moment. In Rewa's case, though, the look was a standoffish one that seemed to read *who are you and what do you want with me?* It was usually an attempt to intimidate whomever it was directed at. However, Chief Ilo did not get that same impression here with Labake. She did not seem to want to trigger intimidation. In fact, she seemed rather timid to him. This was a bit of a surprise to Chief Ilo as none of his girls are timid; they were actually quite the opposite – confident, brazen and sure of themselves. Why was Labake different? He wondered.

As was the culture in which she was raised, Labake bent a knee and curtsied in greeting Chief Ilo. She avoided his eyes and quietly said, "Good Afternoon...sir." Chief Ilo stood for a while and then made an attempt to reach out and embrace her, but Labake drew back abruptly with a question in her eyes. She did not smile nor even try to make him feel welcome. A tear slid down the corner of Benjamin Ilo's eye as he watched her closely.

It was not just Omolabake's reaction to him that made him emotional at that moment; it was the way she appeared non-committal, timid and perhaps even frightened. It was as though something was missing within her. Could it be a result of the ordeal she had recently been through? Chief Ilo wondered. She was not the *lioness* his other girls were, though she looked like them. Something was awry here; Omolabake did not have what they had in terms of presence and gait. She was jittery and appeared to be catching a chill. He withdrew and watched her stumble before she took a seat on the edge of the sofa. She watched him for a moment like one would a complete stranger, then turned away as one would in disgust.

Chief Ilo stood awkwardly for a moment and then sat back down, inching slightly closer to where Labake was. Laide came out at that moment with a glass and jug of water. She placed them gently on the coffee table in front of Chief Ilo and excused herself from the room. Laide thought one could cut the tension in the air with a knife. She knew father and daughter needed some privacy to get acquainted though she suspected the chief had his work cut out for him. She knew this was just a formality for her sister; she was dead set against having a relationship with her father. Ella had been dropped off at Kwame's place as Labake had insisted she did not want her meeting Chief Ilo. Laide entered her bedroom, shut the door and prayed the meeting between Labake and Chief Ilo went well.

Chief Ilo cleared his throat finally and began to speak. "It's great to...to finally meet you, Omolabake...I've been searching for you for some time now. Er...Just as a way of properly introducing myself, I am Benjamin Ilo." Chief Ilo paused for a moment for any reaction from Labake, but there was none. She just sat quietly, looking at him now with that blank expression. "I heard about...the incident at the hotel where you work...I'm so sorry you had to go through that..." Chief Ilo said and deliberately left out the fact that it had been trending news back home in Nigeria. The headlines had read,

> ***ANGRY NIGERIAN HUSBAND DIES ATTEMPTING TO KILL WIFE IN GHANA.***

At the time he first read the headline, he had no inkling that the *wife* in question was his biological daughter. He was even more thankful that no one knew who Labake was. It would have added some more furor to the news and would have been utter *mayhem* if everyone knew whose daughter she really was. He shuddered just thinking of it.

"I was going to fly out to see you in hospital...but Olaide didn't think it was a good time...then there was the fact that you weren't even aware...of my existence at the time. Thank God you're fine now...you are, aren't you? I mean, are you better now?" Chief Ilo asked, hating the fact that he was rambling a bit. It was not his usual style but the present circumstance made him uneasy. Labake gave a slight nod and looked away as though she was saying *what's it to you?*

Chief Ilo prayed silently for the right words to say to her. He felt awash with guilt, which was not helping his thought process. He had played the conversation out several times in his head, but he knew now that it had all been a waste of time. It just seemed rather odd that she was his child, and he was struggling to communicate and even connect with her. She seemed fragile, scared, hurt and delicate all at the same time, and her eyes were haunted too. What was it about her that he could not quite place? Or was he so overwhelmed with guilt that he could not have a *normal* exchange with her, his own daughter? He knew he had to forge ahead, though; it was why he was there.

"Thank God for that...and thank you for agreeing to see me...as I know, I probably don't deserve the opportunity. Let me start by apologizing...profusely that I have been absent from your life since you were born...that's a fact I feel terribly ashamed of." He decided a direct approach would be better as he did not think it would help to patronize her.

"I've had a lot of time to think about it since I found you...I can no longer make the excuse that I was unaware of your existence...as I knew your mother *was* pregnant...she informed me about the pregnancy. What I should have done was to at least find out if she had...if she had terminated it as I'd asked her to...instead of walking away like I did. It was the responsible thing to do...I feel terribly ashamed for my actions and wish there was a way to have sorted things out properly with your mother before she passed away. I am sorry, Omolabake...I'm still trying to forgive myself for that...I'm hoping that we can find a way to move beyond my misdeeds and perhaps...attempt to foster a proper relationship."

Chief Ilo paused again; his eyes danced as they usually did when he was nervous. He hoped Labake would say something, but she had not moved since she sat, and it did not appear as if she was going to. She just sat there and listened with that same blank expression on her face.

Chief Ilo swallowed hard and then took a gulp of the water he had been offered. He expected some reaction from Labake, but he was not getting any whatsoever. She just sat there, silently studying him. He had always had an uncanny ability to read people; it was a special gift which had helped him a lot in business. However, he found it hard to tell anything from Labake's demeanor at that moment. He replaced the glass on the tray and cleared his throat again before he continued.

"I had a heart scare recently...your mother has also appeared to me at intervals...in my dreams...it is obvious now, from the dreams that she wanted me to find you and... perhaps be in your life...I want to be in your life too, dear...I *need* to. I want us to have as close to a normal *father-daughter* relationship as possible. I would also like you to meet the rest of the family...you have a stepmother and three sisters...I would like..."

"Do they know about me?" Labake suddenly asked. It was a raspy whisper, but Chief Ilo heard her clearly.

"Er...not yet, but I'm hoping to set up a family meeting at Christmas to tell them about you...and I hope that you can meet them too..." Chief Ilo said again. It sounded like a question and even a request of some sort.

Something about his general appearance, what he said and how he said it suddenly tugged at Labake's heartstrings at that moment. She nearly even felt sorry for him. Until that moment, she was angry with him, did not want to hear anything he had to say and did not even want to be in the same room as him. She had felt the anger rise within her when he attempted to reach for her when she greeted him. She thought she was going to have to hold herself back, to keep from screaming and yelling at him for all the pain she had known since she was a child and that which she still carried with her as an adult.

Somewhere in her head, Labake even blamed him for what she went through with Vince. Perhaps if he had included her in his life early enough and been the type of father he should have been to her, she would not have ended up with a brute for a husband. Her life would have been different, and she would have probably achieved her dream of pursuing a career in medicine. She would have had better opportunities and helped her family get out of the slum they lived in. She would have gone to better schools, and the list went on. She shook her head as if trying to rid it of the thought when she realized she would not have had Ella. Her most prized possession, one she could not imagine her life without.

Labake realized at that moment that instead of anger, she suddenly felt pity for the chief. She had watched him struggle through what he came to say to her and was aware it could not have been an easy task for him. She sensed deep down that he was truly ashamed of himself and how recklessly he had treated the knowledge that he could possibly have a child somewhere in this big and bad world. She saw the anguish in his eyes as he spoke and imagined the anxiety he was bound to have experienced over everything. She had also seen the tears in his eyes when she came out to meet him. Looking at him now, Labake sensed he was not a mean person; she saw it in his general demeanor.

Labake could not help the connection she felt to Chief Ilo at that moment. Perhaps it was the humble way in which he approached the issue, but she knew she had to find it within her heart to forgive him and knew it would take some time, but she found she desired it. Chief Ilo was clearly a kind man; she had seen it in his eyes, amongst all other emotions. She could not understand what had suddenly come over her, all she knew was that she was tired. Tired of carrying hatred, distrust, anger and animosity within her. She felt an overwhelming need to be kind too, and seek peace. She needed some peace and calmness in her soul, and she was going to reach out and grasp it, no matter what.

After a moment, Labake suddenly rose from where she sat and moved closer to where the Chief was. She sat next to him and began to speak.

"Until now, I was angry with you...I'm supposed to *still* be angry with you...but suddenly, I find that I'm not. My plan was to meet with you this one time, so we could both say we'd actually met and then never communicate with you again. A lot has happened...you missed out on a lot...good *and* bad...*really* bad and ugly too." Labake trailed off and wondered if she should share the dream she had overnight with him. She thought on it silently and then said.

"My mother appeared in my dream last night too. That was the first time since her passing, some eleven years ago. She pleaded with me to hear you out. She begged me to accept your apology...I thought I'd had the dream because I was anxious about our meeting today...now I see. It's what she wants...it was so like her to be gracious and forgiving...that was who she was. Kind-hearted and always willing to give people several chances...even when they'd done her wrong and didn't deserve it. Unfortunately, people like you took advantage of her kindness. In the dream, she pleaded on your behalf, though you abandoned her. If she forgave you...I guess I could try...try and work on forgiving you too. It may take some time, but I *am* willing to try. A lot has happened, and like I said, you've missed out on a lot...for example, you have a nine-year-old granddaughter for starters..." Labake paused and waited for a reaction from her father.

His eyes lit up, and he said, "Really? *Nine*? Where is she?" He looked around the neat room, wondering why he had not seen any traces of a young person in the house since his arrival. Thinking about it now, he remembered that the article he had read on

Labake's shooting had mentioned a child, but that fact had somehow escaped his memory.

"She's not here at the moment; she had a playdate with a family friend. Her name's Ella." Labake stated with some pride, thoroughly enjoying his reaction to having a grandchild.

"That would make *six* grandkids altogether! What a joy to know that," Chief Ilo said. He loved all his grandchildren and was proud to be a grandfather at his age as he had quite a number of friends who were yet to attain the title. "I'd love to meet her soon," he added joyfully. He could not quite believe all Labake had just said to him. It was a dream come true! He was ecstatic to learn that she was willing to at least try to move past his mistakes and absence from her life all these years.

Chief Ilo got emotional at that point. He bent his head, covered his face with both his palms and began to weep uncontrollably. He felt a mixture of emotions as he sobbed. They were pent-up emotions he had bottled in all this time, and they had to be let out. He had been consumed by his need to make things right with Omolabake, and he had. He felt the weight was finally off his shoulders; he had achieved what he set out to. She did not have the spiciness' his other girls had, but she was intelligent, eloquent, present and unequivocal in all she had said. She had demonstrated a type of strength he was not sure any of his other daughters had, and at that moment, he knew for sure that she was his child and he was proud to be her father.

CHAPTER THIRTY

Ralph knew it just was not the right time to discuss Rewa with her father. Chief Ilo seemed pensive, and it was clear he had stuff on his mind he needed to share. He sat opposite Ralph's desk, and Ralph observed that something was desperately wrong. He had not seen him this way before, and he wondered what he needed to say to put his client and friend at ease.

Chief Benjamin Ilo had personally booked this appointment himself. He said he needed to discuss his will. Ralph did not expect that to be an issue seeing as *Prince's Chambers* had been the one to draft the will in the first place. Of course, that had been about thirteen years ago, so why was he here, sitting awkwardly in the chair, shifting as if he had done something wrong? Ralph wondered. Clients amended their wills as and when they deemed fit, he had done it several times and the law did not require them to give their reasons for doing so. He, as the lawyer, was just there to fulfill their wishes.

Suddenly, it struck Ralph that he could be in a precarious position if he pursued a relationship with Rewa, considering she was his client's daughter and also a beneficiary in his will. It had not struck him until now that this could be an issue, particularly because he handled all of Chief Ilo's probate affairs. His relationship with both father and daughter could possibly be deemed a conflict of interest. Lawyers owed their clients extreme confidentiality, and this was something Ralph practiced very seriously. He decided to sleep on what he needed to do about it. He was fond of Rewa and was serious about taking his relationship with her to the next level. He wondered how such a relationship would affect his professional relationship with her father. He decided to hear the chief out first before he did anything about it.

They had greeted one another, and Chief Ilo had commended the new building and Ralph's new chambers when he came into the office, and Ralph had said he had his daughter to thank for the tremendous work she had done. Ralph had seen the chief's face when he mentioned his daughter. He had smiled nervously but said proudly,

"She is really talented, isn't she?" He then got down to the reason he was there.

"As I said on the phone, I'm here to discuss my will and last testament. I'm aware the tabloids have mentioned your *relationship* with my daughter Omorewa, and I'm hoping it wouldn't be a..." Chief Ilo stuttered and then paused cautiously, trying to choose the right words. Ralph decided to step in and help him by asking, "A *conflict of interest*? I have considered that, but you needn't worry yourself at all about that, Chief. As you probably know, my profession requires that I observe absolute confidentiality with my clients and their personal and legal affairs. This is something I've practiced and maintained strictly since I began my career. However, I would totally understand if you wish to take your probate affairs to another firm, particularly if it would make you more comfortable...I guarantee you that our relationship wouldn't be affected in any way should you decide to do so, Chief." Ralph finished politely.

He was aware Chief Ilo had some other legal practitioners he worked with and knew he could easily transfer his probate matters to any of them, but he felt the need to reassure his friend that he would be fine if he chose to do so. Chief Ilo was much older than he was, but they had been friends for a number of years now. They had first met a few years ago at the golf club and had been introduced by a mutual friend when Chief Ilo decided he needed an additional legal eye over his personal affairs. He respected Ralph a lot and appreciated his legal advice too.

Chief Ilo cleared his throat nervously and said, "Er...that shouldn't be a problem, Ralph. I have the utmost confidence in you and your practice, but the reason I'm here involves Omorewa...actually, *all* my children...in fact, my entire family...but the thing is, they don't know it yet, though it's only a matter of time before they do..."

Ralph observed that the chief struggled to get the words out. He looked conflicted and beads of sweat had begun to form on his forehead, making him appear ill suddenly. Ralph got out of his chair to pour him some water from the jug on the side of his large desk. He offered it to him and watched as he gulped it down within seconds. He refilled his glass and returned to his seat behind the desk. He decided to give the chief a moment to gather his thoughts and say what it was he needed to, watching him cautiously still. He was aware that he'd had a heart scare some years back and worried slightly for his health.

Chief Ilo cleared his throat again and said, "I suppose there's no easy way to say this...you see, Ralph, neither my wife nor my children are aware I fathered a child...a *daughter* to be precise, outside my marriage. I had a brief extra-marital affair some twenty-nine years ago...I wasn't aware of her existence myself...well I knew of her conception but didn't quite know her mother had kept the pregnancy until recently..."

Ralph watched as Chief Ilo swallowed hard. He wondered why he was so nervous and appeared rather uncomfortable. It was not unusual for a man of Chief Ilo's stature in society to have illegitimate children. It was not as if Ralph had not dealt with cases like this before. He had actually been surprised, thirteen years ago when the chief had first written his will, that he appeared to have just the three daughters by his wife whom he had provided for generously. Ralph thought it unusual that he had just the one illegitimate child he was now talking about, but he did not show it. He had always maintained an expressionless face whenever he took instructions from his clients and strongly believed that it was not his place to judge anyone. He was there to do his client's bidding, and that was all. As if egged on by Ralph's cool candor, Chief Ilo cleared his throat yet again and continued.

"I would therefore like to amend my will to include my last daughter, *Esther Omolabake Ebodo.*

* * * *

Ralph drove into the Ilo mansion and parked the car at the guest carport. It was Christmas day, and Rewa felt it was a good time to introduce him to the entire Ilo clan. As a result, she invited him over for Christmas lunch with her family. "It isn't a party as such, and no one else would be there except the folks, my sisters, their husbands and kids. You at least get to meet my sister Rien, who's visiting from the States," she said excitedly when she invited him.

Ralph looked forward to meeting Rewa's entire family but could not help feeling slightly nervous at the prospect. He was beginning to fall in love with Rewa and thought she was a great girl. He, of course, wanted to be liked by her family. The fact that she was the daughter of his good friend and client should have made it easier, but it did not. In fact, Chief Ilo was now aware of their budding relationship, but Ralph still felt rather awkward. He was not usually the nervous type, but this was different. He wanted Rewa's family to approve of him and her as a unit and, perhaps, start getting used to having him around too.

Ralph had pondered for a week on his decision to secretly ask Chief Ilo for his daughter's hand in marriage before he proposed to her. He was hoping to catch some quiet time with him while he was here at the Ilo residence today. He had purchased a ring too, thinking he wanted to propose the minute he got Chief Ilo's blessing to marry his daughter. He wanted it to be special and planned to make it a Christmas to remember for Rewa. So why could he not control his nerves? He acted like a foolish teenager; even Israel had teased him about it just before he left home earlier. Israel knew of his plans and, in fact, had been the one to suggest that Ralph proposed today. He thought it would be *romantic*, being Christmas day.

"Parked yet, babe?" Rewa asked over the phone. They had talked on the phone since before Ralph left his house and during the entire duration of the fifteen-minute drive to her parent's home. She had spent the night with her family last night in preparation for their annual family Christmas day lunch.

Rewa had mentioned how excited she was that Ralph was coming over for lunch and had said he did not need to worry about bringing a gift, but Ralph had brought one anyway. It was just the right thing to do; after all, it was Christmas. He had stopped to get the biggest Christmas hamper he could find at a store not too far from where he lived and intended to present it to Chief Ilo and his family.

"Yes, I'm parked, dear," he responded to Rewa's question.

"Okay, I'm on my way down to meet you," Rewa said excitedly. She had not mentioned that Ralph would be joining the family for Christmas lunch. That was deliberate as she was not prepared for the fuss she knew both her mother *and* Sede would make if they had prior notice of Ralph's visit. It was Christmas, and there was going to be a huge variety of food available as usual. She had secretly mentioned to Emeka, the steward, to set an extra place for Ralph at the formal dining room table.

The front doors swung open just as Ralph got to it, hamper in hand.

"Hey, babe!" Rewa said, rushing up to him and planting a kiss on his lips. Ralph returned the kiss and was dragged indoors by Rewa when she said, "Come in and meet everyone. It's a surprise, by the way!" Ralph stopped dead in his tracks and said, "*What*? You mean they aren't expecting me?" He asked her with a slight look of disapproval. He considered it extremely improper to intrude on her family's Christmas lunch. He already felt uncomfortable as it was. What was Rewa thinking?

"Not to worry, babe, *you* are my family's *Christmas surprise*!" Rewa reassured him as she tugged on his arm, gesturing for him to follow her in. *"God knows they've been expecting you for years,"* Rewa mumbled under her breath so Ralph could not hear her. She was like an excited little girl at that moment. Another reason she had refused to say anything to him about the surprise was that she rightly foresaw he would have *flat-out* refused to come along *unannounced* to her parent's house. She was getting to know him better, and it just was not his way.

Too late to back out now, Ralph thought as he followed Rewa, basket in hand, into the large hall, which led straight into an equally large front room. He had never visited Chief Ilo at home and therefore took in his environment with interest as he and Rewa walked in.

"*Hey, family*! for those of you who haven't met him, I'd like to introduce you to Chief Ralph Eke. My...er good friend," Rewa said as they got in. Ralph placed the Christmas gift basket he had brought along for the Ilos on the rugged floor and straightened up to greet Rewa's family, who all appeared surprised to see him.

The first person who appeared to get over her surprise was a young lady who bore some resemblance to Rewa but had short cropped hair and a lighter skin tone than her. "Er...you mean your *boyfriend,* sis." She said as she got off one of the couches in the room and swiftly walked up to Ralph. She ignored his outstretched hand and gave him a hug instead. Rewa smiled coyly and said, "Ralph, meet my rather *rude* younger sister, Omosede." Ralph smiled at her and returned the hug. He had heard quite a bit about Sede and expected some sort of drama from her. Rewa had mentioned she was the most outspoken of the Ilo girls.

"Pleased to meet you Omosede," Ralph said. "*Sede* for short...you can call me Sede, chief," Sede responded, clearly impressed with their new guest. "Please call me Ralph," He responded and watched as she appraised him from head to toe. He almost asked if she needed him to turn around for further assessment, he mused silently. Next to get up and greet him was Rien's husband. He shook his hand and introduced himself, and then there were Rien and Larry, Sede's husband. Ralph recognized Mrs.

Ilo from an event they had both attended. She sat on one of the plush sofas with her sleeping grandson on her lap.

Clearly struggling to get over the surprise of having Ralph in her home, she managed a warm smile. "Pleased to meet you, Chief Eke, er...Rewa, why didn't you mention we were having a guest for lunch? Can someone please go get your father from the den...?" Mrs. Ilo said, still trying to absorb the present situation. She took the hand Ralph stretched to her and shook it.

"Pleased to meet you again, ma," Ralph said. Mrs. Ilo was pleasantly surprised and had heard all about her daughter's budding romance with Ralph Eke. She was so happy about it and had just about managed to keep it to herself. She was tempted to mention it to her friend, *Mrs. Thomas* but thought against it. It was early days yet, she hoped and prayed Rewa's relationship with Chief Eke led to their marriage. She was quite prepared to give her first daughter the biggest society wedding ever to happen in the history of the entire country.

"Please sit, babe, while I go fetch, dad," Rewa said. She wished she had recorded the look of surprise on all their faces, and now it was her father's turn, Rewa mused as she left the room in search of him.

"There's someone here to see you, dad," Rewa stated to her father when she got into the den. She said it with as blank a look as she could manage. Her father turned round in his swivel chair at that moment. He sat with his back to the door, overlooking the garden, in deep thought when his first daughter came into the room.

"Guest?" He asked Rewa with a puzzled look. "On *Christmas day*? Who is it?" He asked Rewa after she nodded in answer to his first question. It was uncommon for anyone he knew to come visiting on Christmas day without some prior warning. He and Mena usually had a *New Year's Day* party when they invited all their friends, but as a matter of tradition, both preferred to spend the Christmas celebration with just their family, and most of his acquaintances knew this.

"Think you should come and see for yourself," Rewa answered and waited for him to rise from his chair. She stretched out her hand and held her father's as they both walked the short distance from the den to the main living room.

"Ralph!" Chief Ilo greeted as he came into the living room with Rewa, "Wow! What a surprise!" Ralph stood to greet Chief Ilo, who, in turn, turned to Rewa and said, "You cheeky girl! You never mentioned Ralph was coming!" Chief Ilo laughed heartily. He was surprised but very pleased Ralph was there. He shifted like he usually did when he was uncomfortable and sat beside Ralph on the sofa. Ralph noticed he still looked slightly pensive and of course, now knew the reason why. He still had not come clean to his family about his illegitimate child. What a burden to carry, he thought, feeling sorry for him.

The conversation carried on between them, and a few minutes later, lunch was ready, and they all proceeded to the grand, formal dining room. It was the one time in the year the large room was used as there was another eating area in the family room, closer to the kitchen, where everyone within the family ate and hung out generally.

Rewa gestured for Ralph to come sit next to her at the table. As usual, there was an array of all kinds of food served. And the platters of food passed round the table as did the light and easy conversation. They talked about politics, local and international. Ralph talked about some controversial case he had worked on and won recently, which was also quite political, and everyone chipped in here and there. It was a great atmosphere, and as was expected, the usual banter between the sisters made for great entertainment, especially to Ralph, who silently watched their interactions with one another.

Rewa felt proud that she was not the only one without a partner at the Christmas table for once. She watched Ralph tackle questions posed to him by her sisters and mother and how he deftly answered them, clearly making an effort to impress them too. He held her hand beneath the table every now and again, and she loved it. She loved how affectionate he was towards her and the attention he paid her, it made her feel important to him, and that made her want to love and respect him right back.

They had dated for nearly three months now, and it had been a smooth ride so far. They got along beautifully and had managed to build a level of intimacy that surprised Rewa. They told each other everything, went out on dates a lot too, and even had a trip planned to Dubai sometime in the New Year. Rewa did not know it, but Ralph was planning a secret *getaway* to Dubai for Valentine's Day.

Chief Ilo was grateful in a way that Ralph was there, in his home, though it had been unplanned. He had thought he needed some moral support of sorts when he shared his news. He had thought on it for weeks now and had decided to let his family in on it on Christmas day. He knew it was a rather odd time to choose to reveal his secret illegitimate child to his wife and children, but he had no choice, and there just did not seem to be a better time. Besides, he wanted to start the New Year on an open, clean slate with *all* his children together. The timing was right for a number of reasons.

First, all three of his daughters were present, under his roof at the same time, as Omorien was home from Texas, visiting with family. He was not quite sure when next that would happen again.

Rien's family was expanding, and there was the possibility that their annual trips would get a lot more difficult with two young children. Rien herself had mentioned that the other day. Benjamin Ilo intended to reveal his secret to *all* of his family in person. The last thing he wanted to do was to have Rien find out over the telephone.

Second, Rien and her family were planning a visit to her parents-in-law, who resided in *Port-Harcourt,* tomorrow – *Boxing Day*. They were all packed and set to leave on the sixty-minute journey to the southern part of the country on one of his private jets. They intended to fly back to Texas after a couple of days with Rien's in-laws as they wanted to be home before the New Year.

Third, Chief Ilo did not want to ruin the days leading up to the festive season for his family as he suspected it was going to be a hard pill to swallow for them all. He had chosen to tell them about it tonight, well after their Christmas lunch, just so the entire day would not be a complete disaster after his revelation. He, however, could not see how that could be avoided. His family's *entire year* was going to be ruined by his revelation, and he knew this was certainly going to be the *Christmas to remember*. He only hoped it would not be the last they shared together as a family.

Again, Chief Ilo had not envisaged the length of time it would take to meet Omolabake the first time, especially because she had been in hospital. He had also wanted to be certain she would be willing to meet with him first before he told his family about her. After he did meet her, he had decided to give her some time to process it all and perhaps get used to having him in her life first before he asked her if she would be willing to meet the rest of his family too. He knew the timing was all wrong, but it could not be put off any longer. He had to do what he had to. Besides, he also had Labake's feelings to consider. If anything, he owed it to her to bring her existence to the knowledge of his family as early as possible. He was tired of the secrets.

Now Chief Ilo had counted the cost of what his *big reveal* could possibly do to his family, but it was inevitable. He was not going to give in to cowardice the way other men in his position had done, leaving their families to find out, after they were dead, that they had fathered illegitimate children. He could not do that to Mena or his girls. They deserved to hear it from him, no matter how difficult it was.

After lunch, Chief Ilo cleared his throat nervously. He had mentioned last night that he would be convening a family meeting with everyone today. He did not want his sons-in-law present and had asked everyone else to meet in his home office. He specifically asked Ralph to join them, causing both his sons-in-law to exchange a certain look.

Chief Ilo had thought about mentioning Labake to Mena first as a sign of respect, but he had decided against it, knowing she would have mentioned it to the girls before he was ready to. He had therefore decided to break the news to them as a group and perhaps have everyone air their opinions openly.

Of course, Mena had enquired of him several times over the course of the last few months if there was anything wrong. She insisted something was *off* with him as he seemed somewhat distant. She had been married to him for almost fifty years and could read him like a book. She had asked if he was sick again or something, as she found his behaviour rather queer. He had been a lot quieter over the past few weeks, was always deep in his thoughts each time she caught him alone, and he was off his food, even when she asked *Chef* to prepare his favourite, *catfish pepper soup*! He tried to set her mind at ease by reassuring her he was perfectly okay, but his Mena was a smart woman; she *knew* something was wrong but decided to stop asking. She, however, monitored his every movement and watched him like a hawk.

Mena, the girls, and Ralph were now all gathered in Chief Ilo's home office, they were all seated, and Chief Ilo could see they were all puzzled as to what the family meeting was going to be about and why Ralph was also present. Rewa looked at Ralph at some point with a question in her eyes. Was her father about to discuss a legal matter? Why had he asked Ralph to join them and none of her brothers-in-law? He was not even aware of Ralph's visit to the house that day, or was he? She found herself wondering now.

Ralph, in turn, looked just as puzzled as Rewa, her mother and sisters too. He had a good guess of what the chief wanted to discuss with his family but wondered why he wanted him there. He did not think he belonged there at that point in time and tried to think of a way to excuse himself, but nothing came to mind. This was a precarious position for him, and he wondered what purpose his presence would serve. He thought he would give it a shot and ask to be excused. He slowly rose from his seat and said,

"Er...seeing as this appears to be a private matter, can I request that I be excused, Sir? I really should be getting back to my son Israel, given it is Christmas and..." He was, however, cut off when Chief Ilo raised his hand and said, "No, please, Ralph, I want you here. I consider you not just my legal representative but also a good friend. Moreover, you're more or less family, given the fact that you and...Omorewa are...are involved." Chief Ilo stuttered as he finished addressing Ralph, who fell silent and sat back down in the chair he occupied next to Rewa.

"What's going on, dad?" Rewa asked. "You're scaring me...us," she said, waving her hand at the others, including her mother, who just sat pensively, looking at her husband intently. *What was he trying to say?* Mena wondered. She had asked him last night as they prepared for bed what the family meeting he mentioned was about, but he said he wanted to discuss it with their children present. She had found that strange too, as they were usually a united front before their girls. Could the family meeting have any correlation with his recent awkward change in behaviour? She had wondered silently but resolved to wait for what he had to say.

Rien got up and moved to her father's side. She rubbed his shoulders reassuringly and looked into his eyes, searching for what it was that clearly bothered him so. "Yes, dad, what's the matter? Are you ill?" She asked in a soft, concerned tone. She was every bit a *daddy's girl* and had always been. Chief Ilo patted her hand and said, "I'm not sick, dear, please...take your seat."

On the other hand, Sede looked at her watch impatiently, wondering what all the fuss was about. She wished her father would just spit whatever was on his mind out. She and Larry, her husband, both worked closely with him. Apart from three of their vessels which had got delayed at sea, everything else was just fine at work, so she knew whatever it was, was not work-related. Her sisters and mother had asked last night if she knew what the meeting was about, but she had said she did not. Everyone knew she was *privy* to most family secrets, but this one *threw her for a loop. I bet it's nothing.* Sede told herself now. Sometimes their father just got *overdramatic* for no obvious reason; she thus was not going to give much thought to whatever it was he was going to say at that moment.

After Rien was back in her seat, Chief Ilo cleared his throat again and started.

"I want you all to know how much I love you. I've worked hard over the years just to ensure that you were all taken care of and that you all wanted for nothing...your mother and me. I expect that you're all aware of this and the other sacrifices I've...we've made to keep us all together, in peace and harmony. It's never been my aim to hurt you or shut any of you out. Hitherto, I believe I have been relatively transparent in...all I've done, there have hardly been any secrets between us as a family...but...something came up recently, and it's pertinent that you all are aware of...of it. Now, I don't want any of you to see me differently, as I am still your father and husband. I haven't changed, but I've always believed in being responsible and doing the responsible thing in every given situation. My heart scare a couple of years ago has also made me realize this is the right thing to do as I do not want any surprises if I...if I happen to pass away suddenly...I mean, no man is promised tomorrow," he paused a bit and shifted uncomfortably in his chair before continuing.

"All that being said...and I know there's no easy way to say what I'm about to, but before I do, I want to beg the forgiveness of my wife, your mother, Philomena. Darling, I have never wanted to hurt you, you are my world, and that's why...I've acted strangely lately...I just didn't know how to tell you..."Chief Ilo trailed off. His voice had begun to shake as he became emotional.

"Tell me *what,* Benny? *What*?" Mrs. Ilo said softly, leaning forward now in her chair. She was alarmed now and looked as though she was going to have a heart attack herself at that moment. Rewa rubbed her mother's thigh gently in an attempt to keep her calm as she also instinctively leaned forward.

You could hear a pin drop in the room as the atmosphere suddenly got charged with so much mystery and suspense. At this point, even Sede leaned forward after that *preamble* by her father. *What's he trying to say? Why is he having a hard time saying it?* She wondered. *It really must be serious.* She concluded within her.

"I...I recently discovered that I fathered an illegitimate child some twenty-nine years ago," Chief Ilo said quietly and looked at his hands which were spread out in front of him on his desk.

For a moment, there was nothing but silence in the room as everyone present, except Ralph, of course, just gawked at Chief Ilo. Then what followed could best be described as a *gasping minute*, after which all of Chief Ilo's girls, including his wife, leaned even more closely towards him in their seats and chorused *"What???"* All in unison, as though a music conductor had just given the choir a cue in a musical performance. Chief Ilo finally raised his head and nodded slowly. He then turned to Mena first and said, "You have a stepdaughter." He turned to all three of his daughters and said, "You have a half-sister."

He leaned back in his leather-bound swivel chair, closed his eyes for a moment and let out a shaky sigh of relief. There, he had told them. Now he waited for his revelation to sink in and the reactions that were sure to follow.

CHAPTER THIRTY-ONE

"Benny, *nooooo way...What??? When? How? Where? Who with*?" Mrs. Ilo asked, looking at her husband as if he was an alien. "You *fathered another child* outside our girls? With whom? When?" She shrieked hysterically. She had gone death pale as what her husband had just revealed dawned on her. First, she was in denial and hoped to be awakened from this horrible nightmare. Then she waited for him to say it was a Christmas Day joke or something, but he did not. Instead, he just sat there at his desk, looking down at his hands like the child who was caught with his hands in the cookie jar.

"This is how you treat me? After almost *fifty* years? You didn't just *have* an affair; you *had a child with another woman! A child* for Pete's sake! And kept it secret *all these years*? Who is she, I ask again? *Answer me!*" Philomena Ilo yelled hysterically at her husband, to the chagrin of all present. Her girls had never seen their parents argue or fight with each other, but none of them dared say a word as the tension in the room could be cut with a knife. Mrs Ilo's eyes were wild with derision. She had begun trembling and looked as though she was about to combust from within.

"We need some answers, Dad, don't just sit there silently..." Rewa was the first to speak. She moved near her mother in an attempt to console her in some way. She was stunned and embarrassed that this was all unfolding with Ralph in the room. Then, as if suddenly remembering that Ralph *was* present, she turned to him and asked, "Did you know about this?" She asked with hot eyes, watching his reaction for an answer. Saying nothing, Ralph looked away uneasily, causing Rewa's anger to flare up. She left her mother for a while and stood looking at Ralph. "You *knew* all this time and said nothing? We've talked every single day, hung out every other day, and you didn't think it fit to mention anything about this to me...?" Rewa asked in a fit of rage. She was astounded by the overwhelming level of betrayal she felt. "Please leave...I need you to leave. This is a *family* matter, and you shouldn't be here right now." Rewa said it in the iciest way possible. She had also begun trembling, her nostrils flared, and her breathing suddenly became labored.

Chief Ilo cleared his throat as if to say something about Ralph leaving but fell silent again when Rewa shot him one of her blank looks. Ralph rose and exited the building without a word.

For the first time in her life, Sede was quiet. She seemed lost and just stared at her father, clearly perplexed. She was the closest to her parents and wondered how she had been unaware of their father's big secret. She was shocked that he would do anything like this as he was the most cautious person she knew. He was not known to be a womanizer. If he was, the tabloids would have aired any known affairs he may have had, but there had never been any such news about him. Sede watched her father and his reaction now, thinking *wonders would never end*. You thought you knew a person, your parent even, only to find you didn't! They had deep secrets!

"Who is the child's mother, Dad, and where are they?" Rien asked softly, finally finding her voice. She had also moved to her mother's side and held her as she whimpered and sobbed in her arms. Mrs. Ilo looked up at her husband, expecting an answer too. Her eye makeup had started running, her face was flushed from her sobbing, and she looked a complete mess. She sniffled into the tissue Rewa handed her distractedly and waited for her husband's answer. She needed to know who he had cheated on her with, to the point of siring a child.

Rewa sat back down, her eyes boring into her father as all four ladies waited with bated breaths for his answer to Rien's question.

Chief Ilo looked up for the first time since he *dropped the bomb* on his family about Omolabake, his illegitimate child. He looked ashen as his eyes settled on his wife and knew he would never forgive himself for how crushed she was at that moment. He hated knowing he had hurt her this way. She had shown him nothing but pure love all these years, and he sometimes felt he did not deserve her as she was childlike in her love for him, trusting him completely through all the years. She had been there when he had nothing, giving up her own wealthy background for his humble one in the beginning. She had naively made sacrifices for him till they built the life they now had. She had given him and raised three beautiful, well-adjusted daughters too. What had he thought when he started the affair with Iyabode? Now he knew he could not make amends with the wife of his youth and was afraid she would leave him. He knew he would die if she decided to and that there was no one else to blame but himself if she did.

He got up from his desk and moved to the seat closest to Mena and Rien. He wondered how close he should get as he desperately needed to take his wife in his hands. Mena had begun sobbing into Rien's chest again as Rien rubbed her back in an attempt to comfort her the way one would a child.

Chief Ilo reached out to stroke her back and said, "My dear...I never meant to hurt you...God knows that's the truth..." He started as his daughters watched him. All three were not just upset at the sudden news that they had a sibling out there somewhere. They were even more upset for their mother, who appeared to be crumbling right before their eyes.

"Don't touch me! Keep your filthy hands to yourself!" Mena yelled at her husband, snatching her arm out of his reach and almost elbowing Rien in the nose as she did. She turned into Rien's chest again and wailed even louder, slobbering all over her youngest daughter's shirt.

Mena had always had a naivety about her that had made Benjamin want to protect and shield her since he first met her. She seemed like a helpless little girl at times and had this way of drawing out compassion from all who met her. Now she just seemed like a shattered little girl whose world had just come crashing down. He had shattered her spirit. Perhaps he was the one she needed protection from, he thought.

"Who is she, Dad?" Rewa asked impatiently, this time with a silent warning in her tone of voice. *Why was he stalling this much?* She wondered.

Chief Ilo shook his head in regret and looked away. He then turned to look at all four of his girls, including Mena, and said, "She was *nobody* really...I mean, it just happened! She meant *nothing* to me...at the time or ever...It shouldn't have happened, I regret it to this day..." Chief Ilo said with remorse written all over his face. He appeared desperate to appease all four women.

"You still haven't answered the question, Dad. Who did you have this child with?" Rewa said with a voice that shook and threatened to explode any minute.

"*Exactly! Why* are you *avoiding* the question?!!" Mrs. Ilo shrieked; blackened tears from her eye make-up ran down her bright red face now.

"We need to know, Dad...*Mum* needs to know," Rien urged her father calmly as she rubbed her mother's back soothingly.

Realizing he could not keep avoiding the inevitable, Chief Ilo cleared his throat and began speaking. "Her name was *Iyabode...was* because she passed away a few years ago. She came to me for help many years ago. She...was unable to feed herself or her child...she was hard working and didn't just want food money...she wanted to start a small food business. What can I say...I was impressed that she didn't want just a handout..."

"So she decided to repay the favor *in kind...with her body*? Listen to yourself *Benny*...you *admired* her!" Mrs. Ilo screamed accusatorily at her husband and wailed even louder. For a moment, Chief Ilo looked confused at the conclusion his wife had drawn. Then he said,

"No, my dear, that wasn't what I said...dear...it wasn't like that at all. She came back a year later to show her appreciation...and one thing led to another..." He earnestly tried to choose his words carefully, but they just came out all wrong.

"How many times...how many times did you sleep with her?" Mrs. Ilo asked, to her husband's embarrassment. He shifted uncomfortably and looked at his girls. He then turned away before saying, "I don't know...she fell pregnant...it was a mistake," he answered, to his wife's horror.

Mrs. Ilo stopped sniffling for a second and glared at her husband in shock. Then, as if she suddenly had an idea, she asked, "You *had* an affair? An *actual* affair with this *nobody*? And you say it didn't mean anything? You got her pregnant and had an illegitimate kid with her...and she didn't mean anything? I hate everything you stand for right now, Benny! You make me *sick*! I can't bear to be in the same room with you! *God!"* Mrs. Ilo exclaimed, then got up and stormed out of the room.

"*Mena*!" Her husband yelled after her, but she left, slamming the door behind her and leaving a strong wind of her perfume in the air.

Chief Ilo sat back down before his daughters in a deflated manner. "I have really ruined things." He spoke what he was thinking out loud and did not even realize it until Sede, who had not spoken a word since they all came in, said quietly, "I'm afraid I have to agree with you on that one, Dad...how old is she?"

Chief Ilo shook his head again in regret. He had expected some reaction and had tried not to dwell on it too much, but Mena's volatile reaction and the look of hatred she shot him were nothing like he had envisaged. He had never seen her look as wounded as she had. He knew for sure now that his marriage was over.

He looked at Sede, seeming confused by her question momentarily. "I don't know...we never talked about that..." He answered, wondering how Sede expected him to know Iyabode's age.

"I meant your illegitimate daughter, dad...how old is she?" Sede asked again.

Chief Ilo opened his mouth to speak, then closed it again as Sede's question sunk in. "Twenty-eight...she'll be twenty-nine next month," he answered quietly. He then turned to his girls and gave them the details of how he recently found Labake and where she was. He also explained how he needed them to meet her and how they were not to take it out on her when they did meet her as she was a product of an affair he had with her mother. She had played no role in how she was conceived or born.

"I wish I could take it all back and do things properly. I regret that I've hurt your mother and you girls too; I never planned to. I'm so, so sorry for putting you all in this position. I will never be able to forgive myself for that," Chief Ilo concluded dejectedly.

"That's ok, Dad. We love you still. I just hope you can make it good with Mum," Rien said. She got up and gave her father a hug as she felt he needed one at that moment. While Sede and Rewa looked on, still perplexed at the magnitude of information they had just absorbed. *What a Christmas this was turning out to be,* she sighed.

After hearing the full story from her father, Rewa felt sorry for him but, at that moment, believed her mother needed to be comforted more. She decided to go in search of her instead.

* * * *

Rewa's phone rang again for the fifth time. Knowing it was Ralph again, she refused to answer it. She felt she could not deal with him now, given the pandemonium her family had been thrown in. She hissed loudly and threw the phone on the table.

"You know the mature thing to do is to speak to him, sis. You can't keep ignoring his phone calls. That's just wrong," Sede said. As much as she was the drama queen in the family, Sede was also the voice of reason. She was analytical and the most objective of them all. It was her best quality, even if Rewa did not feel like she needed to hear it at that moment.

"I agree with Sede, Sis. I know we're all dealing with a bad situation here, but it isn't one that can't be salvaged. Why destroy your relationship with Ralph because of it? It isn't the end of the world if Dad has another child out there...I mean, for a man with the kind of clout he has, I'm surprised there aren't any more illegitimate kids by him! We're all reeling from the shock of it all, and it's the most draining piece of information I ever received, but where do we go from here?" Rien said, spreading her hands.

All three sisters were gathered in Rewa's side of the mansion as they needed some privacy from the husbands, who, by now, had both been clued into the Ilo illegitimate child saga. They had both seen Mrs. Ilo storm out of the den in tears. She had run past them in the living room, heading straight for the stairs. Of course, both their wives had explained the reason moments later, and everyone now wondered what would happen next between Chief Ilo and Chief Mrs. Ilo.

"We can't condone what Dad's done and give him a *pass* because he only had one illegitimate child...besides, how do we know there's only one? There could be others that even he isn't aware of, Rien," Sede said in response to her younger sister.

"I'm not condoning or giving him a free pass, sis. I'm just trying to help us look on the bright side here. It could be far worse...and so far, he has only acknowledged the one illegitimate child, so that'll have to do for us," Rien explained wisely. She had always been the calmer one of the three girls. She was sweet, but in a way, she was just as naïve as their mother, Sede thought within her.

"Anyhow, that's the folk's problem. I'm sure they'll be fine in the long run. Mum just needs time to fully process the whole thing. She'll be good. We'll need to keep an eye on her though 'cause she really is in a bad way," Sede said reassuringly to her sisters.

"You think so, Sede? What if she decides to leave Dad? It would kill him!" Rien mumbled, deep in thought now.

"Don't be silly, sis. No one's leaving anyone. Mum loves him too much to leave. I just wonder how long it'll take her to forgive him though...if she ever does," Sede answered.

"Can't say I blame her if she doesn't forgive him, though; she was *crushed*! She trusted Dad with her whole heart! I've never seen her that way before," Rewa joined in. "Had to give her some pills to help calm her nerves; she really *was* in a bad way." She then frowned when her cell phone began to ring again.

"Really, sis?" Sede said to Rewa in disbelief when she threw the phone on the table again. "Are you going to keep ignoring Ralph's calls? I'm sorry to have to say this, Rewa, but you really need to do some growing up! Like Rien said, there's no need to destroy your relationship over what's going on between the folks because they'll be alright in the long run, like I said. You, however, won't be! You're about to throw a good thing away with a great guy...and for what? If anything, you should respect the fact that he kept Dad's confidence. You *have* heard of *Attorney-Client Privilege,* haven't you? He wouldn't be this great, well-acclaimed lawyer if he went about shooting off his mouth about information his clients give him...it is called *privilege,* sis! He could be disbarred for telling you anything he knew about Dad and his illegitimate child...I mean, think about it!" Sede said sternly to her sister before she left the room in annoyance.

Rewa glared petulantly at the door Sede had just slammed after herself. She was angry with her father, Ralph, and now Sede for her rude comment. It was just one hell of a Christmas, she thought again, sighing.

"*Phew!* The number of slammed doors in this house today...We really need to pray. Everything just seems upside down," Rien said resignedly. She wondered how she would leave tomorrow with the current mayhem going on within her family. First, her mother was distraught and had to be heavily sedated, and her father had locked himself away in the den. Now Sede had left in anger too and Rewa looked as though she could bite someone's head off, any minute soon. *God help us all, please!* She prayed silently.

Rien got up to go sit next to Rewa on the sofa. She had always been the peacemaker in the family though a rebel herself. She reached for Rewa's hands and said softly.

"I know Sede's temper got the better of her, sis, but really, she's right. We cannot let the present circumstance rob us of the things that are lovely in our lives. You said it yourself that Ralph was a great guy. He's clearly trying to make amends and perhaps clarify things to you. Refusing to take his calls isn't just unfair; it could also be deemed immature. He couldn't have mentioned the situation with dad to you; he is his client. You need to understand that, sis. Like Sede said, I think it speaks a lot about the type of person he is. He didn't lose sight of the *privilege* he has with his client, even if he *is* his girlfriend's father..." Rewa interrupted what she was saying at that point.

"But that's the thing! We're a couple. Couldn't he have factored that in somehow? It just still feels like a betrayal to me. I feel like a fool too...I mean, he knew his girlfriend's father had an illegitimate kid, and he never even let on! That's *keeping secrets*. It doesn't feel like *privilege* to me at all, Rien," she said it vehemently, and Rien knew better than to argue with her about it.

"Tensions are high...that's to be expected, given the present situation. Perhaps we all just need to take a break, sleep on stuff and see how we feel in the morning. Please answer his call when next he rings, sis. It's the least you could do and, of course, the polite thing to do too."

That said, Rien gave her eldest sister a reassuring kiss on her cheek and left for her own quarters.

* * * *

Ralph decided to give Rewa one last try. He wanted to satisfy his conscience that he had done enough to reach out to her. If not to explain his precarious position with her father but to at least check on her and see how she was handling the situation with her parents. He wanted to give her the benefit of doubt too, as he refused to believe she would intentionally avoid answering his calls. He had tried her number intermittently through the last couple of days but was yet to speak to her. He thought he would try one more time and then let her be. He thought it unfortunate that things would end this way between them but found the situation was totally out of his hands, especially if Rewa refused to take his calls.

The holidays were still on, and *Princes chambers* was shut down till after the New Year, but Ralph still dropped by at the office daily, as he had a few depositions in the New Year and needed to prepare for them. He had spent a lot of time thinking about all that had happened at the Ilo residence on Christmas Day and decided to relinquish Chief Ilo as a client. There was just too much involved, and he did not want to sabotage his relationship with Rewa by keeping a retainer with her father. He had, of course, had a meeting in person with Chief Ilo to discuss it first and wrote him a formal letter to this effect. At the meeting, Ralph had also formally asked for Rewa's hand in marriage and explained to Chief Ilo that it would indeed be a conflict of interest for them to maintain their business relationship if Rewa did agree to marry him, especially because she was a beneficiary of her father's will.

Chief Ilo had been happy and excited at the news that Ralph intended to ask for his daughter's hand in marriage and had agreed that his probate affairs be transferred to one of his other legal representatives *forthwith*! "I'd rather have you as a member of my family than as my lawyer, *any day*!" He bellowed heartily, clearly pleased with the idea of Ralph marrying Rewa. He only hoped she accepted his proposal, given the current upheaval in the family. He hoped she would not forfeit her relationship with Ralph over his apparent failure to disclose his knowledge about Omolabake's existence.

Rewa finally answered her phone on the third ring. "*Hello,*" she said when she answered. There was no *hey babe or hi hon* this time, like she usually said when she answered his phone calls, but Ralph was relieved she answered his call at all. Now he could at least get the chance to explain things to her.

"How are you, dear?" Ralph asked, adding the term of endearment only because that was what he was used to. "I'm good," Rewa responded flatly. Ralph ignored her tone of voice and carried on. "I've been trying to reach you for days now. I wanted us to talk...about the way we left things the other day, at your parents'. Can we meet somewhere, I mean, I'm at the chambers now, but I can be at your house in ten minutes...that's if you're at your apartment..." Ralph said, pausing for an answer. It was one of those statement-question types of sentences.

"I don't think that's a great idea at the minute...you can say whatever you have to over the phone," Rewa said flatly still.

Ralph was quiet for a moment. He had not expected her to be as cold as she was. He wondered why she seemed so angry with him.

"Rewa, I understand that you may feel upset because you think I kept something that deeply affects you and your family from you. You have to understand that confidentiality goes to the core of what I do. Your father isn't just a good friend of mine; he *was,* more importantly, *my client*. It is essential that I hold in strictest confidentiality matters that come to my knowledge just by virtue of my position as his attorney. I expected you'd understand this. I'm privy to the information your father shared with me *only* because I am his counsel. I'm sure I'd be the last person he shared such information with if I wasn't his lawyer." Ralph paused for a reaction from Rewa.

Instead of feeling appeased by Ralph's explanation, Rewa found that she felt as though he had just told her off and given her *Lecture 101* on Attorney-Client Privilege.

"I don't know why but I feel terribly betrayed and still feel you could have given me a hint or something. I feel like you kept a rather huge secret from me that had to do *with* me, and we were supposed to be in a relationship. I find that scary as it doesn't help trust...we're supposed to be building something here, I don't feel this is a great way to start..." Rewa trailed off.

She had grown to love Ralph deeply but found it unbelievable that they had shared as much as they had together, but he was still able to keep certain things to himself about *her* family. She understood the attorney-client privilege concept but still felt he could have danced around the subject to at least prepare her, but he had not. For her, that made the basis of their relationship questionable, and she found it hard to get passed the feeling of disappointment she felt.

"So, what is it you're saying here, Rewa? What is it you want from me? Perhaps you need some more time to process things and..." Ralph asked but got cut off by Rewa's curt interruption.

"I *do not need more time to process anything*...don't patronize me, Ralph. I'm not a child!" Rewa said vehemently and could feel her anger rising steadily now. She decided she needed to get off the phone before it reached its peak.

"So, where do we go from here?" Ralph asked quietly. He had decided to leave it to her to decide the future of their relationship, seeing as she failed to understand his position on the subject.

"I don't know...I'll ring you," Rewa said for lack of anything better to say. She just needed to get off the phone in that moment as she struggled to contain her temper.

"That's fine, Rewa. Have a good day," Ralph said and ended the call.

In the last few months, he had garnered that Rewa was as sweet as she was *pig-headed*. He had also grown to understand that behind her feistiness was a very soft, sensitive soul, one that could be easily hurt. Ralph had also learned that her bark was far worse than her bite. He did not intend to push the relationship if she refused to understand the ethics of his profession. He decided he was done with her, as much as he did not want to be. He, however, knew he would not divulge any information he received from any of his clients and would do it over and over again whether he dated the said client's daughter or not. If Rewa could not see that, then perhaps they did not belong together after all.

* * * *

"Mena, My dear...I know I've hurt you badly...for that, I will never forgive myself. You've been the best wife a man could ever want. You deserve the very best for all the sacrifices you made for me, and believe it or not; you are the best thing that has ever happened to me. I have never meant to hurt you, dear...*never*. I've loved you since the day I first met you, and I've never stopped loving you...in fact, my love for you grows every day. All I crave is your forgiveness...I'll do anything to make it right between us again...just please forgive me my dear." Chief Ilo pleaded with his wife as he had done every single day for the last three weeks, but she just lay on the bed, motionless, staring into space as though he was not there. He was fast running out of options and did not quite know what else to do to get a reaction, *any* reaction, from his wife. She had not said a word to him since Christmas Day.

The only time he did get a reaction from her was on Christmas evening when he had attempted to come into their quarters of the house to retire for the night. He had hoped that he would be able to get closer to her and perhaps begin to beg for her forgiveness. Her reaction had, however, frightened him. She had got hysterical, screaming for him to get out of her sight. Thankfully the girls were present and had asked him to give her some time and leave. It had taken a good twenty minutes to calm her down. In fact, Dr. Stella, the family physician, had to be called over to the house to give her something stronger than usual to calm her down.

Benjamin Ilo felt sad about his present predicament with his wife. He had never seen her *lose it* the way she had that evening. It could best be described as some kind of *breakdown*. He knew he had destroyed every shred of trust she had for him. He had slept in the guest quarters since that evening and only managed to approach her again a week later, but she was incommunicative. She had shut him down and shut him out, refusing to say anything to him. He was not even certain that she heard what he said at all.

In an attempt to appease her, Chief Ilo ordered the newest *Mercedes-Benz* model and had it delivered to the house, but Mena would not budge. He had also called for her jeweler to send the most expensive diamond jewelry set to the house, but not even that worked. Now he came in every evening to hopefully reassure her of his love, but nothing had changed hitherto. Of course, all the girls were back to their different bases, and he was now left alone to sort his problems out with his wife, but he did not know how.

After he left Mena that evening, Chief Ilo returned to the den. He decided to ring Omorewa. He knew he needed some help in reaching his wife but could not think of how to.

"Hey, Dad, how are you?" Rewa asked after the first ring.

"I'm alright, dear...how was your day?" Chief Ilo answered his first daughter.

"Good, thank you. Has mum come round yet?" She asked. It was the first thing she asked these days. She knew her parents were going through a real rough patch, particularly her mother.

"I'm afraid it's still the same, dear. She just ignores me and acts as though I'm not even there...I feel really bad. I don't know what to do. Besides, I've set up the meeting with Omolabake. She and her daughter, Nuella, will be arriving next weekend, and I don't want it to be awkward for any of you. If your mother is still this way now, Lord knows how she'd be during and after the meeting. I just wish I knew how to get through to her...wish she'd forgive me..." Chief Ilo said, sounding as though he was about to break down in tears.

"Not to worry Dad, I'll have another go at talking to her. Are you eating and taking your medication, though? You know you must...especially now...with the added pressure," Rewa asked, concerned that her father may just have another heart episode, especially now that her mother could not be bothered with him. Mrs. Ilo usually kept a watchful eye on her husband and ensured he ate healthy meals and took all of his medication as and when required. She was, however, too upset to even care at the moment. *It really was a thin line between love and hate,* Rewa thought, thinking not just of the situation with her parents but that between her and Ralph.

"I am, dear. How about you and Ralph? Have you resolved things between yourselves?" Chief Ilo asked, thinking it was sad that a single piece of information about *his* past misdeed appeared to have destroyed not just his relationship with his wife but his daughter's too. He remembered how long he and Mena had prayed for Rewa to find love with a nice young man and settle down. Then how much they had hoped that the tabloids were right, that she was indeed in a relationship with Ralph Eke. Their hopes had all materialized but were now being threatened by his revelation. Maybe he should not have got Ralph involved, he wondered now.

"I don't think that's going anywhere, Dad... it's over between us," Rewa said in a resigned manner. She sighed when she said it. She had not spoken to Ralph since their last conversation and was heartbroken by it. She was, however, quite prepared to leave things the way they were. Perhaps the relationship was doomed from its inception, she thought. There had just been too many interferences from the tabloids, her family and, of course, the business relationship between Ralph and her father. There would always be a conflict of interest, she thought silently.

"Now, that's a shame, dear. You're perfect together! Ralph is a great man and would have made a great husband to you..." Chief Ilo said to his daughter before she interjected by saying,

"*Husband?* Who said anything about us getting married? I don't think we were anywhere near that Dad, besides..." Rewa started, but this time got cut off when her father said,

"Ah, that's where you're wrong, *baby girl*! Ralph came to ask for your hand in marriage already... his plan had been to propose to you on Christmas Day before the *hullabaloo* on the day."

Rewa was surprised to learn that. She had absolutely no inkling that Ralph had planned to take their relationship further.

"Really? Did he say this to you, Dad?" She asked her father in disbelief.

"Yes! He even forfeited the retainer he had with me as a client because he thought it was too much of a conflict of interest to maintain our business relationship if he wanted to pursue one with you. He said he intended to propose to you and marry you if you agreed...so I guess he chose you over me!" Chief Ilo said chuckling, temporarily forgetting his troubles with his wife.

Rewa absorbed this new piece of information her father had just given her and chewed on it momentarily. How had she not seen that their relationship had gotten that serious for Ralph? She had been pretty ecstatic in the weeks leading up to Christmas and had been quite happy for her family to see them together as a couple. However, she was unable to get past the feeling of betrayal she felt that Ralph had not said anything to her about her illegitimate sibling. Perhaps Sede was right when she said his failure to break her father's confidence should be seen as a strength of his character and not as a betrayal of her trust.

Rewa could not deny that she missed Ralph. She had not eaten for three days after Christmas. She had been rather upset and confused about everything that had happened after her father *dropped the bomb* on them and, somehow, had put the blame all on Ralph. For the first time since Christmas, Rewa was beginning to think she had made a grave mistake and had treated him rather unfairly. It was also beginning to dawn on her that she had acted rather immaturely. *Why?* She wondered.

Rewa reassured her father that she would be over to visit her mother in the morning and perhaps have another conversation about the way forward from the present situation. They talked a bit more about the family's scheduled meeting with Omolabake, and then she bade her father a Good Evening, thinking she had a few problems of her own to think about now.

CHAPTER THIRTY-TWO

Earl got into the house, kicked off his shoes, and fell into his old, battered, leather-bound armchair. He sighed as he picked up the TV remote. He flicked through the various channels and sighed again. Concluding there was nothing of interest to watch, he switched the TV off. Even if there was something good on TV, he doubted he was in the right frame of mind to be entertained by it. He was tired but not enough to sleep. He thought about what he could do to while away time and keep from thinking about Labake but could not think of anything. He decided to get up and have a shower, hoping it would help him somehow.

As he stepped into the cold shower, Earl thought about the new hotel building and how it was progressing. They had been at it for eleven months and a few days now. Apart from the rainy season, which interrupted the flow of things, construction had generally been hitch-free. If it carried on this way, they were going to meet their deadline for completion in another five months. Of course, as was to be expected, there had to be a few structural changes here and there, but the work was going at a steady pace. Earl and all the stakeholders of the proposed new hotel were pleased with the progress.

It had been a few weeks since Labake had turned down his marriage proposal, and he could not pretend he was not disappointed by it. Particularly as he had expected something totally different when she asked him to come over to her house. He had rushed to get the engagement ring, thinking he would take advantage of the situation and perhaps propose to her. He figured that her husband, having now passed away, was no longer an impediment to her being with him. As far as he was concerned, it had all worked out great. He loved her, and from the way she had kissed him back on the day she was attacked and nearly killed by her husband, he knew she at least liked him too.

So why had she refused to marry him? She said she was overwhelmed by everything and all, but she had not even asked for some time; she just blatantly refused. Something about the way Labake had explained her refusal had made him decide not to push her or beg her to reconsider marrying him. Earl had concluded that it was not worth it if he had to plead or force Labake to marry him. He needed her to *want* to marry him, to desire him the way he desired her, but she clearly did not. All he could think about as he walked out of her house and life that afternoon was how he had tried to be patient and waited for her all this time, but she clearly was not ready to commit to a more meaningful relationship. He had painfully decided to leave her alone and move on without her. His decision had, however, left him restless.

Kwame and Adia had asked him about Labake and how it was going between them. He had said she was not forthcoming, and he had decided to respect her wishes. It still hurt as he found that even after all the time she spent in the hospital and that which she spent avoiding him after she was discharged from hospital, he still yearned for her. However, he knew he would get over her with time, and he most definitely was not going to be bitter about it.

Earl thought about what Labake had shared about her recently discovering she actually had a biological father for a moment. She really did have a lot to deal with, he thought and decided it was probably for the best that he let her be.

* * * *

"Mummy, I can't find my jeans...the one with the zipper on the sides," Ella announced to Labake from her open bedroom door.

"Then just get whatever one you can find and hurry up! The car would be here any minute Ella. This was why I asked you to start packing the day before yesterday, so we avoided a situation like this. Besides, we're only going to be away for the weekend. All you need is a dress, a pair of jeans and three shirts. Don't forget to pack some underwear too...but hurry!" Labake urged.

The day had finally come to make the trip back home to meet the rest of Chief Ilo's family, which consisted of his wife and three daughters. Labake found that she was quite relaxed about meeting them all. She expected to be nervous and even jittery, but she was not. In fact, she found that she could not wait to meet them all and perhaps even strike up a relationship with them. It was Christmas, and Ella was on holiday from school and coming along to meet her grandfather and the rest of his family.

It had been three months since Labake's first meeting with her biological father. Three months since he flew to Accra to formally introduce himself to her. He had rung her up every day since that first meeting, enquiring about her health and generally keeping their new relationship budding. Labake had learned quite a bit about him, his family, and her real heritage from their conversations. She now knew what exact part of Nigeria she came from – the *Mid-Western* region and of course, she now knew that her maiden name *would* have been *Ilo*. She had learned that apart from Laide, she had an additional three older sisters – *Omorewa, Omosede,* and *Omorien*. She found it uncanny that her own full name, *Omolabake,* matched her sister's, even if they were names from different parts of the country. She had laughed with Chief Ilo about that too. Of course, she had checked all three sisters out on *Facebook* but found just two of them. Omorewa, the eldest, did not have much of a presence on social media.

Labake's relationship with her father had gotten better by the day, and she realized that as long as both parties in a relationship were genuinely willing to *get on* and *move on* from their grievances, love, and respect were easily fostered. She enjoyed her daily conversations with her father and looked forward to them. She had also started referring to him as *Dad* and could not even remember when or how that started. The relationship was not exactly where it could be yet, but they both made an effort, and slowly but surely, Labake was beginning to build some trust for her biological father.

She was thankful she listened to her sister, Laide, but more importantly, Labake was glad she had also taken her mother's advice in her dream. *Maami* had urged her to forgive her father. As usual, *Maami* was right, and even in her death, Labake believed she still looked out for her wellbeing. It was as though *Maami* knew this was the missing piece of the puzzle for her. Labake had found the peace her soul desperately craved once she decided to open up her heart to her biological father. Again, she could not explain how that happened but felt settled in her spirit and, for the first time in her life, felt worthy and as though she mattered. Most of all, she felt she could do and be absolutely anything!

Labake was beginning to catch a glimpse of what *Maami* had possibly seen in her father. Chief Ilo was funny, relatable, kind-hearted, thoughtful, and generous too. He seemed to want to overcompensate for his absence from Labake's life, her willingness to keep the lines of communication open between them, and perhaps for the effort she made in trying to foster a relationship with him.

Labake had been overwhelmed with different gifts from her father since their first meeting. He had mentioned that all his girls got monthly allowances since they were teenagers to date. He had therefore backdated hers from when she was born and credited her bank account, which he had secretly asked Laide for. Labake had been shocked at the lump sum she received and that he had thought it necessary. She became a *millionaire* overnight! She thanked him but said she could not keep the money because, to her, it just did not seem right, but he insisted. He asked her if she wanted to remain in Accra or live in any other place of her choosing.

A week after Labake confirmed her plans to remain in Accra, she received title documents to a property not too far from her current rental in her name! Chief Ilo had purchased a five-bedroom house for her and Ella to live in. Labake had been *flabbergasted* by what she considered an outrageous gesture. Her heart had begun to race, and she felt overwhelmed by all the gifts her father had sent her way, and they kept coming! She had not even thought about receiving anything from him. She was content that she knew who her father was, and that was good enough for her.

Chief Ilo remembered everything she said about pursuing a medical degree *after* he enquired about her dream and what she wanted to do with her life. He instructed her to begin looking for schools online. He had set some money aside for her to study abroad like the rest of his daughters. All she had to do was look for schools, *anywhere* in the world, he said.

Labake had initially been frightened first by the degree of change she was experiencing and second by the opportunities now being made available to her just by reason of her birth! It was way too much for her, *even* her. She thought about her life before her father came into it and the hard times before, during, and after Vince. Was this the turn in her life she had prayed so long for? She had only wanted Vince's violent ways to stop, and she had not ever envisaged the enormity of how her prayers were going to be answered. She had some real difficulty embracing this new affluent lifestyle, so much so that she felt slightly lost and perhaps guilty too. She found it overwhelming and sometimes still battled with the feeling that she was undeserving of it all.

Labake had discussed it all with Laide as usual. Of course, by now, Laide was back at her base in Port Novo. She had left Accra a couple of months ago, once she was sure Labake was back on her feet, able to care for Ella and return to her job at the Hotel.

"This is your new life, Labake; embrace it! God knows you so deserve it too! You've been through a lot, and this is God giving you and Ella the break in life you so deserve. Get used to it; *you are* the daughter of a *multi-billionaire*!" Laide had stated firmly.

"I know, sis...it's just a lot...I mean, it's sudden...I feel like I don't know *how* to be the *daughter of a multi-billionaire*! I mean...I hope he knows I don't care for any of it...we could work on a relationship without all the...without all the extravagant gifts!" Labake said in exasperation.

"Well, I'd learn and get used to it, sis. Chief clearly wants to give you all you missed out on as his daughter. It's almost as though he's paying *Maami* back for all the hard work. Then again, when you look at it, all he's done so far is give you a lump sum of money, buy you a house, and now wants to buy you some education for your dream career...that's what *wealthy fathers* do, sis!" Laide said over the phone and laughed when she realized she was not actually helping matters.

Laide made it sound like a common trend, but the truth was that she knew her sister's life was transitioning in leaps, and she was happy for her. Chief Ilo had even sent *her* a generous sum of money for taking care of his daughter all this time. Laide was not complaining about that or the *all-expenses paid* cruise he had bought her and anyone she chose to go with. He indeed was generous, and she believed Labake was the luckiest person she knew, given all she had been through.

"Oh, he didn't stop there, sis. He's also asked to have Ella enrolled in *Gertrude Hill Private School*!" Labake gasped as she said it. "Can you believe that? He'd clearly done his research...I mean, *Gertrude Hill* is the most prestigious, expensive private school in Ghana!" Labake exclaimed.

"You both deserve it, sis. Just take one day at a time and try to enjoy it, will you?" Laide had asked.

That had been a few weeks ago, and Labake was still reeling from her new opulent way of living. She kept expecting to wake up from this beautiful dream, except it was happening in real time!

Labake had explained it all to Ella. She told her about her Grandfather and how he visited while she was on her playdate with Kwame's girls. She explained how he could not wait to meet her, how she had cousins in Nigeria too, and how plans were underway for them to take a trip to meet them all. Ella was a smart kid and had asked a number of intelligent questions.

"I didn't know I had a Grandfather, Mummy. You never talk about him. Where is he? Did he travel somewhere far away?" She had asked inquisitively. Labake had expected the questions. Ella was just that kind of child. She needed an answer to everything, and Labake believed it was why she was as intelligent as she was. Labake was also aware the questions could not be avoided for much longer now; she knew she had to tell Ella as much of the truth as she could. She was going to be ten soon, and she was not as young as she had been when they first arrived in Ghana. She had been too young to understand what they were going through back then.

After the shooting incident, Ella had suddenly begun to bed-wet and suck her thumb. She had grown slightly quieter for a few months, and the child psychologist they had seen said it was not an unusual reaction for a child, especially after they had witnessed or gone through a traumatic event. He encouraged Labake to give Ella as much attention as possible and engage her in conversations as a means of getting her to talk and perhaps share what she was feeling inside.

It had taken a few weeks, but Ella had become a little more expressive about what she had witnessed. Though the bed-wetting and thumb-sucking had stopped, her boisterous nature had disappeared. Labake knew that was to be expected, considering she was older and perhaps more aware of herself, people and happenings around her generally. She had not expected Ella to get as serious and perhaps even shy as she had in the last few months. She had always had a keen interest in reading but had become even more interested in books and reading. It therefore made living with her a lot quieter than Labake was used to.

"Come sit over here for a second, darling. I need to explain a few things to you," Labake had said. Ella moved closer to her mother on the sofa in response. "You know, darling, until recently, I wasn't aware I had a father either. My mother, *your* Grandma, never mentioned him to me. I never met him as a child. Your Grandma and Grandpa...weren't together when I was born. Your Grandpa wasn't aware that I had been born either. He came looking for me because he had a dream that your Grandma told him about me. It's all complicated, but that's the story. Your Grandpa has a wife and three other daughters too..." Labake explained softly and noticed her daughter's eyes grew wider with that last piece of information.

"So you have *four* sisters all together? *Including* aunty Laide? Wow, mummy, that's a lot of family!" Ella exclaimed in awe.

"Yes, it is, darling, and guess what? They have children too! So, you also have cousins you've never met! There's even one who's about your age, apparently!" Labake provided, causing Ella a few excited gasps. "Wow, *cousins*? I have cousins too?" Ella asked exuberantly.

"You so do! And we're flying out to Nigeria in a few days to meet them all!" Labake said and clapped her hands excitedly. She loved seeing her daughter happy, and this news certainly made her happy. "I'm going to call *Yasmin* right away...to let her know I have cousins like her!" Ella said and bounced off the couch to get her phone. Laide had got her the phone while Labake was in the hospital, so she could communicate with her when she needed to, and Labake had decided to let her keep it. *Yasmin* was Ella's best friend from school. They were so close, and they told each other everything. Suddenly, Ella stopped halfway to her bedroom and said,

"How about my other Grandma...would we be visiting her in Nigeria too?" She asked innocently. Labake had wondered whom she referred to for a second. Then, assuming she was asking about *Maami*, she said, "Your other Grandma died, remember? she's in heaven now...I explained it to you a few years ago," Labake answered.

"I meant my Daddy's mummy...she is Nigeria too, isn't she, and I have cousins on my daddy's side too. I remember playing with them a long time ago," Ella said, surprising Labake, whose mouth hung open at Ella's question *and* revelation.

"You do? You remember your cousin's on your daddy's side of the family?" Labake asked as if to be sure she heard her correctly. Ella had never given any indication that she even had any memory of her early childhood back in Nigeria. How much did she remember? Labake wondered.

Ella nodded and said, "There was *Jessie* and...I can't remember his sister's name, and there was *Paula*...or was it *Pauline*...?" She said it with a lot of concentration on her face. Labake was surprised that she remembered all these things but had never mentioned any of them to her in the last four years.

"It was *Paulette*...you remember *Jessie* and *Paulette*, your cousins? *Uncle Victor's* kids?" Labake asked again in bewilderment.

Ella nodded again and said, "I don't know who *Uncle Victor* is, though. I can't remember him," Ella said. *You remember enough!* Labake thought silently, looking at her daughter as though she was a stranger.

"So, will we see my Grandma when we travel to Nigeria?" Ella asked her mother again. Labake looked away at that moment and mumbled, "We can't...there's no time for that." Still trying to process all Ella had just told her.

The girl was unbelievably smart and intelligent. Labake had not expected her to remember anyone from Vince's family, not to mention their names. She had not even recognized her father when he came for her in Accra! Labake had to admit, though, that Vince had looked different when he suddenly reappeared in their lives again; he had looked crazier, she thought.

Ella was too young, however, to understand that her father's family considered her mother the one person solely responsible for his death. She would find it hard to comprehend how that fact made it virtually impossible for her to ever even think of contacting them when they visited Nigeria. Labake thought she would explain it to Ella again when she was much older. She could then make the choice of her own volition, whether or not to pursue a relationship with her father's family. For now, Labake was happy to leave things as they were.

CHAPTER THIRTY-THREE

Chief Ilo's private jet landed at the private wing of the local airport and both Labake and Ella gathered the few belongings they brought on board and disembarked into the hot, sunny city of Lagos. Just as he had sent a car to pick them up from home in Accra and sent the private jet to fly them from Accra to the city of Lagos, Nigeria, Chief Benjamin Ilo had also sent a car for them with Moses, his Personal Assistant. He had a card in his hand for identification purposes and waited to receive them at the arrival hall. Moses' instruction was to personally check them into the hotel where they were to lodge for the duration of their stay. He was then to leave them to freshen up and then come back for them in time for lunch with the rest of the Ilo family at the Ilo mansion.

Labake felt like royalty as Moses fretted and waited on them hand and foot. He came to the airport with a *Rapid Response* Team of armed, mobile policemen. They rode in a *Hilux* pick-up truck behind them as they travelled in the sleek black SUV with tinted windows.

It was great to be back in her home country, Labake thought as she peered out of the window of the jeep. She did not realize how much she had missed it. The saying, *there's no place like home,* really was true. A lot had clearly changed in the last four years since she had been away. There were new transit buses, and new unfamiliar structures and road works in place. It was obvious the new State government had been busy. As usual, the streets were flooded with people in busy areas, and the Lagos *hustle and bustle* was in full swing. The traffic queues were long, car horns blared, and roadside hawkers did their usual thing as Labake and Ella took it all in.

"It looks different, Mummy," Ella suddenly spoke out loud, interrupting her mother's thoughts. "Yes, it is, darling. You remember it then?" Labake asked.

"Yes. I do. Not a lot, but now it looks more...more colorful," Ella provided. "Really? How so, darling?" Labake asked, curious as to what Ella meant. Had Ella also noticed the new features she had? Labake wondered.

"The buildings look newer and have different colors. I think I'm going to like it here in Nigeria," Ella concluded like she was convinced beyond a shadow of doubt.

Labake smiled at her and stroked her braided head. She was such a clever girl. She had not complained one bit about anything yet, and Labake was thankful that she also seemed to find a sense of identity in the country of her birth, though they had escaped to another when she was much younger.

Labake exhaled now, thinking about how much had happened in the last four years. She remembered the frenzied way she had left Nigeria with her daughter. She remembered how terribly sad, confused, and scared she was, not knowing what the future held for them after she dared to flee from her abusive husband. She remembered how much pain she had been in as they fled. Pain in her body from the beatings and savage rape she endured the evening before, pain in her emotions from six years of verbal and mental abuse. She remembered her inability to think straight due to all the pain she was in at the time.

But look at me now, she thought within her as they headed to the popular *Eko Le Meridian hotel.* Who would believe her story now? That the young, innocent girl, born to an illiterate, poor, single mother of two, who struggled to put her kids through school, who herself was a victim of domestic violence and abuse, would eventually turn out to be the daughter of a wealthy, renowned philanthropist father? How things change, Labake thought. She had fled for her life, poor, broken, and frightened. Now, she was returning in style, more confident and independent, all as a result of who her father was.

Labake suddenly had a thought at that moment. Had it all been worth it? Would she do it all over again? She still felt sad that Vince had lost his life in the process, though he had attempted to take hers. She felt sad for Ella in particular. She would never have her father again, never have him walk her down the aisle when she got married, or be present at any major milestones of her life. Labake turned to look at the back of Ella's head now as she looked out of the car window beside her. She knew Ella missed him and was perhaps confused by her father's actions when she saw him attack and shoot her mother.

Labake knew it was another thing she would have to explain to her daughter when she got older. She needed Ella to get the right perspective on what she had meant to her father and how he had come looking for them *because* he loved her in particular and would never have intentionally hurt her. Ella had indeed been his pride and joy, the only person Labake believed he ever really loved. It was the means through which he had attempted to get her back that had been wrong. Labake needed her daughter to understand that her father loved her very much and had taken the actions he did out of frustration. That was how she hoped Ella would remember him.

That was Labake's last thought as they drove up to the main entrance of the grand hotel, one she could only have ever dreamed she would one day be lodged at.

"Wow, mummy! It's just like *The Dolphin*...bigger even! Are we staying here?" Ella asked Labake as they walked in. Of course, Moses had gone ahead of them to the reception to confirm their reservation and check them in. Thankfully the mobile policemen stayed in their pick-up truck and did not escort them in. It was awkward enough traveling to the hotel with them, Labake thought.

"Yes, we are, darling! We're going to rest and freshen up and then go over to Grandpa's for lunch later," Labake explained to her daughter as they waited for Moses and their room key.

A couple of hours later, Moses returned for them, and they were back in the SUV, mobile policemen on their tail and driving into the Ilo Mansion. Labake was enamored with the size of the property. She and Ella took it all in again and were amazed by the beauty and sheer opulence of the place. She had expected that her father and his family lived in a grand home but what she saw now was way more than she expected. The grounds were well tended and looked like one of those show gardens one paid to visit. She tried not to show that she was in awe but could not help it. She began to wonder if she and Ella looked out of place there and suddenly felt intimidated by the sheer magnitude of her father's home.

Labake had decided to go her usual casual route and wear a pair of skinny blue jeans with a white linen tunic. She had a pair of green flat sandals on her feet. Her thick long hair was swept back in a ponytail, and she had some light make-up on. She had a large, green leather snake print bag on her arm and tiny pearl earrings in her ears. She wanted to create a good first impression with members of her newly discovered family and knew she looked decent but simple. Ella had decided to settle for her denim jumpsuit and looked pretty too in her braids and flats sandals. They had done some clothes shopping before the trip, and both their closets had received a complete *overhaul*. Labake wondered now if they looked the part of the *daughter and granddaughter of a billionaire.* She smiled when she thought of the phrase Laide had coined.

As they came out of the car and walked up the stairs, the double doors swung open, and Chief Ilo himself welcomed them in, guffawing and grabbing them both in warm hugs. "Hi, Dad," Labake greeted, curtsying and Ella followed suit, just as her mother had taught her. "Good Afternoon, sir..." Ella greeted. Chief Ilo squeezed Ella in a tight embrace and said, "You must be Ella! I am *Grandpa*! I've been anxious to meet you, my dear!" He hugged Labake and gave her a peck on each cheek. His eyes danced, suggesting to Labake that he was nervous and perhaps excited too. He seemed quite pleased to have them there, though. Labake greeted the young man standing just behind him; he appeared to be a member of the domestic staff.

"Do come in, my dears. Everyone is in the family room, waiting to meet you." Chief Ilo said as he led the way down a short hall that was just as beautiful as the exterior of the house. There were large gold framed family pictures scattered on the walls, Labake observed as she and Ella followed her father in. Chief Ilo opened the large door to what was the family room and all three of them stepped into a room that had been overdone in gold, Labake observed again. It, however, seemed comfortable and had a lived-in look to it. It appeared every member of the Ilo family was present as there were a number of people in the room.

At first, when they walked in, Labake tried to make out who was who but was not quite certain. They were all seated in various chairs scattered around the room. There were kids playing and running around in the garden; Labake could see them through the large French windows, which showed off a play area for kids. She smiled nervously at the group as they all stared at her and Ella for a moment until Chief Ilo broke the silence and announced, "Hey everyone, this is Omolabake Ebodo and her daughter, Nuella Ebodo, my last child and granddaughter, respectively. Please make them feel welcome." It was a statement laced with a subtle warning, Labake thought as she stood there awkwardly, hand in hand with Ella.

One of the ladies was first to get up and introduce herself, "Hi Omolabake, nice to finally meet you. Welcome to the family! I guess I'm one of your elder sisters. I'm *Omosede,* but everyone calls me *Sede* for short. She smiled at Labake and gave her a warm hug, then did the same with Ella. "What a pretty girl you are, sweetie. To you, I am *Aunty Sede*." She then smiled warmly and said, "Dad was right; we do look alike!" Labake smiled back at her and said, "Nice to meet you Sede...I agree with him too. I certainly look like you."

The next person to come forward was Larry, Sede's husband. Sede introduced him and then said, "Our girls are playing outside. I'll introduce you to them later, especially Nuella. How old are you, sweetie?" Sede asked Ella. "Nine, but I'm going to be ten in March," Ella stated proudly. "That's great as your cousin out there is eleven. Meet everyone else, and then you can go meet and play with them in the garden," Sede said, and Labake knew she liked her instantly.

She was obviously a free spirit and did not seem to have any inhibitions about her.

Next was Omorewa, who remained where she was but stretched out her hand to Labake, indicating that she moved close enough to take the hand she offered. Labake obliged her and moved with Ella to her. Omorewa, unlike her sister Sede, did not even attempt to crack a smile. She said in a rather reserved and unfriendly tone of voice as Labake took her hand, "Hello there, I'm Rewa...Omorewa, the eldest daughter. Nice to meet you." She shook Ella's hand and dropped it like nothing had happened. Labake felt sure that she sensed a bit of hostility there but was not entirely certain as she did not want to misjudge her.

"I am Omorien, the youngest of the sisters," the last of the younger ladies said, getting up to give Labake a warm hug. "I guess I'm not the baby of the family anymore, *thank God!*" She then said, "This is my husband, and that's our first daughter, *Olamide* outside, playing with her cousins, and this is our son *Anjola*, the latest addition to the family." Labake followed her finger and realized for the first time that the baby boy she referred to was being bounced on the eldest woman in the group's lap, his grandmother. Immediately, Labake crossed over to where the elderly woman sat and knelt in greeting. Chief Ilo then cleared his throat at that moment and said, "Omolabake, meet my wife and jewel of inestimable value, *Chief Mrs. Philomena Ilo...*" He said it nervously, and it seemed there was a slight warning directed at his wife in his tone as he made the introduction.

"Good afternoon, ma. It's a pleasure to meet you," Labake greeted. Mrs. Ilo carried on bouncing her grandson on her knee, and without looking at Labake once, she muffled, "Good Afternoon." It was all she said, and Labake knew then and there that there was no love there for her. She had expected some unfriendliness and even hostility from her father's family and had been quite prepared for it. She could not say she blamed them, though. After all, she was a *rude interruption* to their cushy lives. She was the product of an illicit affair that their husband and father had with her mother. She was the one who should not have happened, but hey, Labake thought, she would not have chosen the current circumstance either. In fact, she had done absolutely nothing to bring about the awkward situation they all found themselves in. *It was just what it was.* She got off the floor, and her father led her to one of the empty seats.

"Would you like something to drink, Omolabake? How was the flight over, by the way?" Sede asked as she got up to ring for Emeka, the steward. "It was great. Thank you, Sede," Labake responded politely. Sede then turned to Ella and said, "Nuella sweetie, come to the garden with aunty. Let's introduce you to your cousins." Ella scrambled to her feet and took the hand Sede extended but not before she said, "You can call me *Ella* Aunty Sede. No one calls me by my full name," she said in her usual friendly way. One would have thought she had known *Aunty Sede* for years. Labake mused as she watched them walk out to the garden, hand in hand, talking.

Moments later, lunch was announced, and they all proceeded to the dining room, where all kinds of foods were laid out. Omorien announced that the kids would be eating in the kitchen where their food was being served. That was perhaps to give the adults some privacy, Labake thought.

As they sat to eat, Chief Ilo made light conversation to which all the girls and their husbands joined in. They asked Labake all kinds of questions, particularly Sede and Rien, who appeared quite interested in her and what she had to say. It was clear they were trying to make her feel welcome by including her in the conversation, seeing as neither their mother nor elder sister could be bothered to. Rewa acted as though she could not wait to leave whilst her mother just sat there, quietly toying with her food. She did not seem present in any way; she just appeared to be lost in her own world.

Labake also observed that Mrs. Ilo had not said a word since they sat to eat. She was quiet for the most part and did not acknowledge Labake's presence. In fact, Mrs. Ilo looked like someone whose world had just been shattered, and Labake knew why too. Labake felt somewhat guilty for the way she suspected her father's wife felt, but mostly, she felt sad for her. It clearly was a great shock that her husband had fathered a child outside their marriage, and she obviously had not fully come to terms with it. Labake hoped that in time, she would see it for what it was and move on with her husband, whom Labake believed really did love her. It was obvious from the way he looked at her.

The conversation around the table remained light and, at times, funny too. Everyone else seemed comfortable there except Rewa who interjected once or twice but definitely was not as engaging as her younger sisters. "Do you have any other siblings?" She suddenly asked Labake in a very disinterested way. It was as if she did not really care for an answer. *Why bother asking*? Labake mused within herself but very graciously provided a detailed answer. "Yes, I do, as a matter of fact. I have an elder sister, *Olaide*. She works for the *Ministry of External Affairs* as a diplomat. Her current posting is in the Republic of Benin." Labake answered and noticed the arch in Rewa's eyebrows when she finished. She could not explain why but she was pleased that Rewa appeared impressed by what she had just heard about Laide and her job.

"*Really*? That's interesting. We read about your shooting incident...Dad mentioned that was you. So sorry about that," Rewa added in response with a feigned look of innocence on her face. Everyone at the table, except Mrs. Ilo, of course, gasped, and Labake heard the clanging of silverware as they dropped onto plates. Two or three people round the table had their cutlery slide from their hands in shock at Rewa's insensitive comment.

"*Omorewa Ilo*!" Chief Ilo exclaimed at what he perceived to be his first daughter's rudeness. "*What,* Dad? I only stated out loud what everyone was thinking," Rewa said to her father in a rather blasé manner.

"I apologize on your sister's behalf, Omolabake...God knows we *taught* her better manners than that," Chief Ilo said to Labake and sent Rewa a warning scowl.

"That's alright, Dad...really, it is," Labake assured the others around the table and then said to Rewa. "Thank you, sis, but more importantly, thank God for sparing my life...at least I'm here to tell the story." She smiled sweetly at Rewa, who looked away in embarrassment at that point.

It seemed to Labake as though all present picked their cutlery up again in unison and began eating in silence for a moment. Until Larry, Sede's husband, asked as a way of introducing a new topic to the table, "So, Omolabake, what's it like living in Accra?" Again, Labake felt she heard everyone release their breaths around the table. It was obvious they were all relieved and thankful for Larry's intervention.

At the end of the visit, Labake thought about all that had happened at the Ilo residence on their way back to the hotel. She came to the conclusion that she had somewhat felt welcome in her father's house, for the most part, but deep down, she was relieved when it was time to leave for the hotel. She and her half-sisters had exchanged contact details before she and Ella left them. Labake had, however, decided to stay out of their lives unless they reached out to her. She did not want or need to pursue a relationship with either of them if they were not interested in one with her. She had her father's love, and that was sufficient for her. Maintaining a relationship with him was all that mattered to her.

As far as Labake was concerned, she did not see herself fitting into the Ilo family and did not even care to. All she knew was she had jumped through far too many hurdles in her life to struggle to try and fit into a relationship with *anyone*. Yes, they were related by blood, but that was all there was to it, so far anyway, she told herself silently. They had been born to two very different mothers, their lifestyles and general orientations were different, and Labake was quite happy to return to her own world.

Later that evening, she received a text from Rewa, apologizing for her insensitive comment. It read;

> *DEAR OMOLABAKE, LET ME TAKE THE TIME TO EXTEND MY APOLOGIES TO YOU FOR MY APPARENT INSENSITIVE COMMENT EARLIER. PLEASE NOTE THAT I MEANT NO HARM BY IT. IT WAS GREAT MEETING YOU AND ELLA TODAY. I WISH YOU WELL. LOVE,* ***R****.*

* * * *

A year and a half later, Labake could barely remember what her life had been like before she got introduced to her biological father. A lot had happened in such a short time, and her world had completely changed. She was literally *living the life!* Like Laide had said a week ago. Here she was in Los Angeles, California, a medical student at *UCLA*, finally living her dream! She felt free, happy, and fulfilled all at the same time.

It had not been easy to leave Ella with Laide, but Labake was thankful that the distance between them was not too much. It had been decided that Ella stay with her aunt in Canada while Labake focused on getting her medical degree. It had been a convenient arrangement, especially when Laide got sent to her new post at the High Commission in Toronto, Canada.

Labake was grateful that her sister had again come to her aid and helped register Ella in her new private high school over there. When she had a break from college, Labake usually caught the *red eye* out to see Ella every now and again. She was glad Ella was settled and doing very well in Canada, and so was Laide, who had finally given in to the advances of a nice *Canadian* man, and it appeared their relationship was getting serious. Labake hoped that Laide married and settled with him. *James Harbot II* was a nice Caucasian man, and Labake thought he was perfect for her sister. He had somehow been able to break her defenses and penetrate a place Laide had never let anyone into. Labake was pleased with the way things were going with them. She hoped wedding bells rang soon for them.

Labake herself was now *Mrs. Earl Tetteh,* of course. She had reached out to Earl a few weeks after her return from Nigeria when she felt ready to take their relationship further. He had been pleased to hear from her, and in a matter of weeks, they had started dating properly. They had both traveled to Lagos to meet her father, and Earl had formally asked Chief Ilo for her hand in marriage once she accepted his marriage proposal this time. They had been married in a very quaint ceremony at the Ilo Mansion in Lagos, with all her sisters, including Laide, present. However, Rien had been unable to attend, seeing as she lived outside the country. It had been a lovely affair.

Earl still worked in Accra and traveled to the United States a lot just to be with his wife. Their ultimate plan was for Labake to return to Ghana when she completed her degree, where they planned to settle and live their lives together as man and wife.

CHAPTER THIRTY-FOUR

"P*hilomena,* I've heard all you've said and totally understand how disappointed you feel, but it's time to *wake up, my friend*! There's no point crying over spilt milk; the deed is already done! You've been through all the emotions...denial, anger, depression, even rage, but now it is time to get to the *acceptance* stage. I was there too...the position you're in now. I was distraught like you when *Kanmi* brought two *bastard* children into our family. Yes...I've been where you are now; it was *worse in my case*! My husband's illegitimate children were kids...*literally*! They were five and seven at the time, and their mother was still *very much* in the picture when I was *informed* of them."

Mrs. Ilo looked at *Sara Thomas,* her best friend, in shock. This was the first time her friend of over fifty years had mentioned that her husband had children outside their marriage too. Her mouth hung open for a moment before she eventually found her voice and said. "*Really*? But you never mentioned any of this to me...I thought we were friends!" She looked at her friend now with new eyes, temporarily forgetting her own troubles at that moment.

They were seated in the living room of Mrs. Ilo's quarters as she had not left that part of the Ilo Mansion in weeks. She had been so devastated and depressed by what she considered her husband's unforgivable betrayal and had been in bed for days. She had not even been downstairs once in weeks. She had asked that *Mrs. Thomas* be brought to her quarters today. She was still not in the mood to get all *dolled up* for downstairs as she usually did before her world came undone.

Mrs. Ilo had cried a lot in the last few weeks and had refused to eat for days. She had lost some of her chubbiness and had deep, dark circles around her now puffy eyes. Her friend, Mrs. Thomas, looked at her for a moment, thinking she had aged overnight. She remembered how she had also thought she would never survive the degree of devastation she felt when she discovered her husband's extramarital affair. It was even more devastating that the affair had been with his former secretary, who had now become his second wife and had a couple of little *brats* too! Their family had become polygamous within a *twinkling of an eye,* and she had been helpless to do anything about it.

"Hmmm, my friend, I couldn't mention it to a soul! I was absolutely shattered and terribly embarrassed by the whole thing. Of course, the only people who knew were my kids and my in-laws, as there was so much drama over the other woman becoming his *second wife*! Remember *Amaka*, Kanmi's former secretary? She is the *other* woman here. Can you believe the little *wench* had *two* bastard kids with my husband? And her family insisted that he married her under customary law!

So you see, my friend, my situation was far worse than yours! Do you remember that period when I traveled to spend some time with *Eniola*, my first daughter, in Singapore? Do you remember, about two years ago? I was away for almost a year! I nearly had a nervous breakdown! It hurts still, just thinking about it!" Mrs. Thomas said to her friend's utter astonishment. Mrs. Ilo could not believe she went through all that by herself and failed to mention it to her, as close as they were. Mena believed they shared *everything* with one another until now.

"I wish you'd mentioned it to me, Sarah...at least we would have talked about it, and if anything, I'd have been a shoulder to cry on. I'm so sorry you went through all that. I remember you were in Singapore for quite some time, and I even offered to fly out there to visit you, but you said I needn't bother, seeing as you were planning your trip back home already. I thought you were helping Eniola out with her new baby!" Mena said, still thrown aback by all her friend had just revealed to her.

"Anyway, enough about me, that isn't why I'm here...sorry I've made it about me, but what I was trying to make you see is that there *is* life even after all that...It took me some time to accept what my husband had done, and sometimes I wonder if I would ever truly forgive him for how he broke my heart but hey...*life goes on*! You have to accept what is and prepare to face it head-on. God forbid it, but if anything happens to you and you fall ill and die over this issue, be very clear that *your* Benny *will* move on with his life. Therefore, you need to at least find a way to forgive him, make the most of what's left of your relationship, and keep pushing forward like I did.

Chief...your husband is a good man who made a mistake. He truly loves you but won't be the first to do this, and unfortunately, he certainly won't be the last, either. That's just the sad truth, dear friend," Mrs. Thomas concluded wisely. It had been Rewa who had rang her up for her intervention between her parents and their current issues, seeing as no one else was able to get through to her mother. She knew if anyone could, it would be her best friend of over fifty years.

Mena silently listened to her friend in bewilderment. Sara Thomas was a great friend and had always given great advice, but Mena still reeled from the shock of all she had just divulged about her marriage. She had also seen the pain in her eyes as she shared the details with her. In a way, it made Mena feel better that someone else she knew had been through what she was currently going through and, better still, that she appeared to have survived the experience too. Perhaps there really was life after such a devastating encounter.

* * * *

"I really can't believe you asked her about the incident with her late husband...she almost got killed by him, Rewa. What were you thinking?" Omosede asked disapprovingly a few days after Omolabake's visit. All three sisters were on a three-way video call, discussing the very eventful Christmas they had all had.

"*I know*, right? What were you gunning for exactly, sis? Dad was livid!" Rien added, agreeing with Sede. She had extended her stay beyond the New Year as her father had requested that he wanted her around when Labake met with the family.

"Have to agree, actually. He looked like he could have wrung my neck at that moment!" Rewa said, chuckling. "I don't know, really...I guess it just seemed as though everyone was playing the *perfect happy family* role when we all knew it was far from a perfect situation. I mean, we all knew her story and clearly wanted to know how she got through it, but no one took the plunge to actually ask her. You all then had the nerve to pretend you weren't interested in her response to my comment when you all obviously were! What was that about?" Rewa asked in turn, sticking her hand out in question at her sisters.

"*Anyways*, I quite liked her...to think she'd survived such abuse and still managed to get it together...now that's *Ilo strength* right there! I don't know about you guys, but I'm going to be keeping in touch with her...she *is* our sister, after all. Did you see her uncanny resemblance to us...me in particular? *Uncanny* indeed!" Sede said.

"Yups...Dad certainly has strong genes, doesn't he?" Rien added. "I think I'll keep in touch with her too...there was just something about her and that very smart kid of hers. I really liked them too...I guess our family just got bigger!" Rien exclaimed.

It was funny how they had all been extremely shocked and even upset by their father's indiscretion in having an affair with Labake's mother and how they all now seemed to have decided they were happy to accept and integrate Labake and her child into the family. Rewa thought but remained silent about it.

"Think I owe her an apology. I'll send her a text to say sorry for my *rudeness*. She did seem cool, and Dad seemed quite happy to have her and her daughter around...I almost felt jealous at the level of attention he showered on them," Rewa said, sticking her tongue out cheekily at both her sisters when they both turned to see if she was joking or really meant what she just said.

"Never mind that, sis, how about you and Ralph? A little bird tells me he was planning to propose to you on Christmas Day before all hell broke loose," Sede asked.

"He did!!?" Rien exclaimed, clapping her hands together excitedly. Clearly, she had not heard this piece of information.

Rewa ignored Rien's excitement and asked, "Would that *little bird* happen to be your father? He mentioned it to me the other day too. Apparently, he also went to ask Dad for my hand in marriage...before the *hullabaloo* on Christmas day," Rewa said, sighing. "I don't know, sis. I can't seem to get past the feeling of betrayal I have...I really thought he was *the one,* you know..." Rewa said.

"It would be a shame, sis...not to find out...what if he really *is the one*?" Sede asked her elder sister sadly, suddenly deflated by Rewa's comment.

"*He is*! I can just sense it! I think you should give him a ring sis...he really didn't do anything wrong...and it would really be nice to start planning a wedding. I think that's what we all need as a family right now...it might restore some kind of normalcy again, especially for Mum. Planning your wedding would get her out of the horrible place she's in right now," Rien said wisely.

"*Planning a wedding*? Sorry to disappoint you there, sis, but I'm not getting married...not *yet,* at least," Rewa responded sadly. "Then I don't know about giving him a ring. I feel as though if Ralph really wanted us back together, he would do something about it...I don't want to chase him. I've done that before, and it didn't do well for my psyche...I want to feel wanted by him, you know...like he fought for us...for me even. If I rang him now, I'd never feel as though he really wanted me, and that may affect the relationship in the long run," Rewa said and knew she made sense to herself, if not to her sisters.

"Men aren't always that clued on, sis. They don't always understand that a girl needs to feel wanted by them...perhaps you need to help him. Besides, he did try to contact you several times, remember? He may just be thinking the same thing and waiting for you to show that the relationship was worth something to you," Sede said, thinking her sister needed to get over herself and give

Ralph a call before it got too late. Guys like Chief Ralph Eke did not hang about for too long waiting for a lady to take so much time deciding whether to ring him or not. She, however, did not say anything more on the subject but contemplated giving Ralph a ring herself. She knew Rewa would kill her if she did, though.

* * * *

Rewa had just checked in at the airline counter and gone through immigration and security. As usual, she found the entire exercise rather hectic and wondered why the Lagos International airport always had to be a circus. She was relieved to have gotten through it and now looked forward to finding a comfortable seat within the airline lounge. Her flight to *Abu Dhabi* was to start boarding in another hour and fifteen minutes.

Rewa had planned this trip to Abu Dhabi for weeks now and looked forward to the *International Interior Design Expo* starting in a couple of days. It was going to be a week long, and she planned to explore every new idea and vendor at the exhibition. She thoroughly loved these events and only wished her friend, *Donovan,* was present this year too. They'd had great fun at last year's event, which had been held in *Milan*.

Donovan was a great designer from South Africa, and they had met at last year's event for the first time. This time, he was unable to attend as his father was terminally ill and he did not want to take any chances leaving his side. Rewa wished she had some company at these exhibitions and Expos as it just seemed better with a companion at least. She hoped to meet someone new who was as much fun as Donovan but was determined to have a nice time regardless.

It had been a couple of months since Christmas, February to be precise. In fact, Valentine's Day was in three days, and the *Interior Design Expo* had been themed the *'LOVE EDITION'*. It had been planned to coincide with the *season of love*. *Well, never mind all that* Rewa told herself; she did not have any special person to love at the moment but was planning to love *herself* whilst on this trip. She had all kinds of distractions scheduled for herself in between the Expo and looked forward to all of them. She believed she deserved a time of pampering and leisure, given all that had happened in the last few weeks.

Rewa sighed in relief when she finally found an unoccupied seat in the Lounge. The place was quite busy for February, she thought absent-mindedly. She ordered a *mimosa* as she felt her sugar level needed a boost and moved to the more secluded vacant spot she found, *carry-on luggage* in hand. She had roughly another hour till boarding and decided to relax for the time being.

Rewa thought about all that had happened in recent months within her family and was glad that things appeared to be settling down again, particularly with her parents. Her mother was not quite there yet, but her father was now out of *the dog house,* and back in the bedroom he shared with his wife. Their relationship was still slightly strained, but Rewa was sure that in time, her mother would forgive her *beloved Benny* like Sede had said.

As for Omolabake, their new sister, all three sisters communicated with her via social media, and she responded warmly too. She had recently got remarried at the Ilo mansion, and everyone had been present except Rien, who was back to her base in Texas. Though their mother had refused to play any major role in planning the wedding, it had been a beautiful affair. It had indeed been a *small but quaint* ceremony like Labake had said, and they all thought her new Ghanaian husband was a perfect match for her. Prior to the wedding, Sede had taken it upon herself to plan a *pseudo* bridal shower for her, which had also been fun.

Omolabake was now in Medical School in the United States, and things appeared to be going well for her. In the meantime, all four of them worked on fostering a better bond, but it was early days yet. Rewa was happy for her and wished her well. She prayed she found real peace this time around. She deserved it.

Just as Rewa settled in her seat within the busy airline lounge, she heard that familiar male voice that made her heart want to sing, behind her. "Nice of you to join me finally. I was beginning to wonder if I had the correct departure date." It was Ralph Eke, looking at her as though he had been expecting her. She suddenly realized she was extremely pleased to see him. They had not seen or spoken to one another since that last time after the shambolic Christmas they had, as Rewa had decided she was not going to pursue their relationship any further if he was not going to make any further attempts to either.

Ok girl, play it cool now, she cautioned herself. "Hey Ralph, how are you doing?" Rewa asked with a slight smile on her face. She did not bother to disguise that she was pleased to see him. "We really should stop bumping into each other at airports like this, you know," She said it as though they were old friends, between whom nothing awkward had transpired. Rewa could feel her heart begin to beat faster as they both stared at each other for a moment. Ralph's eyes swept over her denim-clad body appreciatively, then settled on her eyes, holding them with his. Rewa also found him as dashing as ever in khaki pants and a pale blue shirt.

Without another word and with his usual resigned expression, he rose from the seat behind her, walked the short distance to where she was, pulled her up, and enveloped her in a rather warm embrace. He took in the familiar smell of her fragrance and her hair and heard himself say out loud. "*God*, I've missed you!" It was a hushed whisper, riddled with nothing but sheer emotion. He held her tightly for a moment and gave her a peck on the cheek.

Instead of moving back to his seat, Ralph held on to Rewa's hand and studied her intently. On the other hand, she felt a rush of emotions for him too in that instant. Suddenly, she felt as though she would break down and cry in the moment. She realized there and then that she loved him deeper than she had cared to admit and that she would do anything for him. She instinctively drew closer to him and wrapped her arms around his waist in another warm embrace, drinking in his musky cologne. It had always seemed as though they never really had to speak; their raw emotions and actions spoke volumes, meshing them together spiritually, in an unexplainably deep way. It was as though their bodies took over and sent signals and responses to each other without any need for words.

Rewa knew she had made a mistake in letting Ralph walk out of her life. She had let her pride cheat her and keep her away from the man she truly loved and who clearly loved her back and treated her like a princess. What had she been thinking? Why had she done that to herself? Ralph, on the other hand, had been the most mature, gentle and humble man, holding on for quite some time and refusing to let her go before he had finally decided to let her be. Now, he silently thought about how he owed a lot to Rewa's sister, Sede, for giving him another opportunity with the one other woman he truly loved since his first wife.

"Who said anything about *bumping into each other*?" Ralph asked when Rewa finally pulled away. He bent to retrieve her carry-on case from her and led them to where he was seated. *"Huh?"* Rewa asked, having lost the train of their conversation.

"Who said anything about *us bumping into each other*?" Ralph asked again. "My darling, as of now, we are officially travel companions, attending the *'LOVE EDITION'* of the *International Interior Design Expo* in Abu Dhabi for the next one week...*I am your travel buddy*!" Ralph stated and waved one of the Abu Dhabi event leaflets at her.

"What? How did you know about that...or that I'd be attending? And then how..." Rewa began with all the questions, but before she could finish, Ralph said, "Er...there are ways about these things, you know...I have agents all over the place who report events such as these to me...what can I say? I guess I keep my ears close to the ground," Ralph said with a shrug and a cheeky smile on his face.

Rewa could not help smiling back at him. He really was the sweetest guy she knew. Then suddenly, she stopped with a quizzical look first on her face, then her eyes bulged a bit when she realized what was going on. *"Sede!* It was Sede who let you in on this, wasn't it? I'm going to wring her neck when I get back, I promise! It's no wonder she kept asking me about my travel details and all..." Rewa said, still surprised that Sede had furnished Ralph with all the details she had cunningly received from Rewa. "I didn't even realize she was in touch with you...the sneaky little..."

Ralph laughed heartily at Rewa's quick wit and reaction to all of it. Sede had rung him up a couple of weeks ago and said she needed to talk with him. They had met for lunch one afternoon. They had talked about Rewa non-stop, and Sede had encouraged him to give her a ring, stating that Rewa, though hurt, wanted to feel pursued by him and how she now understood why he had kept the information about Omolabake to himself. She urged him to take the plunge as she knew Rewa did love him but was way too stubborn to make the first move.

Somewhere along the conversation they'd had over lunch, Sede had mentioned that Rewa was going to be attending the Expo in Abu Dhabi, and Ralph believed it was a great time to take a well-deserved holiday himself. He had immediately put Sede to work to extract as much travel details and dates from Rewa and had been lucky to find himself a business class seat on the same *Etihad* flight as Rewa. It had worked out beautifully too, as Ralph remembered that he and Rewa never booked that holiday to Dubai, which he had been secretly planning before the Christmas day *catastrophe*.

After Ralph had explained it all to Rewa, she said, "*The little weasel*! I had absolutely no idea! But I know you're busy...how about work? I know how difficult it is to tear you away from the fourth floor..." Rewa said teasingly.

Ralph smiled at her again and thought, *this is exactly why I love you* silently. She was one of the most considerate people he knew. She even cared about his work. "Just thought I deserved a holiday too...besides, one week won't exactly affect anything," Ralph answered. He then fell silent for a few minutes then said,

"I'm sorry for all that happened on Christmas Day. I guess I was in a bit of a dicey situation given my relationship with..." Ralph began, feeling he needed to clear the air, but Rewa stopped him by raising a hand.

"I'm the one who should be apologizing, Ralph. I blew things out of proportion and could have handled things a lot more maturely. I'm sorry for that and...and refusing to take your calls or come to you when I should have. It won't happen again...I promise." She then paused for a bit, looked deep into his eyes, and said. "Do you think...I hate to be forward...but do you think we can...we could try again...I really did miss you. I love you still, and I'd like us to..." This time it was Ralph who interrupted her when he said,

"I didn't even think to ask. I just assumed we'd made up already! I love you, Rewa, even more than I did before. These past few weeks without you have been difficult...say you won't leave again...say it, I want to hear it?" Ralph insisted. Rewa smiled at him shyly and said, "I promise not to leave again, Ralph."

"Do you realize you just betrothed yourself to me?" Ralph asked her. Rewa smiled and said, "Er...I don't know about that...I only repeated what you asked me to say...?" She teased again. "Well, I may as well just pop the question right here and now...you see I've had this ring *burning a hole* in my pocket for quite some time now. I hate to cause a scene, but if you say yes quickly, no one would even notice that this is a marriage proposal!" Ralph said. He got on his knees as discreetly as possible, brought the small, black ring box out, and said, "Omorewa Ilo, will you do me the honor of being my wife?"

Rewa opened her mouth wide, and suddenly, it seemed as though the world stopped and there was just herself and Ralph in the large, overcrowded room. Everything seemed to happen in slow motion. Then suddenly, the pace picked up and the room spun back to reality again. She heard herself say, *"Yes!"* Suddenly the whole room stood in ovation and began clapping riotously. Phone cameras began flashing from every angle of the room as Ralph slipped the beautifully cut diamond ring on Rewa's finger. They were both slightly embarrassed at the raucous they had created right there, at the *Etihad* Airlines *Club House,* within the Lagos International Airport, but they ignored the crowd and embraced each other tightly.

If anyone had mentioned to her earlier that morning that she would be engaged that afternoon and be traveling with her fiancé together on the flight to Abu Dhabi, she would have called them crazy! Rewa thought joyously within her. *Thank You, Jesus!*

Suddenly their flight was announced as ready for boarding. Rewa and Ralph gathered their belongings and left the airport lounge hand in hand with nothing but love and excitement for what the future held.

THE END

ACKNOWLEDGEMENTS

I want to thank God Almighty for giving me the inspiration, gusto, and enablement to write this book. It's taken so long to get here, but I thank God for the ease at which the material poured out of me each time I sat to write, so much that I didn't even know how the stories would end! I thank Him for keeping me and my entire family through the process and keeping us alive for the entire duration.

I want to thank both my parents – ***Chief and Mrs. Fola Akinrinsola,*** for all they invested in my three siblings and me. The confidence instilled in us to go for whatever and just the level of affirmation we had growing up gave us the audacity to even dare. What a legacy! I hope you are both proud of this project.

I want to thank my darling husband, ***Dr. Dayo Brown***. I appreciate your support in getting me to finish this book and your support in all I aspire to be and do. You encouraged, read, edited, corrected, and did the front and back cover illustrations, amongst other things. Since we've been together, my dreams are clearer, in full view and coming to pass one after the other through the grace and help of God. I pray this is also your testimony of me. I love you and pray that we both keep fulfilling divine destiny and purpose in Jesus' Name.

I would also like to thank my siblings (***Abi-Sab, Omobosola, and Iwalesho***), whom I sent brief excerpts for the first time four years after I started work on the book and who encouraged me (by at least taking time out to read it) to finish it and egged me on to keep going, God bless you all. I pray all our endeavors receive a touch from the Almighty in Jesus' Name.

I am also thankful for all my friends to whom I mentioned the book and who were happy to volunteer to read it (even though I chickened out for fear that it would be unreadable and never sent the full book). I say thank you. God bless you for the encouragement.

To all the literary people I consulted and who gave suggestions on *first book* projects, I say thank you for your help.